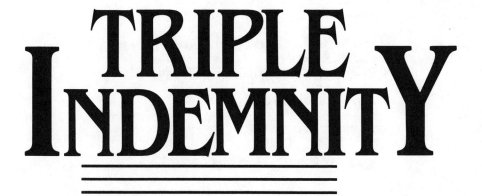

TRIPLE INDEMNITY

by
Judith Richards

ARBOR HOUSE
New York

To our children:
Marc Cline
Trey Cline
Blaise Cline
Cabeth Husbands
Charles Kriel

O NE

Ellen Curry knew, when all was right and the world revolved in a sure orbit, life could be transformed, fate cruel, happiness ephemeral.

Blaise leaned against a kitchen counter, bantering with Richard as he washed fresh vegetables from the garden. They were teasing one another, laughing. But something in the girl's expression was awry.

"How do you spell 'Ochlochnee,' daddy?" Blaise inquired of Richard.

Ellen saw his eyes, chips of ebony, dart like startled ravens. "O-c-h-l-o-c-h-n-e-e."

But it was not his reply Blaise sought—Ellen was sure of it. It was the instant of surprise she elicited when he heard the question.

"It's a small town in south Georgia," Blaise continued. "Primarily agrarian, in the county of Thomas, near the Georgia-Florida state line."

Transfixed, but unsure why, Ellen had a mental image of a

spring shower, a bright lick of light, the unexpected natural event that could strike dead a loved one.

Like a rubber doll . . . cold and plastic to the touch . . .

Rhythm invited cacophony. Order tends to disorder, that was the way of the universe—expanding, exploding, into bottomless pits of black holes. The only sure rule was *change,* and at this moment she sensed the end of happiness.

Richard said, "Why do you ask, Blaise?"

"About what?"

"What are we discussing?"

"I've forgotten—what?"

Richard wheeled around with an expression so alarming Blaise said, "Oh—you mean Ochlochnee?"

Richard strode away, out the door onto the patio, and Blaise lifted her chin a bit, lifted her eyebrows.

Too often of late, such scenes had been played out, the mood suddenly threatening, for reasons Ellen had not understood. Always before, wounded egos could be salved with hugs and kisses. But this time, Blaise had seemed bolder, her intent more sinister like—Ellen thought—like a picador drawing in the bull for a blade between the shoulders.

The girl was at the back door now, observing Richard. In those youthful blue eyes—defiance.

"What was that about, Blaise?"

Blaise glared at the man afar.

"Blaise? What was that about?"

"Daddy probably hasn't had his morning coffee, mama."

Ellen knew the shock of change. A telegram. Arnold dead in Vietnam. The coffin sealed. Metal cold to the fingers and not as heavy as surely it would be if Arnold were truly inside. But he was. The Army said so. Others swore so. Yet for her, Arnold still prowled a distant land. Any day a call would come and he would plead once more, "No divorce . . ."

Tiny fingers curled . . . the flesh blue . . .

How would she explain to Arnold the happiness she had found with another husband? She could imagine pain and resentment as Arnold considered Richard the stepfather to his daughter. But

Arnold was dead. The army buried somebody with his name at Arlington. The survivor benefits came. The flag lay in a triangulated fold in a closet or the attic, wrapped in polyethylene and smelling of mothballs.

"Mama? Are you all right?"

Blaise had turned from the door, owlish eyes behind round spectacles, unblinking blue—

"I was thinking—"

The refrigerator hummed. The girl stared without smiling.

"—of eating breakfast on the patio," Ellen said.

"Kind of cool, isn't it?"

"Daddy wants to."

"Um." Blaise placed cups on a tray, poured milk into a matching creamer. "I'll set the table," she offered.

Ellen moved to the kitchen window, hands trembling. She couldn't remember what she'd been doing. She shook her head, aggravated with herself. Blaise was at the redwood table covering it with a spread. Beyond the girl, dark splotches in the lawn where Richard's feet had disturbed the dew, going to his garden. He was down there now, already dressed for business in a suit, wearing gloves, snipping this plant or that.

Here on Spring Hill, the highest elevation in Mobile, Ellen had a panoramic overview—Blaise, tall for her fourteen years, lithe and thin like Arnold's family, watching Richard, beyond them both a five mile expanse to the east where the steles of civilization rose through early morning miasma. The towering First National Bank building was silhouetted by a sun still unseen over the river, across the bay.

With her two remaining loves in sight, Ellen was uneasy; and letting them go their way was agony. She'd lost something in an Asian land, buried her youth in Arlington and now, at age thirty-five, she feared God more than worshiped him.

—the baby, that innocent flesh—why take the baby?

How would she explain that to Arnold?

Nobody's fault . . . fell in the lake . . .

She put a hand to her chest, breasts aching as if lactating, her throat parched. She was breathless with memory: Arnold lost in

11

war, the drowning of their son four years later. Grief had subsided, but anger was unceasing.

"These emotions are quite normal, Mrs. Curry," the psychiatrist had intoned. "The injustice of loss overtakes us. We are
enraged. We feel we must strike out at something, somebody.
Failing that, we often attack ourselves."

"I blame God!"

"If there is a God," the doctor condescended, "I'm sure he can
bear it. But in any case, stop blaming yourself."

That was when she ceased to see the analyst. She had never
blamed herself. Not for Arnold dying in Vietnam. Not for Tony
drowning in Lake Lanier.

And yet . . .

Blaise was motionless, watching Richard in his garden. The
girl's spectacles gave her the visage of a predatory bird perched
unseen above a prey. Behind those perfect circles cornflower blue
eyes followed Richard as he snipped and discarded severed vege-
tation. What thought created such intensity, such immobility?

Richard was stooped, his back to them, dress trousers rolled to
protect them from dew. Moisture was strewn in a trillion lumi-
nous beads, each sphere reflecting others, capturing an emerging
sun in a cloudless sky.

Richard straightened, stretching, and as he did so Blaise
seemed to, in a single fluid step, move sideways so that as Richard
turned, she was hidden by a post which supported a partial roof
over the patio.

Richard glanced toward the house. Ellen was struck by her own
involuntary response—drawing away, like Blaise. Richard re-
sumed his chore, snipping, discarding, walking between rows of
bean and tomato plants, unaware.

Behind the post, Blaise held her pose, perfectly erect, slender
arms loose at her side. Ellen had seen the girl so immersed that
Blaise was oblivious to everything but the focal point of her observation.

She had once discovered Blaise staring at a photograph of Arnold.

"Handsome man," Ellen had interrupted.

"Is that the way he looked?"

It was a tinted photo of Arnold in dress uniform, captain's bars, medals on his chest. "It's a reasonable likeness. A bit too pink, perhaps. His cheeks weren't as rosy."

"He looks like Tony," Blaise concluded.

It had become a part of Ellen's maternal obligation to create memories, because Blaise did not remember her father. Oh, yes, Blaise had moments locked away like still photographs. "Some are color," Blaise explained, "some are black and white. Some are sharp; the time daddy carried me on his shoulders walking through an airport. Others are fuzzy—impressions, more than memories."

So Ellen recounted stories as they came to mind. She painted images of Arnold in positive strokes. His laughter relieved sadness, his humor leavened life's darker moments. Ellen invented memories for Blaise, telling of their courtship, the early days of marriage, joyful, untethered by worry.

It was not an accurate picture, of course. But why cloud a daughter's illusion with grayer thoughts?

"He must've been a wonderful man," Blaise once sighed, "Tony must be a lot like him."

He was.

"When I watch Tony then," Blaise observed, "it's like seeing daddy when he was a little boy."

The childish comment had become the most comforting and painful single sentence of Ellen's life. She had lost her first husband, father of her child—and yet, through Tony, a genetic reinstatement evolved before her eyes. Arnold's chromosomes recreated the straight black hair with a maddening cowlick no barber ever conquered. Arnold's genes gave Tony a rolling gait when he was especially proud of something, coming to tell his mother. When Tony cocked his head, weren't those Arnold's slate gray eyes sparkling with humor?

Ellen's hand knotted her blouse, the memory so acute, so painful—

. . . sleeping . . . as if chilled only for want of a comforter . . .

Stop it.

. . . hold him, warm him, breath air into those tender lungs . . .
Stop it.
. . . he was limp, not stiff. . . the water was cold . . . revive . . .
Stop! Stop—God!

"Mama?" the cry came from afar.

"Mama!" Blaise had seized Ellen's arms.

"I'm all right, Blaise."

The girl pulled Ellen into her arms, child comforting parent, stroking, murmuring assurances.

"I'm all right, Blaise." Ellen tried to withdraw, but Blaise continued holding her. She felt the girl sob and tears were warm spatters on Ellen's neck. "Blaise, I didn't mean to frighten you."

"I'm not afraid, mama."

"Upset, then."

"I'm not upset."

Ellen laughed huskily, "Nothing wrong with me, nothing wrong with you—why are we hanging onto one another weeping?"

Blaise pulled back, lifted her spectacles and used a dish towel to blot her eyes.

"The biscuits should be done," Ellen said. "How about calling your dad?"

Alone again, she watched the girl descend to the lawn, moving toward Richard. Blaise must've spoken. Richard stood up, waved, and went for his basket of strawberries.

Theirs was a comfortable life, a contented existence. This house with the best view in Mobile, this neighborhood of the affluent and ascending. They had weathered the depths of despair after Tony drowned and Richard's grief had caused his business to fail in Atlanta. They moved here for a new beginning and he was back in the import-export trade—Blaise attended the best school—theirs was a good life.

And yet . . .

Putting dirty dishes in the sink, she saw Richard showing strawberries to Blaise. He put his arm around the girl and she met the embrace.

And yet . . .

Before Arnold was killed, when they were half a world apart, worrying about a disintegrating marriage, talking of divorce, Ellen had suffered a similar vague depression, lying awake nights, haggard for want of sleep—she'd half expected the officers who came to tell her Arnold was dead.

She had felt the same uneasiness before Richard impulsively suggested going to Lake Lanier for a week of vacation. An Atlanta photographer she admired had invited Ellen to come to his gallery opening. At the last instant, she'd determined to go with Richard and the children, but Richard teased her out of the decision.

"You can rent a car and drive to Cummings," he'd insisted. "I'll pick you up at the rental office when you drop it off."

So, she'd stayed to see the photo exhibition. Her last glimpse of Tony alive was a toothy smile and a frenetic wave as they drove away.

Later, motoring toward Lake Lanier, that ominous depression enveloped her and she shoved her foot down on the accelerator. Instead of waiting at the car rental office—she was early—she drove directly to the secluded lake house.

They had just found Tony.

Blaise staggered out of the woods, face bloodless. Richard was screaming, "I told you to watch him, Blaise!"

But when he saw Ellen, Richard wailed, "It was my fault, Ellen! I left them to go to the grocery store for a few minutes. I shouldn't have left them alone. God forgive me—it was my fault!"

Nobody's fault.

For two years, Blaise suffered nightmares, coming awake gurgling as if she'd been immersed, fighting for oxygen. Richard lost interest in his business, almost lost his sanity—their marriage had trembled to its foundations—he still blamed himself.

The back door slammed and Richard entered, grinning, holding up his basket, "Look at those berries!"

"They're beautiful."

15

"Ah," he sniffed the air, "biscuits. I'll have strawberries with my biscuits. How about it, kitten?" He addressed Blaise, "Join me?"

"No, thank you."

"Sun warmed and dew kissed," Richard washed the fruit, appreciatively.

Blaise stared at Richard's back.

"Blaise," Ellen instructed, "get the butter, will you?"

"Blaise! Get the butter!"

Startled, Blaise blinked, nodded.

"A bit testy my dear," Richard admonished without rancor. "That girl goes into oblivion sometimes."

"Did you ever see strawberries finer than these?"

She came up behind him, arms circling his waist. Peering over Richard's shoulder, she saw Blaise doing as told, angry and hurt.

"Damn me," Ellen whispered.

"Make it up with a kiss," Richard advised.

She went out onto the patio. "I'm not myself this morning," she pulled the girl into a hug, kissing first one cheek, then the other. Blaise faked a smile, but her muscles were taut, the affection unanswered.

Richard arrived with a bowl of berries, paused to take a deep inhalation and enjoy the view before sitting at the table. For several minutes they ate in silence.

"I'm debating taking a class in computer science, daddy," Blaise said. "What do you think?"

"It's an up and coming subject." Richard poured coffee.

"I believe it is," Blaise noted. "If it's all right, I'd like to take an evening course at the University of South Alabama. That is, if nobody objects."

"Ellen, do you have any objections to this child educating herself?"

"None."

"I assume," Richard spoke to Blaise, but winked at Ellen, "you have a need other than money?"

"Transportation. But I can get a ride with an older student, I think."

16

Richard lifted a palm, "See, there it is—everything worked out in an instant."

"Not quite, actually," Blaise said. "I need a computer."

"Computer? They don't provide computers?"

"They do. But it would help if I had a computer here at home. I consider it essential, actually."

"I believe we're about to hear a sales pitch," Richard mused. "How much does this essential cost?"

"I'm not sure. Maybe nothing."

"That's cheap enough," Richard sipped coffee.

"There's a machine in the attic," Blaise said, hesitantly.

"Blaise, have you been prowling around up there?" Ellen asked.

"I didn't disturb anything."

"I'd forgotten that," Richard said. "You're right, I had a computer for keeping inventory—it may need repair."

"The keyboard works," Blaise stated. "The video display, too. I'm not sure about the memory, I don't know how to test it. But, I know somebody who might patch it up."

"Could I have the bottom line of this recitation?"

"May I use it, daddy?"

"It's yours."

She leaped to her feet. "Thanks! I know a man who can help me figure it out. He's a computer expert." She kissed Richard brusquely, left him laughing, and bounded into the house.

"For a girl doing poorly in science and mathematics," Ellen said, "I can't imagine Blaise excited about computers."

"Don't get your hopes too high," Richard warned. "Young people today want a computer so they can play *Star Wars*."

Richard gazed toward the eastern horizon, chewing his food with eyes narrowed. "Going to be a beautiful day," he said.

"Before you leave for the office, Richard, roll down your trousers."

He did so absently, looking at the skyline. "I suppose if that equipment doesn't work," he murmured, "we should buy whatever Blaise needs."

"To play games?"

"Even video games are instructional."

"Let's not make any decisions on that," Ellen gathered plates, stacking them. "Her grades are in a slump, her teachers say Blaise daydreams constantly. She mopes. She's melancholy."

"She's going into her teens, Ellen."

"Is that a cause or a symptom?"

It's normal. Listen, I'm having lunch at the International Trade Center today. How about coming down?"

"I've promised to do a photo essay for the *Mobala News*."

The sounds of traffic were a soft moan as the city awakened. Fog was lifting and on the horizon Mobile Bay was a gleaming crescent.

"I'll have to get her some software," Richard thought aloud. "I'll try to remember to call somebody about that."

"Don't get too involved in this until we see whether Blaise is serious, Richard. Remember the guitar lessons."

"I know."

"Darling," Ellen put a hand on his wrist, "we overdo."

He nodded, but she saw he wasn't listening. Ellen turned abruptly, going to the kitchen. Upstairs, she saw a curtain flutter and caught a glimpse of Blaise pulling back.

She left the dishes on the counter and went up to Blaise's room. The girl was still at the window, looking down on Richard below.

"What are you doing, Blaise?"

"Looking outside."

"For what?"

Blaise lifted her shoulders, dropped them. She moved as if to leave and Ellen blocked her way. "Blaise, what's going on?"

"Nothing, mom. I have to go, or I'll be late."

Hurriedly, the girl ran downstairs and a moment later Ellen heard the front door close. The hall clock chimed.

Ellen scanned the room—dirty clothes under the bed, books on the floor, an opened closet door. On a wall were posters of John Denver, Robert Redford, and incongruously, Albert Einstein. The vanity was dusty with bath powder, a tube of colorless lip rouge lay uncapped and drying.

Something was wrong.

She'd learned the hard way with Arnold and Tony—do not defeat intuition with logic. Ellen crossed to the window and peered down. The garden was receiving the first rays of morning sun.

"Ellen?"

Startled, she whirled.

"What are you doing?" Richard inquired.

"Looking out the window."

"At what?"

"Nothing." She paused to kiss him, his dark eyes reflecting curiosity. "I have to hurry, Richard. I'll be late."

She reached the hallway and halted. "Richard, you do love me, don't you?"

"More than life."

"Are you happy with me? With Blaise?"

"More than you know, Ellen. Is something wrong?"

"No. Nothing wrong."

But she knew fear. She knew the portent of change. Even when she couldn't isolate the cause—she knew something was amiss.

T WO

Chapter

Carbon monoxide was a sweetly toxic aroma as Ellen drove through traffic on Government Boulevard. The city was growing rapidly, industry expanding, "snowbirds" fleeing northern climes, more vehicles using the same arteries. From passing cars came the blare of radios, drivers encased in metal cocoons unaware of their volume.

She worried not about text or photo contrast this morning. She worried about Blaise.

The teachers at St. Paul's had reported a shift in temperament. "Blaise isn't interested anymore, Mrs. Curry. She sits and stares out the window. She doesn't turn in assignments, and as you know, that's a new wrinkle for Blaise. She's courteous enough, always has been. But she isn't *here*. Where she is, we don't know—but mentally she isn't in class."

There had been long discussions, labored parental urging, threats of restrictions. Finally, Richard insisted they ease up and let Blaise excel where she excelled, slip where her interests flagged. "Nobody is keen about everything," he'd argued. "There's little

20

point in making the girl miserable because she can't get enthused about algebra."

But it wasn't mathematics alone. Blaise no longer read voraciously. And when she did it was *True Romance*, detective magazines, pulp fiction.

Maybe this professed intrigue with computers was good. Better to study instructional pamphlets than gory sex crimes. Ellen turned into the driveway of a residential structure which was home for the *Mobala News*. She drove beneath a portico constructed in the days of horse and buggy to protect passengers from inclement weather.

"Stop and think about it, Ellen," Richard had recently argued. "Blaise has been attending school for eight years, plus kindergarten makes nine years—she's weary of it."

As he had noted, Blaise *was* becoming a teenager. The girl's beanpole body had developed angular hips, her knees were no longer knobby. Beneath her blouse, the blossoming of womanhood was all too evident. As bone outgrew muscle and tendon, she'd suffered the pangs of growth—clumsiness. It would pass. Was passing. Already she had assumed some of the grace of femininity, and she used her female attributes with a cunning which, to Ellen's eyes, was not altogether intuitive.

Richard thought she worried too much.

"Nothing is wrong with Blaise," he insisted. "She's a healthy girl doing healthy things. She sits and 'sulks' as you put it, because she's trying to come to grips with maturity."

Still seated in her car, Ellen stared at a wall of wisteria that screened this lot from the building next door. A bumblebee inspected blossoms, its legs in pollen jodhpurs.

"Would you care to join the living? Or sit here all day?"

She smiled, opening her car door.

"Do you have these spells often?" Armand Joaquin asked pleasantly.

"Only when I think about children."

Ellen gathered materials to carry inside, but the publisher took them from her arms. "Children are God's way of punishing us for what we did to our parents," Armand observed. "Hence, being wiser than the Almighty, I have invested in proper preventive measures."

"That's what happens when you wait until you're thirty," Ellen joked. "By then you're too smart to do something only the young would dare to try—but, having children is also when one's life begins."

"I'm sure. Did you finish developing the photos?"

"Yes."

"How do they look?"

"All right." Ellen followed him through a storage room, past a typesetter, into the front office. Her subject had been a production of the Joe Jefferson Players theatrical group, amateurs with the talent of professional thespians.

"We're holding the center spread for this," Armand said. "When you finish the copy, give it to Joe so he can set type."

An advertising salesman pulled Armand away and Ellen sat at the "community" desk which was used by anyone who needed it. She pushed things aside, making space for herself.

There was little pay with this job. More free-lance than full-time, she had the option of selecting assignments, accepting or rejecting those suggested by others. But it had served a dire need when they first moved to Mobile. Through the newspaper she met people, stayed active, and her by-line brought attention to her photographic work. She and Armand were the two oldest employees of his enterprise.

A hand shook her shoulder and Ellen turned. "Darling," Armand frowned, "where are you this morning? I was yelling from the back door."

"I'm sorry, Armand."

"Worried about her kid," Armand told his wife, "that's what babies do to you. The brain atrophies, the hair goes gray, hearing fails."

"I'm sorry," Ellen apologized.

"I was saying," Armand enunciated, "we lost an account, so expand your article to fill a double truck spread."

"I'll enlarge the photos."

"Don't neglect the story," Armand spoke, departing. "History of theater, background on the director."

Peggy Joaquin shoved away from her desk and rolled nearer to Ellen. "Blaise isn't in trouble, is she?"

"No." *Not yet.*

Peggy leaned on a corner of Ellen's desk, voice lowered. "I've been trying to talk Armand into starting a family. But he thinks about what a pain in the ass *he* was, and he's sure any kid of ours would have a short tail with a green tuft."

Ellen sorted through photos selecting images to illustrate her text.

"I've thought about pulling the plug," Peggy confided. "Accidents do happen. He couldn't turn back the clock once it started ticking."

Ellen held up a portrait of several black children. "What do you think of this shot, Peggy?"

"Too busy."

"I suppose so."

"I told Armand, he likes the practice, but he doesn't want the natural consequences."

Peggy cast a glance at her husband and returned to Ellen in a whisper, "I might pull the plug and give him a surprise one of these days. We aren't getting any younger."

"You have plenty of time."

"I'm twenty-eight. *Tempus fugit.*"

Ellen forced concentration on the task at hand. She produced a three-thousand-word article, then delivered it to the long-haired youth setting type.

"That's a computer, isn't it?" Ellen questioned.

"Right. Hold the photos, Ellen—all I need is the type." As his fingers moved over the keyboard, words appeared in green on a display before him. He pushed buttons which "reconciled" the text, forming columns.

"Looks complicated," Ellen said.

"Not really. The program came preset."

"What does that mean?"

23

"I can select a font, type size, and feed in the words," he worked as he talked. "The program was already set up to do that, I certainly couldn't have done it." He tossed his head, paused, corrected an error, commenced working again.

"Telephone, Ellen!"

"I'm calling about Blaise," a mature woman's voice announced.

"Yes?"

"She has asked permission to leave school, she was having menstrual pains. I wanted you to know she went home."

"Thank you."

After hanging up, Ellen stood with a hand on the phone. Should she call home? Did that suggest distrust? She could ask how Blaise was feeling.

"Can you do a story on the school board next week, Ellen?" Armand questioned.

"I suppose so."

"I want something on the teacher-incompetency controversy."

"I'll see what I can do."

"We have one of the wealthiest school systems in the nation, more money spent per student than some cities three times our size, and yet the quality of education seems to be lower—why? That's the slant I want."

She dialed the house. The telephone rang, unanswered.

"If nobody needs me," she said, "I'm going home."

"I'll count on you for the school thing," Armand called.

"Right!"

When Ellen entered, the house felt empty, air musty. "Blaise?"

Ellen walked through the kitchen, looking out back. The rear door was latched from inside. She returned to the entrance and climbed carpeted stairs.

"Blaise, darling!"

Silence. She peered into the girl's bedroom. Everything as it had been this morning. Nobody in the bathroom.

Obviously, Blaise had gone elsewhere before coming home. Irritated, Ellen had started for the stairs when she heard a dull thump. She strained to listen, waiting. Another noise. The attic.

She turned the knob slowly, the door scraping the carpet as it swung open. Overhead, the attic was lighted. She started to call Blaise by name, but a humming sound kept her silent. Ellen ascended the steps carefully, stealthily.

The girl was sitting at the computer they'd shipped down from Atlanta. On her right was a manual, the machine topped by a green screen, much like the typesetting display at the newspaper office.

She watched Blaise type with one finger, slowly. Then, back to the manual again, studying instructions. The room was surprisingly cool. Ellen realized Blaise had opened the vents. That explained the recent jump in the cost of utilities!

"Blaise, what are you doing?"

The girl jolted, wheeling to face her mother.

"Are you ill, or not?"

"The usual cramps, mama."

"If you were suffering enough to come home from class, aren't you suffering too much to do anything else?"

"If I have to go to the bathroom, it's right there," Blaise said. "I don't have to advertise it to thirty other students."

Ellen moved toward her and Blaise closed the manual.

"What is that, Blaise?"

"It tells how to set up a program."

"What kind of program?"

"COBOL."

"What is that?"

"Common Business Oriented Language."

Ellen took the manual and flipped pages. Signs, symbols, digits. "What do you do with this, Blaise?"

"If a computer isn't programmed, it's only metal and wires."

Ellen looked around, holding the instructions. Boxes of old receipts, files from Richard's failed business in Atlanta, ledgers and correspondence.

"Does the machine work?"

"I won't know until I complete the program."

Ellen returned the manual and bent to peer at the screen. Nothing made sense. "What is all that?"

"It's the language of the computer."

Visually, Ellen traced the contours of the equipment. She looked behind the machine. "That looks like a special receptacle, Blaise."

"Three-prong plug, just like an electric stove."

"I didn't know there was that kind of wiring up here."

Blaise punched buttons, the television screen went dark.

"Why would anyone put in any special wiring up here?" Ellen questioned.

"A friend of mine did it."

"What?"

"A few weekends ago when you and dad were down at Gulf Shores overnight."

"The night you spent with a friend."

"I did. But during the day, a friend of mine put in the plug. No big deal."

"Tampering with the wiring?"

"The wires were here, mama. All it took was combining circuits."

Blaise met her gaze, with unflickering blue eyes. "Nothing to worry about, mama."

"Who is this friend?"

"He's a student at Southwest Tech. He dropped out of public school last year. His father is an electrician."

"Blaise, I don't want to be critical but this—does Richard know somebody has tampered with the wiring?"

"You say 'tamper' as if the purpose had been to damage it, mama. The machine works. It's on a separate fuse in the box. It's perfectly safe and my friend helps his father do such things all the time."

"Blaise, why do I feel so—so—"

"Suspicious."

"Cautious, certainly."

"You're a mother. It comes with the territory."

"I don't want to be critical unnecessarily."

Blaise shrugged, began placing things in order, pulling a cover over the machine.

"Actually, I want to participate in things you enjoy," Ellen said. "I pictured helping my daughter to knit, or teaching her to sew someday—but this!"

Blaise laughed, throatily. "I don't want to be a seamstress, mama. I might enjoy being a computer programmer."

"And that's marvelous, darling."

An instant of skepticism appeared, vanished. Blaise pushed up her glasses with a long forefinger and stood there, waiting.

"I suppose this is all right," Ellen conceded.

"We did a pretty good job, if I say so myself," Blaise countered genially. "Two of the transistors were weak and I got a friend to replace them. The wiring had to be adjusted and a friend did that. I'm not bothering anybody with anything, I'm doing it myself."

"I see you are and that's fine."

"You're intimidated, mama. That's all. By what you don't understand. By the lights and the gadgets. The computer is only a yes-and-no machine. It doesn't have personality, it isn't going to gain intelligence on its own. It can do only what it has been told to do—and then only to the extent of the ability of the person who programmed it."

"That's intimidating, all right."

Blaise linked her arm with Ellen's and they moved toward the stairs. "I don't know why the thing fascinates me so much, but it does," she said. "It's like looking into my own brain, seeing my own intellect reflected on the video. It's a game, almost."

"I can understand that."

"Then, you don't mind if I continue?"

"No, no, I don't mind."

At the hall, Blaise closed the attic door. Ellen heard the turn of a tumbler. "You're locking the door?"

"Is that all right?"

"But, why?"

"Why not?" Blaise furrowed a smooth brow, smiling. "But if it bothers you, I won't do it."

"We have never isolated one another in this family, have we?"

Blaise unlocked the door. She gave the key to Ellen.

"It's a matter of principle."

"No sweat."

Ellen kissed her and Blaise went to her room, closing the door.

Intimidated. *Perhaps that was it.* Not the resentment of a mother feeling threatened by a maturing daughter—but intimidated!

Intimidated or threatened, the source was the same. It was in the air again, that surge of warning from some subconscious part of her brain.

Despite Blaise's wide-eyed innocence, something was wrong.

T Chapter HREE

Richard washed his hands under a garden hose before coming onto the patio. He sat with Ellen, lit a cigarette and mopped his brow. "What are they doing up there, Ellen?"

"Playing with that machine."

"A strange way for kids to spend Saturday."

"All last week."

"Um."

"Have you met this boy?" Ellen asked.

"No."

"I've seen toads with a healthier complexion. Long stringy hair, glasses that must weigh six ounces—but fortunately he has a nose capable of supporting the weight."

"He must have something," Richard suggested mildly. "Blaise is not indiscriminate about her choice of companions."

"I know precisely what he has. He's two years older, he's already completed the computer course she's taking. The descriptive word Blaise uses most often is 'brain.'"

"Have you been up to check on them?"

"Oh I went. But they didn't see me. They sit there like two gnomes poring over whatever it is they pore over."

"Well," Richard stood up, "let's take a peek. Anytime a youngster is silent this long, I get nervous."

At the top of the stairs, in the attic, Richard frowned a moment. Blaise was digging through several boxes of computer cards.

"Blaise, what are you doing?" he queried.

"Oh, hi, dad. You don't mind if we test the machine with some old cards, do you?"

"Those are probably in some sort of order," Richard said.

"They are," the boy spoke without turning to look at the adults.

"Dad, this is Herman Krause. My dad, Richard Curry."

"Divorce, I take it." Herman still had not faced them.

"My first dad died," Blaise replied. She brightened, "Herman says I don't have to program the computer! It's already programmed. We were just checking it out."

Richard's face darkened. He moved nearer to stand behind Herman. "You know about this thing, do you, Herman?"

"Yeah. IBM System-thirty-two. It didn't stay on the market long. Batch oriented. Sixteen- to thirty-two-K capacity."

"You lost me, Herman," Richard acknowledged.

"Thirty-two-K means," Blaise elaborated, "the machine can hold thirty-two thousand bits."

"Bytes," Herman amended. "A byte is eight bits. It's limited, and that's why it didn't stay on the market very long. Came out in 1974 and IBM replaced it a couple of years later. Ready, Blaise?"

Ellen was startled by Richard's expression as he watched Blaise place a stack of the cards in the chute at one end of the machine.

Herman continued, "The data is all on punched cards, which is now an antiquated system. Here we go—"

Eyes bright, Blaise grinned as Herman leaned over the keyboard. "What we want, let us say," he muttered, "is inventory on hand. You did get these cards from the box marked inventory, right?"

"Right," Blaise said.

He pushed a button. The machine made a fluttering noise and the cards disappeared in a few seconds. Herman reached down to retrieve them and absently gave them back to Blaise. On the screen was the word WAIT.

"Now, let's see what we have here," Herman whispered. He pushed another button. Green lines of text flowed across the screen. "That's one of the problems right there," Herman said. "Relatively slow."

"It works!" Blaise exulted.

"Not as good as electronic storage, not as fast," Herman intoned. "But it beat bookkeeping by hand, at the time."

Richard glowered at the screen and when Blaise touched his arm excitedly, he nodded grimly. "That's interesting, darling."

"This stuff is all old," Blaise said. "Do you mind if I use it for practice, daddy?"

"What can you learn by doing that?" Richard questioned.

Herman looked up, glasses reflecting light overhead. "You're in the import-export business, obviously."

"Yes."

"Half a million net was some kind of business. Still at it?"

Ellen sensed discomfort. "Yes," Richard replied, "same business. Blaise, be certain to put those cards exactly where you found them. Those are for tax purposes."

"Outdated," Herman surmised. "Except in case of fraud, the IRS can't go back that far."

"You seem to know a great deal about such matters," Richard said, crisply.

"It's how I make my bread. You need a programmer with your business?"

"My business is already functioning."

"Hah, yeah," Herman said, "but how efficiently? I could take a look for you—no charge."

"Thanks for the offer. Blaise, don't you think you've spent

enough time in a dark attic for one day? Maybe Herman would enjoy some lemonade."

"Can't take the acidity," Herman noted. "Sours my juices. Got to go anyway. Any questions?"

Blaise put a hand on his shoulder, "I'll call if I need anything else."

"Always glad to help a hacker," Herman arose on two incredibly bowed legs and walked eggbeater fashion across the room, Blaise's arm around his shoulder.

Richard reached over and shut off the machine.

"Is something wrong, Richard?"

"No. He's right, these are outdated records."

"Blaise would understand if you forbade her to—"

"No," Richard sounded irritable, "don't worry about it."

Richard turned off the lights as he followed Ellen down the attic steps. He closed the door, then asked, "Where is the key?"

"I took it. It's downstairs in the den, on your desk. Do you need to lock it?"

"I was only curious."

When they reached the kitchen, Blaise was making herself a sandwich. "He's a brain, isn't he, dad?"

"It's difficult to judge on a subject about which I know so little," Richard said. His tone made Blaise look up.

"I know he seems a bit odd," she stated. "He's not very popular with other students."

"He goes to your school with hair that long?"

"No. He's a sophomore at the university."

"Seventeen, you said—how can he be in college?"

Ellen watched the girl shift to cautious responses. "He has an I.Q. of one sixty," she explained. "He's a brain, like I said."

"Um," Richard turned on a heel. "Well, the world needs such types."

"Put you off, right?" Blaise asked.

"Charm and grace are not his strongest attributes," Ellen offered.

"I guess not," Blaise said. "Hey! Anybody else want a peanut butter and banana sandwich?"

But Richard was already out the back door now, letting it slam shut. Blaise watched through the kitchen window as he left the patio, went to his tool shed and began to gather what he needed for gardening.

"Pissed him off," Blaise murmured.

"What?" Ellen demanded. "What did you say?"

"Kissed him off, I said."

"That's not what you said and don't say that again."

Blaise had a disarming way of meeting conflict.

"How about a sandwich, mama? I'll make it."

"No."

"Gracious," Blaise made a prim mouth. "Everybody is so tense today."

In the days to follow, Ellen witnessed a procession of "Hermans." Blaise had joined a computer club at the university, which seemed restricted to the most talented of the Herman types.

"A pretty seedy looking lot," Richard grumped.

"Does the possession of 'brains' preclude other civilized qualities?"

"They live in a world all their own, daddy," Blaise placated. "But they're the mobies."

"Mobies?"

"Biggies."

"As in Moby Dick, I assume."

"I'm not sure," Blaise said. "But don't judge them by their manners, daddy. Last week, Herman got a call from a company in Lucedale, Mississippi and he earned $2,000 correcting a bagbiter."

"Which is?"

"Something failed in the machine," Blaise said. "Herman said it wasn't crufty, but nobody there could—" she paused, "Crufty means 'overcomplicated.' Anyway, Herman said it was just a dump and—"

Richard threw up a hand.

"Dump is what happens when the memory overloads," Blaise explained. "It begins to print out nonsense. Herman said the frotz was—"

"Hey!" Richard leaped to his feet. "If your purpose is to be ostentatious, Blaise, you fail. Slang is an indication of communications breakdown."

"A frotz is an electronic black box," Blaise responded, more subdued. "It isn't slang, daddy. It's jargon."

"Yes, well, when one's language interferes with one's capacity to be understood, it is pretentious and infuriating. Incidentally," Richard snapped, "I've decided to clear out all those business records in the attic and—"

"Daddy! Why?"

"It's junk, that's why. It's clutter. It will give you more room to move about."

"But I'm using it."

"For what purpose, Blaise?"

"It's all I have to work with."

"How can you learn anything from junk records?"

"But I do! I see orders that came in, the transaction which followed, the goods shipped out, billing processes, accounts receivable—"

Richard's black eyes darted here, there, turned to Ellen. "The place is a fire hazard and machines create heat."

"There's no heat," Blaise countered. "The computer is solid-state, transistorized—there are no vacuum tubes and that is what used to make so much heat."

"Nevertheless, there have been a dozen people going up there and I found a cigarette butt on the floor yesterday."

"That won't happen again," Blaise insisted. "I told that boy never to smoke up there again—it's bad for the computer."

"Damn it, Blaise!" Richard snapped. "I'm trying to accommodate you, but I won't allow juvenile games to present us with hazards, is that understood?"

"But, daddy, I'm being very careful. I'm sorry about the cigarette. That won't happen again, I swear it."

"The junk goes out."

"Daddy," Blaise choked, paused, took a breath, "daddy, please don't be angry. I'm learning something very important. I was showing off, using words to impress you. I thought it would show you how much I'm learning. This is a good thing I'm doing, daddy. Mama? Really! It's interesting and exciting, but it is also good. I know Herman and the others look odd to you, but they're in parse—"

Blaise winced. "They understand everything," she said. "They're teaching me and they aren't on the make."

"Blaise!"

"They don't even see my body, mama. They see my brain! They admire what's really me."

Richard returned to his chair.

"Daddy—please?"

"I'll think about it, Blaise."

"Look," Blaise reasoned, "the problem with the computer is like Herman said, it's slow, but that's okay—I'm slow. But its greatest shortcoming is a matter of storage. Data is stored several ways—on cards with holes punched in them, like the one upstairs. Or on paper tape with holes punched in it, and on reels. Or on magnetic tape. The new systems have magnetic cores—little wires with doughnut shaped rings which are magnetized, and that forms the storage, the memory. I don't have that. I have cards. But without your old business cards and records, I would have nothing!"

"I'll buy you some new cards then."

"No, daddy—then I'd need a machine to make the holes in them and—it isn't worth investing in it. This machine is outdated already. For me, right now, it's fine. But—don't you see? If I can use what's up there, I will learn a tremendous amount of things. Just running the cards through, I learn analysis, accounting, even programming, because I'm figuring out how to use this system and make it more efficient."

"What do you think, Ellen?"

"Dear Lord, Richard—I don't understand a word of this!"

"All right, Blaise," he said. "For the time being, you may continue. But the decision is temporary. No more smoking in the attic—no nonsense from your friends. Understood?"

"Yessir. Thank you, daddy."

He arose, paused for the obligatory kiss of peace, then left the room. Instantly, Blaise's face hardened.

"Blaise, your expression resembles insolence."

"I didn't mean for it to be," she said. "I wasn't thinking about daddy just then. I mean—not about *this* daddy."

"Blaise, sit down with me."

The girl sat.

"I know you think Arnold, your father, was the perfect man," Ellen said. "I've helped to create that impression. Your father was indeed a wonderful man. But at moments like this, when you and Richard have had a disagreement, I see your thoughts as if they were printed across your forehead: 'this isn't what my real father would have done.' Am I right?"

Blaise swallowed.

"You are doing yourself a disservice and being unfair to Richard. It is unrealistic to indulge in these little fantasies, Blaise. Arnold could have been a tyrant with a girl of your wit and intelligence, or too indulgent—who knows how war and time would have altered him? But in any case, he couldn't love you more, want to please you more than Richard. Richard adores you, darling. He may worry a bit but that's an indication of love."

Eyes downcast, Blaise nodded.

"When you stare after Richard with such an unforgiving expression," Ellen said, "I want to shake you. Richard hardly ever refuses anything you or I ask. It is unfair of you—and it would be unfair of me—to demand that he compete with a person whose faults we no longer remember. Arnold was not perfect. Nobody is."

"I'm not stupid, mama."

"Of course you aren't."

"Mama—do you ever—" Blaise gazed past Ellen at a wall. "Do you ever think about how Tony would be?"

Ellen felt her chest constrict. She answered with as much control as she could muster, "Tony is six years old forever, Blaise."

"I—sometimes I—" the girl started to stand and Ellen grabbed her wrist.

"Some of that day is so sharp I can hear the birds chirping as daddy and I walked the bank of the lake," Blaise said. "Some of it is not clear at all. I'm not sure what is real and what isn't, anymore."

"That's nature's way of protecting us from pain, darling."

"When I first realized Tony was gone, after daddy left to go to the grocery store—I ran from room to room, looking, calling. Tony never wandered off. I couldn't make him stay away from me—remember? He'd be right behind me when I turned around, talking ninety miles an hour. You remember that, don't you?"

"Yes," the word came as a bubble of sound.

"Why did he go off that day, then?" Blaise wailed. "Why sneak off? And why did he go where we found him?"

"Maybe he was looking for Richard," Ellen said weakly.

"I'm upsetting you," Blaise said. "I'm sorry."

"If you feel you must talk about it—"

"The first couple of years I just hated myself for letting it happen. But now, I keep asking questions—and mama, I can't remember how much was true. How far *was* he from the cottage, really?"

"Blaise—"

The girl leaned forward, face intense, "I was making up the beds, like daddy had asked. When I realized Tony was gone, I ran all over looking for him."

"Blaise, please—"

"I ran up the road, to the top of the hill—I saw—"

"Hey!" Richard spoke from the doorway. "What's happening in here with you two?"

"Nothing, daddy."

"It sounded as though you're having a fight."

"No sir."

"Well, I have made a decision, Blaise—and this one isn't temporary."

She waited apprehensively.

"I'm going to invest in your future, my love," Richard said. "Monday, we're going shopping for computers. Nothing old-fashioned, nothing out of mode—how's that for lingo?"

"Buy me a new one?"

"Brand new and with whatever memory storage you need. You have impressed me, and I admit it—your interest seems genuine."

"It is, daddy."

"Then so be it."

"Wait a minute, Richard," Ellen interjected.

"I'll charge it off as a tax deduction, Ellen. Blaise can consider it hers, but the books will show it as a business cost."

"Can you do that?" Ellen questioned.

"Done all the time! I think it's an honest assumption that Blaise may end up being my number one stock controller someday."

Blaise blinked behind her glasses. "A new computer costs lots of money, daddy."

"What is a lot?" Ellen asked.

"From a thousand dollars to—six thousand is what I need."

"Six thousand dollars!"

"Worth it," Richard concluded. "That's as cheap as two years of college, maybe cheaper."

"Richard, we need to think about this."

"My mind is made up, Ellen. Unless you veto it."

"No, of course not. But that's such a huge sum."

"Worth it," Richard said sharply. "Blaise is right, she is doing a good thing. She isn't smoking pot and slinging quarters into video games at the arcade."

"Six thousand dollars," Ellen breathed.

Richard gave a quick nod. "Going to my garden," he said.

Ellen repeated, "Six thousand dollars! Blaise, are you actually that interested?"

"It's very important to me, mama. Maybe the most important thing in my life."

F Chapter OUR

Impetuously, Richard had abandoned his garden, suggesting, "Let's go to Gulf Shores and spend the night."

"Do I have to?" Blaise had demurred. "My computer club meets this evening."

"Uh-oh," Richard feigned, "we'll be alone, Ellen."

The sun was almost down now, the highway latticed by shadow patterns of loblolly pines. Richard drove, relaxed, but preoccupied. When he caught her looking at him, he winked, patted Ellen's knee.

It had always been one of his most endearing traits to suddenly cast aside the world and do something unexpected.

"Richard, is everything all right?"

"What could be wrong?"

"I don't know."

He patted her knee again, absently.

The Gulf State Lodge was part of Alabama's park system. Each two-story unit formed eight rooms, all with a view of the Gulf and white sandy beaches. It was one of their favorite retreats.

"Blaise will be all right," he said, as if she'd asked.

"I wasn't worrying about her being alone."

His hand patted, eyes on the road.

"Be all right," he murmured, sing-song.

"I meant," Ellen queried, "is anything wrong with you? With us?"

Now she had his attention. "Of course not."

She clasped his hand tightly. "I'm very zealous where our happiness is concerned," she said. "For so many years I was not happy—now that I am, I fear any threat no matter how remote."

"Don't poison the moment with dire portent, Ellen."

"I've told myself almost the same thing. I don't want to do that, either. But I've seen you tense lately, mostly because of Blaise."

"There's nothing wrong between Blaise and me."

"That's what I wanted to know."

He squeezed her hand, pulled free. "We ought to buy a place down here on the Gulf," he said. "We both enjoy it."

"Outside of monetary consideration," Ellen replied, "we don't spend enough time here to warrant such a purchase."

"People ought to enjoy the fruits of their labors," he said. "Business has been good."

"That good?"

"Pretty good," he said. "Ah, here we are!"

For dinner they had superb trout almondine with an excellent California chablis. The tourists did not come en masse until late May and for now the restaurant was subdued. From their table they could see patrons in a lighted pool and beyond, nearer the surf, lovers as silhouettes strolling in the twilight.

Richard had been in a good mood all evening, dreaming about owning a beach home in the area. On every trip he did this—always concluding, "But you can't beat this for the price, can you?"

"No upkeep, no insurance, no preparation for hurricanes," Ellen always reminded.

"You're right," he said. "This place serves our needs nicely."

He lifted his wine in a silent toast and took a sip, exhaling appreciatively. As Ellen stared across the Gulf, her ears were filled with "Lara's Theme" from *Zhivago*. Instantly, she clamped her teeth fiercely. The unsought memory engulfed her.

Blaise was a baby and they were in Montreal for *Expo-67*. In an open-air, downtown cafe. A strolling musician paused at their table, playing his accordion—the same song. Arnold was so proud of Blaise. He insisted on holding her, showing her to anyone who wished to look. The next three years were the happiest she and Arnold had ever known.

"I'm sorry," Ellen responded to Richard's touch. "What did you say?"

"Where away, my love?"

"Nothing, I—it was—the song that was playing brought back a memory."

Richard smiled, waiting to hear.

"When Blaise was four months old," Ellen said. "Arnold and I took her to Montreal for *Expo-67*. A musician was playing the same song in a cafe—playing for Arnold and the baby."

Richard threw back his head as if to nod, waiting.

"I was remembering how happy things were. How proud Arnold was. He couldn't keep his hands off Blaise—showing her to people as if she were a personal engineering accomplishment all his own."

She laughed and shook her head. "He always said he wanted only baby girls and Blaise was the perfect first child. She knew the feel of him, the sound of his voice—she would lie in a crib without a whimper until she heard him come home. Then she'd scream until he came to pick her up. She had him trained."

Richard held his pose, chin lifted.

"Those were the only three happy years we had, really," Ellen said, softly. "When Tony was born, everything changed. Arnold had always said he didn't want a boy and he meant it. More than I knew, he meant it. Then Tony was born, that's when the trouble began."

"The impotence."

"Yes."

"Father-son libido thing," Richard said, repeating her own terse summation from years ago.

"Yes."

He sipped wine.

"If Tony had been a girl—"

"You'd still be Mrs. Meredith," Richard said.

"Arnold wouldn't be dead."

"Ah, love, do you believe that?" Richard chided, gently. "You believe you caused Arnold to die in Vietnam? Because you were going to be divorced. Because Arnold was crying long-distance, begging you not to leave him—crying for his babies."

"Yes, he did that."

"Using your emotions, you know."

"I know he was."

"Punishing you for having borne a son, and Arnold couldn't stand the male competition for your affections."

"That's what the doctor said."

"But it's good to remember the better moments," Richard said. "Putting things in perspective. It never distresses me when you remember the positive things about Arnold. I get upset only when you linger over the sad things."

"Even good moments can be sad," Ellen said.

"Sure, we all have happy memories which sadden us later, but that's healthy. Lingering over bad memories is self-destructive."

"But we all do it," Ellen parroted.

"No, I never do. Never." He said it so adamantly. So positively. Richard twirled his glass, sending wine up the sides of the vessel. "If my decision is bad, and I later suffer for it, I never abuse myself for having done it. Understand?"

"I think so."

"Remorse is a cancer," Richard stated. "It eats away confidence, wastes emotional energy. The past cannot be altered, therefore worrying about something out of the past is self-destructive."

"Nothing—no regrets about anything?"

"Nothing." He downed his wine in a swallow. Pulling back a cuff, he said, "Think we ought to check in with Blaise?"

"I thought we weren't going to worry about her."

"Preventive worry is not the same thing," he grinned. "Call her and tell her you love her—that's the way to do it."

Back in the motel room, Richard sat on the balcony, doors open wide to admit a fresh southerly breeze, while Ellen dialed Blaise.

The telephone rang several times before Blaise lifted the receiver, shouting breathlessly.

"Where were you, Blaise?"

"In the attic."

"I was calling—" Ellen smiled at Richard, "to say I love you and we wish you were here."

"Fibber," Blaise laughed. "But thank you."

Ellen heard voices in the background. "Who's there, Blaise?"

"Herman and some of the computer club members. Mom, I met the most fan*tas*tic guy tonight. He's twenty-six, but you wouldn't know it—handsome, a brain!"

"It's a little late for guests, isn't it, Blaise?"

"They're about to go. Anyway, he offered to let me use his computers in return for doing some clerical work."

"Clerical work?"

"You know, filing, billing, correspondence. He is a security analyst, and mama, he knows computers from the floor up. He's phenomenal, really."

Blaise spoke nearer the receiver, voice lowered, "He didn't say it, mama, but I think he did time for computer crime. Or maybe he was with the CIA—something he won't discuss, I know that. He's got a computer business in his house."

"His house?"

"That's where we met tonight. It was a super meeting—we're thinking about forming a crash club like they have at Cal Tech."

"Blaise, it's after eleven and I think it's too late for company, don't you?"

"Oh, sure. They're waiting to leave."

"We're at the Gulf State Lodge if you need us."

"I know. Kiss-kiss, mama."

When Ellen hung up she found Richard listening with eyes narrowed. "Everything is all right, Richard," she said.

"The company?"

"Some of the computer club members."

"That Herman boy—seventeen is a lot older than fourteen, Ellen."

"Blaise said they were just leaving."

After her shower, toweling dry, Ellen heard Richard dialing the telephone. A few moments later, he hung up without speaking.

"Are you trying to call Blaise?" Ellen queried.

"Yes. No answer."

"If they're out in the driveway, she can't hear the telephone."

Richard paced a step, turned. "It's been fifteen minutes since you called."

"You know how children say good-bye, Richard. They might stand in the driveway half an hour. If you're worried about the boys—don't. One of them is a man."

"Man?"

"Twenty-six years old, Blaise said."

"What manner of man that age associates with children?"

"Teachers."

"Oh."

"Call again," Ellen suggested, intuitively. "Or, better yet, I will."

The phone was answered on the first ring. "They're gone, mama."

"See you tomorrow, Blaise. I love you."

She laughed giddily. "I love you, mama. You two have fun and forget about me."

"We're having fun. Good night."

Cradling the phone, Ellen said, "They're gone."

"She says."

Taken aback, Ellen said, "Blaise wouldn't lie. She never has before."

In the dark, balcony doors open, the surf was a lulling roar in the distance. Bathed, powdered and filled with anticipation, Ellen had been waiting for Richard to finish a cigarette. He lay on his back, one hand beneath his head, silent.

Ellen stroked his chest, kissed his shoulder. She must have

44

dozed. A few minutes later he awoke her, getting up to go out and sit on the balcony again.

He wasn't thinking about love.

Ellen drifted away to sleep with the rumble of waves soothing her mind.

She awoke to a massaging stroke and the scent of coffee. Richard kissed her neck, her face, whispering, "Good morning, beautiful woman—time to wake up."

He was dressed, clean shaven.

"I went up to the restaurant and got a carafe of coffee, and it's delicious—I've already had some."

Ellen stretched luxuriously. Richard shaped pillows against the headboard and helped her sit up. He gave her a cup as she covered a yawn and stared blearily at the seascape. She blinked away sleep, gazing around the room.

"You took out the suitcases?"

"Except yours. I was going out for coffee and made double purpose of the trip."

"Aren't you going swimming?"

"No, my love," Richard sat on the side of the bed, a hand on her thigh. "In fact, if you don't mind, I'd like to go home this morning."

"Oh," she was disappointed. "The weather is so beautiful."

"Tell you what," Richard bargained, "we'll come back next weekend and have two nights and two days of this."

"All right, if you wish."

She drank coffee slowly, aware that he was watching each sip. "Are you in a hurry, Richard?"

"A slow hurry. But drink your coffee."

"No, I'll get dressed right away."

As Ellen went about her bath, she heard him pacing the room. *Going early to surprise Blaise?*

Mildly distraught, she dressed. Richard was already at the door, ready to depart.

He drove faster than the speed limit. Not fifty words passed between them during the trip back to Mobile.

When they reached the house, Richard noted Herman's cut-down, topless vehicle and grunted derisively. Ellen saw him touch the hood as he walked by. "Still warm, so he came this morning," Richard noted.

"Richard, really now—Blaise wouldn't have lied about having guests here overnight."

"I didn't say she would, Ellen."

"Then, what—"

He went through the front door in long strides. Voices in the kitchen made Richard halt on the stairs and turn. He and Ellen reached the back room together. A large suitcase sat on the floor. Herman lifted his upper lip and chin at the same time, peering through glasses steamed by hot cocoa.

"Hi!" Blaise called. She was at the stove, cooking. "Want some eggs, you two?"

Sheepishly, Richard fluttered a hand, "Coffee, if you have some."

"Won't take but a minute," Blaise said.

"Good morning, Herman," Richard said, gruffly.

The boy slurped hot chocolate and answered with a curt nod.

"Would you like me to finish cooking, Blaise?" Ellen asked.

"Nope. Don't feel guilty now, mama."

"Guilty? About what?"

"Leaving me alone and untended."

"I'll make coffee," Ellen stated.

Richard had gone to a telephone and Ellen could hear the tone of voice he used when conducting business.

"Tan didn't take?" Herman inquired.

"No moon," Ellen said.

Blaise laughed. She put a plate of horribly mangled eggs before him and Herman ate sightlessly.

"Blaise," Richard returned, "I've called the office for a truck and driver. We're going to get all that junk out of the attic today."

"No sweat. Maybe Herman and I can help."

Herman raised his head in mid-chew. "Uh, that's kind of bad for my back."

"I'll help, though," Blaise said cordially.

"Good," Richard smiled. "I'm glad it hasn't ruined your plans."

"Not at all. Watch the coffee, mama, it's going to boil."

Ellen seized the pot and pulled it off the stove.

"Well then," Richard glowed, "it's all settled. What's in the suitcase?"

"My mini," Herman said.

"Computer," Blaise elucidated.

"So small?"

"Smaller, lighter, faster, the state of the art has changed since you bought the beast upstairs," Herman said.

"Mind if I see it?" Richard asked.

Herman lifted his case to the table and opened it. The video screen was a separate thing but smaller than the one in the attic.

"We're going to buy Blaise a computer tomorrow," Richard said. "Is this a good one?"

"Twenty-K altogether."

"Twenty—thousand?"

"Plus various components which interface with other pieces."

The meaning of the past few moments finally dawned on Ellen. "You're going to haul away stuff today, Richard?"

"Today. It's got to go and this is as good a time as any."

"I can clean the place before my new equipment comes," Blaise noted.

"Right!" Richard clasped her to him affectionately.

"Seems a shame to throw away all that's up there," Ellen said. "It's like a part of our past."

"It's only pieces of paper, Ellen," Richard said. "About three hundred pounds of it."

"That's the beauty of these new units," Herman explained. "You have an attic full of records. Bulky, heavy, difficult to store."

"That's true," Richard agreed.

"And you see," Herman lifted a pliable piece of plastic, "this is a floppy disc. Your system uses punched cards. My machine uses these. In a box which weighs less than ten pounds, I can store all the data in your attic. That's the advantage of the new micro-computers."

Richard was transfixed, staring at Blaise. The girl busied herself gathering utensils to put in the dishwasher.

"The state of computer art changes so rapidly," Herman continued, "you ought to have your system evaluated every couple of years. You could be wasting thousands of dollars on poorly designed programs which slow real-time use. You might add a terminal, change your retrieval system and still have fundamentally the same—"

"How long have you been here, Herman?"

"Sir?"

"How long have you been here this morning?"

"Couple hours, maybe." Herman leaned to see around Richard, looking at Blaise. She was motionless.

"Got here about—seven?" Richard asked.

"Ohhh!" Herman's mouth opened wide. "I get it! Ah hah! Oh no, Mr. Curry, none of that. You don't have to worry about that with me."

"I'm glad to hear it, Herman."

"No sir, not me," Herman shoved spectacles up the bridge of his nose. The glasses were greasy, speckled with lint.

"My interests are intellectual, Mr. Curry," Herman said. "I don't *frobnicate*."

"That means," Blaise hastened, "to adjust or turn something— like a knob—"

Richard held the hapless boy in a penetrating glare.

"Not me, Mr. Curry," Herman insisted. "When Blaise is with me, we're straight."

Herman got his suitcase and moved toward the door, "See you soon, Blaise."

They heard the portal close and Blaise chewed her lip.

"Hey," Richard grinned, "for the first time I felt like the father of a teen-ager."

F IVE
Chapter

May 13th. It fell on Thursday in 1971. Today was—

Ellen turned in bed, peering at the clock radio. Richard had left without waking her. Later, he would call. Send flowers. Ask her for lunch. Every year the same since Tony—

Thursday. 7:30 A.M.

She could taste again the bile that rose in her throat that morning eleven years ago. There had been no labor pains. Those didn't begin until evening. She'd awakened to hear Paul Harvey's newscast on the radio.

North Vietnamese forces attacked A Shau Valley . . . heavy casualties . . . Paris peace talks began today for the fourth year . . . please God, stop the war . . . please God, protect Arnold . . .

Arnold was dead, now.

Tony about to be born eleven years ago—dead, now.

She sat up feeling heavy, disconsolate. She was breathing shallowly, as if her lungs were impeded by the bulk of a baby in her belly. She saw her image in the mirror on the bedroom door. She looked exhausted, pale. Where was the youth that drew taut the flesh of her face? Where had the decade gone?

The telephone rang and she fumbled the receiver, lifting it.

"Good morning sleeping beauty!"

"Richard, will you love me when I'm old?"

He laughed. "Every little crepe. How do you feel?"

"Feel all right."

"I want to take you to the Malaga Inn for lunch," he said. "Caesar's salad, filet mignon."

"Sounds good."

"Shall I pick you up?"

"I have to turn in a story for *Mobala News*," she said. "I'll meet you there."

"Make yourself beautiful and smell good," Richard purred. "I want to show you off."

She hung up and sat looking at herself in the mirror. Her hair was never true blonde, just a lackluster brown which fell straight to her shoulders. She put a hand on her abdomen. *He was right there*, eleven years ago.

Rising as if weary, she shuffled to the bathroom and stood over the lavatory. Were the wrinkles friendly ones? Or tired? Her eyes gazed back in yellow-flecked blue—sometimes aqua, sometimes topaz—now amber and sad. "Always so sad," Richard had once remarked, having just met her. "I've seen cocker spaniels with the same expression."

She brushed her hair with a heavy hand, paused to examine her face again. The wrinkles were sorrow lines. Etched not by time so much as circumstance. She had seen the beginning of such wrinkles in Blaise's face, too. Sorrow was the India ink of the soul. Once applied, it stained the countenance for life.

She took a long hot soaking bath, hoping to ease muscles aching from tension. It was a mistake, enervating. She followed the tub with a cold shower.

No sooner had she dressed than the doorbell rang. *Flowers*. Yellow roses. Every year—

She arranged them in a vase, the aroma suddenly cloying, nauseating, funereal. Laboriously, she dialed Richard's office. "The roses are lovely!"

"I'm glad. See you at lunch."

When she hung up, a shudder traversed her body and she swallowed a temptation to be ill. Richard meant well. Solicitous, never once mentioning Tony—none of them did that—but on Tony's birthday, Richard's effort to mask the event with gaiety was a mistake.

She wandered through the downstairs, took her coffee on the patio listening to mockingbirds quarreling with the squirrels. Thursday then, Thursday now. She had been so worried about Arnold. At noon, her time, he had called. No, he wasn't at A Shau Valley. He was in Saigon. No, he wasn't hurt—how did she feel? Be sure to let him know if it was a girl!

Well. It wasn't a girl. It was Tony. She had telephoned even before getting out of the hospital bed.

"A boy?"

"Yes, and he looks like his daddy!"

"A boy."

She used all the adjectives she'd heard Arnold use to describe Blaise, three years earlier. The tiny feet, the toes like peas in a pod, the wizened red face—

"Damn."

"Don't be silly, Arnold Anthony," she'd laughed. "You have a son and a namesake."

"Yeah," his voice faded on the transoceanic line.

When Arnold came home on leave three months later, everything had changed. He ignored the baby except when it was foisted on him. He showed Tony to no one unless compelled to do so. There was no rising for early morning diaper changes this time. No rocking and crooning to put the infant to sleep. At first she'd attributed it to the war—who knew what mysterious things happened to the psyche in combat? He was not loving. He was brusque and impatient—except with Blaise. At age three, she was her father's focal point. Arnold left Tony to Ellen; Blaise was his child.

A year later, supposedly home for good, the rift between them widened. Not once did they successfully make love. Not once. Six months afterward, Arnold had stunned her by volunteering for another tour of duty in Vietnam, and she began to think seriously of divorce.

The decision was wrought over dozens of hours of angry, recriminating telephone calls. Letters came in batches from Arnold, pleading, accusing, blaming Ellen for his impotence, referring to Tony as "the kid."

"All right, then," Arnold had finally screamed on the telephone, "get a divorce!"

Two days later he was killed.

She had burned all the letters. She had tried to bury the unpleasantries at Arlington where Arnold was given a military funeral. "He would've been a general someday," an officer lamented.

She was in the attic. Without consciously determining to be here, she was standing at the top of the stairs. Blaise's new equipment dominated one end of the room, a red light glowing to indicate it was on. "Never turn it off," Blaise had advised. A slight hum came from the machine, even when idle.

In the three weeks since the new machine arrived, the attic had become Blaise's domain. For several days men had come and gone, connecting telephone lines, testing this or that.

"Richard, this must've cost a fortune," Ellen resisted.

"If I'd bought a computer to do what Blaise said she needed," Richard confessed, "it *would've* cost a fortune."

Ellen overheard a technician telling Blaise, "You have half a million dollars worth of computer."

"What!"

"Not really, mama," Blaise howled. "My terminal is connected to daddy's computer and *it* cost half a million."

"You're telling me that Richard owns a piece of equipment that cost so much?"

"Sure!" Blaise said. "Didn't you know that?"

"No."

When Ellen asked him, Richard shrugged, "It wouldn't occur to me to tell you something like that. But yes, it cost about half a million."

For the first time, she realized how little she knew about the import-export business, how seldom Richard spoke of anything relating to his work. Her reaction seemed to puzzle him. "You've been to the office many times, darling. You're welcome to come down and question my auditors."

"Of course not, Richard—I was just stunned! The place looks like any office—I never considered it, before."

"There's no stock warehoused there," he suggested. "Maybe it's difficult for you to visualize a thousand tons of stock when it's only listed as digits on paper."

Ellen still stood at the top of the stairs. The computer was not a single piece of equipment, but several. Blaise had given her a quick tour, speaking of central processing units, interface connections, retrievals—gibberish.

About a week after everything was installed, Ellen had come up to discover Blaise and Richard playing Space Invaders.

The thing was a toy which engrossed them both.

"But there are more serious aspects to it," Richard had explained. "Now Blaise can reach my office computer by telephone line. For all practical purposes, she truly does have a half million dollar piece of equipment."

"Won't it interfere with your office work?"

"No. She could use the computer for hours and nobody else would even know it. She has a password to gain access to my machine."

"Suppose everybody in your office is trying to reach the machine at the same time?" Ellen had questioned.

"Twenty people can be using the computer at the same second," Richard explained. "The computer works at very high speed. It divides up a second into a twentieth of a second and none of the twenty people are ever aware that there are nineteen others also using the same second. That's how thousands of people can use these 'time-sharing' computers. People work slowly, the machine does not. It divides the time into split seconds. Believe me, Blaise isn't interfering with my business. It was cheaper to do that than to buy her any of these home machines they're offering. Besides, I have a service contract if her terminal needs repair. I did the smart thing. It's a deduction, too."

Ellen had heard Richard and Blaise speaking of milliseconds, a thousandth of a second; and microseconds, a *millionth*.

"Daddy knows a lot more about computers than I thought," Blaise confided to Ellen. "I think he's been playing a trick on me, pretending not to know things. He said his computer can accept a single-digit code in a millisecond and respond in four."

It had been confusing, slightly frustrating, to be shut out so completely as Ellen was from such discussions.

"That's how we feel when you talk about photography sometimes, mama," Blaise had countered. "I'll tell you the same thing you tell me—try learning about it."

But there was something foreign about the computer. Something as alien and cold as a far planet. Even now, sitting there humming softly, it seemed to sense her presence. Ellen found no pleasure in the thing.

She couldn't think why she'd come up here.

She was breathless. Crossing the room, she felt the air stir as the thermostat caused the air conditioner to click on and blow up through vents. She'd complained to Richard about the increase in the electric bill that would ensue.

"The equipment is delicate, Ellen," he'd said. "We can afford it—"

Yes. Of course. If he owned a half million dollar machine, perhaps they could!

She had promised herself she wouldn't do this again. She had sworn not to come up here on this date looking for—Ellen moved toward a corner of the attic even as she thought this. The way was deliberately blocked by boxes of old *National Geographic* magazines, issues of *American Photographer*. Into this area she had piled sealed cartons of discarded clothing and other items they never used anymore.

There it was.

She squeezed through a narrow passage and stood over a

steamer trunk—the kind that rested on one end so it opened into two halves. Part of it was drawers. The other half was for hanging clothing—Tony's clothing.

She knelt, chest aching, and opened the bottom drawer. His shirts, short pants, a pair of scuffed shoes worn on the outside of the heels. The next drawer: a baby book listing weight at birth— his birth certificate with a tiny print of his foot.

She moved things around, looking for the scrapbook. It was filled with snapshots, mostly—playing with Blaise, first tooth, first tooth missing—where was it? She couldn't find it. She went through the other two drawers—toys, Tony's favorite tractor with a rusty scoop.

She began again with the bottom drawer—surely she put the scrapbook back after looking at it last year! Blaise, perhaps—

Ellen stood up, dragging the heavy trunk away from the wall to see behind it. There was a small opening there. Where the roof adjoined the floor. Maybe it fell in there. She hauled the trunk completely aside and knelt to look into the darkened nook. She saw—something.

She had to stoop to get through, bumping things in the dark, feeling ahead of herself. But once cleared, she was in an alcove boxed by two adjoining parts of the roof and sheltered from the rest of the room. It had once been a dormer. A window threw yellow shafts of light toward rising motes of dust.

As her eyes adjusted to the dim light, she saw a child's table and two chairs—a dining room suite in miniature, given to Blaise on her third Christmas. Ellen blinked, kneeling, and whispered, "Oh, dear God."

On the tiny table, a cake with white icing, a single slice missing. Beside it, eleven partially burned candles lying in a jar cap. A glass with a filmy residue of milk.

"Oh, Blaise, darling," Ellen moaned.

She must've been here this morning, before school. The milk was not completely evaporated, the cake still fairly fresh. On one of the small chairs, a boy's shirt. Trousers were draped across the seat, the pants leg touching the floor. It was as if the owner had evaporated, leaving the clothing as it fell.

On the floor, crumpled gift wrapping and remnants of a ribbon and bow. Placed before the empty clothes, as if to Tony's spirit, an inexpensive battery-operated pocket calculator—the kind of thing that would fascinate an eleven-year-old boy.

Ellen lifted an unsealed envelope. Birthday card. It was signed with a flowing script, "All my love, Blaise."

She tried to put everything where she'd discovered it. Turning to leave, Ellen found pictures from the scrapbook tacked to the bare rafters. No air conditioning reached this area and the photos curled around pins tacking each corner.

Trembling from emotion and strain, she pushed the trunk into position again, covering the hideaway. Faintly, she could hear the telephone ringing downstairs. It quit. She took the time to stack the boxes again, blocking entry as it had been before.

Her legs weak, she gripped the handrail tightly, descending the steps. Passing the master bedroom, she glanced at the clock. She was to have met Richard at noon. She was already thirty minutes late, covered with dust. Perspiration soaked her blouse. She called the Malaga and had Richard paged—but he'd already left.

The front door flew open and Richard stood there, legs spread, face dark. "Are you all right?"

Her mouth opened. Her lips moved, but nothing came. Richard reached her in two strides and grabbed her shoulders. "What is wrong?" he demanded.

"I—Richard—I love you!"

"What happened, Ellen?"

"I love you, Richard."

He shook her slightly, "Tell me!"

"It's Blaise."

"Is she hurt?"

"No, no. She—"

He turned her, wrapped an arm around her waist for support, and took Ellen into the kitchen. He pulled out a chair and eased her into it.

But in that moment, she'd had time to think, to reconsider. Remembering in quick flashes the deep abysmal depression Richard had suffered after Tony died. Remembering how he wept himself to sleep in silent, bed-shaking sobs. Remembering how he loved that boy—loved Tony as Arnold had loved Blaise—

"What is it now," Richard asked, more softly, kneeling before her.

"I'm being silly, Richard."

"Not silly," he replied, gruffly. He embraced her with both arms and rocked her gently to and fro. "Not silly at all," he murmured. "Everything is all right. All right."

And she wept. As never before.

S Chapter
SIX

Ellen awoke and lay motionless, listening. Beside her, snoring softly, Richard slumbered with a hairy arm outstretched. Bumped her, awoke her—something had. She could hear the electrical whirr of her bedside clock, the numerals glowing red in the dark. In the backyard, a mockingbird imitated a nightingale. A neighbor's dog barked, fell silent.

The ceiling creaked. *Blaise, in the attic.*

Ellen lay with her eyes closed, weary, her sleep less than complete. Every morning before dawn, Blaise was up there. "It's quiet and cool at that hour, mama," Blaise had explained. "Am I making too much noise?"

Ellen could hear the gentle rat-tat-tap of the keyboard. The dog barked again, quit.

A few days ago, Richard had scanned one of Blaise's new books. "You always wanted her to study," he said, "well, take a look at what she's reading these days."

It was Kurt R. Stehling's *Computers and You.* Beside Blaise's bed, a copy of *Computers and Society* by Rothman and Mosmann. She concentrated on *The Computer Age* published by the Massachusetts Institute of Technology. She had requested a subscription to *Omni* magazine which she devoured when it came. No longer was she engrossed in pulp fiction.

"As I prophesied," Richard had gloated, "this was a good investment. This is college level stuff, Ellen."

She couldn't deny that. In every room was proof. Van Tassel's *The Compleat Computer* was water-spotted from reading in the tub. Blaise had become monomaniacal about the subject. As once she'd anticipated holidays, now she lived for the weekly meeting of her computer club. She was no longer interested in movies, television, or anything else that distracted from her single-minded pursuit of that damnable machine.

Richard turned in his sleep, teeth grinding. Overhead, the floor of the attic revealed Blaise's presence.

"You pay the price for a child like Blaise," a teacher once observed to Ellen. "Emotional strain to a parent is directly proportionate to the intelligence quotient of the progeny."

Ellen had tried to joke away the tutor's remark, "I don't complain so long as Blaise isn't a bad student."

"Einstein was a 'bad' student."

"I was referring to deportment."

"Blaise is never a disciplinary problem," the teacher had affirmed. "She's too smart to get caught doing something wrong."

Ellen found no comfort in that.

In an effort to sleep longer, Ellen tried to purge her mind of thought. Richard stirred restlessly, striking her with an elbow. The ceiling groaned under Blaise's weight.

Ellen had a mental vision of Tony's clothes draped over a miniature chair, of the cake and card. Two days after the boy's birthday she went back to see it, and all was gone.

A shrine, she had come to think of it. An altar devoted to the memory of Tony.

It struck her, lying there, they rarely talked about Arnold, or Tony. Mention of either made Richard uneasy. And Blaise—"I'm upsetting you, mama."

Blaise must've felt, if nobody else would pay homage to Tony, she would. Privately, constructing a fantasy around a party, with an appropriate gift, a loving card, a whispered rendition of *Happy Birthday*.

"Are you awake, Ellen?"

"Yes, Richard. Do you need something?"

He stroked her leg, drawing her nearer with gentle tugs. His breath was warm against her bare back and he breathed in short exhalations which slowly evened out until he was snoring again.

Perhaps if they had continued to attend church, the girl would have had the succor of organized worship, a confirmation of belief in life after death—

But Blaise believed in life after death, why else "the shrine"? The setting suggested Blaise was trying to commune with Tony's spirit. As if to reaffirm his existence. If they were a religious family, she could have prayed for Tony in church, instead of staging a birthday party in the attic.

Religion was supposed to comfort the believer in moments of inexplicable loss. But that was the very reason she had abandoned it. Church services had become unbearable. How could she vow allegiance to a God that would take a child's life so needlessly?

Was she then to blame for Blaise's clandestine and pitiful party to a departed soul? If they'd continued going to church—

Even as she thought it, Ellen knew she couldn't have done it then, couldn't do it now. How could she pray to a being she feared? If there was a God, he would be less disturbed by absence than hypocrisy.

Was a mock birthday celebration a hint of warped reality?

"Ellen, darling, are you ill?"

"No, Richard."

"You're trembling. Bad dreams?"

"No. I'm sorry I disturbed you."

He rolled onto his back. "How about my going to start the coffee and let's watch the sun come up?"

"Yes," she said. "That would be nice."

She felt him slide off the bed, heard him yawn, a gritty noise

60

like sand in the bottom of a baking tin as he scratched. He fumbled for slippers, yawning again before leaving the room.

It was not easy being a child, especially an only child. Ellen remembered her own difficult youth, loved but dominated, pampered but controlled. Every decision had two steps: desire to take action followed by concern for her parents' response. Parents made mistakes. Even when they knew what they should do. Ellen couldn't bear to listen to Blaise's thoughts about Tony and she couldn't take her to church. She could provide no outlet for Blaise's feeling for Tony.

The first predawn illumination cast a gray pall on the ceiling and she stared at it, listening to Blaise overhead, the machine responding to keyboard queries.

If Blaise felt the memories of her father and Tony were being neglected, what harm could come of letting the girl indulge in respectful reveries of her own?

She heard Richard ascending the stairs. She pretended to sleep, but he wasn't fooled, laughing softly as he put a tray on the bedside table. He patted her posterior, cooing, "Time to wake, my sweet, time to rise . . . " He massaged the small of her back, murmuring, "Wake up, wake up, sleepyhead."

He placed her pillows, helped her sit up. He presented a steaming cup of coffee and pulled a chair to sit close by.

"Nobody is as beautiful as you at this hour," he said.

She dismissed it with the wave of one hand.

"My sexy sweetie," he said. Then he let her succumb to "early morning stupor," drinking his own coffee, watching cognizance dawn in her eyes.

She saw Richard gaze upward as Blaise walked across the attic floor.

"I ought to insulate the floor," he said. "It would make it quieter down here."

Blaise couldn't go to Richard; couldn't come to Ellen. Richard's parents had died in an air crash in Nepal soon after World War II. Ellen's parents too, gone.

The only grandparent remaining was Arnold's mother, dividing her time between New York and a home in Jamaica. Her visits were annual, usually in June, in transit from one clime to another.

Like church attendance, Mother Meredith was something Ellen avoided. Not blatantly. But she didn't encourage the woman to visit, never pleaded for an extension when she did.

"What's on your mind this morning, darling?" Richard inquired pleasantly.

"Thinking about Mother Meredith."

They had never dissuaded Arnold's mother from coming. Richard certainly never complained. If he resented her—and he did— he endured the woman with stoic forbearance. It was unfortunate that Mother Meredith brought renewed grief as part of her baggage. Looking for photographs of Arnold, asking for them if the pictures were not where she expected them.

"Is she coming?" Richard asked.

"You're going to Aruba as usual, aren't you?" Ellen countered.

"Next week, in fact."

"I was thinking about asking Mother Meredith to come early and stay longer."

"Um."

"For Blaise's benefit," Ellen said. "Time is getting away, Mother Meredith is older, Blaise maturing."

He sipped coffee, listening without expression.

"To give them time to talk," Ellen said. "They don't really know one another."

Richard drew his shoulders forward as if to ease muscles between his shoulder blades.

"Since Mother Meredith is Blaise's only blood tie to the family tree, for whatever that's worth," Ellen said, "I thought it might be beneficial."

"Fine with me," he said.

"Your parents are dead," she observed.

"Killed in an air crash. Nepal."

"Yes, I know. And my parents are gone. So that only leaves Mother Meredith as a link to what is past."

He reached over and patted her leg. "Do it," he smiled.

Blaise passed overhead and a moment later the staccato tap of the machine beat a monotonous tattoo. "If that machine were male," Richard grunted, "I'd have it neutered."

"Eighteen more days of school," Blaise lamented. "I'm getting varicose veins of the eyeballs from study."

"Staring at the video," Herman Krause asserted. "The incidence of cataracts among programmers is considerably higher than the general population."

"Thanks a lot, Herman," Blaise said.

"It isn't absolutely conclusive, Mrs. Curry," Herman attempted.

"Less time at the video wouldn't hurt Blaise's personality," Ellen said. "Before school, after school, into the night—"

"Daddy," Blaise interjected, "there's a seminar next week at the University of Southern Mississippi. It costs a hundred dollars and lasts three days. That includes room and meals, so it isn't all that expensive. May I go?"

"Mother Meredith is coming next week," Richard said.

"I went to that same seminar last year," Herman spoke to Blaise. "You won't be missing much. It was either elementary BASIC or abstract theory, algorithms and such."

"Mother Meredith is coming earlier this year," Blaise noted.

"And staying longer," Ellen said.

Blaise took Herman's glasses and dipped them in soapy detergent. The boy squinted with the expression of a mole. "Did you complete your flow chart, Blaise?"

"I threw it away."

"Jesus! Excuse me, Mr. and Mrs. Curry. Blaise, we spent a week on that!"

"GIGO, Herman," Blaise replied. Then to Ellen, "Garbage in, garbage out—it means, if you give the computer incorrect information it will give back incorrect output."

Richard loosened his tie, drumming the kitchen table with the tips of his fingers, a sure sign of boredom.

"When's your flight to Aruba, Richard?"

"Wednesday."

"Hey!" Blaise exulted, "Maybe we can take Mother Meredith to daddy's office and show her the computer."

"I doubt she will find much to appreciate in a machine. But you may go, if you wish."

Blaise returned Herman's glasses and he took them without thanks, looking around the room. "Ah so," he said. "There you are."

"Would you like a martini, Ellen?"

"Aruba," Herman's pupils loomed large. "Where's Aruba?"

"It's an island off the coast of Venezuela," Blaise said. "Wind-blown, dry as a bone, nothing but cactus and diva-diva trees."

"And a business," Richard reminded.

"You import things from there?"

"Entrepôt, Herman," Richard stated. "Warehouses, packing facilities, reshipment."

"Hence the half million dollar computer."

"Hence," Richard confirmed.

"Don't you ever wash your glasses, Herman?" Blaise chided.

"When I take a bath." The boy crossed one bowed leg over the other. He had a hole in his shoe. "Listen, I'd like to go down to see Mr. Curry's computer when you go."

"I don't want the office disrupted with a lot of visitors," Richard said.

"Oh," Herman was stung. "Okay."

"Herman," Blaise altered tone, coyly, "how about giving me a ride to Kim's place. I promised to help him post some data."

The hurt seemed to deepen. Herman twisted his lips, staring at the floor.

"Who is Kim?" Richard asked.

"Has a computer business," Blaise said, offhandedly. "You remember, I told you I was doing some work for him."

"What rate of pay?"

"No pay," Herman sneered. "He uses people like Blaise."

"In return for computer time, Herman. His has functions mine doesn't have."

"Kim Jensen doesn't have anything that will do what your dad's will do. He's sucking you in."

"I ask again," Richard persisted, "who is he?"

"He wants everybody to think he once committed a computer crime," Herman scoffed.

"Why would he want that?"

"Good for business. He fancies himself a computer security specialist. He doesn't know as much about computers as—"

"Hey!" Blaise interrupted. "You're jealous. Well, okay, be jealous—but don't screw me up with my folks."

"Easy, you two," Ellen soothed.

"He may end up in jail," Herman snapped. "He has the criminal mind for it."

"Maybe you ought to explain that," Richard said.

"Okay, all right I will. A criminal is one of three types. An honest man makes a mistake and commits a crime. Drunk driver accused of negligent homicide, is an example."

Richard stood at the bar making a pitcher of martinis. He mixed gin and Vermouth with his back to them.

"Second type is too lazy to work and he commits a crime, gets caught, serves time, commits another crime. He enjoys crime. It's exciting. Nothing you can do will change that. He can be a dumb ass, or brilliant—it's like gambling. It beats the dull day-by-day routine of working for a living."

"The third type?" Richard asked amicably.

"The one-timer. The kind of man who kills his wife for her insurance."

Ellen saw Richard pause. Blaise focused on a point somewhere beyond the kitchen window.

"Getting rid of a bad wife is only part of his motive," Herman said. "He's after the insurance and greed is the motive." He looked from Richard to Blaise. "Did I say something wrong?"

"Which type is this fellow Kim?" Richard questioned.

"He enjoys crime. Beating the system, he calls it. Given a choice between making a million dollars legally, or the same amount illegally, he would go for the crime because it's exhilarating."

"What crime has he committed, Herman?"

"Crashing computers. That's how he gets business. He crashes a bank's computer, goes in with their most private and confidential data and says, 'If I could do this, anybody can.' Then he tries to sell them his services as a security analyst."

"He does it successfully, daddy," Blaise said. "That's what's eating at Herman."

"But he doesn't actually steal anything," Richard noted.

"Yes, he does," Herman insisted. "When he taps into a time-sharing computer, he's stealing time that's sold by the hour."

"As I understand that," Richard said, "they have difficulty getting a conviction for stealing *time*."

"It's illegal," Herman railed. "It's invasion of privacy if nothing else."

"What's illegal in one place," Richard said, "may be perfectly acceptable somewhere else."

A painful lull. Blaise continued to stare across the patio.

"Kim breaks the law when he violates somebody else's computer," Herman said. "It may not be as serious as killing someone for insurance, but it is a crime."

"Let's have our drinks on the patio, Ellen," Richard said, brusquely.

Ellen and Richard sat at the patio table and he poured a drink for each of them, garnishing his with onion, hers with olive. His dark eyes were veiled, troubled.

"Herman suffers from foot-in-mouth," Ellen said.

"He's trying to stake out his territory and protect it from this other man," Richard said. "Jealousy is obvious."

"You can relate to that, surely."

"I have never related to boys," Richard replied. "I know what they're thinking. Their ulterior motives. Boys are devious, selfish." He downed his drink, poured another. "Herman is a bit possessive of Blaise, don't you think?"

"If he is, there's nothing to be concerned about. She isn't allowing it."

Unexpectedly, Richard brightened. "If I delay my trip to Aruba for a couple of weeks, how would you like to go with me? We could take a cruise, sail up through the Antilles, end up in the Bahamas and fly home from there."

"Do you want to do that?"

"What's the point in having money, if we don't enjoy it?"

"I wasn't aware we weren't enjoying what we have."

"You never ask for anything," Richard said. "Is that because you want for nothing, or because you think we can't afford it?"

She lifted her palms, mouth open.

"You don't seem to think we have enough money for certain things. Do you think I'm still operating on your money—Arnold's money and—"

Tony's insurance.

"I never think about it, Richard. What difference does it make?"

"Well, if you don't know it," he spoke gruffly, "business is good. I'm grossing high and netting even better. We're doing quite well, you and I. But here we are in the same house at the same address as when we first came to Mobile."

"I love this house."

"I like it too. But we could have a beach house if we wanted it. We could have—whatever—within reason, of course. What do you want, Ellen?"

"Richard, I'm happy. Incredibly contented!"

He sighed, poured another martini. Inside, the young people continued to squabble. The sun had reached a nadir, ready to disappear. Shadows lay in cool deep pools across the yard.

"I always come back to practicalities, don't I?" Richard remarked.

"Usually. What is it this time?"

He lifted his eyebrows, lips pursing. "Who would water my garden?"

"If that's the most we have to worry about," Ellen laughed, "we have no grounds for complaint."

His face flowed into a sorrowful, almost pained expression.

"That's it," he said. "That's all we have to worry about."

Chapter

SEVEN

Ellen skinned a shin getting dressed in the dark, letting Richard sleep a while longer. When she reached the kitchen, Arnold's mother was there, wearing a tailored skirt, jacket and jewelry, waiting for service. Herman was with her. God only knew what he might have said before Ellen arrived. Blaise was surly for want of rest—she'd stayed up late studying for final exams.

"Do you want breakfast, Herman?" Blaise offered.

He was diagonal to the floor, his weight suspended by an elbow hung on the bar. "I can always eat."

As Blaise put dishes before her, Mother Meredith spoke, "Don't you have a proper cup and saucer, dear? Drinking coffee from a mug is for truck drivers."

A moment later she questioned, "Paper napkins?"

When Richard entered it was with his "Here's Company" geniality, but he was harried, getting ready to catch his flight to Aruba.

Mother Meredith dabbed rouged lips, apprehensively watching

Herman wolf eggs and bacon. Caught staring, she smiled tightly.

"Nothing but coffee, Ellen," Richard dictated. Herman bumped him with a jutting arm, dicing his toast into swabbing wedges.

The telephone rang and Blaise grabbed it.

"You look nice today, Mother Meredith," Richard said.

"I believe we're going to your office, or some such."

Blaise spoke into the receiver, "Who?"

"There isn't much to see," Richard warned.

"It will please Blaise."

"Daddy," Blaise extended the phone, "I think this is for you."

Richard went into the hall to answer and Blaise returned to the table. "It may be a wrong number. Some old man asked for Ralph, then for Richard."

Herman stretched his legs beneath the table, leaning back. "That was okay," he said. His tongue felt for food remnants between teeth and cheek.

"One lousy test," Blaise complained. "I have to go to school for one lousy hour."

"How are your ballet lessons coming these days?" Mother Meredith inquired.

"I quit."

The grandmother's hazel eyes registered disapproval. "Are you progressing with the piano? Any recitals?"

"I gave it up, Mother Meredith."

"More coffee?" Ellen interceded. She saw Richard hurry up the stairs two at a time.

"As soon as I get home," Blaise was explaining, "we'll go to daddy's office, Mother Meredith."

Richard appeared, luggage in hand, face taut, and it seemed to Ellen, slighty pale. "I have a business emergency," he said. "I need to take the Lincoln and I must leave at once."

"What is it?"

"A shipment of perishables in Nashville without proper bills of lading. Nothing serious." He attempted a smile. "But I must go immediately."

He kissed Blaise, winked at Mother Meredith reassuringly.

"Can't you catch a plane, Richard?"

"I'll need a vehicle when I get there."

"What about cash? The banks will open in an hour."

"I have credit cards." His response was curt.

He kissed Ellen distractedly. As she stood watching him drive away, he didn't glance back to see her wave. When she turned, Blaise was at the door observing.

"Isn't daddy going to Aruba?"

"No. You're going to be late for class, Blaise."

"Herman is giving me a ride."

He was in his car, gunning the motor, creating plumes of exhaust from rumbling tail pipes.

Mother Meredith waited as before, still sitting in the kitchen, back straight, one hand in her lap, food uneaten.

"Blaise looks like Arnold, doesn't she, Ellen?"

"She has his forehead and chin."

"Not as much resemblance as Tony, of course," the grandmother remarked. "That boy was from the same mold."

Ellen gathered breakfast dishes.

"May I help you, Ellen?"

"No, thank you. It will only take a minute."

"Remember how busy the house used to be in Atlanta?" Mother Meredith helped anyway. "Blaise's friends, Tony's little chums. Everybody congregated around those two."

"Much like this morning," Ellen conceded.

"Oh, much more so. The children had Arnold's gregarious nature—how he loved people."

Ellen perceived a tremor in her voice.

"When you were living in Washington, when Arnold was with the Pentagon, there were parties for holidays, soirees at the yacht club, openings at the Kennedy Center. Arnold had a calendar to keep track of social engagements."

"Yes, I remember."

"He loved people," Mother Meredith delivered dishes to Ellen at the sink and stood there. Ellen could smell perfume by Worth.

"I haven't seen any of Blaise's friends," Mother Meredith said. "Except this boy Herman."

"Blaise has fallen in love with computers," Ellen explained. "Herman has a like interest."

Ellen washed while Mother Meredith dried.

"Blaise tells me she no longer plays tennis, Ellen. Doesn't your country club have good courts?"

"We aren't members of a country club."

"Arnold loved the yacht club when he was a boy," Mother Meredith said. "It could be cold enough to freeze your earlobes, but he was out there ready to sail when the wind blew."

"We don't own a boat." Ellen repressed her resentment.

"You and Arnold were always in the midst of it," Mother Meredith recalled. "Season tickets to the opera, the symphony and theater. Doesn't Blaise enjoy such things?"

"We live a different life style these days."

"Of course, Arnold grew up with all that," Mother Meredith touched her coiffure. "He counted among his friends the son of the governor of New York, daughters of financiers, people prominent in the social register."

"We go to the Joe Jefferson Playhouse for legitimate theater," Ellen defended herself. "We support the symphony and touring roadshows from New York. Now and then. As things appeal to us."

Mother Meredith moved from cabinet to cupboard seeking cup hooks. "Friends made in prep school and West Point became enduring relationships," she said. "I still receive Christmas cards from Arnold's childhood friends."

Ellen was silent. Mother Meredith spoke wistfully, "I can't help worrying about—things."

"About what, Mother Meredith?"

"You've changed, dear. In Atlanta, after Arnold—you knew so many talented people. Photographers, artists, writers."

Desperate for identity, for a new life.

". . . giving shows of your photography at the Nexus Gallery . . . "

Without a crowd, Arnold was miserable.

". . . he planned, even when Blaise was in diapers—Montessori schools, dance, music . . . "

71

A masquerade. A social facade to cover his impotence.

"...wanted his children to know the right people, move in circles of affluence..."

The army was a mother. Told Arnold what to do and when.

"...do all your own household chores?"

"With only three of us, it isn't difficult."

"How industrious." Mother Meredith took a breath. "Arnold used to say, 'Rank has its privileges.'"

"I enjoy my house, Mother Meredith. Creating a clean, contented home."

"I'm certain it's good for your character, too."

"Mother Meredith, if you were male I'd say that was a sexist comment."

"I didn't mean it that way," Mother Meredith replied. She folded a dish towel and placed it on the counter. "Was last evening a typical one?"

"In terms of activity? More or less."

"Blaise secluded in the attic with her machine. You and Richard listening to music on a phonograph."

"I hope you weren't bored."

"Not at all. Goodness no! It only seemed such a contrast."

"Compared to Westchester, I'm sure Mobile appears provincial."

"I must seem critical, Ellen, and I'm not. My concern about this new insularity is mostly for the benefit of Blaise."

"Insularity?"

"I see you live comfortably, modestly. There are merits to that. But how good is it for Blaise to seclude herself in a garret with a piece of equipment and—"

"I agree with you. It's Blaise's nature to become completely engrossed with novel things. Experience has shown that, given time, it will pass."

"It extends beyond that, doesn't it?" Mother Meredith seemed pained. "You yourself don't seem to have friends here like you did. Do you like this city?"

"Very much. And we do have friends."

"Your neighbors?"

"The neighbors are mostly older couples whose children are grown and married."

"You are happy, aren't you dear?" It was a statement.

"Incredibly happy."

"So it isn't you, or your man I'm concerned about."

"Blaise devotes more time to that computer than I like, Mother Meredith. But it seems wise to let it run its course."

Mother Meredith clasped ringed fingers, put her hands in her lap and sat at the table again. "These formative years are so crucial, Ellen. Talents honed, education received."

"Blaise goes to the finest school—"

"I am referring more to that which is absorbed by osmosis than that which is pounded into her."

"I don't understand."

"Culture finds its own level, Ellen. Like good manners, it is either second nature or awkwardly acquired. I'm thinking of cotillions and debutantes. Social status is a natural consequence of childhood associations. Like using linen napkins, and saucers with cups."

"Blaise is not lacking in social grace."

"The boys dated are the swains who become husbands of tomorrow," she persisted. Ellen saw the woman's little finger quiver. "I look at Herman," she said. "That poor boy is genetically deprived."

"Mother Meredith! That is most unkind of you."

"The words sound more cruel than I intended," she said. "Perhaps I'm not articulating well. Please accept what I say, not as criticism, Ellen. But if Blaise never sees you wear the fine jewelry Arnold gave, never experiences the give and take of intellectual conversation between witty and charming people—"

Ellen sat at the table and they looked at one another as if tormented. "When Arnold was alive," Ellen said, "he was gone much of the time. Like most military wives I followed after, from post to post."

"His career was demanding, of course."

"When he was overseas," Ellen said, "I had two children and a household to manage, virtually alone. But I assumed those duties always knowing Arnold would be back to take command again."

"I see that, I empathize with—"

"Then as a widow," Ellen persisted, "I found myself facing awesome decisions with nobody to consult. Accountants, taxes, what to sell and what to keep. I didn't know stocks from bonds from debentures."

"You could have called our family attorney, Ellen."

"No, I couldn't. I had to learn about those things. In addition to buying groceries, immunization for the children, illnesses and dental appointments, I had to worry about my own future. I was swamped by chores, always behind. I had two bewildered children, the complexities of Arnold's estate—"

Mother Meredith's chin quivered, a tear ran down her cheek.

"I was being destroyed, Mother Meredith. My concept of myself was one of ineptitude, inadequacy. I couldn't seem to cope with the things all widows must confront."

Mother Meredith drew a shuddering breath.

"Richard saved me," Ellen said. "He accepted my children as his own and that was a lot. He shored up my insecurities and quieted my fears. He took over the stock portfolio, managed the liquidation of remaining properties. After we were married he even took over the household accounts."

"I wasn't censuring Richard."

"I'm not defending him, either. But he isn't Arnold, Mother Meredith. He isn't gregarious. He prefers quiet evenings listening to Strauss waltzes. If Blaise or I wanted to have a party, Richard would acquiesce. But it isn't something he requires."

"He seems to be a nice man."

"He's generous, considerate, attentive. We want for nothing. But what Richard wants and enjoys must be considered here, too. This is his home, we are his family now, this is his domain."

"I don't know how to communicate what I feel without sounding selfish," Mother Meredith regained control of her emotions. "I envision Blaise as Arnold would have wanted her to be. She has her inheritance coming at age twenty-one, more at twenty-five; by the time she is thirty-five she will have so much, Ellen. As my heir, she—"

"And she will handle it well, Mother Meredith! Blaise is intelligent, business-oriented—the computer is testimonial to that."

"To Blaise goes all our family has accumulated for several generations, Ellen. I fear the advantages of it are being cast aside."

"You mean societal affiliations?"

"My grandfather told me, when fortune fails, the wealth of a man is friends and associates. Business reversals are inevitable. It happened to Great-Grandfather Meredith during the potato famine. It happened to grandfather when whaling fleets were made obsolete by oil, and to Arnold's father during the crash of 1929. Had it not been for friends and business contacts, the Merediths might have become destitute. To whom would Blaise turn? Herman?"

"Herman may own a company like Xerox someday, Mother Meredith."

"If she could come to New York and visit me, I could introduce her to proper young men and—"

"You're welcome to invite her."

"I did."

"And?"

Mother Meredith lifted her eyebrows, let them fall. "We are as strangers," she said. "I ask Blaise if she ever thinks of her father and I can feel the child shrinking away from me. I ask what is happening to her annuities and she shrugs it off, saying Richard handles those things."

"He does," Ellen took the woman's hand. It was cold, waxen. "Richard says we're doing quite well with our investments. He's talking about purchasing a beach house. He asked if I wanted to take a cruise. He's conservative, Mother Meredith, but that's what Arnold's grandfather would have wanted."

The front door slammed and the two women drew apart.

"A-double-okay!" Blaise shrieked. Oblivious to her grandmother's tears, Blaise hugged one, then the other. "When you get an 'A' from Miss Donna DeVries," she smirked, "you know it's perfect. Not a comma, not a semicolon, not a word misplaced. Nothing! Besides, she hates me."

"That's not true, Blaise."

"Despises me," Blaise insisted, gleefully. "Well! Are we ready to go to daddy's office?"

Herman was hanging on the kitchen counter again, waiting.

"Herman is coming with us, mama," Blaise advised. "Daddy said he didn't want his office disrupted, and Herman has sworn he won't offer unsolicited advice."

Driving toward town on Government Boulevard, Mother Meredith rode in the back seat with Blaise. Herman was up front with Ellen. "He didn't have to go to Vietnam," Mother Meredith was saying. "But Arnold had a deep patriotism, an unabiding affection for his flag."

"Yes ma'am."

"We made the supreme sacrifice, didn't we, darling?" Mother Meredith patted Blaise on the leg. "He didn't have to go back, but he did."

Ellen turned south on Water Street, the pavement broken, fences guarding both sides of the lane. Ships loomed at dock and the shrill of industrial construction was piercing. Richard's office was an imposing yellow brick edifice. Bordered on one side by a salvage yard, on the other by a marine supply house. Across the river the davits and cranes of Alabama Dry Dock formed a tatted pattern of structural steel lace against the sky.

"We've been expecting you," the youthful office manager greeted them. "I'm Bradley Pearson, Mrs. Curry."

Introductions completed, Bradley seemed uncomfortable as he gestured toward the general office area. "There isn't much to see. But Mr. Curry said he thought you were primarily interested in the computers."

"Yes," Blaise said.

They passed between men and women employees who looked up briefly, or not at all. They rode a small elevator to the second floor. Stepping out, Ellen was astounded.

The entire level was enclosed behind glass except for a perimeter walkway which allowed a visitor to traverse the area without entering the central part of the room.

Bradley tried to give personality to the sterile scene. "Air-conditioned, dust free. Do you know anything about computers, Mrs. Curry?"

"The children do."

Bradley eyed Herman who had wandered ahead, looking through the glass. "The central processing unit is the piece of equipment at the center of the complex," Bradley said. "There are connecting terminals—"

A long row of machines held reels of tape which turned in sporadic whirls, halting, starting, stopping. "Retrieval of stored data . . ."

Technicians in white smocks moved about like interns in a hospital nursery, checking heartbeat and respiration of first this baby, then that. One man made notes on a clipboard, monitoring dials.

". . . transmitted via satellite from London . . ."

Blaise listened with intensity, eyes alight, a child in a zoo getting her first glimpse at the wonders of the world. So concentrated was she, Bradley had begun to confine his remarks to Blaise alone. But Herman was not too far distant to hear every word, despite his apparent insouciance. Beneath Ellen's feet, the floor was vibrant. She could hear the whirr of machines, the steady pulse of electronic gadgets. The reels were rotating, mystical, moving by some predetermined plan, stop-go-stop-go.

". . . relayed from the Orient, underwater cable and microwave . . ."

Ellen had never been up here before. Never had cause to. Her impression of Richard's business was based on the cramped general offices below, clerks and accountants quietly pursuing their mathematical tasks. Richard's private office was small, austere, functional, the only exception being several Dean Mosher pen and ink drawings framed over a credenza.

" . . . products purchased in one nation, shipped to Aruba, unpacked, repackaged, shipped anew . . . "

Blaise asked something and Ellen watched the office manager's expression alter to a more serious, but pleased countenance. His reply was business argot, "Cost differential, per unit, increased proportionately at each step of the production process . . ."

Ahead of them, licking his teeth, thumbs hung in his trouser pockets, Herman was a study of indifference. But he turned as Bradley spoke, "Calculations based on the present value of anticipated future earnings."

"Discounted cash flow," Herman interjected.

"Exactly!" Bradley grinned at Ellen. "These young people are a pleasant surprise to me. They know what this is."

Mother Meredith was not the least interested. She kept a discreet distance from the tour guide, her demeanor that of a city dweller in a musty museum of fossils.

"What does Blaise get out of this?" Mother Meredith questioned Ellen.

"I'm not sure. I try to think of it as an educational toy."

"What does anyone get out of such machines?"

"Only what one puts into them," Bradley responded.

Surprised that he'd overheard, Mother Meredith fell back even further, pulling Ellen away from the children and the office manager.

"She spends hours at it, Ellen. Doing what?"

"Some sort of mathematical computation, I assume."

"If she were going to a far galaxy, such devotion would be understandable. But after you play with numbers for a while—what else is there?"

Mother Meredith watched garbed technicians peering at meters and blinking lights. "More than what she gets out of it," Mother Meredith intoned, "I'd like to know what she's putting into it."

Chapter EIGHT

"How long has daddy been in Nashville?" Blaise asked.
Ellen dusted living room furniture with lemon oil. "He's not in Nashville anymore."

"Where is he?"

"Blaise, you're dropping crumbs on the carpet. Please go in the kitchen to eat your sandwich."

"Sorry." Blaise followed to an étagère, "Where did you say daddy is?"

"The last time he telephoned, Miami."

"Is he going to Aruba?"

"I don't know. Blaise, go to the kitchen with that food."

Blaise gulped the last of it and smiled around full cheeks. Mother Meredith was upstairs in the hallway running the vacuum cleaner.

"Mother Meredith wants me to go to Jamaica with her, mom. I don't want to though."

"How about helping Mother Meredith vacuum, Blaise?"

"Won't let me. Says she'll suffer if you suffer but there's no need both of us suffering."

"Nevertheless, you vacuum this room. Those are your food particles."

"She said," Blaise continued, "she wanted me to visit her in Westchester, too. We'd go to New York and shop at Saks, she said. Take in some shows, play the tourist, things like that. I don't want to though."

"I think Mother Meredith is through upstairs, Blaise. Go get the vacuum and do this room."

"She told me how lonely she was in Kingston," Blaise kept up as Ellen moved to other furniture. "She gave me a sales pitch on calypso music and native festivities. Talked about the blue-green waters and beautiful beaches. But I said, no."

"Sounds like fun," Ellen said noncommittally.

"Then why is she so bored, which she says she is when she's down there?"

"Her scope of friends is limited, Blaise. Your presence would help her extend her own circle."

"Are you suggesting I should go?"

"That isn't my decision. Are you going to do as I asked and get the vacuum?"

"I hear it running again, mom. She's not finished. If you were me, would you go visit Mother Meredith?"

"I don't know."

"Fibber," Blaise said, softly.

Ellen ignored the girl. Thinking of Richard. So terse on the phone last night. All week long, in fact. He'd called from Nashville, troubles compounded. Something about import duties and mislabeled goods. Then he'd telephoned from the Omni Hotel in Miami Beach. Miami was a port of entry, he'd explained. He was immersed in government red tape. It would be another week before he could come home.

It was not what he said, but the tone of his voice which upset her. He had failed to ask about Mother Meredith, or Blaise.

"You know what she's doing, don't you?" Blaise had lowered her voice, standing very near.

"Vacuuming the hall carpet."

"She's trying to put her stamp on me. She wants me to dress frilly and act like a rich snot."

"What?"

"Rich tot," Blaise said. "Go to afternoon tea and play lawn croquet with other—rich people."

"What's wrong with that?"

"Rich people are boring, mama."

"Blaise, that's unkind to Mother Meredith."

"Only because it's true. But I didn't act disrespectful to her."

"I should hope not. I think you're misjudging your grand-mother's motives."

"I asked her!"

Richard staying away because of Mother Meredith? Ellen asked him.

"No, no," he'd insisted. "Please apologize in my behalf, Ellen. I wish I could be there, believe me."

"You know what she said, mama?" Blaise whispered.

"What?"

"She wanted me to drink from a proper cup and saucer. Use a cloth napkin."

"Incidentally, I put the Lennox china in the cupboard to use while Mother Meredith is here."

"She said she wanted me to meet healthy young men of good stock," Blaise labored. "It sounded like we were going to a nursery and pick out oak trees."

"Her intentions are good, Blaise."

"She asked me if I'd ever eaten caviar, escargot, truffles—do you know what that is, mama?"

"Yes, of course."

"Fish eggs," Blaise grimaced, "snails and a fungus!"

Ellen laughed softly.

"We don't speak the same language, mama. We certainly don't eat the same foods. She told me about a place where she could get pâté de foie gras, and insisted I learn how to say that. Well, the reason it's in French is because of what it is."

Ellen laughed again, wiping the frames of paintings.

"But you talk about those super hot dogs from the Dog House, or pizza, or salty boiled peanuts, and Mother Meredith acts like we're living out of garbage cans."

Mother Meredith entered and sat hard on a hassock. She looked at her hands as if they were diseased. "All that noise makes my ears ring," she said. Her head was bound in a borrowed bandana. She wore a pair of Ellen's slacks which were too small in the waist, secured by one of Richard's belts and covered by a blouse that hung outside of the pants.

"Go get the vacuum, Blaise," Ellen commanded.

"That's the first time I ever saw you sweat, Mother Meredith," Blaise said in passing.

"Good Lord," the grandmother moaned, "it's true. My hairdo will be ruined, Ellen."

"Blaise said you invited her to Westchester and Jamaica."

"To no avail. We're leagues apart, that child and I. One must admire the pragmatism of the girl, though," Mother Meredith dabbed her upper lip with a sleeve. "For every offer I made, she had a counteroffer."

"Oh?"

"I tried to pique her interest with descriptions of Rudolf Nureyev and Charlene Gehm in Nijinsky's *The Afternoon of a Faun*," Mother Meredith reported. "Blaise responded by inviting me to see Willie Nelson at the municipal auditorium week after next."

"Did you accept?"

"I did."

"You did?"

"Which means I'll have to invent some disaster. I just learned he's a—we saw a movie last night—he plays a string instrument and talks about keno girls who can suck the chrome off a trailer hitch."

"Apparently there's a disparity of culture," Ellen offered.

"Chasm," Mother Meredith said. "We talk like a Greek in an Athens bazaar, understanding nothing, but eager to make a sale. Blaise has no concept of the most rudimentary things."

"Such as pâté de foie gras."

"Indeed."

Blaise brought in the vacuum cleaner and the noise of the machine chased them out. Mother Meredith accompanied Ellen into the kitchen. Despite her labors, she still smelled of Worth.

"I may as well be practical about this," Mother Meredith concluded. "Blaise isn't coming to me."

"It takes time, Mother Meredith."

"My world sounds as alien to her as hers sounds to me," the grandmother conceded. "I cannot imagine a person putting a trailer hitch in her mouth. Blaise cannot conceive of eating goose liver or beluga roe."

"I'm sure there must be more important middle ground—"

"So I've decided to move here."

Ellen blinked hard. "Move here?"

"If I go away and come back next year, will things have changed?" Mother Meredith questioned.

"I—I don't know. Possibly. Blaise will mature."

"My moving here was one of her counteroffers," Mother Meredith said. "Actually, I think it's the only way I'll be able to put my stamp on that child. I told her as much."

"So she said."

Mother Meredith's face contorted, "I must expect to endure some rather bizarre experiences such as this man Willie Nelson."

"Mother Meredith, do you think you'd be happy here?"

"My husband's grandfather spent eight years in Dhahran, Yemen. It was desolate, the people were unfriendly, the weather was hot and humid. But Grandfather Meredith said a place is what one makes of it. If he could exist in Yemen long enough to tie up coffee concessions, I can survive in Mobile, Alabama long enough to see my granddaughter educated to civilized ways."

"Mobile is so different from all you've known."

"Be that as it may," Mother Meredith held out an arm as Blaise joined them, pulling the girl to her. "Blaise and I are going house hunting."

"Car hunting," Blaise amended.

"Yes. First an automobile, then a house."

Blaise smiled at Ellen, eyes wide behind her glasses. "I'm going to teach Mother Meredith about life, mama."

What would Richard say? Annual visits were one thing. But residency!

"... Herman will drive us to the car dealers, Mother Meredith..."

"First to a hairdresser, my dear," Mother Meredith replied. "I can't go anywhere looking like this. Perhaps you'd like an appointment, too?"

"Sure!"

Ellen listened to them going upstairs together, laughing like two children in a conspiracy.

"Oh dear," she murmured. "Oh dear, oh dear."

Ellen went to the attic, and unnoticed, stood there a few minutes watching Blaise. The girl was transcribing something from a notebook, typing information on the keyboard. With each touch of the keys, the glowing green screen of the cathode ray tube reflected what Blaise had done. It seemed to have no sense. A random word here or there was legible, but overall it was gibberish.

"Blaise?"

"Hi mom," she replied as if she'd known Ellen was present.

"What exactly does that thing do?"

"Computes. Analyzes. Depends on the program."

"Give me an example."

Blaise wheeled around her secretary-type chair and gazed at her mother. "Are you getting interested in computers, mama?"

"I can hardly ignore it."

"No," Blaise said, soberly. "I suppose not. Pull up a seat, then."

Ellen did so, sitting at Blaise's side.

"You know how to type, mama?"

"Yes."

"That's all this is—a typewriter. You strike a key and it makes a letter appear on the screen. That way you can see if you've made a mistake."

"Where does the information go?"

"Nowhere, until I make it happen. But first, we type out a problem. Let's say daddy bought pressed cane trays from Taiwan, which he did. He bought four tons to be shipped in bulk."

Ellen watched these terms appear as Blaise typed.

"Now," Blaise continued, softly, "there are approximately seventeen thousand trays per ton, multiplied by four tons—"

Ellen felt a tingle begin at the base of her neck and radiate down her spine. She watched those nimble, lean fingers flick across the keyboard, constructing a problem.

"Multiplied by—"

The machine was almost silent, except for a faint hum. It was a green-eyed cyclops meeting Blaise's gaze, the information appearing as white letters across the screen.

"Less breakage or other damage—"

Ellen realized, suddenly, Blaise could sit there and see anyone behind her reflected in the video display. Yet the child had continued working as if alone.

"Which gives us a base cost per unit of—"

Under Blaise's elbow was a ring-binder of ruled paper, such as that used in her school work. Across the room, in a partially closed cardboard box, more notebooks like it.

"There," Blaise sat back. "This is how it works. We have bought all these pressed cane trays at this price and they are going to Aruba. We'll feed this information into the computer, and when we know it, we'll add shipping, handling, insurance and other costs. That means each tray costs us a total of forty cents."

"Forty cents," Ellen said, dumbly.

"I'm making up the figures, mama. But that's about right."

"A person could do all that with a simple adding machine, Blaise."

"Sure they could."

"Then why spend a fortune on a computer?"

"Because you don't have to do this but once, mama. The machine stores this much information in the computer memory. As we learn new costs, we add it in. Let's say one whole ton gets lost and the insurance rates double."

Ellen watched these hypothetical figures typed in.

"Now we learn that daddy paid not forty cents, but nearly seventy cents per tray. Then he gets a good deal on pressed cane bowls, maybe salad forks, and he wants to combine these in one retail package."

Her fingers flew over the typewriter, Blaise pushed buttons and a moment later announced, "He has spent a total of ninety cents per retail unit. Every step of the way he knows what his cost has been, what price he must get, how much profit he will make; and according to daddy's office manager, they also compute the depreciating value of the money when it finally comes in. This is only one item. Daddy's business handles thousands of items from all over the world. He can tell at a glance where a product was bought, where it is at the moment, how well it sold in retail stores. The computer does all that and keeps him abreast of cash flow, in and out."

"That's remarkable, I suppose."

"Without it," Blaise said, "he couldn't operate with less than fifty employees. There would be tons of paper stored, file cabinets overflowing, and human error."

"This is what you do the whole time you're up here, Blaise?'

"Talk to the computer," Blaise acknowledged.

"Talk?"

"I have to use the computer language, but yes. The computer speaks in numbers only." She punched a few keys and the screen glowed, **READY**. Blaise typed more and suddenly the screen was filled with numbers. Zeros and the numeral one over and over.

"What does all that signify?" Ellen asked.

"The letter 'A' is number 10 0001," Blaise wrote it on her pad. "The letter 'B' is 10 0011. The letter 'C' is 10 0111. And so forth through the entire alphabet. There's a six-digit number for each letter. It's called binary code, which means two numbers are used, *zero* and *one*. It's all that's required. But when I type a letter it shows up on the screen as a letter until I feed it to the computer which translates the letter into numbers."

"I'm confused."

Blaise chewed her lip. *So serious.*

"And this is what you do the entire time you're up here?"

"Things like this."

"But what do you learn from it?"

"How to do it better. How to make the computer tell me what I wish to know. That means giving it the proper instructions."

"May I ask it a question?" Ellen inquired.

Blaise seemed to be probing, looking from one of Ellen's eyes to the other.

"I won't hurt the machine," Ellen added.

"What do you want to know, mama?"

"Ask it what the price of beef will be next week." Ellen expected a smile, derisive laughter, some response of loving disdain, perhaps. But Blaise pushed a button and cleared the screen. She typed: COST: BEEF.

The machine did nothing until Blaise pushed a button. They waited, waited, waited.

IMPROPER INPUT.

"The machine doesn't know, mama."

"Why did it take so long?"

"It was searching thousands of miles of memory data for the word 'beef.' It isn't in there."

"How do you know what to ask?"

"I ask," Blaise said, "only that which I've already answered by putting in the data the computer needs to evaluate a question."

"Well," Ellen stood up. "I'd like to say 'How interesting' but it seems incredibly boring to me."

"That's how photography seems to me," Blaise said.

As Ellen reached the stairs, she turned, "Anybody could reach Richard's computer if they had a telephone line?"

"If they knew the code. I have to type in my code before daddy's computer will respond to the keyboard."

"What is your code?" Ellen asked.

"The word 'chaser.' "

"Chaser," Ellen mused. "Which only signifies the proper numbers, I assume."

"You're learning, mama," Blaise said solemnly.

But going downstairs, Ellen felt less than informed. Whatever Blaise was doing, to the girl it was not a game. She was protective of her machine, reticent about sharing it. Yet, as far as Ellen could see, Blaise knew what she was doing.

"Is Blaise coming down to join us?" Mother Meredith asked as Ellen reached the patio.

"I don't think so."

Mother Meredith nodded, troubled. "It isn't normal for a girl to devote so much time to such a lonely pursuit, Ellen."

The lights of the city were beginning to appear in the gloaming. The distant hum of traffic was a drone.

"When is Richard coming home, Ellen?"

"He called today. Maybe next Wednesday. He isn't certain."

"It's been over two weeks."

He had telephoned from south Florida again, not Miami, but Ellen wasn't sure where. Problems continued. Richard had stated he was delayed and that was that. He didn't want to talk about it. He didn't have anything else to say. *Not coming.*

Ellen had not told him Mother Meredith was still here. Richard hadn't asked. She did not speak of Mother Meredith's decision to move to Mobile. That she was looking for a home. That she had bought a new Mercedes.

But then, Richard hadn't give her a chance.

"What about clothing for yourself, Richard?"

"Don't worry about me, Ellen."

"But I do worry."

"Don't," he said. "I can buy clothes as I need them."

"I miss you," Ellen had tried to turn the mood.

"Miss you," he'd replied. "I won't be calling again until I'm on my way back to Mobile."

"Is there anything I could do to help?"

"What would that be, Ellen?" His tone was dangerously close to sarcasm.

"Anything you ask, Richard."

"Nothing."

She'd hung up feeling acutely uneasy. As if she'd done something, or stood accused of something she hadn't fully grasped.

In a prior telephone conversation she'd complained about his unexpected absence and Richard seemed angry as he replied. "We've had very few emergencies in our association, Ellen."

Association!

Mother Meredith seemed lost in thought, but she wrinkled her brow an instant, inhaling before a sigh. "If somebody doesn't water Richard's garden," she said, "it will all be dead when he comes home."

N Chapter NINE

After three weeks, Richard returned. Ellen saw his troubles were not over. Although he denied it, pensive silence belied assurances. If she persisted, he became restless, brusque, finally irritable. His words, "There's nothing to concern you," were not comforting. To which he added, "You worry too much, Ellen."

Yes. True.

She watched his garden choke with weeds, the plants, seared by June heat, dying for lack of moisture. She saw him preoccupied, unhearing if she called, not listening as she spoke. She found herself reflecting his mood, snapping at Blaise unreasonably, hurrying the child away to visit Mother Meredith.

Deep in the pit of her stomach, the acid ache of indigestion couldn't be alleviated. She was lying awake, pretending sleep, with Richard lying awake in the dark beside her.

It was like the period after Tony died, when Richard constantly relived the moment.

"You found the body, Mr. Curry?"

"Yes."

"Floating face down, you say."

Blaise had sat there, eyes glazed.

"You felt for a pulse, did you?"

"Yes."

"Did you try mouth-to-mouth resuscitation?"

"Yes."

The officer wore sunglasses, tiny mirrors which threw back one's face as a contorted oval, a paraboloid image of agony. "Then what did you do?"

"Carried—brought him to the house."

"The girl was with you when you found the boy, Mr. Curry?"

"Yes."

A muscle in Richard's cheek began to twitch. He massaged it with a forefinger, but it quivered anew.

"The girl had been left alone with the boy, you said."

"Yes."

Ellen remembered how dry her eyes became, burning, tear ducts devoid of fluids. She remembered the way Blaise sat there staring at Richard, responding to the officer's questions after a pause as if to assimilate breath and muscle coordination—each word a whispery affirmation of all Richard stated.

The morgue. The casket. The funeral home. The high tenor of the youthful minister giving a eulogy for a child he barely knew. The graveside ceremony. The flowers—a sweet aroma riding a gentle breeze. The friends. Weeping women with no words to say, hugs and sobs.

In the week that Richard had been back, she found herself parroting words she'd used after Tony died. To ease Richard through the tragedy, she'd seized upon every positive thing—the weather, the way he had dressed that day, her love for him. Like a blind man repairing a dike, she felt for emotional crevices, using logic to chink his wounds. She'd bolstered, teased, loved—she'd saved her own sanity by devoting every thought to Richard's utter depression. But beneath her smiles and behind twinkling eyes, she'd suffered.

She was suffering now.

"What're you thinking about, handsome man?"

"Nothing."

"If your mind were a lake I'd swim in it, Richard."

No smile.

"You know what we ought to do?" she asked, brightly. "We ought to go look at some beach houses."

But they didn't.

Richard sat on the patio, coffee gone cold, tie loose, staring across the dying garden at the shimmer of summer heat undulating up from the city below. He came home late, without calling. A few times his breath smelled from liquor.

Like after Tony—

So she'd slipped back into the pattern of up-tempo conversation. No probing questions. Only patter which was superficially cheerful. Commenting on anything positive, anything good.

But there was a toll to pay, an emotionally exacting toll. She began losing weight within a few days. She was cranky with Mother Meredith, short-tempered with Blaise. She had rebuked Herman for leaving a mess in the kitchen. Only with Richard was she ebullient, ever vigilant to remain so. And her muscles strained from the sustained charade. A dull headache lingered, temples pulsing.

It was especially difficult since Ellen had no idea why he was acting this way. A direct approach was construed as assault and he became defensive. She was restricted to oblique inquiries.

"Your office manager, Bradley Pearson, seems like a capable young man."

An almost imperceptible shrug, "Yes. He is."

"Blaise was enthralled with the computer equipment. Even Herman, trying so diligently to seem unconcerned."

"I told Blaise not to take Herman."

"He resisted playing the expert," Ellen reported. "I think Mr. Pearson was impressed with both Blaise and Herman."

"He was."

"He said business was very good these days."

"Best ever."

So it wasn't a business slump.

"With credit getting so tight and lending rates high," she'd said, "what will that do to you?"

"I don't run on credit. It won't affect us."

"Do you think the recession will get worse?"

"Importing and exporting allows us to do business where business is good, Ellen. I'm not worried about recession."

Then what?

Suddenly, he would lurch up from some mental abyss, "This is ridiculous! Let's go out to eat, Ellen."

She'd hear him whistling in the shower, grinning when she pulled back the curtain to receive a watery kiss.

But in a restaurant, sipping wine, as if an unseen mist enveloped him, he would succumb again and stare at nothing, present in body only.

"Have I told you lately how much I love you, Richard?"

He took her hand between his, patted.

"You are my life."

He kissed her fingers.

"You resurrected me, you know," she said.

"And you: me," he replied.

Fortunately, Blaise was with Mother Meredith most of every day now that school was out for the summer. They pored over wallpapers, studied color tints, searched through galleries of antiques, planning renovations of a rambling two-story Tudor home Mother Meredith had purchased. Gardeners, painters and repairmen went about their duties while Mother Meredith walked among them dressed as if to greet a member of a foreign legation.

"Do you resent Mother Meredith moving to Mobile, Richard?"

"Don't be ridiculous."

"She is thoughtless where you're concerned, sometimes."

"Consider the source, Ellen. You have another husband. She cannot acquire another son."

"I haven't tried to curtail the time Blaise spends with Mother

Meredith," Ellen remarked. "They seem to be good for one another. What do you think?"

"Unless Mother Meredith takes up smoking pot and entertaining young men in sandals, she can't be bad for Blaise."

If Richard missed Blaise around the house, he didn't mention it. Mother Meredith invited them over to see work in progress. Richard went without complaint. His only observation: "A phone in every room."

"And a sauna on both floors," Ellen noted.

As they drove home again, he ebbed away, moving like an automaton from place to place, almost sulking.

Blaise announced that Mother Meredith was driving to New York and wanted her to go. Was that all right?

"Have fun," Richard said.

"We're not going to hurry," Mother Meredith warned. "Going to Atlanta, then to Chattanooga to see Lookout Mountain. Then up the Skyline Drive across the Smoky Mountains."

"Have fun," Richard repeated.

"I'm planning to select certain pieces of furniture to ship down here," Mother Meredith explained to Ellen. "Not much, but a few things. We may be gone two weeks. It would be a shame not to go to the city while we're there. We'll make the rounds."

Make the rounds.

Ellen heard the term shortly after she and Arnold announced their engagement. To Mother Meredith, it involved shopping at Lord and Taylor, Saks, and Tiffany's. Dinner at Four Seasons. Broadway shows and nightclubs which catered to "personal friends" of the Meredith family.

Already Ellen had detected changes in Blaise. Her visit to a hairdresser had been radical. From long straight tresses, Blaise had been styled to a short, bouncy coiffure. Easier to manage, contoured to high cheek bones. A few days later, the round spectacles were gone and Blaise wore designer glasses which accentuated her blue eyes even more. She'd begun to speak of contact lenses.

Richard didn't seem to notice.

"Blaise may bend to Mother Meredith after all," Ellen dared to remark.

"It works both ways," Richard grunted. "You never saw Mother Meredith in slacks and a checkered blouse before. I heard her humming a country music song the other day."

A few days later, Richard's depression vanished. Just as it had happened after Tony's death. Like a sun appearing at dawn following weeks of stormy weather, the air felt cleansed, the world renewed, birds sang.

Richard brought coffee to her bedside and awoke Ellen with kisses and strokes. "Time to wake up my sweet," he murmured. "Wake up, wake up . . ."

He pulled a chair near the bed, sitting there smiling as she became aware. He winked appreciatively. "Beautiful as always," he said.

And as she had reacted when it happened before, Ellen gratefully accepted the transformation, almost afraid to question how it came to be.

That evening, with Blaise and Mother Meredith already gone, Richard mentioned that he still must go to Aruba. She was prepared to accompany him, if asked. She really didn't want to. She wanted to accept a new writing and photo assignment. She wanted to clean her darkroom, replace stale chemicals, put her avocation in order.

Richard didn't ask.

Ellen sat in Armand Joaquin's cluttered office as the young publisher tapped his teeth with an unsharpened pencil. "The article on incompetent teachers was a winner," he noted. "Stirred up a stink, helped the move to have teachers tested and made the National Education Association mad as hell."

"Thank you," she said.

"What we need is more of the same," Armand declared. "How about a piece on the victims of crimes and the inefficient, lazy and inadequate judges who try their cases, failure of the criminal judicial system—"

"That's not for me, Armand."

"Give that one to somebody else, Peggy," Armand instructed his wife. "Okay, Ellen, how about the current effect of school busing. Cost of fuel, equipment, the way the country is forced to employ private buses for lack of funds, the vehicles are overcrowded and unsafe and—"

"I don't think so, Armand."

"Um. Okay, let me see then. How about the environmentalist's view of drilling for oil in Mobile Bay?" Seeing Ellen's expression, Armand shook his head in reply to his own query.

"There's the controversy between local shrimpers and Vietnamese boatmen who are competing with one another."

"No."

"Tennessee-Tombigbee waterway," Armand offered. "Tell how the Corps of Engineers go from one boondoggle to another."

"That's out of my field completely."

Glowering, Armand turned to Peggy. "Any ideas?"

"The city auditorium is selling liquor during concerts," Peggy suggested. "That's competing with local private enterprise."

"I've written an editorial about it already," Armand replied.

"I'll tell you what I'd like to do, Armand," Ellen said. "An article on computers."

"Computers?"

"They're used by the university hospital in health care. The city traffic department plots the timing of street lights by computer. You get billed by the utilities, telephone company and banks according to computer tabulations. You have one back there setting type for your newspaper."

"Controversy, Ellen—where's the controversy?"

"The article could be informational, Armand," Peggy suggested.

"A paper like this needs more than information, Peg. Something like the teacher incompetency thing—we had an order for a hundred copies from the school board alone."

"What are computers," Ellen continued. "What can they do, where are they leading us?"

"Science fiction approach," Armand grumped.

"No. Reality. A friend of Blaise's mentioned that someday

computers may expand their own memory capacity in the form of growing crystals."

"That's frightening," Peggy said.

"I hear my daughter and her friends talking about computers that get smarter and smarter, learning as people do, by experience. Blaise says technology is all that keeps computers from attaining some rather phenomenal accomplishments."

"Wait a minute!" Armand narowed his eyes. "John Lawrence with the local FBI was talking about computers recently. Computers and *crime*."

Ellen repeated fragments of conversations she'd overheard, "A day may come when people have computers inserted into the body to accentuate native intelligence, to control radical shifts of mood caused by erratic hormonal and chemical flows. They're designing computers which will become public information centers. Years ago, every factory had its own electric power plant and water supply. Now they tap into municipal systems. In the same way, the average citizen may soon be connected to information banks with home computers."

Armand was pawing through a desk drawer, a pencil clamped between perfect white teeth. He spoke around the obstacle, "Why would anybody want to have such a computer connection?"

"To read your newspaper," Ellen said. "The cost of postage continues to climb. Someday you may be paid a fee for every person who calls up your newspaper on their video screen. Mail may become obsolete. Letters will be typed at home and held in a national computer until called for by the recipient."

Armand consulted a note he'd found. "John Lawrence was talking to me about the rising incidence of computer crime. The laws are lax, culprits go free—how's that for an angle?"

"Computers could be the best, or the worst thing to happen to mankind," Ellen labored. "It will depend on the people who program and operate the machines, in the same way we are at the mercy of men who handle nuclear power today."

Armand arched black eyebrows and thought aloud, "Lawrence was after something, those guys always are. Wanted me to put the squeeze on somebody he couldn't reach legally."

"Computers are the repository of all man's technical knowledge," Ellen continued. "The machines hold in their memories what man must know to go to the moon, launch a nuclear attack, making lightning swift decisions on whether to remain at peace, or go to war."

"Yeah, yeah," Armand said, irritably. "All that's good, but no controversy—it isn't something the man on the street can relate to. But crime, right here at home, hitting him in his pocketbook, anybody understands that."

Ellen spoke now to Peggy, "I watch Blaise go up to the attic and stay there for hours poring over data, analyzing, programming the machine to do more and more functions. Blaise is probably a typical intelligent girl. If she becomes that engrossed, other young people must be equally as interested. I admit, I don't understand what the thing does. It scares me not to know. I could bring a fresh approach to the subject as I find out—and I intend to find out."

"The guy's name is on the tip of my tongue," Armand pondered. "He rips off the public; a real threat, according to John Lawrence."

"If my daughter had one of those things in the attic," Peggy said to Ellen, "I'd go up and unplug it."

"I may," Ellen agreed. "If I don't like what I discover."

"Jensen!" Armand snapped his fingers. "Kim Jensen! A computer thief in the guise of a security analyst. Now that could be good—the menacing threat of a local man gaining mastery over our lives with technological skill. The FBI is interested in him— how about that for an article? If Jensen is a crook, let's nail him."

"Kim Jensen," Ellen said, softly. "I've heard Blaise speak of him."

Armand rubbed his palms briskly. "Right you are! That's your assignment then. Use Blaise as your opening gambit."

When she returned home, the house dark, Ellen entered and stood listening to silence. Richard in Aruba. Blaise and Mother Meredith making their way northward to New York. For at least two weeks she'd be here alone. She had all the books Blaise had gathered. She had the intelligence and now, the drive to learn about the subject at hand. There would never be a more propitious moment.

She went upstairs, leaving the lower level dark. The air in the attic felt heavy. She turned on lights and stood over the equipment. "I don't know what you are," she said aloud, "but I'm going to find out."

She sought a point for beginning, walking along shelves where Blaise kept manuals and books. Her toe struck the cardboard box filled with notebooks and Ellen stooped to open it.

She selected a notebook, turned pages held by a spiral of wire. In a left-hand column was a date. Every line had a date. The first one, three years ago. Beside the date, on every entry, a word, sentence, or phrase.

It had a vague familiarity.

Ellen scanned pages, Blaise's handwriting sometimes fluid and artful, other times cramped and almost illegible.

May 12: Ochlochnee/Oklocknee/awk-lach-nee.

May 13: Panacea bridge . . . girl: Betty Sue.

Ellen dug down in the box for another binder. The same. Dates, phrases.

She could tell by the handwriting, this was not a new endeavor. From a ten-year-old's scrawl to more practiced penmanship. Page after page of dates and notes—but of what?

She perused other notebooks, searching for intelligent, cogent —a shiver swept over her.

She'd found a notebook dated a few months ago. The phrases, place names, sentences, *all Richard's!*

January 11: *contradiction, private schools*, Blaise had written. Another date, a similar notation: *contra-public sch yrs.*

Copious notes of statements by Richard—for what reason?

Ellen sat on the floor, notebook in hand. Like everyone, Richard told tales to make a point, not necessarily relate facts. He had contradicted himself, Ellen recalled, first claiming to be chary of private schools because they were "so regimented, restricting intellectual growth." He'd cited his own experiences. And yes, Ellen remembered other conversations about childhood trauma, hunger, and a ghetto school.

Page, after page, after page after—

She stared at the machine, its red light glowing.

Blaise had been at the keyboard with one of these notebooks. Feeding in material such as this?

She heard the telephone downstairs, but didn't go for it. She sat at the swivel chair Blaise used, and examined the keyboard. Ellen pushed a button and the screen grew bright a moment, dimmed to a matt green.

She typed with one finger, slowly: **CHASE**

Instantly the screen replied: **READY**

Ellen typed: **JAN 11**

She waited.

Nothing.

She cleared the screen as she'd seen Blasise do. She typed again: **JANUARY 11: WHAT?**

Nothing. As if the machine were mocking her. Like a child testing a parent, waiting to see the consequences.

Ellen typed again, rapidly: **JUST YOU WAIT CYCLOPS.**

Nothing.

She needed help. Needed to know what this was about. What was wrong with Richard? What was Blaise doing with these comments, accumulated over several years? She cleared the screen, turned off the video display.

Whatever it was—she was after it.

Being passive had gotten her nowhere.

T EN *Chapter*

Ellen had never violated Richard's den. She had never gone through Blaise's bedroom. But now, systematically, she read correspondence, checked lists of long distance telephone calls, searching Richard's rolltop mahogany desk.

Enough was enough. She was tired of worry, weary of uncertainty.

The telephone rang.

"Mrs. Curry, please hold the line for Mr. Denny at First National Bank."

Ellen hung up. She pulled contents from a lower desk file drawer, examining folders one at a time.

The telephone again.

"Mrs. Curry? This is First National Bank. We must've been cut off. Please hold the line for—"

"Wait a minute," Ellen said, sharply. "I don't know Mr. Denny."

"Oh, I'm very sorry, Mrs. Curry. It was—"

A man's voice broke into the conversation, "Mrs. Curry? Good morning! This is Norris Denny—we've never met, but I hope to change that."

Ellen modulated her tone, "What may I do for you, Mr. Denny?"

"My wife and I met your delightful mother-in-law at the country club last week," Denny said. "We'd like to invite you and your husband to join us as our guests for dinner one night next week."

"My husband is out of town," Ellen explained. "Perhaps you could call back?"

"More than happy to do so. Welcome to Mobile, Mrs. Curry."

She hung up, irritated. That was the fifth call in two days with invitations generated by Mother Meredith. As if, somehow, she and Richard had been overlooked. As if to rectify the slight and admit them to the stratum of society Mother Meredith called her own.

It was Richard's bent to be orderly. Folders A-Z and subheadings by subject, cross-indexed by names . . .

The doorbell. Ellen considered ignoring it, but it might be Herman.

It was. He stood there uncertain, hesitating only because Ellen had called for him whereas he usually came of his own accord.

"I need your help, Herman," Ellen said, bluntly.

"Something wrong, Mrs. Curry?"

"Have you had breakfast?"

"I can always eat."

"Then go feed yourself. I'll be in the den."

"I'm not that hungry, Mrs. Curry. Is something the matter?"

Ellen led him into the kitchen, talking as she made sandwiches. "I'm having trouble with Blaise's computer, Herman."

"Her computer?"

"I have been reading the manuals, but I can't seem to get anything out of the machine."

His pupils were magnified, skeptical.

"You helped her program the thing, so I knew you'd know how to work it."

"I helped some," he hedged.

Ellen placed pimento cheese sandwiches, cold cuts and condiments on the table. She indicated a chair, "Sit down, Herman. Let's eat before we do anything else."

"I'm not really all that—"

"Sit down, Herman."

"Yes ma'am."

"What I need from you is a crash course in operating that machine, Herman. I can expect that, can't I?"

"Well, see, Mrs. Curry—it's like invading somebody's privacy when you go into their computer."

"I'm sure Blaise would agree. But a mother has a right to such things, doesn't she?"

"I don't know, Mrs. Curry. It's like reading a diary that doesn't belong to you."

Ellen smiled sweetly as he swallowed food. "But you will help me, won't you?"

"If you tell me to. I mean, how could I say no, if you *told* me to?"

"Would you care for milk?" Ellen inquired. "Or would you prefer iced tea?"

"Coke," he said.

Herman sat at the console, the cathode ray tube a viridescent glow. His nose wrinkled as he peered down myopically. "What's her code word, Mrs. Curry?"

"Chase."

"It's a six-letter code."

"She told me 'chase.' "

Herman typed that much. READY appeared on the screen. Nothing happened. "Let's try CHASED," Herman typed. "No," he murmured. "CHASEN." Then, "CHASER."

The video display responded: START.

"That's it," Herman said. "Okay, Mrs. Curry, what are we looking for?"

"I don't know."

He squinted up at her, glasses reflective. "Then what do you want?"

"I want to know what's in the machine."

Herman pushed his tongue beneath his upper lip. "That could be anything. You'd have to have the codes Blaise used to put data in. Otherwise, you'll be calling up things with no logical sequence."

"Such as?"

"Let me see." Herman typed SCAN: TOTAL 10101010. He pushed a button.

The screen filled with numbers, letters, symbols. As they watched, the lines appeared, changed, reappeared in different positions. Herman pressed a key and the changes halted. He selected a sequence, typed it and pressed the start button again.

TICAL: THAI: EQV 231.5 GRAINS = APPX ½ OZ = UNCOINED SILVER = 100 SANTANG REPLACED BY BAHT. FORMER SILVER COIN AND MONETARY UNIT SIAM.

"It's about the value of some foreign currency," Herman said. "I must've tapped into Mr. Curry's data."

"You can do that?"

"Evidently. I doubt Blaise would put this stuff into her storage unit."

He pushed the start button and the screen presented the mass of symbols, letters and numbers again, changing rapidly. "Yeah," Herman said. "Dollars, rubles, pounds. It's listing the value of money around the world. Boy, he must do a whopping business, Mrs. Curry."

"Does anyone at the office know we're doing this?" Ellen questioned.

"Not likely. They might have a monitor, but I doubt it." Herman cleared the screen. He typed other numbers at random. Stocks. Shipping terms. Products. Flight schedules. Telephone numbers—Ellen cried, "Hold it!"

She put a hand on the boy's shoulder, leaning nearer to study the information displayed. "Those are telephone calls," Herman explained. "See, a new one is coming on the screen now. Everytime a call is made, the computer records the number, the time, and probably pays the telephone bill."

It was one number in particular that caught Ellen's eye. (615) area code. *Tennessee.* She'd seen that number downstairs in Richard's desk. She also saw it—

"Herman," Ellen said, "do you think you could figure out Blaise's codes?"

"There's no telling how many codes are in this machine, Mrs. Curry. Hundreds, maybe thousands. Somewhere in all that is Blaise's stuff. It would take weeks, months!"

"Will you try? I'm going downstairs for a few minutes. Keep at it, will you?"

"Blaise will never speak to me again, Mrs. Curry. And I can tell you, Mr. Curry will be boiling mad if he finds out I was wandering through his business records."

"I vow never to tell them, if you vow the same," Ellen said, seriously.

Herman flashed a toothy grin. "I so vow," he said. Then, as Ellen reached the stairs, she heard him wheeze, "Wow-ee."

In Blaise's room, in the closet, a notebook similar to those upstairs. Herein, Blaise had a list of telephone numbers. Two of them from Tennessee. One number was the motel where Richard stayed, recently. The other—circled—was on the computer.

When Ellen returned, she said, "Herman, show me those telephone numbers again."

"What numbers?"

"The ones you had on the screen awhile ago."

"I don't know what I typed, Mrs. Curry."

"Oh, Herman!"

"I didn't know we were looking for telephone numbers."

"Write down the codes from now on, Herman. Keep track of what you're doing."

"But I'm not doing anything but poking around."

Ellen turned on a heel, frustrated. "You're right, this could take weeks or months."

"Blaise has to have some kind of code book," Herman suggested. "If you could find that, we would be able to reach everything, go back to it as we want to."

Ellen ransacked shelves, pulled away the steamer trunk and crawled in with the toy table and chairs. She went through boxes of odds and ends. "How big would it be, Herman?"

"It could be one piece of paper."

"Stuck in a magazine or book."

"Or a mathematical sequence that would call up the code on the screen," Herman confessed.

The complexities were staggering. Ellen didn't know the value of anything Herman brought to the screen as he arbitrarily selected numbers to type on the keyboard. Often, even knowing the code Herman had penetrated, the information was incomprehensible. It might be general, such as the monetary units worldwide—or specific, such a *tical* and the value of that one coin.

Hours passed and Herman's list grew ponderous. He was following a mathematical progression now, looking at the information only long enough to identify the subject before going to the next numerical code.

By the time they quit, night had fallen and Ellen had a raging headache. She and Herman sat on the patio, exhausted, stars winking in the heavens, the city an amber glow before them.

"You want me to come back tomorrow, Mrs. Curry?"

"If you will, Herman."

His silhouette seemed frail in proportion to the size of his head. Ellen heard him slurp the last of his orange juice.

"This is how Kim Jensen does it," Herman said. "He'd take just what we got today, go to Mr. Curry and convince him he needed electronic security services."

"Maybe he does need it, Herman."

"If you didn't have 'chaser' you couldn't have done it," Herman stood up. "Stealing from honest folks is easy, Mrs. Curry. The tricky part is stealing from wary customers. Most businesses don't try to hide anything except the most confidential data. You can believe we haven't touched Mr. Curry's confidential stuff— no more than we've reached Blaise's input. That's the hard part."

"But you will try?"

"I'll try."

"Thank you, Herman."

"No sweat."

As he left her, Ellen compressed her lips. Maybe what she needed was a crook. Somebody like—Kim Jensen.

After a long soak in a hot bath, Ellen sat in her bedroom, belatedly unsure of what they'd done today. What was she after? What damage might come of such meddling? Herman was right, Richard would be furious if he discovered she had allowed that boy to pry into the business computer.

The telephone rang and Ellen answered, knowing it would be Mother Meredith or Blaise.

"We'll arrive in New York by next week," Mother Meredith reported.

"Next week? Have you had car trouble?"

"No, no," Mother Meredith replied, cheerfully. "We've dawdled here and there as we wished. Went to your former haunts in Atlanta—"

"Atlanta?"

"The cottage up at Lake Lanier."

"Oh. I see."

"Natural enough, Ellen," Mother Meredith lowered her voice. "Blaise wanted to do it and I couldn't think why not."

"You're right, it's natural enough."

"Then," Mother Meredith lifted her tone again, "we went to Nashville and toured Andrew Jackson's home at Old Hickory."

"Nashville," Ellen said, leadenly.

"Went to see an old friend at Gallatin."

Ellen heard Blaise yelling something. "What friend, Mother Meredith?"

Blaise came on the line, "Hi, mom!"

"Hi, yourself. What friend?"

"Not a friend of ours, mama," Blaise said. "One of my classmates—her mother—asked me to stop in and see *her* old friend if we happened to be going through Tennessee."

"Who is this classmate?"

"It doesn't matter though," Blaise continued. "He wasn't there anymore. Do you want to say 'bye' to Mother Meredith?"

"Yes."

"Love you, mom."

"I love you, Blaise."

Mother Meredith came back on the telephone, extolling the joys of what they'd experienced, the places they went, the restaurants they'd tried. She spoke of hazy mountains and huge mushrooms growing in damp virgin forests.

Holding the receiver to her ear with a shoulder, Ellen only half listened, trying to find a note she'd written to herself. Ah—here—the telephone number from Blaise's closet notebook.

As soon as the call was ended, Ellen dialed the Tennessee telephone number.

"Old Hickory Convalescent Home."

"Convalescent home?" Ellen asked.

"Yes ma'am; Old Hickory."

"Where—where are you located, exactly?"

"Right outside Gallatin, ma'am."

"Near Nashville?"

"Yes ma'am. Where are you calling from?"

Ellen hung up, feeling numbed. *Old friend . . .*

Blaise had lied. It was, so far as Ellen knew, the first time the child had not been truthful. Hurt turned to anger and ebbed to resentment. The number came from Richard's telephone charge card. Someone Richard knew. Blaise had evidently maneuvered Mother Meredith into driving there. Gullible grandmother and conniving daughter. Damn that girl! She had no reason to lie, now or ever.

Ellen donned a robe and in slippered feet went to the attic. She sat at the console, flicked the video switch.

CHASER

START

SCAN: Ellen paused. *What?* Impetuously, she typed, RICHARD CURRY.

To her surprise, the machine responded: SPECIFIC OR GEN-
ERAL.

She typed, GENERAL. She pushed the start button.

Horrified, she saw the screen fill with five-letter words—JKLTV
MRNPL MLLVW SYDLP . . .

Had she broken this thing?

Ellen cleared the screen, following Herman's lessons from earlier today. She requested the same data, but this time typed SPE-
CIFIC. She pushed the start button.

Nothing.

Well? What was wrong?

Exasperated, she cleared the screen. She tried to remember the
steps Herman took in calling for data.

Once more she typed: RICHARD CURRY. She added, TEN-
NESSEE.

INADEQUATE the screen glowed.

"You hunk of junk," Ellen seethed. She cleared the screen.

ARE YOU THERE? she typed.

To her surprise, the screen replied: GOOD EVENING.

Somebody down at the office? Ellen considered shutting the
thing off, going away, forever disclaiming any knowledge.

WHERE ARE YOU? she typed.

YOU TELL ME.

An employee, probably, playing games on company time.

DON'T YOU HAVE WORK TO DO? Ellen questioned.

DO YOU?

Incensed, she stared at the screen. Methodically, she typed,
PLEASE GO AWAY.

WHY DO YOU WANT ME TO GO AWAY?

Ellen wrote, YOU HAVE OTHER DUTIES. DO THEM.

WHY DO YOU ASK THAT?

GET OFF THE LINE.

HOW DO YOU FEEL? the screen asked.

GET OFF THIS LINE, Ellen commanded, typing firmly.

TELL ME WHY YOU SAY THAT?

She had no idea how this thing operated. Suppose she had inadvertently connected herself with a teletype machine? The typist at the other end of the line could be downtown, or around the world from her. Richard had intercontinental lines, she'd heard the office manager speak of them. ". . . transmitted via satellite . . ."

She had no idea who was there. More importantly, did they know where she was?

DO YOU KNOW ME? Ellen typed.

TELL ME MORE.

Ellen shut it off. Trembling, she debated how she would explain this to Richard if called upon to do so. Or to Blaise, if the girl angrily demanded a reason for such trespass.

Be logical!

The employee at the office was not likely to tattle about this. He or she was wasting time at company expense, wasn't he—or she? Richard would blame the employee more quickly than he'd blame Ellen.

She had a disturbed feeling, as if she'd discovered someone listening in on a telephone party line. It was the principle of the thing.

She went downstairs to the bedroom and dialed Richard's office.

"This is Mrs. Curry," Ellen identified herself, curtly. "Who is there, please?"

"This is the night watchman, Mrs. Curry."

"Who is in the office at this hour?"

"Nobody, Mrs. Curry. The place is locked up."

"What about the computer room?"

"There's nobody in the building, Mrs. Curry."

"Somebody is there!"

"I just walked my rounds, Mrs. Curry." The man's voice suggested apprehension. "But let me go see."

Ellen waited. Waited. Waited.

The man came on the telephone again. "Mrs. Curry, I'm the only one here. The alarms didn't go off. Nobody used the elevator, or walked the halls."

"How do you know that?" Ellen demanded.

110

"Because they would break the electric eyes and set off alarms here and at the police station. There's nobody here. Nobody but me."

"I see. I'm sorry. Thank you."

She sat with a hand on the receiver, ears humming with the pulse of her own blood. The room felt smaller. The house larger, emptier—

She swallowed and it seemed inordinately loud. She tied her robe tighter, walked to the hallway and strained to hear even the most distant noise.

This is a good house. Comfortable house. Safe house. She mumbled reassurances to herself, going to the attic steps. The light upstairs formed a yellow rectangle overhead, the steps dark brown, the elevation seemed a hundred yards away.

When she reached the computer again, she flicked the switch with quivering fingers and sat at the console.

CHASER
START

She typed, ARE YOU STILL THERE?

Nothing.

She cleared the screen, tried anew: HELLO?

Nothing.

Her head was streaking with pain, stabbing through her skull, wrenching muscles at the nape of her neck. Tension.

Somehow, she had typed a code. She had broken through with a code of some kind. Ellen massaged her cheeks and pressed fingertips to her temples. *Relax. Relax!*

She had been sitting here . . . had asked for information on Richard . . . the answer was five-letter nonsense. She had asked for general . . . specific . . . became disgusted with the machine.

"You hunk of junk," she had said.

. . . and frustrated, she had typed, ARE YOU THERE?

She did it now.

GOOD EVENING.

Breathless, she stared at the screen. She typed, GOOD EVENING TO YOU.

Nothing. Ellen typed, HOW ARE YOU?

YOU TELL ME.

Her chest was constricting, her hands slippery with perspiration. She typed, one-slow-letter-at-a-time: WHO ARE YOU?

With a gasp, she read the reply.

I AM TONY.

Chapter
ELEVEN

Most of the night Ellen had stayed awake, forcing herself to bed only to doze and toss fitfully. Several times she'd returned to the computer to question: **ARE YOU THERE?**

What kind of macabre game had Blaise engineered? What would be Richard's reaction if he discovered it?

It was obvious Herman was a plodder, going from one numerical code to the next, a single digit at a time. And that was what Ellen lacked—time.

During the night she'd found Kim Jensen's residential and office numbers in the telephone directory. They were one and the same, an address adjacent to the Jesuit, Spring Hill College campus. Ellen had to restrain herself from calling before dawn. She took a long shower, examined puffy flesh in the bathroom mirror. She looked ragged and worn.

Impatience overcame her shortly before seven and Ellen drove to the address telling herself she'd wait before entering. English ivy obscured burgundy red brick, manicured around portals, the roof of the two-story structure a green terra cotta tile.

She noted the hour, but went to the front door anyway. A small brass plaque announced: JENSEN COMPUCODE. Ellen rang the bell and waited. Footsteps inside. She could feel the eye of someone at the one-way peephole, examining her.

The door opened and a shirtless man stood there in bleached blue jeans, open sandals with no socks. Thick dark hair was a hirsute tornado tapering from chest to abdomen as if swirling out of the navel.

"Kim Jensen?"

"Correct."

"I'm Ellen Curry."

Chocolate eyes assessed her. "I'm Blaise Meredith's mother."

He acknowledged this with a nod, but made no move to clear the way.

"Blaise has been coming here to work with you, I believe."

"Yes."

"I'd like to talk with you, Kim."

"All right," he said. Then, pointedly added, "Ellen."

When he made no move to step aside, Ellen asked, piqued, "Do you mind if I come in?"

He extended a hand toward the interior. All the hall doors were shut, transoms closed. Passing through the dimly lighted corridor, Ellen was surprised by heavy ornate, eighteenth century French furniture.

She entered a living room, or office, she couldn't be sure. A massive rocaille desk dominated one corner. Bookshelves behind glass. Two file cabinets and a video display were starkly modern amid the otherwise baroque setting. Beneath an oil painting, an IBM electronic typewriter. As she gazed up at the rococo frame and picture, Jensen said, *Polyphemus and Galatea.*

"Original?" Ellen asked, facetiously.

"Annibale Carracci," he replied, seriously. "It's a detail from the frescoes in the Palazzo Farnese in Rome. Polyphemus was a Cyclops who murdered Acis in jealousy over Galatea. He was ultimately blinded by Odysseus."

"You have an interest in mythology?" Ellen questioned.

"Only insofar as it relates to being murdered by a one-eyed lover."

As Ellen turned, she was startled by a completely naked young woman who arose from a couch to amble lazily from the room.

"I wasn't expecting you," Jensen said without apology. "About Blaise?"

Face flaming, Ellen blustered, "She has a computer at home. I want to know what's in it."

He lifted his chin slightly.

"I've been told you have the ability to 'crash' a computer. Is that true?"

"Yes."

"I want you to crash my daughter's computer."

"I do this for a living, Ellen."

"So I understand."

"My fee is $100 an hour with a minimum of a $1,000. If it takes twenty minutes, or ten hours, $1,000."

She felt uneasy, out of her element, flustered and embarrassed by the naked woman, put off by this bare-chested ungracious—

"Your terms are acceptable," she said tersely. "I insist that everything, including my coming here, remain confidential."

"That goes without saying."

She was angry—no, not angry, acutely discomfited, and he was doing nothing to ameliorate it. Ellen questioned, acidly, "Do I merit some information for the sum of $1,000?"

She saw a glint of humor, or was it condescension?

"What are your qualifications?" Ellen demanded.

"I can do what you want."

"Is that a guarantee?"

"I can guarantee that I will do it sooner or later—perhaps not in twenty minutes or ten hours."

"I see. Open-ended and therefore potentially endless."

The humor vanished and he took a step toward her. Ellen felt distinctly threatened. "Suppose," he said, softly, "you accord me the same respect you seem to expect."

"Let me ask you," Ellen countered, "do your usual clients find you under these office conditions?"

"Most of my clients don't show up unannounced. Those who do are my friends, well aware that this is my home as well as my office."

He was near enough to be smelled. It was a clean, masculine aroma, reminiscent of Arnold, the scent of a male who is moderate in his vices, accustomed to exercise and good health.

"May I offer you coffee, Ellen?"

His use of her first name was galling. But now, she saw he was not as young as she'd expected and she had called him Kim.

"How old are you, Kim?"

"How old are you?'

"Thirty-five."

"Five behind you. What do you take in your coffee?"

"My daughter told me you were younger."

"Bingo. I tell everybody under twenty that I am. To them, anyone over twenty-five is old. Coffee?"

"Cream and sugar, please."

He stepped to the door and without raising his voice requested that coffee be served. Then, as an afterthought, "Maybe you should get dressed."

He pulled on a shirt, buttoned it to the sternum. If Richard knew that Blaise had been consorting with—

"Sit down, Ellen."

"When could you begin work on Blaise's computer?"

"Tonight would be convenient. Is there a time factor?"

"No more than two weeks. My husband and Blaise are both gone. I don't want them to know."

"No problem."

For lack of anything to say, Ellen commented, "Your desk is nice."

"It belonged to Jean Baptiste Rochambeau when he was marshal of France from 1791 to 1807. I took it in lieu of a fee," Kim said. "I have no idea of the value, but the previous owner was going to prison and his priorities were in a state of flux."

The girl entered with a tray. She wore a sheer dress that was more transparency than substance. Kim said, "Thank you, Gwen."

The pot was heavy sterling silver, with matching pitcher and sugar bowl. "Another honorarium?" she asked.

"It was my mother's. What are you after in Blaise's computer, Ellen?"

"I want to know what it contains."

"What is the make and model?"

"I haven't noticed. Her terminal is connected to her father's office machines. Is that important?"

"It gives me an idea of capacity and complexity."

"The office computers would fill a room," she looked around, "as big as the downstairs of this house."

He sat on a corner of his desk, hands clasped loosely. Hair on the back of his fingers was wavy, like the hair of his head and chest.

"What do you expect to find in there?" he asked.

"I don't know anymore."

"Meaning, you thought you knew at one time?"

"I can't make sense—there's a —I don't understand how the thing works." The cup clattered in her saucer and Ellen clamped it with both hands, putting it down.

"Something in it is upsetting you," he surmised.

"A boy who helped to program it, Herman Krause, showed me how to call up information."

"Herman," Kim said without expression.

"Herman didn't want to, but I coerced him."

"I know about Herman's ethics."

"But we don't have Blaise's codes," Ellen said. "We were trying random numbers, getting data mostly from Richard's business computer."

"Richard is your husband?"

"My husband. And Herman said there might be hundreds or thousands of codes. He said it might take weeks or months."

"It might."

"I don't have that much time."

He circled his desk, sandals scuffing the floor. "First of all, Ellen, you and I need to be candid. It will expedite matters considerably. Do you suspect your husband of having an affair?"

"Good God, no!"

"But you suspect Blaise of some impropriety."

"No. Well, not until recently."

"What do you suspect her of?"

"I don't know."

He smacked his lips softly and Ellen thought she read impatience in caramel irises. "Look here, Ellen, this is like going to a doctor. You have a pain in your gut but you don't tell the doctor and he has to diagnose a malady without knowing the symptoms."

"No, no, it isn't that! I honestly don't know whether anything is wrong. Blaise lied to me last evening for no real reason and she's been obsessed with this machine. All I want from you is the codes. I want access. A meddling mother, that's all."

"Have you asked her to give you a demonstration?"

"I don't want to defend my motives. I want to know what Blaise is doing for the same preventive reasons any mother wants to know her daughter's activities."

"Wants to know her obsessions," Kim said.

"She eats, sleeps and dreams of nothing else!" Ellen snapped. "Once past she'll probably never give it another thought. But until then, I want to know how her many hours are spent."

"All right."

"A lie is a tiny indication of deceit in more meaningful ways," Ellen said. It sounded like an alibi and she felt herself blushing.

"Have you discussed this with your husband?"

Ellen stalled, poking through her purse for a tissue. He pushed a box across the desk to her.

"Because Blaise's terminal is connected to my husband's business computers," Ellen said, "it may be necessary to violate his confidential material. That's why I don't want him to know. He would be understandably upset."

"That's true," Kim said.

"I've been told that poses no problem for you," Ellen said curtly.

"I crash computers every day," he acknowledged, evenly. "But I don't do it as a means of helping a blackmailer gain leverage. I don't do it for $1,000, or any price, if it hurts the owner of the computer."

"Richard would not understand," Ellen said.

"I crash computers to demonstrate the need for security precautions," Kim said. "Having proven that, I promptly forget the data and move along to the next potential customer."

"He would resent my doing this," Ellen said. "But he would recover. I am thinking of him by concealing my actions."

Ellen could see he didn't believe it. She continued, "For personal reasons, some of the things Blaise has been doing would prove very painful for my husband. My motive is to circumvent pain, not incur it."

"Suppose I drop by this evening to get a check from you, and I'll look over this computer system?"

"That's fine."

"I do most of my investigative work at night," Kim stood up, his mien more professional. "Is there any limitation on the number of hours I may stay?"

"No."

He ushered her toward the exit. "Whatever Blaise had in her computer, knowing her as I do, I doubt you have anything to worry about."

"You feel you know her well?"

"I see she's bright, a very quick study. She grasped theory rapidly in class. Those who are good at this have a flair for it and I see she has that."

He held open the front door but didn't move out onto the steps. Traffic along Old Shell Road was increasing and he watched cars go by as he spoke. "Like most intelligent people, Blaise has curiosity and the greater intelligence, the greater the curiosity. She obviously gets that from you." He tempered the accusation with a smile which was surprisingly effective. "I differ with you on whether this is a passing phase," he said. "Blaise has the ability and she has tenacity. I think you're witnessing the beginning of a promising career."

"She's never been prone to tedium before," Ellen replied.

"Is that how you see computers?" he mused. "Sometime I'll

have to show you what those machines can do. I admit that programming is dull work. But Blaise isn't like Herman. He's structuring himself for inevitable unemployment, because programming is all he cares about."

"I would have assumed that's where the career is found."

"Hell no. A day will come when every conceivable computer program is perfected and for sale at a local store. The end is in sight for programmers and they're already worried about what to do in the next couple of decades."

"For you, then," Ellen questioned, "what is the allure?"

"Protection," Kim said. "Fighting off the government. Helping businessmen and individuals keep free of despots who are exerting more and more pressures every day of your life. If the public only knew what is happening, how close they are to disaster."

Behind him, Ellen glimpsed the scantily clad young woman crossing the hallway, her legs backlighted as she opened the door to a closed room.

"I should expect you this evening at what time, Kim?"

"When do you normally eat dinner?"

"You tell me the time and I'll meet your schedule."

"That was an invitation to join me for dinner."

"No," she said, firmly. "Come prepared to work, please."

"Say about seven then."

Ellen walked away, feeling his eyes on her, appraising shape and stride. He was distasteful. But according to Herman, Kim Jensen was precisely what she needed—at any cost.

Kim watched until Ellen reached her late model Buick. Blaise must favor her father. Yet, in the poetry of motion, the daughter took after her mother. The girl had an air of authority, the assurance of the rich which only upbringing could instill. She certainly took that from the mother.

He closed the door, turned a dead bolt and reset the alarm. Gwen crossed the hall, arms laden with computer tapes, taking them to storage. He chuckled to himself, reliving the shock of Ellen's face when the lissome lass arose to walk from the room. Gwen had fallen asleep on the couch at some wee hour, after too many tequilas, too much exertion.

He went into the auxiliary room where he kept most of his outdated equipment—functional, but slower than the Intertec. It was here that he allowed students to play their games, learning, practicing, in return for labor expended in his behalf.

He went directly to Blaise's bin. Her floppy discs were there. He withdrew them and sat at the console, activating the CRT, inserting the disc for recall. He set it for scan and let it run. Business. Import-export, apparently.

"Want some coffee or breakfast or anything, Kim?"

"No, babe."

She massaged his shoulders, standing behind him, looking at the flicker of information on the video display.

"I'm going to take a shower and shave my legs, hon," Gwen said. "Is that all right?"

"Sure."

"Playtime's over, right?" she nibbled his earlobe.

" 'Fraid so, babe. Go away now."

She smacked his ear so loudly it hurt and scampered away before he could strike with a behind-his-chair swing at her legs.

More business records. Bank transactions. Shipped goods, purchase price, markup, discount rates, currency values.

He leaned forward, elbows on his knees, hands clasped, watching the material appear, evaporate, more data coming.

Another disc.

More of the same. Loans, cancelled checks, payments made. Blaise came here and worked in return for computer time, but why? Her father's machine obviously exceeded anything he had. Yet, she performed long hours at menial chores, never complaining, never shirking her duty to give labor in return for time granted.

He inserted another disc, watching the flow of common business oriented language symbols. Another disc—mathematical graphs and business indexes, escalating payment schedules for lines of credit.

He whistled softly—$500,000, depreciated by—taxes paid, $50,000 federal and—

He'd seen the girl sit here for hours, going over data again and again and again. For what? It was such mundane office data. He thought of Ellen's word, "tedium." Certainly this was it.

He heard the commode flush upstairs, a tap of water pipes in the walls as Gwen began her shower. Absently, he made a mental note to call that kid who had replaced the frozen pipes last winter. The things rattled every time anybody turned a faucet.

Another disc.

Why would a pretty, pert, lively kid like Blaise come here to pore over junk like this? Day after day, the same outdated records from five years ago. He inserted another disc. The pipes shuddered behind plaster as Gwen adjusted water flow upstairs.

He taught a class at the university to keep in touch with the state of the art, but more importantly to keep in touch with students whose labors he needed, cheaply. Trading computer time for the humdrum task of billing and updating batch systems was—hello?

He stopped the disc an instant after it began.

Five-letter nonsense.

Code.

Blaise's or her father's?

He sucked his cheek between his teeth and bit it. He let the disc run, stopped it again. All five-letter code. He returned to the beginning and wrote two lines of the encoded text on a piece of paper.

If it were something encrypted by Blaise's father, the key could be exceedingly complex. Blaise would not be capable of more than a simple routine.

He allowed the computer to scan all the way to the end. He judged the capacity of the disc at approximately twelve thousand bytes. Three hundred words to a typed page, which was about two thousand bytes. The disc would represent six typed pages of information.

He patched in another machine, setting up a clean disc to duplicate Blaise's coded one. A few minutes later he had the same information. He replaced Blaise's floppy discs as he'd found them.

She came here twice a week, sometimes more. It occurred to him that she elected to come on the very nights when other students did not, weekends usually. He knew his appeal to adolescents. Common between professors and freshmen girls. He was not above using masculine attributes for luring girls into work. Never touch them, never—but at that age the girls weren't after more than a sexy wink, and fatherly attention was as flattering as a beau's.

He returned to his office, sat at the desk and pondered the inscrutable five-letter ciphers. The first order of business seemed to be here, break this and he would be ahead. He had a code-analyzer program that could run through various combinations, if need be. Although, usually, he could do it "off-time," thinking about a code as he wiled away minutes between other projects.

So, okay, he had $1,000 coming from Ellen Curry. She looked like she could afford it. Like a mechanical Merlin, what he had to sell was magic. How far would he get telling people how simple this was? Did a lawyer show his client where to buy forms to file for divorce, or make a will? Did a chemist admit his formula for steak sauce was merely the combining of catsup and Worcestershire with a dab of Heinz Fifty-Seven?

Kim could, and would, take ten hours to tell the lady what any idiot could learn in a few minutes.

Gwen came in, draped both breasts over his forehead and said, "Guess who?"

"Twiggy."

She laughed, throatily, and bent to kiss the top of his head.

"Have you ever met Blaise?" he asked.

"Who is she?"

"One of the students."

"I'm not allowed here when students come around, remember?"

"This one comes by unexpectedly," Kim said. "Tall for her age, about fifteen or so. Educated, stuck-up kind of. Uses the word 'brain' to describe everything from a genius to a moron."

"Yeah, I met her."

He wheeled his desk chair to face the woman. "What did you think of her?"

Gwen lifted golden shoulders and dropped them. "She is a little girl. I don't pay much attention to little girls. Now, if I'd thought you and she—"

He grabbed the finger she waggled. "Have you ever talked to her about anything at all?"

"I'm not supposed to—"

"But have you?"

"Maybe once or twice."

"What does she talk about?"

"Jee-me-nee, Kim, I can't remember that."

"Okay." He pulled her down, kissed her.

He couldn't remember either, except these indistinct impressions which accrue when you're around strangers long enough. Blaise was aloof, pampered, but lonely. That was his impression.

"She did ask me a funny question one time," Gwen stood at the kitchen door now.

"Yeah? What?"

Gwen drew a breath as if to speak at length. She moistened full lips in preparation.

"She asked me," Gwen said, "how long does it take a person to drown . . ."

T<small>Chapter</small> WELVE

On a piece of paper, Kim copied five-letter code words as they appeared on Blaise's floppy disc. He wrote the entire alphabet across the page, and under it the alphabet again, but moved so that "B" was over "A." It was the simplest of codes, one a child might use in the mistaken belief that it was "secret." When the five-letter words still made no sense, he did it again, adjusting the lower alphabet so "C" was over "A." If he did it twenty-six times, he'd know if this was the key.

"The FBI is here, Kim," Gwen spoke around the door.

"Come in, John."

The handshake was as practiced as the man's posture. The agent sat down as if weary. "How goes it, Kim?"

Kim adjusted the alphabet so "D" was over "A."

"You look busy," John Lawrence said.

"You look like J. Edgar Hoover," Kim responded.

"No," John replied, soberly, "narrow ties are out. What're you doing?"

"Playing anagrams. What's on your mind, John?"

The agent leaned nearer. "Wondered if you knew anything about Regalia Boat Works."

"Some."

"Specifically," John said, "contracts for shrimp trawlers to parties unknown in the Caribbean."

"John, John," Kim murmured, shaking his head.

"Hey, Kim, we're on the same side you know."

"No dice, John."

"Listen, Kim," John's tone hardened, "let's lay it on the table. Every day you break the law and we turn our backs. Every damned day you go pilfering some guy's files and you do it over telephone lines, which makes it a federal crime."

Kim adjusted "E" over "A."

"You deliberately withhold evidence that might solve a crime—not a misdemeanor, but a felony!"

"Nothing I could say would be admissible in court."

"No, but we might uncover corroborating evidence if we knew where to look."

"Then crash Regalia's computers on your own."

"Things could get tough, you know," John's smile was a grimace. "Suppose they put a tap on your lines?"

"Suppose they do, John. I'm in the business of knowing such things."

"Suppose the word got out just what you do?"

"Wish it would. Send me a copy of the public relations release for my files."

"Sonofabitch," John snarled. "You know, pal, you hide behind this so-called morality, this code of ethics, and you break more federal and state laws in a week than most of the birds we're after."

He tried "F" over "A."

The agent stood, paced a step and turned, "DEA hauled in two bodies last week from another hijacked boat. A Regalia trawler was seen departing the vicinity."

Kim adjusted to the next letter.

After a moment of silence, John said, "I presume Regalia contracted you for security."

"Don't be insulting."

"Is it possible to insult you?"

"Anytime a government snoop comes asking for collusion, I'm insulted. Go to NCIC! Go to CIA." He lowered his voice and eyes, "Go to hell, John."

"This country is undergoing a surge of violent crimes as never before in history and your attitude is a contributing factor, Kim. I have to tell you, it hurts my respect for you."

"John, last week a man came to me unsolicited. He said his car had been stolen two years ago. The state police recovered the vehicle, but they neglected to remove the listing from the national computers. The man who owned the car was later arrested for stealing his own automobile. No real problem, he identified himself, proved ownership. But that was not the end of it."

"And?"

"And the only tiny lingering problem is that he now has an arrest record which showed up when he applied for insurance. It showed up on his credit rating. It did not say he was falsely arrested for stealing his own car, it stated he was arrested for car theft. No disposition was mentioned."

"Damnation, Kim, he can apply to get that removed."

"Yep. They'd comply too. Then he'd have to get it removed from the insurance company computer. He'd have to get it removed from the National Credit Association computers. God knows where."

"I don't guess it occurred to you that he would never have gotten the vehicle back at all if it hadn't been for such computers."

"It occurred to me." He moved the alphabet anew. "Nobody is advocating the destruction of the crime computers. But I think most people would like them efficiently operated. Most people don't have a preference for which crook rips them off. They're ripped off, either way."

John put his knuckles on the desk top and leaned on straight arms. "Kim, the keystone to justice is rational judgment. Regalia is smuggling tons of dope, protected by equipment as sophisticated as any we possess. I need a bit of information. How are they laundering their money?"

"Sorry."

"Goddamn it," John moved toward the door in three angry strides. "Don't call yourself an American, Kim."

"I am, though."

"Not a loyal one. If you'd seen the two bodies they dragged out of—"

Kim was on his feet in an instant. "I'm not a Democrat or a Republican," he said softly. "I'm not a conservative or a liberal. I'm a realist, John. Americans need have no fear of Russia or China. They have a far more ominous threat right here at home, bureaucrats and politicians using law and crime as an excuse to steal away our privacy and liberty. Get out of here."

Abruptly, the agent's expression melted. "Handball Thursday night?"

"I'm not sure."

"Angry with me, right?"

"Yes. But that's not the hitch. I agreed to check a computer program in the evenings. I'll call you."

The agent cuffed him gently on the shoulder.

Gwen saw the man to the door, set the bolt and alarm and came back smiling. "Your mama called. She got in a new shipment and wants to show you."

He studied his watch. "Tell her we'll be there around two."

"Goody."

Kim drove as Gwen filed her fingernails with an emery board. Crossing the causeway, she squinted out at Mobile Bay and sighed. "I wish we lived on the water," she said.

"Humidity is bad for the equipment."

She was humming a Christmas carol despite summer heat. Kim was thinking of Blaise. Her code in his top pocket, unsolved.

Why was the girl so absorbed by business records? What about that had upset Ellen Curry? The woman had lied to him, if only by omission. She'd invited him in to her husband's business records and correctly warned that he would be angry. He would be *very* angry.

He turned south on "scenic" Highway 98 toward Fairhope, the

bay a shimmering mirror off to his right. Gwen had changed tunes. The subject: snow.

"Dashing through the snow," she sang softly.

"Did you get Mrs. Curry's bank records, Gwen?"

"Balance floats," Gwen replied. "If it drops below $1,000, a deposit is drafted from a business account. I put all that on your desk, didn't you see it?"

"I was interrupted by John."

Through the town of artists, Fairhope, on to Point Clear. His mother and father had moved here from Pasadena while Kim was in Vietnam. Dad retired his chair of history, they closed up the family home and settled on the eastern shore of Mobile Bay. Their antique business grew out of a quandary—what furniture to sell, what to store, what to do with the balance of their lives.

Mentally, he placed "R" over "A" and superimposed it above the five-letter code words he'd memorized.

"John made a pass at me," Gwen noted.

"Um-hm."

"Tried to brush against me going through the door."

"What was the business account, Gwen?"

"Curry import-export business, the balance is $42,619. Don't you care that he made a pass at me?"

"Maybe he stumbled."

"If he'd tripped, he'd have smothered. I wasn't wearing a bra."

Kim turned through a picket fence and parked next to his father's 1947 mint condition Chevrolet.

The antique store was a converted home across from Punta Clara Kitchens which specialized in pecan pralines and other candies. Built in a day of no electricity, the house stood high off the ground to make it cool, and protect the interior from flooding which a hurricane might bring. Inside, despite floor-to-ceiling wavy glass windows, it was dark and pleasant. The odor was of ancient things: metals caught in a state of corrosion, the lacquer of refinished pieces, the musty, solid scent of wood and leather, of polish and paint removers being employed on "used" stock in a back room.

"Gimme smooch," mother said, and planted one on his lips. She kissed Gwen and the two women laughed easily.

Mother brushed back hair the color of cornsilk, her forehead dappled with perspiration. "Wait until you see what we got in from London, Kim." She led the way, but not hurriedly, through narrow aisles. She paused to flick away a mote of dust, to admire a particular item before moving along. Gwen was a reflection of the older woman, *oohing* and *aahing* in unison and intensity to match mother's appreciation.

"This should've sold before now," mother caressed a table. "Solid cherry, original handmade brass screws. Cheap at the price, too."

When they reached the aftermost room, dad was rubbing an oak sideboard with smooth, even strokes. At his elbow, on top of the piece, a half-finished New York *Times* crossword.

"I know you prefer French," mother said. She opened doors of a shipping container and positioned a lamp to see inside. "But there was a confluence of French and English styles in certain periods. Take a look at that headboard, Kim."

"It's beautiful."

"Not a crack in it," dad said.

"I was thinking about your upstairs bedroom," mother related. "The one with a Howard Johnson's bed in it."

"How much are you asking, mother?"

"It cost us $1,500, plus shipping—"

"It's worth twice that."

"You think so?"

Dad joined them, wiping spectacles on the tail of his shirt. "$1,600 is your price," he offered.

"I don't like it," Gwen said. "All those little gargoyles staring down with their fangs showing."

The women went to fetch tea and dad watched Gwen depart. Caught at it, he grinned. "Being on a diet doesn't kill your appetite for sweets."

"I heard that!" mother hollered.

Kim withdrew the code from his pocket and presented it.

Dad adjusted his glasses to peer through bifocals at combinations tried thus far. "It isn't staggered alphabet," he said.

"No, it isn't."

"Did you try a fence rail?"

"No."

Dad got a pencil and toyed with letter combinations.

"Iced tea with mint," Gwen announced, placing it on an upturned crate.

"Have you run it through a decoder, Kim?" dad inquired.

"Not yet."

Mother was trying to instill respect for the headboard, telling Gwen the history of the bed, probable period and craftsman.

"I don't want anything staring at me with its mouth open," Gwen said.

Dad stroked his mustache, scribbled, erased, wrote another combination.

"We have guests, Stuart," mother declared.

"He's doing that for me, mother."

"He can do it tonight then—Stuart, we have guests."

Dad nodded, unheedingly. He tried another approach.

"I think it's because I was nearly eaten by a dog," Gwen explained to Mother. "I had bad dreams about dogs coming at me when I was a child—slobbering and licking and showing their teeth. They may have been smiling dogs, for all I know—but it makes me nervous to have things stare with their mouths open."

Mother set her jaw and avoided eye contact.

"It could be a modified Polybius," dad spoke to himself. He drew a grid, five squares across and five down. Each square had a letter. Each line a number.

"I don't like tongues lolling either," Gwen was saying.

Mother shot a glance at Kim, but he studiously ignored her.

The Curry home, on Ashley Drive, was not imposing. Kim pulled into the driveway. He saw the front door open as he stepped out.

"Punctual," Ellen said. "I like that."

This morning he'd thought of her as older; flesh sagged, eyes puffed. Now he guessed she'd come to him after a sleepless night. She wore slacks, a silk shirt, espadrilles. Her hair was clean, brushed. The yellow pupils had given way to cerulean, picking up the hue of her blouse.

He removed a microcomputer from the trunk of his car and carried a case with several floppy discs.

"What is all that?" Ellen questioned.

"No need us toiling when this will do it for us," he said. He followed her upstairs, then to the attic. *Nice butt.*

The floor was littered with books, magazines, pieces of ruled notebook paper. "I was looking for Blaise's codes," Ellen said. "Please, sit down."

He activated the CRT. On the console was a list of codes Herman had already penetrated. Reflected in the video display, he saw Ellen behind him, hands clasped, face tight.

"Might as well relax," he suggested. "This will take some time."

He set up his computer, interfaced with Blaise's terminal, followed Herman's guide and gave the code word to the office computer: CHASER.

START

"I've been here before," Kim said. "I never forget a machine. I remember, Blaise asked how to bypass her own computer to reach her father's. Let me show you."

He cleared the screen. He could feel Ellen touching the back of his swivel chair. He typed: CHASE.

The screen replied: READY.

"There are two computers involved," he said. "The key to Blaise's is five letters. To go to the one downtown, you add the letter "R." She probably uses her own machine to prepare data, then feeds it to your husband's machine when it's like she wants it. All right, let's see what we can get out of this one."

He put a disc in his machine, set it to try three-letter codes up to, but not including the letter "R."

He sat back, watching the video screen.

"What's happening?" Ellen asked.

"My computer is trying every combination possible. When it hits a wrong one, it keeps going. If it gets the right one, it will stop, print out the entry code and we'll have access."

"It's that simple?"

"It is, if you're a computer."

"So," Ellen said, "we wait."

"Yep."

She twisted under his gaze, but he continued looking at her. She was, could be, an attractive woman. Time and circumstance had given character to her features. There were clues to tough events in her past, clustered at the corners of the eyes. "Life lines," mother called them, bought with emotional currency.

"Mobile your home?" he asked.

"I grew up in Georgia. Near Atlanta."

He checked the progress of his machine.

"Go to school there?"

"High school in Decatur, just outside Atlanta. College at Agnes Scott."

"What was your major?"

"Kim, I don't feel like idle chitchat."

He returned to the CRT, watching the screen for proof of access.

"Art," Ellen said.

"Modern?"

"General."

He kept his back to her. He could see her mirrored in the protective glass of the cathode ray tube.

"My thesis," she said, "was on late sixteenth century Italian."

"Then you knew *Polyphemus and Galatea*."

"Yes."

"Sorry for the slight. I'm accustomed to students who ask questions in a frank effort to learn."

The scrape of a window sash made both of them turn. Herman crawled in.

"That's a strange means of access, Herman," Kim said.

The nearsighted boy wheeled.

"A second-story job if ever I saw it," Kim chided. "Is it ethical to crawl through the window of a house like that?"

"Mrs. Curry, what is he doing here?"

"He's helping, Herman."

"You're making a big mistake," Herman railed. "Mr. Curry would be mad enough for me messing with his computer—but this man—this is a mistake!"

"Condemnation from a sneak who enters by stealth," Kim said, genially.

Face flaming, Herman advanced with malice, "I saw your car and the lights. I came up the ladder to see what's going on. I've been coming here to help."

The computer stopped. The screen glowed: START.

"That's the access to Mr. Curry's computer," Herman declared.

"I see that, Herman. Interesting." Kim reset his programmed disc to search further. "Evidently Blaise doesn't use her machine for storage. She reaches her own computer only by way of her father's, if she does."

"I could've told you that," Herman grumbled. "She isn't stupid, you know."

"No, she isn't," Kim agreed.

"If getting into Blaise's machine were that simple," Herman said, "I'd have done it long ago."

"Which means what?" Ellen questioned.

"It means there could be tens of thousands of code possibilities," Herman sneered.

The telephone was ringing. Ellen left to answer and Kim asked Herman, "Have you connected an interceptor to this machine?"

"No. I *know* how to get into Mr. Curry's machine."

"We could defeat the program by cancelling it," Kim said. "But then, Blaise would find out."

"Mr. Curry certainly would."

Ellen yelled up the steps, "The call is for you, Kim."

"Watch the screen for an intercept, Herman."

"I told you, there won't be one."

Downstairs, Kim reached an extension, Ellen standing nearby, listening.

"This is your pappy," dad said. "I broke that code."

"Good for you."

"It was a staggered alphabet after all, but the key is a short sentence followed by all the letters of the alphabet which aren't in the sentence."

Kim glanced at Ellen, waiting.

"Read it to me, dad."

"No guilt has BM." dad enunciated, "followed by *CDEF* and so forth."

"I knew you could do it."

"Nothing to it once I worked out the key. There weren't many words to work with, but I decoded what you gave me."

"What did it say?"

He heard dad rustling a paper, mumbling to himself.

"It's a quotation, Kim," dad drew it out, enjoying his victory. "William Shakespeare. I don't know the play and passage, but it's the Bard."

"Read it, dad."

" 'The Devil hath power to assume a pleasing shape.' "

After a long moment, dad queried, "Did you get it, Kim?"

"Yes," Kim said. "I got it."

T Chapter HIRTEEN

Underestimating people was a rarity for him, but Kim had misjudged Blaise Meredith. She had learned her computer, shown inventiveness in the programming, and her access codes were still inviolate despite his best efforts.

He sat in a tub Gwen had drawn for him, a rolled towel his pillow, body covered with a thick blanket of suds. Gwen loved bubbles.

"Cost of living is about $2,000 a month," Gwen sat on the closed lid of the commode, reporting. "You want the breakdown of utilities, food, clothing?"

"No."

He'd come home after midnight, leaving Herman in the attic listing sequential codes and subject. It seemed the only way.

"Two automobiles, both late models," Gwen turned a page, reciting. "Lincoln Continental and Buick. You want the price and optional equipment included?"

"No."

He'd returned to Blaise's floppy disc of codes, with the key in hand. After that, it was simple. Now he knew what the girl was doing.

"Life insurance under the group plan, so-called family plan," Gwen continued. She paused to remove gum from her mouth which she wrapped in tissue before discarding it in the commode.

He chuckled.

"What's funny?" Gwen questioned.

"Wrapping your gum before flushing it."

"People walk around down at the sewage plant too," Gwen rationalized. She returned to her notes. "Credit cards include all major ones, *American Express, Master Charge, Visa, Carte Blanche*—you want a list of all these?"

"No."

He laved water to his face, sighed with a sputter and closed his eyes.

For $1,000 he'd agreed to reveal the contents of Blaise's computer. But should he?

". . . major purchases at Lillie Rubin, Raphael's—you want all the other clothing stores?"

"No, Gwen."

"Don't get impatient, Kim! You said you wanted it all and I have it."

"I'm not impatient. Go on."

He had a policy in this business. Never hurt the owner of a computer. No matter what he discovered, no matter the nature of the data, it was not his to disseminate; he had no business accumulating it. He did what he did to prove the necessity for computer security.

In the course of surreptitious investigating, he'd uncovered things. Regalia boats was a recent example. But it was not *his*. He shouldn't have known. He would not use illicit access to incriminate anybody. He sold security, not threats.

Shouldn't have taken this job.

He'd seen at the outset that her search was personal. Ellen Curry was looking for an EDP detective, not an analyst. Electronic data processing was, as Herman had claimed last night, a diary.

Now he had created a dilemma for himself: do as he'd said and tell Ellen Curry all he'd learned? Or tell her what she wanted to know, and no more?

What did she want to know?

"Everything in that computer," she'd claimed.

He'd spent several hours before dawn decoding Blaise's disc. He saw what she'd surmised, he followed her deductions, recognized her conclusions. Even then, he didn't accept it. He'd run the same business tapes she'd run. He tracked the machinations of finance in the same way she'd tracked it. But he did so skeptically, the devil's advocate, accepting nothing until he'd proven it to himself.

There was no business. That was the bottom line. Merchandise bought, shipped, labeled and priced for retail, goods rerouted, marked up, placed on consignment. Gross monies held in account, bills paid, invoices satisfied—everything was there, but there was no business. It was all paper. No goods bought, none sold.

At the end of Blaise's coded summation, the final sentence posed the question: "Why pay $50,000 in taxes for a business that did not exist?"

Kim didn't know why. But Richard Curry had done it. He'd fabricated a $500,000 gross, depreciated equipment that wasn't there, declared a first net of $150,000, and paid $50,000 in taxes.

It was a superb case of electronic sleuthing. Any accountant would have to admire the tenacity Blaise had exhibited, chasing every transaction from inception to final disposition.

". . . two major credit cards, seldom used but issued in duplicate with cards possessed by Mr. Curry," Gwen sat with shapely legs crossed, kicking absently as she read.

The hoax might have been part of a securities scam. But there were no stockholders. It was a privately held, solely owned company, unincorporated, and no laws had been broken. Or it could have been engineered to defraud a lending institution. Yet every loan was repaid promptly and in full. He had violated no tax laws. The Internal Revenue Service certainly wasn't going to nail him for paying $50,000 in taxes needlessly.

Who but Richard Curry had lost anything? And why?

Gwen paused to push another stick of gum in her mouth. When Kim looked at her she perceived his expression as impatience and chewed in very rapid movements to make the substance pliable.

"Real properties include the single family residence on Ashley Drive . . ."

Kim closed his eyes again. Pondering the onus of his responsibility in all this.

Suppose he informed Ellen that her daughter had discovered their Atlanta business was a sham?

Did Ellen know it? If so, how comfortable would she be sharing the information with him? Worse, what if she did not know, and this was more likely. It meant, then, the man she had married was not what he'd seemed.

And perhaps that was Richard's only motive. All's fair in love and war and he saw Ellen Curry as unapproachable unless he walked in similar financial circles.

Yet Richard was *not* without money. The loans and business shenanigans aside, the man began with a sum of cash. His initial deposit in the Atlanta bank was in excess of $150,000.

"As for the grandmother," Gwen began.

"Forget that for now, Gwen. Call Mrs. Curry. I want to see her on a business matter over lunch."

Gwen darted pellucid sea green eyes at him and he saw her tongue push against one cheek.

"Business, Gwen," he explained softly.

"Keep your pants zipped, Kimbrough."

"Do the same with your lip, Gwendolyn. Call her."

Did he have an obligation to tell Ellen all he knew? It was a moral question. He had decided it was not his decision to make.

Gwen returned with glee. "She said, no."

"Damn it," he came out of the tub so rapidly water sloshed

overboard, bubbles spreading across tile. He wrapped a towel around his waist and went to dial Ellen's home number.

"I told your girl I wouldn't do that," Ellen explained haughtily. "I've tried to set our limitations in subtle ways, but you seem to miss the nuance."

He made his voice the proper mix of business and anger, "The meeting is business," he said. "You'll be paying for it. I'll expect you to be at Roussos."

"Don't go without cash then. I won't be there," Ellen snapped.

"Listen, lady. You seem to be laboring under the delusion I'm after more than your money. I'm not, I assure you. If you can't make lunch, consider our transaction ended."

He put the receiver down firmly and turned to find Gwen contemplating him. As he walked past her going back to the bath, Gwen said, "Now I'm really worried."

She followed, "When you can't break a code, that makes you rabid. I know you, Kim."

"Don't be ludicrous."

"You always want what you can't have," Gwen cried. "You would marry me if I said you couldn't!"

"Stick to data gathering, Gwen. Psychology isn't your field of expertise."

"I don't have to be a psychologist to know about you," she countered. "I have your mother to tell me."

He got back into the tub and began bathing in earnest. Gwen snatched the washcloth and scrubbed his back.

"You think I'm dumb, Kim."

"That's not true."

"Because I'm agreeable, because I don't complain. Because I'm pliant and easy to get along with."

"Wash a little lower," he mandated.

"I see the way you look at me when I sing Christmas songs," Gwen said. "Well, for your information, I sing them because it makes me feel cooler."

When he laughed, she slapped his back. She dipped water and returned to scrubbing.

140

"Ellen Curry is a married woman of limited appeal," he said. "She doesn't have your magnificent legs, or your sexy eyes. She never saw breasts as pretty—"

"Talk about my mind."

"And you have a fine mind."

She was kneeling now, sitting back on her legs. "Do you love me a little, Kim?"

"Sure, babe."

He pulled her to him and kissed her. But when she drew away, doubt clouded her eyes and her lip quivered. "Hey," he said genuinely, "you can always find things to worry about needlessly. Ellen Curry is one of them."

"I hope so, Kimbrough. That would be very painful."

He smiled, pulled her over for another kiss. But even as he did it, he had a mental image of Ellen Curry, so damn sure he was out to seduce her.

Gwen was right. Inaccessibility gave the most unlikely things irresistible allure.

When Kim arrived at Roussos, Ellen was waiting. Every fiber of the woman's body suggested displeasure and suspicion.

"What's my limit?" Kim inquired.

"What do you mean?"

"Since you're paying for lunch, what's the budget?"

"Sate yourself if you wish," Ellen said harshly.

He smiled up at the waiter. "I can't decide between shrimp rémoulade and West Indies salad. Give me both. Also, fried crab claws, broiled snapper throat with lemon butter. What have you in a good white wine?"

The waiter suggested several as Ellen glowered at the menu.

"Any good Moselle will do," Kim concluded. Then, with a *tsk,* "I jumped ahead of you, Ellen, forgive me. What will you have?"

"A shrimp salad is fine."

Their order completed, he rested an elbow on the table and smiled congenially. "Majored in art," he said.

"Yes."

"Agnes Scott. That's a pretty exclusive school. What kind of work did your parents do?"

Resentfully, "My father was an art restorer. My mother was a housewife."

"Noble professions both," Kim said. He sat back as wine was poured. He swirled it, sniffed, tasted and nodded. He waited as Ellen was served.

"How long have you been married to Richard?"

"You asked for a business meeting," Ellen bristled. "That's what I'm here to conduct. Your personal questions are not appreciated."

"This is business. How long have you known Richard?"

She turned away, eyes flashing yellow darts.

"Let me ask you a question, Ellen. Suppose you were a doctor and you knew a patient had a fatal disease. Would you tell the patient?"

He saw fear in her eyes and added, "This relates to nothing. It's rhetorical."

"It would depend on the patient."

"Suppose you had the fatal disease. Would you want to be told?"

"Absolutely."

"Would you tell your husband and Blaise?"

"That—it depends on many things. What's your point?"

"That is my point. How much information to divulge is not always a simple matter. I agreed to crash Blaise's computer."

"Which you have not done, after six hours and twenty minutes."

"Another question," Kim persisted. "Suppose you discovered your best friend's husband was having an affair. Would you tell her?"

"Is *this* rhetorical?"

"It is."

"It would depend on the man and the woman."

"Her emotional stability?"

"If telling her would help, I might tell," Ellen said curtly. "If telling would only exacerbate a bad situation, I would say nothing."

"That makes my point, too."

"I see it is the nature of your profession to play word games, Kim. If you have a point, I'm missing it."

"To be more specific," Kim said. "If you discovered your father was having an affair, and you do know this woman—she's your mother, would you tell her?"

"No."

"My point then," he stated, "before you can make a judgment on what to tell, or not tell, you must know the persons involved. Hence, my question, how long have you known Richard?"

"The only question apropos," Ellen countered, "is whether you are honorable. You took my check for $1,000. It was fee paid for service not yet rendered. I expect, for my $1,000, all results uncovered."

"Which is, knowing what Blaise is doing."

"Positively."

He sipped wine, rolling it on his tongue. "In my line of work, I uncover illegal things every day."

"Blaise, or Richard?" Ellen demanded.

"No businessman in America can pursue a commercial venture without breaking a law."

"That is poppycock."

"That is *true*," Kim asserted. "The tax codes are deliberately ambiguous because IRS wants it that way. No American then is free of a tax audit threat, and a tax audit cannot be called harassment. Because the laws are so constructed, it is impossible to stay completely legal. They can always find something you've done wrong. It's a form of tyranny and the creeps at IRS love it."

"Richard has broken a tax law?"

"I just said he couldn't avoid it."

"Well, I can live with that," Ellen said sharply. Heads turned and she lowered her voice, gripping the napkin in her lap. "Now, damn you, tell me what you know, if anything."

"Suppose," Kim said, "you discovered your husband was a criminal?"

Impatiently, she jerked her head aside.

"Let's say he ripped off a businessman in Africa."

"I could live with that, too."

"What if he ripped off the First National Bank in Mobile?"

"You bastard," she started to rise and he grabbed her wrist.

"I'm not playing games, Ellen."

"I think you are, Kim. Obfuscating the issue for lack of ability."

"What I'm trying to do," Kim said evenly, "is determine whether my obligation covers destroying your marriage, or saving it. Whether I should reveal a crime, or ignore it. Whether I should shake your confidence in your daughter and perhaps wreck your home, or protect you from yourself."

"Is this rhetorical?"

He released her. "It may be. I don't know yet."

"Then let me be the judge of that. If you know something, say it! If you don't, consider our business agreement ended."

He sighed, poking shrimp rémoulade with a fork. "I know what Blaise has been doing."

"Then tell me."

"She's been investigating your husband's business."

Ellen laughed derisively. He saw her lips twist, discolor, her face a mix of relief and fury. "Is that what you've discovered, Kim? That Blaise is investigating her father? You—you idiot!"

"She's done a remarkable job, actually."

Ellen shoved fists into her lap. "Blaise has always been enthralled with Richard. She has an insatiable curiosity regarding him because she is constantly comparing Richard to her biological father. She plies him with questions, keeps notes on his every reply. She's in love with him! I don't know whether to scream or weep. If this is normal operating procedure I predict yours will be a short and unsavory future."

"How long have you known Richard, Ellen?"

"We've been married seven years."

"Were you involved with his business in Atlanta?"

"No."

"How long had you known him before you married?"

"Go to hell."

"Days? Weeks? Months?"

"I'll pay the check," Ellen made a move to stand and he grabbed her wrist again.

"Look," he said gently, "I don't give a damn if you walk out. I almost wish you would. I shouldn't have taken this job in the first place and to tell the truth, I don't know why I did it. I don't need the money or the turmoil. And I don't need you and your silly feminine suspicions."

"If you won't tell me what is in that machine, I'll get someone who will," Ellen said.

"Good! Goddamn it, good! Then it's his problem and yours, not mine."

He felt her ease back into the chair.

"Kim," her voice wavered, "give me the bottom line if there is one."

"All right. Blaise recorded all her father's old business records. She's been using my computers to run the data over and over again. I couldn't see why, still don't know *why*, but I have discovered what she was learning. She had a floppy disc filled with five-letter codes."

Ellen jerked slightly.

"My father and I broke the code," Kim said. "It was more or less a summation of all she'd learned about the Atlanta business."

"Something illegal?" Ellen whispered.

"If it is, I can't figure it," Kim admitted. "But I didn't take Blaise's deduction at face value. I was up all night running the business data to confirm it for myself. Your husband, apparently, established an intricate business of importing and exporting— orders, sales, even paid taxes on it. Like most businesses, he borrowed money, which he always repaid promptly when due."

"Then, what?"

"Nobody lost anything. Except Richard."

"Oh," she moaned. "Well, see, my son—Tony—Tony drowned and Richard went into a deep depression, blamed himself. That's when the business went downhill. Oh, God, why have I subjected myself to this?"

"Ellen," Kim leaned nearer, "Richard started his business with $150,000 cash. But there was *no* business. No orders, no sales, no bills. It was all paper, nothing more."

"What're you talking about?"

"Blaise summed it up with a very interesting question," Kim said. "Why would a man pay $50,000 taxes on a business that never existed?"

F*Chapter* OURTEEN

Without invitation, Kim followed Ellen home. As if he had not parked behind her, she went inside. Entering, he heard her on the telephone, "When do you expect Mrs. Meredith to return?" He reached the stairs and paused. "Tell them," Ellen said, "I'm going out of town for a couple of days. I don't want Blaise to worry if she tries to call home."

In the attic, Herman's hunched form cut a dark silhouette in the green light from the CRT. His list of codes accumulated as he continued to follow a mathematical progression from one to the next.

"Because we crashed Mr. Curry's computer," Herman spoke without greeting, "he is going to skin me alive and roll me in salt. But I'm not you, Kim Jensen. Because you violated his computer, he's going to kill you. For what you're trying to do with Mrs. Curry—"

"Lock your jaw, Herman." He looked over the codes Herman had identified and marked one with a finger.

"It'll be a slow death," Herman muttered. "Gut shot. Eviscerated."

"Feed this code into the computer, Herman."

"Hell no! That's Mr. Curry's confidential—"

Kim lifted the boy by one arm, moved him aside. He sat at the console, cleared the CRT and typed, **FINANCIAL: WORTH.** He heard Ellen's footsteps behind him.

"He'll hang you up by the heel tendons and let you bleed," Herman persisted.

The screen filled with data. Bank account numbers, deposits—Berlin, Bern, Boston . . .

"Mrs. Curry," Herman's voice rose in terror, "this is going too far."

Ellen was leaning over his shoulder as Kim typed: **NET WORTH.**

"THIRTY-TWO MILLION SIX HUNDRED THOUSAND—"

Ellen snapped off the CRT and the green light vanished. Kim looked up into hard, cold eyes.

"Herman is right," she said. "Enough."

Gleefully, Herman reclaimed the swivel chair.

"Herman do you need anything more from Kim?" Ellen questioned.

"Nothing I can't work out myself."

He was about to be dismissed. He forced nonchalance, "Have you run into any five-letter cipher codes, Herman?"

"Yes, but I can break that."

Kim shrugged for Ellen's benefit, "I know the key to those ciphers."

"I've paid for service," Ellen spoke to Herman. "Take advantage of it."

Herman cleared the screen, called up the five-letter ciphers. "Okay, Jensen. What's the key?"

"The code is a staggered alphabet," Kim advised. "The key is a short sentence, Herman. Write this down: No guilt has BM."

With peripheral vision, he caught Ellen's reaction.

". . . followed by all the letters of the alphabet that aren't in that sentence," Kim instructed. "CDE—skip GHI—JKPQ, like that."

Herman placed the normal alphabet below the code. "N is A," Herman mumbled, "O is B; G is C."

"You've got it," Kim said pleasantly. "Decode a few words to be sure."

As Ellen watched, Kim followed Herman's laborious scrawl, "The Devil hath . . ."

"That's it," Kim announced. "The rest of the sentence is 'power to assume a pleasing shape.'"

Ellen's eyes flowed to gold, like water sweeping away sand in a miner's flash pan.

"I enjoyed lunch," he smiled. "If you need anything else, Ellen, feel free to call."

Herman snickered.

As they reached the downstairs, Kim tried to stall, "I overheard you on the telephone when I came in. Can't reach Blaise?"

"She and her grandmother have taken a trip."

"Sounds like you plan to do the same."

"Yes."

"Be gone long?"

"A couple of days. Thanks for your help, Kim." She was trying to usher him out the door.

"Are you flying, or driving?"

"Driving." When he did not move, she asked, "Do I owe you more money?"

"No, no—when are you leaving?"

"Immediately," she said.

"I could take off a few days myself, if you need a driver or companion."

"No."

"I wouldn't mind."

"But I would. Thank you, Kim," she motioned him toward the exit.

"Listen, Ellen, I don't know any way to say this but to say it. There are some intriguing and unanswered questions here and I will be happy to—"

"You've done your job. Thank you."

He quelled anger. "I can't just walk away from a challenge," he said. "It's my nature to go for it—you know what I mean?"

"Good-bye, Kim." She closed the door.

He backed around Herman's jalopy. The twerp would have every access code in due time. Kim drove with his subconscious in command of the vehicle.

He'd seen her reaction to the net worth. Thirty-two million six hundred thousand—and she hadn't known it.

A following driver blew his horn; the traffic light had changed. Kim turned onto Old Shell Road toward home and office.

No guilt has BM. It had no significance to him, but it rocked the mother. And the sentence, The Devil hath power—

Maybe the kid needed psychiatric help. Rich kids suffered peculiar mental strains, a phenomenon he had never fully appreciated. He pulled into his driveway, around behind the building, parked in the garage.

Nobody made $32 million without attracting attention. But who'd ever heard of Richard Curry? There were no articles in *Fortune* magazine. He served on no board of directors locally. They lived a quiet, unpretentious life in moderate circumstances.

Illegal. It had to be something illegal. Kim let himself in the rear door. Telephone ringing. Gwen's voice came down the hallway, answering.

He had enough information to impress Richard Curry with the need for computer security. The man would be hot about *how* Kim gained access, but that was normal when a computer owner found his personal data spread before him by a stranger.

"FBI calling," Gwen hollered.

"Not here!"

"John," Gwen said sweetly, "Kim says he isn't here." She blew him a kiss with pouted lips. "John," she said, "Kim would know he isn't here, better than I would."

He sat at his desk, making notes. When Gwen joined him he spoke without looking up. "I want all the information you can get on Richard Curry. From birth certificate to now."

"I already tried to find that, Kim—"

"Try again, babe. Here's the access code to his office computer. You'll have to break his security codes, program the thing to ignore your entry, and start compiling a code book."

"That could take weeks."

"It could," Kim smiled. "On the other hand, you might find out who has access to the code book at Mr. Curry's office and buy it."

"Is Curry a customer?"

"He will be. Nobody ever needed us more." He leaned back, hands clasped behind his head. "Get me a round trip ticket to Aruba and a couple of thousand dollars in traveler's checks."

"I don't suppose I can go with you?"

"Not this time. I also need the micro and clean discs. One suit, slacks and loafers, mix and match to make space for equipment in the suitcase."

Her petulant expression made him wiggle a beckoning finger and she came to sit in his lap. "This is a big one, babe. Bigger than any contract we have—big enough to sacrifice everything else to get it."

She stroked hair from his forehead, kissed it.

"I don't know who this man is, or what he's been doing," Kim mused. "But he's in trouble and doesn't know it. His wife is laying his bones bare in his absence, and when he comes back, he'd better be prepared to explain a lot of things."

"Mrs. Curry fired you." Gwen kissed his forehead.

"My job was done."

"Fired you," Gwen murmured.

"Yes."

"Goody," she said.

Old Hickory Convalescent Home was not what Ellen had expected. Carefully tended lawns spread around a stone and rustic wood structure. Putting greens were pools of manicured turf punctuated by flags. Tennis courts, swimming pool, a courteous guard at the gate who issued a parking permit for visitors. As she walked toward the entrance over fieldstone paving, she saw elderly men and women having drinks on a terrace, watching games of shuffleboard. Their clothing and demeanor suggested wealth and leisure.

The foyer was more that of a luxury resort hotel than a nursing home. But she noted a nurse pushing a wheelchair, and others confined to playing cards. From hidden speakers came a string orchestra playing semi-classical music. The corridors were carpeted, potted palms graced spacious walkways.

At the desk, Ellen introduced herself, "I'm Ellen Curry from Mobile, Alabama."

"Oh, Mrs. Curry, how nice to meet you."

"My husband was here a few weeks ago—"

"Won't you come in, Mrs. Curry?" The regal male voice came from a door marked, Director.

"How do you do?" Ellen shook his hand and received five limp fingers and a courtly nod.

"I'm sorry for the misunderstanding with Mr. Curry," the director stated. His accent was a blend of American and British inflection. "I assume you have come for his personal belongings?"

"What did Mr. Curry leave?" Ellen inquired carefully.

"Various toilet articles, a few items of clothing. Again I say, we all regret the circumstances of this unfortunate matter."

"I'd like to hear about it," she said.

"As I told your husband, and later, your daughter," the director laced fingers across his vest, "we offer a tranquil haven for a refined clientele. Our services include medical assistance only in emergencies, or upon request. But not for—" he winced for emphasis, "mental aberrations."

"Mental aberrations."

"I realize Mr. Curry cannot be held accountable for the progression of such a condition."

"Your name is?" Ellen smiled.

"Forgive me. Hardy."

"Yes. Mr. Hardy, what is the mental aberration?"

"Goodness knows, I'm not a psychiatrist," Hardy said, primly. "Goodness knows we are prepared to endure eccentricities. We strive wholly to please."

152

"I'm sure."

"When Mr. Curry demanded Chivas Regal, Glenfiddich, and Dom Perignon, we were only too happy to comply. Our clients have cultured certain tastes and we must always strive to oblige."

Ellen nodded, expression fixed, heart hammering.

"The tirade—and forgive me, Mrs. Curry, it was nothing less—was over caviar from the Caspian Sea! Caviar from the Black Sea would not do, Mr. Curry insisted. It had to be Caspian. We tried to explain the difficulties these days between Iran and the United States but he'd have none of it. Caspian! Well dear me, when it became physical violence—"

"My husband became physically violent?"

"Gracious no! I refer to his brother, Ralph Curry."

Brother? "Oh. Of course."

"Mr. Richard Curry has been nothing less than gracious," Hardy said. "Over these past five years he has always come when summoned, a man with the patience of Job!"

"Yes, he's patient."

"He reasoned, he cajoled, he tried to pacify Mr. Ralph Curry, but—" Hardy threw up pink hands, let them fall to his desk, palms down.

"I haven't seen Ralph in years," Ellen feigned. "What is he like these days?"

"On a good day, nobody is more compatible," Hardy stated. "He returns from Europe or the Orient with gifts, he sends the residents postcards and mementos. No man had a more commanding presence. With that head of white hair, mustache, and rumbling baritone voice, he charmed the ladies and held the men spellbound with tales of kings and courts, tsars and tsarinas. Manifestations, of course, but witty and entertaining."

Hardy withdrew a handkerchief from his breast pocket and dabbed his upper lip. "As I've said, we will go to extremes to accommodate our residents. But each year Mr. Curry's attitude has become more argumentative, more narrow and less compliant. Do you understand?"

"I think so."

"When your daughter and her charming grandmother came to make inquiry, I told them how much we regretted having to expel him."

"Where is he now, Mr. Hardy?"

"Mr. Richard Curry offered several appealing choices, but the Virgin Islands seemed to be the final decision. I had recommended an establishment capable of handling Mr. Ralph's problem. Which is to say, he'd have the illusion of freedom, but when in the grips of one of his moods, attacks, whatever such things are called—then there would be attendants capable of dealing with it."

"A psychiatric hospital, you mean."

Hardy winced again. "It sounds so harsh, doesn't it?"

"Did my daughter and Mrs. Meredith get to see Ralph?"

"Oh no. He was gone. They were on their way to Ochlochnee, Georgia from here."

Ellen smiled, nodding pleasantly. "Ochlochnee," she said.

"Your daughter said she was gathering material for a genealogical chart and since that was his hometown, they indicated they were going there."

"Other than these periods of turmoil," Ellen probed, "is Ralph in good health?"

"Not a day passes that he isn't in the spa or swimming before breakfast. He looks years younger than his age."

"Oh?"

"Gracious, yes. But for the white hair, he could be forty. He toyed with coloration, but decided against it, I was told. As well you might guess," Mr. Hardy said, "we could not survive here without referrals. I do hope we have not imperiled our reputation with you and your family."

"I don't think so."

"I told the grandmother—I'm sorry, her name escapes me—"

"Meredith."

"I told Mrs. Meredith we cater to a select clientele such as she. Nevertheless, she seemed quite perturbed that we had evicted a relative. She insisted on talking to Mr. Ralph's friends to reassure herself."

"His friends?"

"Dr. Whatley, Mrs. Rhomack, various others."

"I see."

"I dare to hope we assuaged Mrs. Meredith's trepidations. She indicated as much before leaving, but perhaps that was courtesy."

"Mother Meredith isn't known for meretricious behavior."

Hardy laughed shrilly. "I surmised as much."

As she arose to leave, the director asked again about the "personal belongings" but Ellen declined to take them. She inquired about the "friends" he'd mentioned and Mr. Hardy explained that they were away on an Aegean cruise.

As she drove southward toward Georgia, Ellen fought her pounding heart. Mother Meredith had joined Blaise in this. Whether by collusion or in the mistaken belief that she was being helpful, the grandmother was sowing seeds of poisonous fruit. What did that child know, or think she knew? What was she after?

It occurred to Ellen that it might serve Mother Meredith's interest to see Blaise alienated from Richard. Surely she had connived with Blaise at Old Hickory, "demanding" to speak to Ralph's friends! To reassure herself!

Ellen reached to turn on headlights in the gathering gloom of evening. Without Mother Meredith to lend credence to her story, Blaise would have learned nothing.

She swerved around a slower vehicle, knuckles white from gripping the steering wheel. Richard had lied. By omission, if not commission. A brother! Why would he hide such a thing? An embarrassment to the family, a potential source of worry to Ellen? It must've been that. Richard had always gone to whatever length necessary to protect her from worry, hadn't he?

"There's an explanation to all this," she said aloud. Richard would sit her down. He would give a perfectly logical and loving explanation. He hadn't wanted to burden her, he'd say. He hadn't wanted her to feel obligated to visit, or send notes and gifts, which surely she would've done had she known Ralph existed. Every lie by omission was out of concern for her, he'd say. He had tried to protect her, he'd say.

Thirty-two million dollars . . .

Well, had she ever asked about business? Did she not willingly eschew her own personal financial problems when they first met? Still—such a sum—such an astounding sum as $32 million! She tried to shake it off, to reconcile another "omission," but that coupled with the unknown brother were now doubly worrisome. If he'd known she cared, Richard would have revealed all. He'd told her they could afford a beach house, hadn't he? He'd urged her to take a Caribbean vacation, hadn't he?

The four-lane stretched away through Georgia foothills, by-passing towns and cities.

Mother Meredith had conveniently forgotten to mention that she and Blaise had been to Ochlochnee, Georgia. Ellen had found it on the map, a village, no more, located near the Florida state line.

If there was any deception here, it was less from Richard than from Blaise.

Incongruously, she thought of Kim Jensen. Something about the man was disturbing. He had appeal and lacked it at the same instant. Cocky, confident, too damned cocky. His dark eyes were slightly mocking, and she resented the way he looked her over every time they met.

He didn't even eat that expensive shrimp rémoulade—

Ellen rounded a roaring trailer-truck and then watched in her mirror as he stayed too close behind her.

Anger surged. She slammed the steering wheel with the flat of a hand. Blaise was so preoccupied with Tony's death . . . programming that machine to answer in the boy's name . . . the ritualistic birthday party . . .

Was she determined to destroy their happiness?

Ellen considered her alternatives. Confronting Blaise, calmly demanding an accounting for lies and subterfuge.

But would that change anything?

Take the girl to a counselor, have her tested for psychological—

Nonsense. Blaise wasn't ill. She was devious!

Or, was all this a fragment of a larger and more ominous fate?

Was this, like Arnold's death, Tony's drowning, something beyond Ellen's control?

She bent forward, peering up through the windshield.

"Are you there?" she demanded.

YOU TELL ME.

She sat back, lowered her speed with deliberate will. Arnold had once accused her of treating symptoms, rather than the disease. He was blaming her for his impotence, refusing her requests that he see a doctor. It would go on his military record, he had claimed. It would damage his career. Besides, he'd said, it was only symptomatic of deeper problems . . .

Very well. No more would she be averted by symptoms. She would find the root core, the disease, and by whatever means necessary she would eradicate it.

So now she tracked the spoor that Blaise had tracked before her. What devil was their prey; what pleasing shape would he take?

F Chapter IFTEEN

Ellen drove slowly, past dark windows and unpainted store-fronts with sheet metal roofs. Ochlochnee was divided by rusting rails of the Atlantic Coast Line, both sides equally hot, dusty, pavement broken, sidewalks buckled. The abandoned depot was a decaying memorial to the day when America was mostly agrarian and railroads were the arteries through which all commerce flowed.

She stopped at a service station with old-fashioned pumps: regular, ethyl, and kerosene. The attendant leaned down, smelling of lubricants, "Help you, lady?"

"I'm looking for information about a family that once lived here. The Currys."

He brushed away gnats with a lazy wave, squinting across the top of the car. "Don't know anybody by that name. You tried the post office, I reckon."

"Where is it?"

"Across the tracks. In the feed and seed store with the hardware sign."

A small black boy with no shoes ran past, rolling a worn automobile tire, his feet slapping hot tar, his hand slapping rubber. He stole a glance at Ellen and they traded smiles.

The post office was a cubicle behind a latticed iron grill. The floors were wide planks worn into uneven valleys by shuffling feet. "I'm looking for information about a family named Curry," Ellen said. "Ralph Curry."

The woman in the cage plopped a fatty forearm on the counter, "The Pee-Oh can't give out that information," she said.

"Perhaps you could direct me to someone who might?"

The postmistress pursed a hairy upper lip jeweled by beads of perspiration. "I been living here all my life," she said. "If anybody knows anybody it's me. Not that everybody doesn't know Ralph Curry."

Pressing her point, Ellen said, "Could you tell me where they lived? I'm trying to locate relatives."

"Other than Ralph's first wife, there ain't any. Not to my recollection anyhow. Works over in Cairo at the pickle place. Cairo Pickles, you've heard of them."

"Yes."

"She's married again." The postmistress shouted at the ceiling, "What is Betty Sue Curry's new name, Charlie?"

The reply came from shadows toward the rear, behind sacks of feed. "She was a Smith."

"I ain't talking about used to, I'm talking about now."

"Still is," the man's voice said. "Smith. Married her cousin or some such."

"He don't know that," the postmistress said. "Charlie don't know his elbow from a knothole."

"I know that much," the man intoned. "Smith!"

"Do you have her address?" Ellen inquired.

"You'd have to ask in Cairo," the woman reported. "But the Pee-Oh won't help you over there."

"Ask the banker," the unseen man droned.

"He knows a mite more than Charlie, but only a mite."

"He knows that much," the man called.

"I'm actually seeking information about the entire family," Ellen persisted. "Do the parents still live here?"

"Dead."

"Buried at Pentecostal Church," the man supplied.

"The ashes is," the postmistress said. "Buried two sacks in a regular coffin. They couldn't know which was which. Burned to a crisp."

"Cremated?"

"In the car wreck."

"The parents of Ralph Curry died in an auto accident?"

"It ain't for me to say that Rood was drinking," the postmistress allowed.

"But he was," came the voice.

"More than likely. Ran into the hind end of a propane gas truck over in Whigham late one night. Knocked off the nozzle and spewed gas through the window-shield and it was like a blow torch."

"It was."

"Rendered both Rood—that's what everybody called Ralph's daddy, Rood—rendered Rood and Stell down to nubbins."

"Ain't no need to describe it," the man said.

"Folks come from as far away as Atlanta," the woman elaborated. "So I reckon Rood and Stell had some friends."

"Enough said," the man admonished.

"This lady ain't no Pee-Oh dick! Charlie worries they're going to take away the mail drop. Which is easy for him to worry about, he don't put a finger to nothing behind this cage. Come payday at the silica plant or the mill and I write money orders until my arthritis aches like a boil."

"Two hundred a week easy to come by," the man drawled.

"It is if you ain't licking stamps and filling out forms!" the woman yelled. "You sitting back there on the john reading some magazine you slipped out of a mail shuck!"

Ellen heard the flush of a toilet.

"I went to school with Stell," the postmistress said. "Rood

couldn't be content no matter what. One day had them riding in a flashy car, the next day they'd be eating skillet bread and fatback. Did you notice that big house with white columns north of town?"

"I don't believe so."

" 'Cause it ain't there," the man appeared. He hooked thumbs in wide suspenders and snapped them against a barrel belly. "This woman ain't been further than the door in so long she don't know the place burned to the ground ten years ago."

"I knew that. But it slipped my mind. Anyhow. Rood built that for Stell and Ralph, Junior. He lost it six, seven times and paid higher to get it back, over and over."

"None of our business," the man said.

"What kind of work did Mr. Curry do?"

The postmistress and man laughed together.

Ellen tried to smile.

"Rood never worked a minute of his life."

"Oh? I heard he traveled extensively."

"Must've been talking to Ralph then. That boy lied to explain the rich times, alibied to explain the bad. He said his daddy was a spy. He said his daddy was with the FBI. He said his daddy was a big businessman gone broke."

"Made a heap of money," the man added.

"And lost it all. Stell come in here many a time in feed sack skirts, still wearing that diamond ring, before Rood had to hock it."

"Many a time with furry collars and skin colored hose, too," the man recalled.

"You ain't related, are you?" the postmistress asked belatedly.

Ellen held her smile, "Did you know Ralph's brother, Richard?"

"Didn't know he had a brother."

"Didn't."

"The lady said he did."

"Maybe so then," the man turned to walk away.

"You could see old man Murphy at the bank next door," the postmistress suggested. "He knew Rood and Stell longer than us."

Ellen stepped into blistering heat, the air dry and suffocating. The boy with the tire passed, hand slapping, feet beating double-time. Through the soles of her shoes she could feel hot pavement. How could that child stand it with bare feet?

The glass in the door rattled as Ellen admitted herself to the Ochlochnee bank. A sign in the window said, "Pay utilities here."

"Mr. Murphy?"

The elderly man started to rise from behind a desk and Ellen insisted, "Please don't get up. May I see you for a few minutes? My name is Ellen Curry. I'm from Mobile. I am looking for people who might be relatives."

"You're doing a genealogical chart too, are you?" his eyes suggested bemused skepticism.

"My daughter has been here, obviously."

"And Mrs. Meredith. She is your mother-in-law?"

"Yes. My first husband died in—"

"She told me."

Ellen sat down at his bidding. He withdrew a pocketwatch and looked at Roman numerals a moment before closing it.

"Interesting lady, Mrs. Meredith," he said.

"I hope they didn't inconvenience you."

"She came asking about Rood Curry and she made me think of him before she got around to the question."

"In what way is that?"

"She commenced dropping names the second she came in the door," he chuckled. "Chairman of the Board at Chase Manhattan Bank, president of E. F. Hutton, senators and congressmen. I always knew Rood was about to go bust when he came in here spouting famous names."

Ellen could feel her face coloring.

"Not that Mrs. Meredith isn't what she seems to be," the banker said. "Wealthy people have a shine you can't get overnight. Driving her Mercedes car, two carat diamond ring shooting fire. Lisle knit, perfect fit clothes—soft leather handbag."

"You're very observant, Mr. Murphy."

"When you're accustomed to doing business with folks who

have to chew their leather to make it flexible," he said, "you tend to notice imported calf. Monogram on her hanky. She oozed money. Besides, she wasn't after any. The new rich smell new. The old rich smell rich. Poor folks smell poor even with diamonds and lisle suits."

"Do you mind telling me what you told Mrs. Meredith and my daughter?"

"I did business with Rood Curry for thirty years," he said. "He stung me more than once and I still liked him. Rood used to say, if he died broke, folks would claim he was too worthless to get a job and too lazy to keep it. But if he died rich, they'd say he was the hardest working man they ever knew, never quit no matter how many times he failed."

The banker's jowls jiggled as he dropped his gaze.

"Well," he murmured, "he died worthless."

"What was his occupation, Mr. Murphy?"

"Rood? He had about four years of schooling, I think. He could figure the board feet in a standing pine, or a whole forest, if you wanted it. He could give you the quantity of a silo. He could tell you about constellations and galactic gases, but he couldn't tell you from one minute to the next what he did for a living. He used to say, he did what he could, and he could do what was necessary."

"An entrepreneur," Ellen suggested.

"He'd like that word." Mr. Murphy showed his dentures with a smile. "He admitted he was a promoter and I've been told he was a good one. Lot of people had less complimentary terms. Laboring folks don't trust a man who makes his way with wits. That's what Rood did. He'd buy an option on a thousand acres. He'd sell the timber to pay for the land. He'd borrow a fortune to start a housing development, set up federal loans, haul in a trailer and a sales crew and just about that time he'd need $100 to pay the original owner the balance he owed for the option. Sometimes it worked, though."

"Mr. Murphy, did you know Ralph Curry?"

"Most fondly."

"Do you know where I can find Betty Sue Smith?"

"I told your daughter, that lady doesn't need any grief."

"That isn't my intention, I assure you."

"What is your intention, Mrs. Curry?"

"I'm trying to learn about the family."

"Does Ralph want that?"

"I don't know."

Folds appeared as he pressed chin to chest. "Ralph is a man who tore himself free from everything in this town," Mr. Murphy said. "After Rood and Stell were killed, he worked across the street at the service station every weekend until he finished high school. He delivered milk before dawn, and did manual labor at Dawes Silica Mining Company until dark. He married Betty Sue and stood by that girl even after the divorce. If Betty Sue needed anything, Ralph would get it if he could. That boy came in here to borrow $250 and it took him four years to pay it off, but he was here every Friday with cash in hand, skinny as a beanpole from overwork. He was determined to be a better daddy than his daddy had been to him, and God help him, he adored his baby and gave up a lot of dreams to stay here and support Betty Sue because she had a child."

"Believe me, I don't want to cause her any discomfort."

"Nobody who ever knew Ralph Curry has a bad word to say about him," the banker continued. "He got knocked down again and again—by the community, by an early marriage, by a child; but he always did what was honorable."

"When was the last time you saw him, Mr. Murphy?"

"Years and years. But he hasn't changed, I'd bet on it." He turned a rotary desk file, stopping at Smith. "Seeing you will be painful to Betty Sue."

"Did you tell my daughter and Mrs. Meredith where she is?"

"No, I didn't. They came in here trying to bluff me with tall tales. The girl said they were doing a genealogical chart of the family and Mrs. Meredith confirmed it. In one breath they tell me Ralph is having some kind of mental problems, that he's been in a rest home in Tennessee, that he's gone to the Virgin Islands to a hospital. Then they say they don't know him."

Ellen covered distress, but he saw it.

"Mrs. Curry, I admire Ralph. He's a wonderful man. He'll come bouncing back from any mental problems just like he's bounced back from a thousand other problems in his life. He's solid stock, despite his daddy's reputation around here."

"Thank you, Mr. Murphy."

"Because it's you, I won't place myself in a position of judging whether or not to protect Betty Sue. I see you are a refined, genteel lady. I'm trusting you to do nothing that would hurt somebody Ralph cares about."

"I will not disappoint you."

"All right," he said brusquely. "She's in Cairo, which is near here. She works in the packing department at the pickle processing plant. Her husband—she's been married several times—ran off and left her with a house full of children a couple of years ago."

He gave Ellen an address, a telephone number "belonging to a neighbor."

As she stood up to leave, the banker said, again, "That lady doesn't need any grief."

"No," Ellen agreed. "She doesn't."

The address was a city street, but the neighborhood was rural. Frame dwellings perched on concrete block foundations; rusting hulks of vehicles littered driveways. Children of all ages played in the unpaved street, shirtless, shoeless, their complexions ruddy from a scarcity of hot water and good soap.

She was surrounded by curious children sucking dirty thumbs the moment she stepped out of the car. Ellen stooped, reached for one child, but he edged away and cast a sidelong glance at a sister who said, "What you want?"

"I'm looking for Mrs. Betty Sue Smith."

"She in the house."

Ellen climbed the steps to a high porch before she realized the woman had been behind a screened door watching the entire time.

"Mrs. Smith, I'm Ellen Curry. May I come in?"

"Mr. Murphy called and told me you was coming." The

woman's voice was a high-pitched whine. Ellen heard the flick of a latch, the door spring groaning as the door opened.

She smelled beans cooking. The couch was covered with a greasy looking, red ribbed bedspread. Tufting showed through a tear.

In the paucity of light, it took a moment to see the woman. About Ellen's age, her skin drawn tight across firm cheeks, eyes pale and lifeless. The nipples of her breasts pushed against thin cotton. As they contemplated one another, Ellen felt compelled to say, "The children out front are yours?"

"Four of them."

"They're beautiful."

Betty Sue Smith indicated a wall, "My oldest ones are gone. Married, moved, away in service, those still living."

A moment passed before she offered, "Take a seat if you want to."

Ellen sat on the edge of the couch.

"Would you like iced tea?"

"No thank you, Betty Sue. May I call you Betty Sue?"

"Sure. You are Ellen."

"Yes."

The woman sat on the other end of the couch and only now did Ellen see she wore rubber boots.

"I just come from work," Betty Sue said. "I must smell like sour brine."

"I appreciate you seeing me on such short notice."

"I dreaded it, I admit that."

"But, why?"

"I always imagined you'd be beautiful. You are."

Ellen flustered, "But how do you—why would you think about me at all?"

"Your girl favors you," Betty Sue said.

"You met Blaise then."

"Her and her grandmama. Blaise come in a spell, but her grandmama stayed in the car. Afraid somebody would scratch it, I reckon."

"What did Blaise want, Betty Sue?"

"Same as you, I expect."

"I don't understand."

"You come about Ralph, didn't you?"

"Yes."

Betty Sue shrugged as if trying to wipe one ear with a shoulder. Ellen saw tears in her eyes.

"I don't rightly know what I'll do if Ralph is truly sick. I never went to him for nothing, but he was always there to help me. Sometimes he'd send me money just when I needed it most. My baby Cheryl needed her teeth fixed and like from God here come money from Ralph."

Ellen saw a young face pressed against the screen door, listening.

"I wasn't no good for Ralph and I knowed it," Betty Sue whispered. "Dragging him down and killing him with worry after the baby was born. We was too young to be a mama and a daddy, but that's what it was and Ralph never complained. He tried to save so we could get ahead, and I had my appendix took out one time, my tonsils the next. The baby was sick a lot. But Ralph never complained. Then, when Ralphy was three—"

"Ralphy his son?"

"Yes—" from contralto to soprano, the woman's voice rose. "Ralph loved that boy. He worked all the harder. He wasn't going to do to Ralphy what was done to him by Mr. Curry. He was going to love him and send him to good schools. He was going to—"

Ellen felt suffocated, the woman sobbing, staring at stained plywood walls, a plaster crucifix.

"When the baby died," Betty Sue said, "Ralph nigh about died too. Crying at night until his throat was raw. One night I woke up and he was beating his fists on the wall so hard they were bleeding. Screaming, like he was crazy—"

More faces at the screen door now and Ellen saw wide eyes, noses pushing on mesh.

"Ralph come to me and said, 'Betty Sue, I'm going to die if I can't be something more in life. I have to divorce you or I'm going to die, and I won't be any good to you dead.' "

Ellen's hands felt ice cold, the air thick, heavy with stale cooking aromas.

"Mama?" a voice at the door.

"Go away, Darnell, and take them young ones with you. I'm all right."

"I'm thirsty, mama."

"Do like I told you."

But nobody moved away. Ellen found a tissue in her purse and offered it.

"He took $5,000 and left me $5,000," Betty Sue wiped her nose. "He promised to look after me if ever he made any money, and he always did too. Like money from God, when I needed it."

"I understand."

"How bad off is he?" Betty Sue asked.

"I don't think very bad at all," Ellen said. "He has good days and some bad moods, that's all."

"That's what Blaise said."

"What did you tell Blaise, Betty Sue?"

"What I'm telling you. How it was. Where Ralph went after Ralphy died."

"Where did he go?"

"He married that lady in Michigan. She and him had a baby boy, just like with Ralph and me. Then, just like with me, that boy died—"

Betty Sue threw back her head, staring up at the ceiling. "Ralph told me he was cursed by God, cursed to lose people he loved most."

"He came to you after this second child died?"

"To give me some money."

"I see."

"First Ralphy," Betty Sue moaned. "Then his second son. He swore he'd never have another child. Going to give up everything and put the past behind him. He was going to use the insurance money to go into a business he'd thought of—"

"Insurance money?"

"From the boy getting killed."

Ellen tried to speak. Her ears were humming, head drumming . . .

"He was going to be a new man," Betty Sue said. "He divorced Wynette. That was his wife in Michigan."

"Betty Sue, do you know Ralph's brother?"

"He doesn't have a brother."

"Richard—"

"Ralph Richard Curry," Betty Sue said. "He doesn't call himself Ralph anymore."

Betty Sue took a framed photo from the wall. "See," she displayed a youthful, but unmistakable image. "That's Ralph—to you, he's Richard. To me, he's Ralph."

S Chapter IXTEEN

His flight landed before dawn and Kim drove home through a thick fog. When he arrived, Gwen was upstairs in the bathroom, her gargle trilling down the hall. He sneaked in, put his luggage at the foot of the bed mother had sold him. Gwen had stuffed cotton balls in the gaping mouths of the carved gargoyles. He stepped around the bathroom door.

"Sexy," he said softly. She spewed mouthwash.

"You made me swallow some of that!" she cried.

He encircled her nude body with his arms and she leaned away to spit into the lavatory. "You aren't supposed to swallow that stuff," she said.

"I missed you, woman."

She pushed back, dabbing her breasts with a towel. "How was Aruba?"

"Windy. Dry. You smell good."

"I have several pieces of news for you," she said. He kissed her neck, shoulder.

"You broke Curry's access code," he guessed.

"Bought the code book from a new employee."

"Good work." He moved to go lower. "Gimme sugar."

"Some guy with *Mobala News* wants to talk to you," she said.

"Hey, you luscious thing, do I get some attention?"

"Sure." She kissed him.

"Gee, that was wonderful."

"Did you bring me anything?"

He affected a pained expression, "Aruba is not the Paris of the Caribbean. We'll go out for lunch."

"You have a busy day ahead."

"When I tell you about Richard Curry, you will know the insignificance of all else."

Something in her green eyes made him pause. "I'm being punished because I went? Because I didn't bring you a gift?"

"John Lawrence has been coming around every day."

"He's after your body."

"That's true." She circled him, began dressing. "He's not such a prude when you get to know him."

"Don't get to know him."

"Your parents delivered the bed."

"I liked it better without the cotton balls." He nibbled her shoulder.

"Kim, I need to talk to you."

"Talk," he said, undeterred.

"Your whiskers are scratching me."

He pursed his lips, continuing.

"The newspaper man was asking about Ellen Curry."

"She writes for the paper."

"She was supposed to write an article on computers and she didn't do it," Gwen said. "He was asking questions about what we do."

He paused, irritated. Began again.

The telephone rang. She tapped him on the shoulder. When he released her, she went into the hallway.

"Oh, hi, John." Her voice lilted. "Thank you," she said. "I enjoyed it, too. Thanks for helping with the bed."

Kim looked around the room.

"Yes, he's here," Gwen related. She called, "Kim, can you speak with John Lawrence?"

"No."

"He says he's busy, John."

When she returned, Gwen went to the closet for clothes. "John helped your folks and me bring the bed upstairs."

"Okay," he heard his own surliness.

"So tell me what you found out in Aruba," Gwen pulled slacks over long legs.

"Curry has a huge warehouse complex. Several, in fact. He hires a couple hundred people there, mostly descendants of the Carib Indians. Ever heard of them?"

"Cannibals."

"They used to be. How did you know that?"

"John told me."

"John knows I was in Aruba? Just what the hell does John know?"

"That the Carib Indians ate people, that's all."

He threw back bedding, looking at the sheet. The dryer wrinkles suggested fresh linen.

"You were saying?" Gwen questioned.

"The Europeans wiped out the Caribs throughout the islands, except in Aruba. Now the Indians are the majority of the population. Curry hires them, from common laborer to top management. They love the guy."

"Did you get any recipes?"

He watched her, unsmiling. "When I offered a bribe to a warehouse manager, he threatened to knock my head off. Curry operates on the same labor-management precepts of the Japanese."

"Profit sharing, employee input," Gwen affirmed.

"Yes. Gwen, what is John after from you?"

"I think you're right," she buttoned her blouse. "My body."

"That's enough to make the sap rise," he agreed, "but what else?"

"Regalia Boat Works, things like that."

"Did you tell him anything?"

She smiled, disarmingly. "You know better than that. What else did you learn in Aruba?"

"Curry's business is mostly in Oranjestad, which is a port city. He owns a small villa overlooking Eagle Beach, but stays in a suite he leases year round at Manchebo Beach Hotel. He doesn't run around with women, he doesn't gamble, he doesn't give big parties. He's known for philanthropy to local causes."

"Let's go downstairs and I'll make coffee," Gwen suggested. Her hips were perfectly molded for the slacks. He followed her as she said, "Go on, I'm listening."

"Curry's got a business, all right. Owns a dock for incoming shipments, drays for transporting goods, machinery for vacuum sealing packages. To the local officials he's in the business of entrepôt, warehousing and reshipment. But what he exports doesn't tally with his imports. I think he's a criminal. A smuggler."

"Not a smuggler," Gwen said.

"Oh? Did John tell you that, too?"

She turned from the coffee pot, bemused. "It's in his computers."

"Don't be coquettish," he said irritably, "I'm not in the mood. Suppose you tell me what's generating that smug attitude?"

"I could be wrong," she plugged in the percolator. "Mr. Curry may be a smuggler, but I don't think so. I traced one of his normal transactions yesterday. He bought 250,000 cases of green bottles from the Holmegaard glass works in Denmark. He bought 20,000 heavy duty corrugated shipping containers in New Bedford, Massachusetts which he sent to Italy for imprinting. He ordered very expensive specialized printing from an engraver in Turin. The containers and the specialty printing arrived as one shipment in Aruba. From Norway he received 300,000 liters of a product listed as 'alcohol base solvent.' The solvent was shipped in casks and cost fifty cents a liter."

"So?"

"Each transaction by itself is meaningless," she said. "But when he exported 20,000 cases of bottled, unlabeled solvent, I noticed the specialty printing was shipped to the same buyer."

"So?" Kim demanded.

"He isn't a smuggler. He's a counterfeiter."

"Counterfeiting what?"

"Everything but money, evidently. In the case of the green bottles, the 'solvent' and the packaging, I couldn't figure it out until I learned what was imprinted on the containers. The solvent is Scotch. He's counterfeiting Cutty Sark Scotch. The specialty printing was the labels."

"Are you positive?"

Gwen scooped sugar into a bowl. "He also sells Bisquit V.S. Cognac. It wholesales for twenty-five dollars in a white Haviland Limoges porcelain decanter shaped like a keg with hand painted clusters of grapes. That's a cheapy. There's Hennessy Fine Champagne Cognac in Baccarat crystal decanters for $90. Remy Martin Louis XIII Grande Champagne Cognac, also Baccarat crystal decanter, at $150. Perfection Cognac in hand cut Daum crystal decanter packed in a velvet lined oak box and supposed to be a hundred years old, unblended, including a signed Carzou lithograph, a package he sells for $1,000. He only sold a few thousand of those. But it's all fake."

"Good God."

"He sells Chivas Regal twenty-one year old Scotch, Glenfiddich Single Malt, twenty-five year old Scotch; Haig Pinch with a silver medallion label—"

"God almighty!" Kim jumped to his feet. "I saw no Scotch coming in and I saw Scotch going out, so I thought he was smuggling!"

"Besides the liquors," Gwen poured two cups of coffee, "he sells gallons and gallons of counterfeit perfume at $50 an ounce. He has a printer in Taiwan who seizes every best-selling novel and replicates it in any language. He handles top recording albums and moves tons of them. That's how he made $32 million. But Curry has broken no law here that you could prove. He insulates himself with jobbers and wholesalers, middlemen who handle everybody except his suppliers."

The telephone was ringing. Gwen went to his office and hollered, "For you, Kim."

"No."

"For you," she said, sing-song.

"Hello!"

"This is Ellen Curry. I need to see you."

"Yeah? Well, I'm busy at the moment."

"Then," she said, crisply, "I'll state my business on the telephone."

Gwen put his coffee on the desk.

"I want to hire you."

"For what?"

"To do a complete investigation of my husband. I want you to work with a detective agency I intend to engage."

"That won't be possible."

"Why not?"

"Conflict of interest," he said. "I intend to offer my services to your husband."

"I don't want you to do that."

"The gentleman needs computer security like he needs oxygen."

"I must see you."

He looked up and Gwen was at the door, troubled. "How about next week sometime," he suggested.

"Today, godddamn you."

"Today, today," he mused. "My calendar is—"

The telephone slammed in his ear and he laughed softly.

"That was a mistake," Gwen said.

"What the hell is eating you, Gwendolyn?" he asked jovially. "The lady fired me and now she's trying to rehire me."

"We have troubles, Kim."

"Not unless you told John Lawrence something out of school."

"No," she replied, seriously, "it isn't John, although he may be causing it. It's the newspaper man."

"I'll tend to the public relations, babe."

"A court couldn't gather enough evidence against you to bring in an indictment," Gwen warned. "But a newspaper presents information to the jury out there," she swept the air, indicating the world.

"The coffee is good," he patted his knee, beckoning.

"An editor can take one of two directions," Gwen stood fast. "He can present you as a charlatan, an electronic voyeur, invading the bank accounts and privacy of helpless businessmen, or he can make you seem a stalwart against political abuse, trying to alert the public to what government is doing to them with unregulated computer information."

"I'll take care of it, Gwendolyn."

So dark was her expression, he went to her and took her hands. "Babe, don't let some local yellow sheet journalist shake you up. Watch your backside with John Lawrence, he's the man who could hurt us. He takes you out and pumps your sweet cranium, drawing off thoughts without you knowing it."

"I'm not stupid, Kim."

"He's a pro, babe. He can interrogate me while playing a hard set of handball, so smoothly, so subtly, I have to stay alert every second. You do the same, and we'll be all right."

"The newspaperman—"

"Forget it! I'll take care of him."

As she turned to leave the room, Kim joked, "Is it true a wife cannot be forced to testify against her husband?"

Without a second of hesitation, she answered over her shoulder, "It's true, Kimbrough. Unless she volunteers."

"I understand you have quite a business," Armand Joaquin flashed symmetrical teeth.

"What we do is not for public scrutiny," Kim said lugubriously. "But I'll help you as much as I can."

"I'm not after any trade secrets."

"Nor am I withholding any."

"I believe we have mutual friends," the newspaperman accepted coffee from Gwen. "The Currys."

"I know *Mrs.* Curry and her daughter, Blaise. I've never met Mr. Curry."

"Ellen was going to do this article, but she's been out of town, evidently. It sounded like an intriguing idea, so I began checking about. It's astonishing the way computers have invaded so much of our lives, unseen and unsuspected."

"That's correct."

Armand surveyed the office, his eyes obsidian in the dim light. "I went to several law enforcement agencies asking about the incidence of computer crime."

"It's a growing problem."

"Fellow at the FBI—what was his name?" Armand gazed up at the ceiling a moment, dismissed the thought. "He said you might be able to give me some information about such things."

Kim launched into his standard sales pitch. He was accustomed to confronting angry men whose data he had acquired. He was inured to insults and intimidation. He usually went away the victor, the customer a believer, if not subscriber to electronic security. This Cajun bastard should have stayed in the bayou.

"In the private sector," Kim related, "such as credit bureaus, individuals compile records for a profit. In the government, they gather similar information for the purpose of tabulating funding, keeping up with the growth of commerce, to levy taxes, and other worthwhile pursuits. But in both the private and government sectors, all too often, the end result is to punish people with the knowledge they've gained."

"As an example?" Armand asked.

"The largest credit bureau in America is Credit Data Corporation in California, Illinois and New York, primarily. They keep files on twenty-seven million citizens. They have access to one hundred million more through other credit bureaus. That's most of the people in this nation over the age of twenty. Then there's Retail Credit Company in Atlanta, with over thirteen hundred offices and seven thousand so-called inspectors who do investigative work. They have files on forty-eight million Americans. Among the things they report are a subject's drinking habits, including the reasons he drinks; any domestic difficulties, neighbor's criticism of 'character or morals' and whether the subject's living conditions are crowded, or dirty."

"Who cares?" Armand questioned.

"For legitimate reasons, few people care. Employers ostensibly. For automobile insurers the investigators will offer their opinions on whether the subject is 'antagonistic or anti-social' in behavior, whether he lives in a good neighborhood."

"I would think such information is important, if you're financing a car," Armand opined.

"For employers," Kim continued, "they offer reports on whether a subject belongs to any subversive organization, including radical groups, but not excluding the Knights of Columbus, the Primitive Baptist Church, and the John Birch Society."

Armand chuckled.

"Congress probed into the reliability of such investigative reporting," Kim said. "Retail Credit assured Congress that the inspectors were carefully trained, with 'unusual inspection ability'. But Congress discovered the investigators were paid barely above minimum wage, preparing two to sixteen reports a day, which Retail Credit sold for from $2 to $200 apiece. Half the investigators had no more than high school education and another thirty percent were college dropouts."

"Boo on the credit bureaus," Armand suggested, amiably.

"Congress also discovered the information was drawn from public records such as newspapers, with little if any confirmation and seldom any corroboration."

"Boo, boo," Armand crooned.

"All dossiers of the public compilers are available to the government compilers," Kim said. "Not only financing agencies such as Veteran's Administration and Federal Housing Administration, but also the IRS, FBI, CIA, and other government agencies requesting it. These agencies seldom attempt to verify anything. They accept the data as presented."

"Boo on the government," Armand noted.

"Did you know IRS can command the post office to supply the name and address of anyone sending mail to a taxpayer, a matter that has become a part of your computerized permanent record?"

"Didn't know that," Armand replied, genially. He gave the appearance of a man amused, but unimpressed.

"Are you aware of the seven hundred and fifty government

178

computer banks which store information from cradle to grave, without laws to protect you from what they say about you, or the number of years they may retain information, and that you may not be able to correct information that is false? They got their information from your neighbors when you applied for insurance. You are a newspaperman, so if your competitor happens to think you are a bit radical, that information may be in a government computer somewhere. All your banking records are there, registration of automobiles, licenses for hunting, guns, business, and permits to drive a car, build a home, add onto your office. You aren't protected by the Fourteenth Amendment. The government agencies can trade it around, right or wrong, and affect your credit standing, your ability to progress in the military or even, in the case of government contracts, such erroneous information can get you fired."

"Boo on them too."

Sonofabitch. Kim clasped his hands atop his desk, face pleasant. "Politicans make up their mailing lists from cross-indexed computers. That way, they don't offend anybody. You get a letter taking one view, your neighbor another view of the same issue. If they find your editorials disturbing, through the maze of computers available to them, they can force a tax audit, question your advertisers, impugn your reputation by innuendo. How would the community react to an agent investigating your loyalty, or morals? Against this you have no recourse."

"How many times does that happen?"

"Many times. In fact, Armand, the only safe man is a criminal. He doesn't usually buy insurance, make a loan, or operate a licensed business. Did you know most questions on a Census Bureau form are put there to help business and you are not required to answer them?"

"Everybody has to answer the census. That's the law."

"You don't have to say you have a flush toilet, or that you've been married more than once, and that your first marriage ended because your spouse died. You don't have to say how much you pay in rent, what your monthly utility bill is, and whether you worked last week. You don't have to tell them you have a dishwasher, and whether it's built-in or portable. You don't have to say your means of transportation is car, taxi, bus, or train. Nor do you have to describe the state of your health and the duration of any disability. That's there for some government snoop. There is no law that says you must reveal such things about yourself. Although the politicians mention criminal penalties, they neglect to mention the purpose of a census is to count people, not toilets."

"Boo on the census."

Kim quenched a flash fire of anger, continued amicably, "The Department of Health and Human Services asked the Census Bureau to send out a questionnaire which was designed to look like an official census inquiry. It asks how many times you call your parents. How much do you spend on gifts for your granchildren? How many newspapers and magazines do you buy each month? Do you wear false teeth? How often do you go to a barber shop or beauty parlor? Would you say you are happy, fairly happy, very happy, or not too happy these days?"

"What kind of crap is that?" Armand asked, skeptically.

Kim pulled a copy from a drawer and presented it. "Some bureaucrat spends tax dollars to gather information that he will use to petition Congress for additional funding and more powers. The hazard is this: whatever the answers, they go into computers which never forget it. Forever. Because computers are now so fast, working at the speed of light, they can retrieve your personal data in seconds. Before computers, storing such data would have taken all the warehouses in the world and all the clerks in the world would be required to find it in the files. Now they store reams of information within the space of an inch of tape and the scanner can locate it in microseconds. We're in danger, Armand. We're one step from a police state. We're already being subjected to government abuse of private information. They're trying to convince us we are un-American if we don't cooperate. That's the ultimate insult and the last step to a regulated society in which each individual is forced to conform to the norm—do what the computer says is the norm—be like the median, the average, the general populace."

"You really believe all that," Armand scoffed.

"You'd better believe it," Kim replied. "Your freedom is being stolen away and when you realize it, it will be too late. They'll have you, psychologically, financially, occupationally, maritally. They already use the information to aim propaganda at this country, playing to public fears, paranoias, and individual fanaticism. They play us like a concert orchestra. Fear the Russians! Fear the Chinese! The biggest threat is our own government, and this is whether you are American or Russian or any other industrialized, computerized society. Fear your own government, Armand. They're the ones who'll get you."

The newspaperman tapped his teeth with a pencil, his gaze steady, "Mind if I look at your equipment?"

"Gwen will be happy to give you a tour."

"Oh, that was such an exciting interview," Gwen gushed, taking the man's arm. "You asked such good questions!"

"Thanks. Been doing it a long time."

As they left his office, Kim sat back. John Lawrence had set him up.

If they were monitoring him, they knew about Ellen and Blaise. They knew about Richard Curry . . .

Chapter SEVENTEEN

Ellen scrambled eggs. Herman was at the kitchen table babbling about his work in the attic. She responded with practiced verbal sounds of a mother fending juvenile nonsense, answering without answering, smiling as if attentive. She was thinking of Ochlochnee.

Like a bird in a dropped egg, her world had suddenly become threatened, her security in doubt. She could be sure of nothing at this moment, except that Richard was not the man she thought she knew. His present wealth, his previous marriages—and two sons, dear God! What could he possibly say about concealing two marriages and children by both?

She had devoted her evenings to Betty Sue, the woman coming home exhausted by long hours of toil, reeking of brine. Ellen had taken them to a restaurant for catfish dinners. She had driven the children to school, easing Betty Sue's life even if only for a day.

From their conversations tiny motes had assembled until Ellen saw Richard as he had been, a boy becoming a man in a harsh world. Not one word did Betty Sue speak that was uncomplimentary. She'd recalled her marriage to Richard wistfully, as if the first nuptial was still her best. As if Richard had never been meant to be hers, and she'd been privileged to have him for a short while.

"Of what did Ralphy die, Betty Sue?"

"Fever, the doctor said."

"What caused the fever?"

"Might've been bad water. The doctor said it might've been something Ralphy found in a tin can in the yard. You know how little boys always drink things they oughtn't. One time coal oil, another time bleach."

"It happened more than once?"

"Had to watch him every instant. He was sickly anyhow. Doctor said it was fever."

With Betty Sue working at the pickle processing plant in Cairo by day, Ellen had gone to the school Richard attended off and on from first grade through graduation. The principal was a young, red-faced, overweight man. School was closed, he said, which was obvious. But there was no harm in Ellen using the library.

In aging school annuals she found pictures of Ralph Richard Curry. He wore a two-piece suit in one photo, patched overalls in another. In the eighth grade he was the school dandy, grinning at Ellen from the photo, wearing a sports jacket and silk ascot, matching kerchief tucked in a pocket. In the ninth grade, there was no photo. In the tenth grade, none. He was maturing in the eleventh grade with more of the features she recognized in her husband of today. He was class president that year, pictured in an informal pose with a laughing moonfaced girl who must've been, even at that moment, harboring the seeds of impending motherhood.

"He married me because we had to," Betty Sue confessed. "It happened and we had it to do, that's all."

"Mrs. Curry—"

Called back to cognizance, she turned to Herman at the table. He swabbed his plate with toast. "Aren't you eating, Mrs. Curry?"

"No. Please. Help yourself."

"As I was saying about those access codes—"

Ellen had found a retired teacher. The former tutor sat on a shaded porch, her eyes incredibly bright and alert, two youthful orbs in an ancient setting. Her shoulders wrapped in a shawl, despite the heat, she remembered not only Richard, but his parents. She'd taught them all, Mrs. Langham said.

"More comes with blood than life," the teacher laughed musically. "Walking, talking, mannerisms. Dimples and temper and a glint in the eye. Many a child, I taught his mama and his grandmama too. I could walk into first grade class and pick which child was whose because I had seen that impish look before!"

Of Stella Curry, "She was sweet when Rood had money and no less sweet without. I was at their fancy house north of town when the trucks came to repossess everything. Stell sat at the breakfast table eating Cheerios, wearing a low-cut mink-trimmed evening dress. Neither she nor Rood batted an eye as they carried out grand pianos—they had two—bedroom furniture. The table and our chairs were the last items to go. Stell was nonchalant the whole time. It was amazing to me."

The teacher recalled Richard's father painfully, "Ralph was his daddy Rood in every way save one," Mrs. Langham chirped. "He craved money, same as Rood. But when he got it if he did, Ralph wasn't going to throw it away like Rood."

She rocked, amused by mental images. "Ralph told me one time," the teacher reported, "he didn't care so much for money, but he didn't care to be without it, either."

She laughed, a sound akin to soft mallets on a xylophone. "I asked him why he wanted to be rich, then? I said, 'Enough is aplenty, isn't it?' "

Ellen waited for the answer.

"He said it wasn't for him. He said it was for his children."

The woman's expression grew pensive. "Long time ago," she said. "A long time before Ralph had cause to think of children."

Ellen had drawn on a comment made by Betty Sue. "Was he a moody child, Mrs. Langham?"

Sparkling eyes faded. "Anybody whose life vacillated like his had to be insecure. Some men gamble with dice. Rood gambled with everything he had. One venture after another. Up and down. Midas to misery, Plutus to poverty. Ralph never trusted money. He knew how easily it could vanish. He never trusted his father's fortunes, either, but he loved that old reprobate. Made up fantasies about Rood consorting with millionaires, traveling around the world. Childish lies. He had to draw pride from some tale, so he invented them."

The doorbell brought Ellen back from afar. She passed Herman as he took the last of the scrambled eggs onto his plate.

"Morning, Ellen," Armand Joaquin greeted her.

"Come in, Armand. Have you met Herman Krause?"

The boy threw his head back to peer through slipped spectacles.

"Would you care for coffee, Armand?"

"Thank you." The publisher tried not to watch Herman eating. "I've been following up on your idea about computers. It's still your article if you want it."

"I'm—I've had some personal problems lately that have taken my time."

"A fellow from the FBI came to see me."

Herman looked up, mid-chew.

"He mentioned your name," Armand said to Ellen.

"In regard to what?"

"A passing comment. Reads your articles, I gather."

Herman ate more slowly.

"He indicated an official interest in a gent named Jensen," Armand said. "You know him, don't you?"

"Yes."

Herman's pose made Ellen think of a fox testing the air.

"So," Armand lifted his voice, "I went over and interviewed this Jensen. His girl, sexy, dumb blonde type—you know her?"

"Gwen."

"Well," Armand concluded, "she isn't dumb. I found out she holds a degree in computer science."

Herman turned magnified eyes from Ellen to his food again.

"Jensen sells computer security," Armand continued. "I can't write about something I don't understand. Perhaps you could enlighten me."

"I don't know much myself, Armand."

"How does computer security work?"

Ellen looked to the boy, "Herman?"

"If you can reach a computer by an outside line," Herman said hesitantly, "it isn't secure. The only secure computer is one nobody can reach."

"Gwen said they offer scramblers."

"You can scramble signals between terminal and computer to create electronic garble," Herman replied. "But anything one machine can encode, another machine can decode."

"What is the value of what Jensen offers?" Armand questioned.

"He belittles programmers," Herman said slyly, "but all he sells is tricky programming. More difficult access codes, mostly. He can encrypt data so that, as an operator types on a standard keyboard the machine puts it in as a coded message. But that's easy to break with another computer."

"What protects the data, then?"

"Nothing, really," Herman looked to Ellen for permission to be candid, but she gave no sign of assent. "The government has a group in the Pentagon called ZARF," Herman related. "If a company like Honeywell or IBM claims to have an unbreakable computer code, ZARF's job is to test it. So far, no computer has proved inviolate."

"Why?"

"Because," Herman said, "all you have to do is program the computer to ignore its own safeguards. Then you can make it work for you. That's what Kim Jensen does."

"According to my sources," Armand confided, "Jensen violates computers with regularity."

"Most executives don't understand how a computer works," Herman said. "Jensen gets random data and takes it to the owner, claiming security is required. They get frightened, sign a contract, and Jensen reprograms the access codes so they are more difficult to bypass. But it can still be done."

"It seems to me he's selling protection the way the underworld does," Armand stated. "Pay us and you'll be all right; don't pay us and you have troubles."

Herman looked away without reply.

"What do you think of Jensen, Ellen?" Armand inquired.

"I don't know him well."

"Is he a man of scruples?"

"I couldn't say."

Armand turned to Herman, but the boy said nothing.

In the uncomfortable silence, the telephone rang. Ellen excused herself. It was Mother Meredith's attorney returning Ellen's call from earlier this morning.

"I've been trying to reach Mrs. Meredith and my daughter for several days," she explained. "The housekeeper wouldn't give me any information. I hoped you could help me."

The man's voice had a cultured New England accent, "Is this an emergency, Mrs. Curry?"

"No emergency," Ellen exacted concern. "But I am worried about their welfare. It isn't like either of them not to call."

"I will telephone the housekeeper and confirm your position in the family," the attorney offered. "Will you be at this number?"

"Yes."

When she returned to the kitchen table, Herman and Armand still sat in silence.

"Armand, what do you plan to write about Kim Jensen?"

"Maybe nothing."

"For a while," Ellen said, "could you wait on that article?"

"Why don't you write it, Ellen?"

"I might. Eventually."

He studied her face. Then, smiling, "I never trust a government initiative," he said. "In that way, I am like Jensen. Bureaucrats are as much anathema to me as to him. But the best reporter must be a skeptic without cynicism. He must have the courage to be persistent. He retains a child's curiosity about the world, people, events, and never loses the capacity to be awed, amused, or appalled. But mostly, he develops a sixth sense. With nothing to substantiate his suspicions, he gets a whiff of something in the air, know what I mean?"

"Yes, I do."

Armand pushed away his cup of coffee. "There are exposés to be found everywhere. I make it a policy not to undertake one without a complete investigation. I've started many a one, only to drop it because it served no purpose except to make trouble needlessly. The end result should be, I think, an article that brings change for the public good. If this is another self-serving government ploy to bypass the law and bring pressure on a businessman, forget it. If it is the only way to stop Jensen from a practice that is injurious to the public, then we should consider exposing it."

Ellen hesitated, debating a reply.

"Good to meet you, Herman," Armand rose to his feet. "Are you a student?"

"The university."

"Computers, I assume."

"Yes."

When they reached the front door, Armand looked back past Ellen to be certain they were alone. "Want to talk about it, Ellen?"

"Not yet."

"May I help?"

"Do you know a good detective, Armand? I've never hired one."

"I'm the best detective you ever met, Ellen."

"It's personal."

"And the most discreet."

"It seems so unsavory," Ellen said huskily.

"Detectives are," Armand took her hand. "Detectives must sneak and pry. Reporters state their business up front and proceed to sneak and pry, if necessary. They claim to be writing an article, but they don't have to."

She felt her face warming.

"Is there something you'd like me to write an article about, Ellen?"

"Possibly. I'll let you know, Armand."

He kissed her on the cheek—he'd never done it before—and squeezed her hand before releasing it. She stood there until he drove away.

In the kitchen, Herman waited, smirking. "They're going to get Kim Jensen, finally."

"Herman, I want you to finish up in the attic and get out of there."

"Yes ma'am, Mrs. Curry."

"When you have finished, leave the front door key on the desk in the den if I'm not here."

As she gathered dishes, Herman said, "Going to nail Kim Jensen at last."

When she did not respond, Herman left the room.

Ellen caught the telephone on the first ring.

"Well hello there," Richard's voice came from afar.

"Hello yourself."

"I've been trying to reach you for days, my darling. I had begun to worry."

"I'm sorry, Richard. I've been out of town."

His voice faded a moment, the line filled with interference. ". . . love you, you know," he said.

"I hope you do, Richard. Where are you?"

"Singapore. But I'm flying back to Aruba tonight. I'm calling to tell you I've been delayed another week."

"Oh? Why?"

"Same thing, those bills of lading they caught in Nashville. Nothing to be concerned about, however. I miss you, Ellen."

"I miss you."

"Are you all right? You don't sound yourself."

"I'm fine."

"And Blaise?"

"I wouldn't know," Ellen said crisply. "She and Mother Meredith have been too busy to telephone. I haven't talked to them."

"Like me," Richard soothed, "they may have been trying to call while you were gone. Gone where, by the way?"

"Driving, wandering. Tennessee, Georgia."

She couldn't believe her casual tone, as if nothing were amiss, as if the world was the old world yet.

"Good for you!" he said. "How would you like to wander down to Aruba for a few days of hugs and kisses?"

"I—I can't, Richard. I agreed to write an article for Armand Joaquin."

"Oh. I see."

"It's about minerals in the southeastern states," Ellen said, with unexpected inspiration. "Gold in Dahlonega, Georgia. Coal in north Alabama. Salt in Louisiana."

"You prefer that to my body?" Richard teased.

Ellen waited for the interference to clear. "I'm having difficulty finding a source for silica," she said, carefully.

"Silica?"

She pressed the telephone to her ear, alert for inflections.

"Did you say silica?" Richard asked.

"Yes, silica. It's used in—"

"I know what it is," His voice altered. "There are other minerals to write about. Marble in Sylacauga, bauxite around Abbeville. But, Ellen, can't that wait? Meet me in Aruba."

"Somebody suggested south Georgia for silica," Ellen felt sweat in her palm.

"We could spend a week at the villa, have dinner at the Manchebo Hotel each evening."

"There's a place at Thomasville, Georgia," Ellen forced the words. "Near Cairo, Georgia."

The burn of sunspots distorted the signal somewhere around the globe. When it eased, she added, "Dawes Silica Mining Company is the place."

"Better check your facts, Ellen."

"Oh?"

"They're out of business."

"Out of business," she said. "How do you know that? Do you know the area?"

"I know the area quite well. You won't come to Aruba then?"

"I would like to, Richard. I'd gotten bored and was looking for some activity when I agreed to take on this article for Armand."

No reply.

"When it's finished, maybe I could fly down then."

"I'll be home as soon as I can, Ellen."

"As you might suppose," she warned, "this is going to take some traveling."

"Obviously."

Long long pause.

"Ellen," his voice seemed weaker, "Have I ever told you how important you are to me? You are the most astonishing thing that has ever happened in my life."

She responded as if by rote, "You resurrected me, Richard."

"No matter what accomplishment I may ever attain," he said, "it could not come near that of earning your love."

She was trembling.

"I love you," he said, softly. "I love you, I love you."

The line whirred, crackled, the connection broken. She hung up, waiting with a pounding heart to see if he would call back. But he didn't.

When she turned, Herman was on the stairs.

"How much longer before you're through up there, Herman?" she asked, too severely.

"Another day or two."

"I want to pay you for your services, Herman," Ellen went into the den after her checkbook in the desk.

"No, Mrs. Curry."

"I paid Kim Jensen," she said brusquely. "The least I can do is pay you."

"No."

Why was she being curt to him? She tried to compose herself at the desk before turning to apologize. He was gone.

The telephone rang and Ellen grabbed it. "Hello!"

"This is Mrs. Meredith's attorney."

"Did you locate them?"

"I am told they are en route to Michigan, Mrs. Curry. According to the housekeeper, they are on vacation, calling only sporadically if at all. But so far as anyone knows, they are safe, fit, and enjoying themselves."

"Thank you."

"I find it refreshing to see a generation gap closed," the attorney chuckled. "I have difficulty relating to my own children, much less grandchildren."

Instantly, a remark by Richard came to mind.

I have difficulty relating to boys, Richard had said.

And there had been two boys . . . before there was Tony . . .

Chapter EIGHTEEN

Ellen sat on the side of her bed. Ten o'clock at night. She heard Herman moving in the attic overhead.

The telephone sounded a fourth ring.

"Hi, mom."

"Hello, Blaise. Where are you?"

"Saginaw, Michigan."

"Why haven't you telephoned, darling?"

"We've been driving until late each evening. I hope we didn't make you worry, mom. Do you want to speak with Mother Meredith?"

"You and I need to talk, first."

"Is daddy there?" *Wary.*

"No."

"What do you want to talk about?"

"I want you to come home, Blaise."

After a pause, Blaise altered her tone to adolescent excitement, "We've been having a wonderful time, mama. We went to the

Catskills, to Niagara Falls. We're in Saginaw, tonight, and tomorrow we're going to Chicago."

"Please, Blaise. Come home."

Long pause. "You've been in my computer, haven't you, mama?"

"Yes."

Air rushed in Ellen's ear as Blaise exhaled. The girl spoke aside to her grandmother, "She knows."

"Obviously," Ellen struggled, "there have been some misunderstandings. A touch of fantasy, perhaps."

"I wasn't trying to hurt you, mom."

"I know that, Blaise. That's the one thing I do know."

"I was going crazy, mama. Ever since Tony—I've been going crazy."

"I'm sorry you had to bear that burden alone, Blaise."

"I was seeing things, mama."

"What I want you to know now," Ellen said, "is that I am more than your mother. I am your friend. I am your ally."

Blaise sobbed.

"Ellen?" Mother Meredith came on the line.

"Mother Meredith," Ellen's voice broke, "please come home."

"We should be through in Chicago by—"

"Immediately, Mother Meredith. Bring Blaise home tomorrow morning."

"Ellen, dear—"

"Mother Meredith, this is a terrible thing you've done."

"I didn't realize what I was getting into, Ellen. But now that I am in it—"

"You had no right. The result may be irreparable."

"Ellen, I hear the frustration and anger in your voice."

"What license have you to investigate anything where my family is concerned?"

"Did you know Richard's business in Atlanta was no business at all, Ellen? Did you know he was living a deception at the time you met him?"

"Yes, I know it."

"Dear Ellen, I don't want to cause you pain. But to understand what we're doing, I must speak frankly. Did you know Richard was twice married before—"

"I know that!"

"Ellen—there were two sons before—"

"Damn you!" Ellen seethed. "I know that, too. How dare you do this with only Arnold as your excuse?"

"What would you have me do, Ellen? Bring this child home to mendacity and fear? I tell you again, I did not know what she was doing, thinking, but once into it, I could hardly refuse to help. One does what one must," Mother Meredith said. "Confronted with these facts as Blaise presented them, what course have I but to prove or dispel them? Surely you don't want the kind of scene that could ensue if we all sat down to discuss this with Richard. Better that Blaise see the error of her suspicions. Better that she come home begging forgiveness for them than to come home afraid."

"What are you doing in Saginaw, Mother Meredith?"

"We came to see his second wife. She doesn't live here any longer. She's in Chicago."

Ellen could hear Blaise, weeping.

"May I make a suggestion?" Mother Meredith asked. "Why don't you fly to Chicago and join us? Let's talk. Let's see what we can find together. It would be difficult for you, I know. But I'm sure Blaise would concur."

"If we're wrong," Ellen said, "Richard will see all of this as a horrible collusion."

"If we're wrong, Ellen, it will be a horrible collusion. Better that, than that we're not wrong."

Herman's footsteps creaked attic floorboards. Ellen took deep draughts of air, forcing calm.

"I want you to understand," Mother Meredith said, "I pray all of this is other than it seems. I loathe the circumstance, despise the role I am filling. But Ellen, Ellen, what would you have had me do?"

"I don't know."

"We won't go talk to this woman until after you arrive,"

Mother Meredith offered. "We'll meet you at O'Hare. Will you come?"

"I'll catch the next flight."

Blaise came on the telephone, "I love you, mama."

"I love you, Blaise."

"I was going crazy, mama. I had to——"

"We'll talk tomorrow, Blaise. Don't worry. We'll work everything out."

But after they hung up, Ellen asked aloud, "How will we work things out?"

The clock in his office chimed the half hour and Kim sat at his desk trying to make sense of what Gwen had shown him.

"Richard Curry and Ralph Curry are not the same person," Gwen said. "They have separate credit cards. The billing for both goes to the office account, but they're in different parts of the world at the same time."

She pointed to data on the computer readout. "Ralph Curry is in Paris, London, Antwerp, Vienna. Richard Curry is in New York, San Francisco, New Orleans. Ralph Curry spends money on the best wines, gourmet meals, expensive hotel suites. Richard Curry is a steak and potatoes man, flies second class, seldom expending more than $100 a day for everything, taxis, food, lodging."

"Ralph might be an employee," Kim suggested.

"That's what I thought," Gwen noted. "But his bills are paid as personal, nondeductible expenses."

"Two separate accounts," Kim said. "I don't know, Gwen. The kind of business Curry is in, this could be one of his agents. Maybe Ralph is an employee using Richard's name."

"Why would he allow that?"

"To hide an affair. So Richard would appear to be working, when in fact he's halfway around the world on a fling."

"Yeah," Gwen pursed her lips, thoughtfully. "But I got an impression of two life styles here."

"How are you coming on his personal background?"

"Precious little," Gwen said. "So I'm running down Ralph, now."

The doorbell made them look at one another. "Who at this hour?" Gwen questioned.

He listened as she walked down the hall, then swore softly when he heard John Lawrence's voice.

"Come in, John," Kim said.

The FBI agent sat with an arm thrown over the back of his chair, legs extended, grinning.

"What may I do for you, John?"

"Hell, can't this be social?"

"It could be. But it isn't."

"Coffee?" Gwen inquired.

"We won't be long," Kim said. "Will we, John?"

"Who knows? Make mine black, you incredible edible."

Kim folded the Curry data and put it in his desk drawer. John gazed open-mouthed as Gwen walked into the kitchen. "Those slacks are vessels of liquid motion," he said.

"State your business, John."

The agent lit a cigarette, tossed the spent match at an ashtray. He missed.

"I don't need to tell you the value of propaganda. Or of public relations."

Kim put a forefinger to his lip, waiting.

"It is within my power to make a trade," John mused. "I have a friend with the press who is making inquiries about you. He's a bulldog, Kim. Gets a bite, never lets go, inching toward the throat until—"

Gwen delivered coffee and sat down.

"I could shoo him off," John offered.

"In return for?"

"Gossip. Hearsay."

"Concerning Regalia Boats."

"Yes indeed."

Kim watched the man wink at Gwen.

"I don't want to play dirty with you, Kim," John said. "But the judiciary being what it is today, we do what we can."

"John, so long as I don't impart any information, this is between Regalia Boats and me. But the moment I divulge any data, I subject myself to potential charges including wiretapping, invasion of privacy, theft of commercial—"

"What we say will be held in strictest confidence," John interrupted.

"And if I don't cooperate?"

"Ah me," John put aside his cup. "Why must we be at odds? The underworld and the police have evolved a system of symbiotic exchange, why not you and I?"

"If I don't cooperate?"

"Then I'm going to play hardball, Kim."

Kim tilted back in his chair, "Gwendolyn, what can we do for John?"

She blinked green eyes. "Overdraw his bank accounts," she smiled. "Have his car repossessed."

Kim gazed at the ceiling.

"Program the computers to order a tax audit by depositing huge sums in his savings accounts," Gwen suggested. "His driver's license could be revoked—it would show up on NCIC."

"That's good," Kim agreed.

"Order sixty or seventy subscriptions to magazines." Gwen said. "Everything from *Scientific American* to *Penthouse.*"

"That's good."

"Foul up his credit card bills. Telephone bills. His utility bills."

"I like that," Kim said.

"Who do you think you're kidding?" John scoffed.

"Those are for fun," Kim said, "for sicking the newspaper on me. But, Gwen, if we have to play hardball, what next?"

"Well," she sighed, "I heard about a fellow who started getting death benefits at the age of thirty. It took him months to straighten it out. A computer at Personnel might stop pay altogether. He could be transferred to Seattle or—"

"Won't work, Kim," John smiled, but his eyes didn't.

"Then of course," Kim said, "we could go back ten years or so. Your mother could have been worried about little things. You felt uncomfortable when boys clipped their fingernails in your presence. You liked to sleep with her at age twelve. The way you played dolls. Material somehow overlooked during your security clearance."

"He could've been a member of the Ku Klux Klan," Gwen added.

John's lips twisted.

"Why must we be at odds, John?" Kim questioned. "You are an honest man who has stooped to unsavory measures. You wouldn't crash Regalia's computers on your own and I won't crash them for you. Even if—you hear me, John—even if a reporter tries to fry me."

"Good coffee, Gwen," John said.

"Mountain grown." She smiled.

"Been missing you at the racquet club, Kim."

"I'll try to be there Thursday."

John stood up, clapped his thighs, then extended one hand to shake. "Thanks for the coffee."

"Good night, John."

Gwen lingered at the door, flirting to salve John's ego. They agreed to have lunch together.

She returned, gathered dishes and took them away.

"I was wondering," Kim mocked, "would you have lunch with me tomorrow?"

"Back to Curry," she admonished. "What now?"

"Two things, babe. You get what you can on Ralph. I'll take care of Richard. I think it's time to make a pitch."

It was the next day before the call went through. Kim sat in his office, ankles crossed, heels atop his desk, waiting for Richard Curry to answer.

"Mr. Curry will be with you in a moment, sir."

"Thank you."

Gwen was in the back room, placing long distance calls to computers, crashers in other cities, chasing public records. She had learned this morning that Ralph was a recent resident in a convalescent retreat near Nashville.

"One more minute, please," the woman's voice came over the line.

"Hello?" the man was winded, breathless.

"Is this Richard Curry?"

"Are you the police?"

"Why would you ask that, Mr. Curry?"

"I was met outside upon my arrival," he replied. "They indicated this was urgent. Is something wrong?"

He had to handle this so the prospect did not become an enemy. Yet he must present a certain ominous threat. "This does not regard your family, Mr. Curry. This is a business call."

"In which case," Curry said, sharply, "I will turn you over to my secretary—"

"And yet, in a manner of speaking, it does concern your family," Kim intoned.

He waited through a long silence. Curry said, "I'm not in my office. Where may I call you?"

"I'll hold."

Gwen appeared in the door, a computer readout in hand. "Not now, babe," Kim said.

Curry came on the line again, strictly business and agitated. "What is your name, please?"

"Jensen. Kim Jensen."

"Mr. Jensen, I only now arrived from Beatrix Airport. Forgive me, I thought I had a problem."

"A man who orders bottles from Scotland," Kim began, "who orders specialized printing from Turin, who orders alcohol base solvent shipped in casks—"

He let it sink in.

"A man in your line of work," he said, "requires specialized associates."

Curry's reply was cold, brittle, "What is your specialty, Mr. Jensen?"

"Security."

"I feel quite secure."

"Computer security."

Pause. "Oh, yes. Jensen. I recall the name now."

200

"You have troubles close to home that you don't know about, Mr. Curry. More trouble than you might imagine. You don't want people to peruse your financial transactions. My job is to see that they don't learn about bank accounts in Bern, Boston, Berlin. With a net worth of $32.6 million, you have need of my services. I considered the need great enough to label it 'urgent.' Thus this call."

"Where are you, Jensen?"

"Mobile."

"Where can you be reached?"

He gave the telephone number and address.

"Let me think it over," Curry said.

"As an astute businessman," Kim persisted, "you know the imperative of time. Damage has been done, but with swift action, I can block further trespass. Within the hour, as a matter of fact."

"Your fee?"

"Generally it's based on a small fraction of the net income. If you stop to consider the ramifications of public access to private data, the cost is minimal. It's like paying a guard service to patrol warehouses, maintain alarms, insure sanctity of possessions."

He smiled at Gwen. She listened, soberly.

He had set the hook, now he must dull the barb. "Mr. Curry, in the event you determine my services are not for you—this is not a strong-arm tactic. I'm a businessman with a service to offer. If you avail yourself of it, fine. If not, I forget the matter entirely."

"Commendable."

"When shall I expect you?" Kim asked.

"Very soon, Mr. Jensen. Very soon."

N*Chapter* INETEEN

On the flight from Mobile to Chicago, Ellen fought tension, taking aspirin, and still her head ached. She formulated a response to fabricated conversations which might transpire. When they spied one another in the rush of passengers, Blaise hesitated, then ran into Ellen's arms, "I'm sorry, mama."

Mother Meredith, gloved hands clasped, stood by anxiously. Her expression and demeanor reminiscent of the day they'd buried Arnold at Arlington. Stricken by tragedy, Mother Meredith maintained a forced composure. "We're staying at The Tremont Hotel," she said.

Driving from O'Hare Airport in Mother Meredith's Mercedes, the schism was painfully obvious. Chitchat about trivia, excruciating lulls, Blaise mute as her grandmother attempted to be cordial.

Only when they were settled in their suite did they begin to communicate.

"First," Mother Meredith mandated, "let us clear the air. Blaise, you tell your mother what you think, and why."

"I had to do this, mama."

"I'll try to understand that, Blaise."

"After Tony died, I kept having the same dream, reliving the day it happened. I thought I'd gone crazy. Blaming myself. Daddy blamed me when he first saw me, 'I told you to look after him.' " he said.

"He didn't mean that, Blaise."

"Don't tell me that!" Blaise shrieked. "He didn't have to blame me, anyway. I blamed myself a thousand times. How did Tony get away from me? He never did that before. I kept thinking about how far he'd gotten from the cottage. Thinking about how deep the water was where we found him. Maybe I imagined it, I told myself. Maybe it was farther away. Maybe the water was deeper. So I asked Mother Meredith to take me there."

Mother Meredith's chin trembled.

"The water was knee-deep, mama. That's how deep it was."

"It's a lake, Blaise. The water table fluctuates as they allow a runoff."

"It was knee-deep," Blaise insisted, evenly. "Daddy's pants got wet from the knees down when he picked up Tony. Daddy's knees haven't changed. That's the way I remembered it, too. When we went back, I waded out and it *was* knee-deep. How could Tony drown in water so shallow, I asked myself? It wasn't so far from the cottage, either. If he'd yelled, I would've heard him."

Blaise wrung slender fingers. "The more time that passed, the less sure I was of what I'd seen. My dreams became as real as the day it happened and things got blurred in my memory. A man running away with pants wet from the knees down—"

"Oh, Blaise, God—"

"I kept seeing crazy things in my dreams. Things that couldn't be."

Mother Meredith, gloves still on, sat on the edge of a bed, her back as straight as a rod.

"I wasn't guilty of killing Tony, mama."

"Of course you weren't."

"I wasn't guilty, but I felt guilty. I had to know."

"We should've talked more, Blaise—"

"Mama, please. Please! Don't make platitudes, all right? Don't try to make me feel better. It's too late to make me feel better. Then—then, I kept catching daddy in fibs. He said he grew up on a farm. He said he lived in a city. He said they made their own fishing flies in the mountains. He said he ran a trotline across a river, for catfish."

"All of which could be true, Blaise."

"I know that, mama. I know people who live a lot in a little time do many things at once. But daddy never would give me a straight answer about his parents."

"Blaise," Mother Meredith prompted. "when did you begin keeping the notebooks?"

"After Tony died. Trying to keep everything straight. It got to be a habit. Writing down everything just as I remembered it. First about that day. Then about my thoughts. Then about daddy. It was confusing because there were so many contradictions. He claimed to be rich, but poor at the same minute, for example."

"That may have been true, also, Blaise."

Blaise nodded. "I know."

"Don't you imagine Richard will have an explanation for everything?" Ellen reasoned.

"He may. But mama, when I got the computer and began working with his Atlanta business records, I saw he didn't ever have a business. He borrowed money and borrowed more money to repay his loans. From banks in California to banks in Atlanta, borrowing to pay for borrowed money. And he paid $50,000 in taxes. Why would he do that?"

"I'm sure he could tell us, Blaise."

"Maybe," Blaise's voice fell. "Maybe not. Maybe he wanted to look successful without being successful."

"Why, Blaise?"

"We had money, didn't we?" Blaise asked. "If daddy had money, too—who would ever suspect anything if—"

"Blaise!" Ellen leaped to her feet. "Now listen to me, Blaise. I see these things, too. But Richard—whatever Richard may have done, he loved Tony. Loved him! Don't you remember how close they were? Don't you remember how—"

"Two other times he was married, mama. Two other little boys died."

Ellen sank to her chair again, shaking.

"The insurance was—"

"Stop, Blaise."

"I'm sorry, mama. I have to know. I have to know!"

"I cannot—this cannot be," Ellen said. "I will not believe this."

"Who is Ralph, mama?"

"I don't know."

"Daddy was an only child."

"An uncle, a cousin—"

"Daddy pays all his bills, mama. And Ralph spends an awful lot of money. They meet once or twice a year."

"How can you know that?"

"When they both have hotel bills at the same hotel, when they both eat meals at the same restaurant—they're together!"

"We're being unfair to Richard," Ellen declared. "If we're wrong, this will destroy us as a family."

"The onus is his, Ellen," Mother Meredith said. "The prevarications are his!"

"You saw what he was before he met us," Ellen cried. "He was poor. He was trapped; ambitious. He was—he *is* a good man."

"Mama," Blaise was firm, "I wish this were not true. I wish it for you, not me. I'll grow up and move away. You need daddy."

"There has to be a rational explanation," Ellen insisted.

"You know about Betty Sue?" Mother Meredith queried.

"Yes, I went to see her, Mother Meredith."

"Have you always known?"

Ellen shook her head.

"The baby died of fever," Mother Meredith said. "The doctor attributed it to foul water. Very well, that is not conclusive."

Blaise came to sit beside Ellen, taking her mother's hand.

"This second wife here in Chicago," Mother Meredith stated, "is not of the same ilk."

"What do you mean?"

"She lives on the lake shore. A lot sells for $5,000 a front foot in that area. The house must have cost $500,000 twenty years ago.

Her children attend a military academy. Her present husband is old aristocracy, politically powerful and socially prominent."

"How do you know these things?" Ellen demanded.

"I hired a detective, Ellen."

"He sent you to Saginaw, too."

"We knew she wasn't there. We went looking for the marriage record. We went to see where they had lived, she and Richard. A nice home in Saginaw, too. She was the child of influential people. She met Richard much as you met him. He was operating an import-export business even then."

"But if you're wrong—"

"Mama," Blaise was so near Ellen could feel the child's breath, "I want to be wrong, mama. I don't want to be right."

"We all want to be wrong," Mother Meredith confirmed. "But hoping won't make it so. We must know. This is too grave to turn away."

For several minutes they said nothing more, Blaise held Ellen's hand. The two of them cried.

"After we speak with this second wife," Mother Meredith said, "we will have to come to grips with the possibility that we are right."

"When are we going to see her?" Blaise asked.

Mother Meredith stood, tugged gloves up her wrists. "She's expecting us within the hour."

Blaise read a map as Mother Meredith drove. When they reached the address, they passed through an electrically operated gate and the vehicle climbed a winding paved drive. Two Great Dane dogs bounded out in full voice, loping alongside the automobile, sounding the alarm.

Wynette Weyman was waiting outside a shaded stone and stucco home. She leashed the two dogs and gave them to a servant. Only then did they get out of the car.

"Mrs. Weyman, I am married to Richard Curry," Ellen began.

"Yes, Ellen, I know that. Please call me Wynette."

As introductions went round, the woman nodded briskly, then took them inside. They passed through a formal living room, down a short hall, into a den with one massive glass wall which afforded a magnificent view of the lake.

"May I offer you anything?" Wynette inquired. "How about a cold drink, young lady?"

"Please," Blaise said.

Wynette rang a bell and a uniformed maid answered.

"Tea for us," Wynette instructed. "A cola for Miss Meredith."

"Yes ma'am."

They sat in leather chairs. Wynette looked at Ellen, unsmiling. "I presume you did not know about me," she said.

"Not until recently."

"I told Ralph he was making a mistake. But he wanted one hundred percent cleavage from all that was past. A decision he had made long before he met you."

"How long were you married?"

"Four years."

"You met in Saginaw?"

"Aspen, Colorado. He moved to Saginaw because of me. That was my childhood home."

"Did you know about Betty Sue?" Blaise asked.

Startled, Wynette's face flushed. "Yes. I knew."

"Before you were married?" Blaise questioned.

"Yes, before."

The maid brought tea.

"I may save all of us time," Wynette said, "if I anticipate some of your curiosity. After Ricky died—"

"Ricky?"

"Our son. You didn't know about him, either? Oh dear."

"Yes," Ellen said. "I knew. I didn't know his name."

"Ralphy was the first son," Wynette explained. "Ricky was ours. Since Ralphy was deceased, why not have our son bear the same name? Ralph made quite a point of it, but we would call *our* son Richard—it became Ricky."

"I see."

"It took a long time for Ralph to get over the death of his first born," Wynette said. "He blamed himself. He blamed poverty, mostly, but he blamed himself for that, too. Then after Ricky died, he saw that money was not a savior even when it was available to buy the finest medical care. Ricky's death destroyed our marriage."

"What did he die of?" Blaise asked.

Wynette ignored her, directing all remarks to Ellen. "Ricky was very special in his own right. But because of Ralphy, Ricky was extra special to Ralph. He wouldn't let the child out of his sight. He wanted the crib in our bedroom for the first year. He neglected his business to spend time with our boy. I say our boy— Ricky was his father's son through and through. Nothing was too good for him. Time was too precious to be away from him. Ralph was always vigilant for any threat—he had electricians cover the receptacles in the rooms. He forbade the use of extension cords. He became furious with me for turning my back on the baby's stroller in a public market one day. Fear made the love all the more keen, I suppose. It made death all the more severe when it occurred."

"How old was Ricky?" Ellen questioned.

"Thirty-nine months." Wynette swallowed, added softly, "Seventeen days. Eleven hours. Fourteen minutes."

"I'm sorry, Wynette," Ellen blustered. "I lost my own baby boy—"

"Yes," the woman said, "I know. Ralph came to see me, nearly mad. He said he was cursed, even when it was not his son by blood. He'd already sworn he would never have another child. But he loved your son, Ellen. Fearfully, but totally."

"May I ask a question?" Blaise requested.

"Why didn't he tell you about me?" Wynette spoke only to Ellen. "He did not tell you because he had made two determinations regarding his life. First, that he would have nothing whatsoever to do with his past, except where obligations were concerned. He continues to assist Betty Sue. He has no respect for people who fail in their familial responsibilities. The second determination was, he would take any gamble at any cost to become wealthy— which was ironic, because that was the kind of things his own father had done repeatedly, with disastrous results."

"He had financial resources of his own when you met him?" Mother Meredith asked.

"He was building in those days," Wynette stated. "He had meager, but adequate capitalization when we met. However, we were partners in more than marriage. My family assisted us. I had certain investments bequeathed to me—but what has that to do with you, Ellen?"

"I'm not sure."

"But there was insurance," Blaise said, huskily.

Ellen saw suspicion creep into the woman's eyes. "What exactly is the purpose of this meeting?" Wynette asked Ellen.

"It's so terrible—"

"Do you think—the insurance is—are you suggesting the insurance was a consideration?"

"Was it?" Mother Meredith asked, quietly.

"Positively not!"

"Don't be angry, Wynette," Ellen implored. "This is so painful for me that I—"

"Positively not!" Wynette was on her feet, glaring. "Had I known, I would not have agreed to see you."

"Let us state the facts," Mother Meredith said, calmly. "Let us tell you what brings us here. We need to know the truth, Wynette. I'm sure you want the truth, too."

"How could you come to me with such a reprehensible and cruel suggestion?" Wynette seethed. "I see that Ralph has not been wise by withholding his past marriages. When you called, I assumed this was a fit of jealousy—a curiosity natural to any woman—"

"There were three children," Mother Meredith attempted.

"In the sad event that you do not know it," Wynette cried at Ellen, "you happen to be married to a remarkable man. He loves you, if he loves you, with all his being. Isn't he generous?"

"He is," Ellen quavered.

"Doesn't he devote his life to you? To—" she flung a hand at Blaise.

"He does, Wynette."

"Each child," Mother Meredith persisted, "died with an appreciable amount of insurance—"

"Shut up!" Wynette shouted. "You cannot come into my home with these terrible accusations. I won't allow it."

The maid appeared in the hallway.

"You're right, Wynette," Ellen stood up. "This is an unforgivable thing to do."

"Ralph went insane after Ricky—every day I had to talk him away from the brink of self-destruction! That man has borne a burden so monumental—"

"How did he die?" Blaise demanded.

"—if he knew you asked these things—if he knew you were here, asking these things, making these horrible insinuations—"

"How did he die?" Blaise screamed.

"Mrs. Weyman?" The maid's voice was a tremulous contralto.

"How?" Blaise cried.

"In my arms, you ungrateful child. In my arms! It was not Ralph who killed Ricky. It was me!"

Ellen reached for her and the woman tore away.

"Mrs. Weyman, you want me to call the police or somebody?" the maid questioned.

Gasping, Wynette stood with mouth agape. "I ran out—going shopping—the baby was riding his tricycle on the terrace—got in the car—I looked. I think I looked. I swore I looked—Ralph was aways saying, look before you back the car, Wynette—look under and behind—"

"I'm so sorry, Wynette," Ellen whispered.

They moved toward the door. The maid sidled away from them.

When Ellen looked back, the woman was immobile, staring at the lake.

Kim wrote a check in the amount of $50 and gave it to his guest. "Pleasure doing business with you," the man grinned. "If you need anything else, gimme a call."

"Thank you."

"I'm going to hold you to your word now," the man waggled

the check at Kim. "If anybody finds out I passed along those account numbers, my ass is ale."

"All our transactions are confidential," Kim said.

"The only reason I did this was because those suckers wouldn't give me a lousy fin a week raise."

"You've done your employer no harm," Kim eased him toward the door. "In fact, although he'll never know it, you may have done him a favor."

"I wouldn't know about that. But mum's the word."

"Mum," Kim said.

When he locked the door and reset the alarm, Gwen spoke behind him, "I've got the data on Ralph Curry."

"Let's sit in my office, babe." The telephone rang. "Don't answer it," he spoke over his shoulder. "This is more important."

Gwen positioned herself across the desk from him, licking her lips as she mentally prepared her report. He saw the lace of a half-slip and got a vivid mental image of this morning when she was dressing.

"The Ralph Curry who lived in a convalescent home is not the Ralph Curry I'm talking about," she said.

"Which Ralph is it, then?"

"Ralph Richard Curry, born in Ochlochnee, Georgia, son of a promoter named Ralph Richard Curry, son of Stella nee Burns, grandson of—"

"Richard Curry's first name is Ralph?"

"Yep."

Kim clasped hands behind his head, put his feet on the desk, waiting.

"Richard Curry's father was known as 'Rood' and he didn't have but one son. So we still don't know who the Ralph Curry is in Nashville."

"Okay, babe, go ahead with it."

"You aren't going to like it."

"Damn it, get on with it," Kim growled amiably.

"Probably what's wrong with Ellen Curry is, she found out her husband has been married twice before and she didn't know it."

"How do *you* know?"

"It isn't on the marriage records in Atlanta. Each party must state their previous marital status, if any, and Mr. Curry got their marriage license under false pretenses. He was married two times, but didn't admit it."

Kim laughed.

"Also," Gwen said, "she probably discovered he had other children."

"Yeah?"

"A son in Ochlochnee, Georgia. Another son in Michigan by the second wife."

"The rascal," Kim mused.

"They're dead," Gwen reported softly.

"Dead?"

"First son by disease. Second son by accident."

Her expression drove him to a conclusion, "Insurance?"

"Ten thousand on the first son," Gwen affirmed. "Two hundred thousand on the second son."

"And then—Tony."

"Yep."

"Dear God," Kim wheezed. "Murder."

T Chapter WENTY

Herman Krause cleaned his spectacles with a paper napkin, put them on again, and squinted at notes he'd made over the past few weeks. He shoved aside bits and pieces of a radio he was constructing from spare parts. *Something wrong, but what?*

He was a plodder and knew it. Step by painfully logical step he drew conclusions by trial and error, until he reached the point of pivot upon which all else revolved.

On a wall hung a poster Blaise had given him: COMPUTER PROGRAMMERS DO IT BY THE NUMBERS.

It was the only tangible proof he had of their association. He did not think of it as "friendship" lest it bring him emotional pain when, inevitably, Blaise abandoned him. She'd never perceived him as a boyfriend, anyway. Nor for that matter, did he think of her as anything other than "a kid."

She'd approached him at a computer club meeting and he saw it was his brain she craved. Realistically, it was all he had to offer. His consciously created image was born of necessity: clothing purchased at the St. Vincent de Paul thrift shop, brogans for durability. So he'd fashioned an ambience he secretly likened to Albert Einstein. He was too busy mentally to be concerned with the mundane. But, someday, when he finished college, when he knew computers from theory to the last transistor, conductor, and capacitor, when he had the education to design microchips and forge ahead in the field of self-breeding crystals . . .

He shook off loneliness. Missed Daoud. The miserable Iranian had seldom bathed, hated American food, loved Khomeini and got himself deported—but he was company.

He rummaged in a cupboard for the peanut butter and examined rye bread for mold. A bit of penicillin couldn't hurt. He covered the fungus with tablespoons of crunchy brown spread and returned to his notes atop the Formica kitchen table.

He remembered things Blaise had said, when they were first getting to know one another. "Have you ever had anything bad happen to you?" she'd asked. "Something so bad you couldn't shake it off?"

She meant Tony. The drowning.

But she didn't mean *Tony*. She *meant* the drowning.

She'd needed help structuring her programs. He'd agreed, knowing her purpose to be ulterior, knowing she was using him. She bought hot dogs and plied him with pizza and what else had he to discuss but computers, anyway?

Something wrong.

He sucked peanut butter from the roof of his mouth, plodding, plodding, through the notes he'd made regarding Blaise and her endeavors.

Daddy. Notebooks filled with comments by *daddy*. Daddy had no business in Atlanta, daddy was guilty of shading the facts from his past. Who wasn't? And daddy contradicted himself—who didn't? —and daddy was—

What?

He spooned more peanut butter from the jar, eating it sans bread. The mold hadn't helped the flavor.

He remembered asking Blaise what she wanted the computer to do. Until he knew that, he'd told her, he couldn't help establish a program.

"I want it to compare things," she'd said.

"Numbers, statistics, graphs?"

"Things people have said," Blaise replied.

That's what she had in all those notebooks. Things people had said. Things daddy said. Things said about daddy. He and Blaise compared names of people, places, things—Ochlochnee, Cairo, Atlanta; wines, foods—

To teach Blaise the precepts of turning numbers into verbal response, he'd helped her construct I AM TONY. It was a program similar to Joseph Weizenbaum's DOCTOR, and Dr. Ken Colby's psychotic brainchild, PARRY. The computer was programmed to respond to certain key words . . . Who are you? I AM TONY. If the question stumped the memory banks, the computer responded, YOU TELL ME.

She learned quickly. She'd shown promise far beyond her chronological years. That was what motivation did for you. When he saw that life was toil without education, he'd struggled to complete high school early and with the highest possible grades to earn a scholarship. When he saw his parents and all their relatives spading hard packed and mineral deficient soil for food, Herman had vowed to lift himself from the slavery of workaday existence.

He was a plodder. Plodding now, constructing the jigsaw puzzle of human reason. From remarks made in his presence, from personal observations. Mrs. Curry was stunned to learn her husband's net worth. She knew nothing of the business, obviously.

Mr. Curry was an assimilator. He gathered components and constructed a package for sale. His business was one of gestalt thinking, buy a piece here, another piece there, and turn the fragments into a whole, saleable commodity.

But Blaise had known all that early on. She had learned that the Atlanta business was no business even before she got her own computer terminal. Access to Mr. Curry's computers neither confirmed nor denied that fact. Yet out of all those early records, she had selected items to feed into her comparative program. In a business of no real transactions, only a few checks had been dispersed—one, the first one, for $5,000 cash. Thereafter, like sums were paid to Ralph Curry.

Blaise had said she had no relatives, except Mother Meredith. Then who was Ralph Curry?

That had become her quest. It had nothing to do with Mr. Curry's business at all!

He picked peanut butter from between his teeth, staring at the notes, seeking an overview, seeking a clue to *why* Blaise did all this.

Be-jeeze!

But no, it couldn't be!

Yet—look here, look here—yet—

He stood up so abruptly the chair fell over backward. Suppose he was right? What did it mean? Suppose—oh, hell, that couldn't be—yet, yet—

His hands trembled as he locked the front door behind himself. Up to now he had done only what asked. He had not been prying. He had not violated Mr. Curry's computer except upon the express wishes of Mrs. Curry.

And yet, be-jeeze!

He pumped the accelerator to prime the 1952 Ford carburetor, which served the 1962 Mercury engine in this cut-down Plymouth body. He turned the key and twin glass pipes rumbled comfortingly.

Don't speed. Cops preyed upon students living in these university housing areas, which was good, because it was rip-off city for thefts. The key to staying victimless was to own nothing, a feat he'd accomplished to a safe degree. Herman drove past a billboard: HILLSDALE HEIGHTS. Or, rather, now that students had removed selected letters: LSD HEIGHTS.

He had to go back. Go up the outside ladder and into the attic. He was positive Mrs. Curry wouldn't be angry, despite the fact she'd told him to get finished and get gone. He'd left the house key on a desk in their den, as requested. But he'd also used the attic window for access several times.

This was too important. He had to go back. Had to be certain.

Plodding had done it. Putting his mind on the same course Blaise had followed—*watch the traffic, Krause!* He drove with a forefinger pinning spectacles to the bridge of his nose.

Kim Jensen had a flair for the end results, for psychology, but he, Herman, knew how things worked!

Assuming he was right.

Jeeze—suppose he was right?

He drove toward the Curry home, afraid, but elated.

Suppose he was right?

What then?

Rounding a corner onto Ashley Drive, Herman thought he saw a light in the Curry home. But when he entered the driveway, the light was gone. Must've been a reflection. No other cars. He circled the house to one side in deepening darkness, a chirp of crickets punctuated by tree frogs welcoming the night. The ladder, built onto the wall permanently to serve as a fire escape, rose thirty feet to the uppermost floor. It passed no windows except the one that entered the attic.

He paused, listening. Turning, he had a view of the city, beyond the patio, past Mr. Curry's weed infested garden. Thought he'd heard a thump from inside. Wood contracting, perhaps. He continued, hand over hand, to treetop level. Carefully, he lifted the window, sash weights bumping within the frame. He crawled into the black interior and felt his way across the room to the stairway light. Ah, much better. He went to the terminal, activated the CRT display, and pulled his chair closer. Below, more sound of expanded structure responding to the cool of evening, almost like random footsteps.

He typed in the access code and requested: RALPH CURRY, GENERAL.

Nothing.

But how could that be? He'd seen data on Ralph Curry throughout. A list of checks payable to him, places he'd been, hotels where he'd stayed.

He paused, head cocked, listening again. Then, admonishing himself for being distracted, he went to the pile of notebooks, thumbing through pages for material he remembered seeing. Not this one. Not this—here! He took the pages to better light near the console and studied the penciled scrawl.

He was certain his deduction was correct. The question was, how would Blaise have filed it in the memory bank? He returned to the glowing green display and cancelled the last command. The screen advised: **READY.**

Herman typed, **RICHARD CURRY, GENERAL.**

The screen filled, information flowing, appearing, disappearing—he cancelled it.

How would she think? Think like Blaise would think.

Another noise below drew his eyes to the shadowed stairwell and for a moment, heart racing, he strained to hear anything afar. *Come on, Krause! Get with it and get out of here.*

Think as Blaise would think . . .

He typed: **DADDY.**

READY

"Ah so," he crooned softly.

GENERAL

The screen began to fill and there was the data from the notebooks. Each sentence had a code. He selected one and typed a command: **FOOD COMPARE**

And there it was—the whole key—

DADDY below which was listed meats, vegetables, condiments, sweets (none) and beverages. It was, Herman knew from the notebooks, a compilation of everything Blaise had ever heard her father mention in the way of food, everything she'd ever seen him eat, the seasonings he selected, the beverages he preferred.

The stairs creaked and goosebumps erupted. Herman turned, calling, "Hello? Anybody there?"

Silence.

Get through. Get out.

In one of the notebooks he'd seen a reference—

He froze, staring at the video display, watching for a reflection. His nerves were crawling, he was trembling with excitement, he almost had it now—a few more minutes and—

The room plunged into darkness. Only the green of the CRT provided illumination. Herman pushed up his spectacles, shivering, and walked to the stairs. He flicked the switch—was it up or down, before? It was a two-way switch, controlled here at the top, and down at the bottom of the stairs. He stooped, staring down the steps into utter darkness below. Might have been a surge in power. Faulty breaker in the fuse box, perhaps.

Five more minutes and he'd have this solved.

He went to the console, glancing backward to see that he remained alone. He heard a murmur of wind in the eaves—was the wind blowing when he arrived?

He typed: DADDY TOO.

The lights went out again and Herman swore softly. He watched data fill the screen.

Footsteps for sure now.

That damned Jensen playing spook—just like him—

"Hey, Jensen!" he hollered. "Come on up, wise guy. I got it figured out now. Blaise thinks her daddy killed—"

He turned in the dark and his voice died in a shudder. He blinked his eyes rapidly, trying to adjust to the black interior. He wiped a sleeve across his spectacles to clear away—

"Who is there?" he asked.

No reply.

"Hello? Anybody there?"

A whispery inhaling, exhaling—a dim visage beyond his range of sight—a glint of green on the metallic blade of—

Herman flung his chair at the dark, scrambling for the keyboard: ARE YOU THERE

GOOD EVENING

An arm came around his neck, his spectacles flew and he heard them break as he kicked for leverage, being lifted, powerfully lifted, choked by—

His fingers thrashed the keyboard . . . clawing for the arm, gasping for air . . .

He had to warn them . . .

Had to warn them . . .

The hot searing plunge of a blade took his breath and Herman held the console with the grip of a terrified man. Again the blade came down and he plodded, typing, WH—

He felt the searing blade and a warm ooze of life juices; coming again, this time as if in slow motion—

O-AR—

He wouldn't let go of the console, anchored, his fingers moving by touch, practiced touch, typing . . .

E-YO

One more . . .

—U—

He heard a scream and he was flung aside.

He fell, turned in agony—but he would have imagined the pain would have been greater—

Another scream and he saw the blurred image reel away into the dark.

"You know what I've done, don't you?" Kim said, gutturally. "I've told Curry they've been in his computer. I've told him I've been in it!"

"You think he might try to hurt us?" Gwen questioned.

"If he killed three children—"

Gwen shivered with a low moan.

"I've put Ellen Curry in jeopardy," Kim said. "She's in danger and doesn't know it. Call their house, Gwen, and get her on the telephone."

He'd never owned a pistol. Too many students coming and going during the school year. He couldn't afford the chance of accident.

"There's no answer, Kim."

"Could be out of town."

"Or shopping," Gwen suggested.

"Well, damn it," Kim stood up, paced the office. "Okay, look, I have to go over there. If I haven't telephoned in say, thirty minutes, you call the police and send them over. I could stall Satan half an hour . . ."

"Be careful, Kim."

He drove filled with apprehension. Should have waited. Too precipitous. A fine mess he had made.

He turned into the driveway and slammed the steering wheel with a hand. Herman Krause's car. He'd forgotten about that twerp. Kim went to the front door and rang the bell insistently.

He stepped out into the yard looking up at the attic. A faintly visible green light. The CRT was on. It was not likely the boy would come to the door, if he wouldn't answer the telephone. Kim tried the portal. Locked. He went around to the patio. When he pulled the sliding glass door it moved. Broken. He stuck his head inside, calling, "Anybody here? Hello!"

He stepped in, found the light switch and returned to examine the damaged glass frame. It had been forced, as with a crowbar. Didn't Herman have a key?

He remembered the night the boy came through an attic window. Maybe Ellen forgot *her* key and she forced entry.

He turned on lights as he moved through the house, checking rooms as he went, calling repeatedly, "Hello? Anybody home?"

In the den he found house keys on the desk and a note in Herman's handwriting, "Blaise, call Herman when you come home."

Kim went into the hallway, hollered up the stairs, "Anybody up there?"

He climbed carpeted steps slowly, a sixth sense foreboding, a sense that had served him well in Vietnam. Never ignore an inkling of—

He paused, listening. He turned on the upstairs light, holding his breath, listening. Outside, the sound of a car. A neighbor, maybe—here he was in a house with a forced lock! He ran on tiptoes down the hall to the attic door. If that was Richard Curry pulling into the driveway, he was in trouble! So was Herman, up there oblivious to what was happening.

Kim mounted the steps in the dark, afraid another light would be a clue to his progress, if viewed from outside.

The CRT *was* on.

He felt something crunch underfoot, broken glass. Kim groped his way through the room toward the console. His foot bumped something and he stepped around it. He stared at the console.

I AM TONY

What the hell?

Now he did hear something—downstairs, a male voice calling, "Ellen? Are you up there?"

His eyes adjusting to the dark, Kim moved so he wouldn't be

backlighted by the green illumination from the CRT. He bumped—

He felt below him and gasped.

He shut his eyes tightly, trying to hurry night vision. Dear God! Herman Krause!

"Ellen?"

Blood. Kim reached for the boy's throat, feeling for a pulse . . .

The lights came on and for an instant he was blinded, concentrating on the ghastly sight before him, Herman staring with sightless eyes, the floor covered with—

He heard ascending feet, irritation in the man's voice, "Is anybody up here?"

Veins collapsed beneath his touch. The floor was a crimson pool. Kim wiped his hands on his trousers, steeling himself for combat, all the instincts of a marine coming back, adrenaline flowing.

He stood to face his adversary.

"My God almighty!" the man yelled.

"Richard Curry?"

"Who are you?"

"Are you Richard Curry?"

"Yes."

"Too many people know, Curry," Kim reasoned. "Too many people know. Your game is over."

Chapter
TWENTY-ONE

The detective had dark circles under deeply set eyes, asking questions in a somnolent monotone.

"Which airline?"

"Eastern."

Men brought Herman down from the attic, his body covered, strapped to a stretcher, a pale hand exposed.

"Coming from where?"

"Aruba."

In the instant following shock, Richard Curry had turned to run, Kim had thought to flee—and Richard let him! But Curry raced from room to room, screaming, "Ellen! Blaise!" Frantically, he'd approached each closed door with unmitigated fear, throwing wide the portal anticipating horror, wheeling to fall on his knees, peering under beds.

"What kind of business is that in Aruba?"

"Import-export."

"Where is Aruba, exactly?"

Through the opened front door came the slash of revolving

blue lights, uniformed men keeping the curious at bay. A forensic team was in the kitchen examining the broken door, in the attic dusting for fingerprints.

"What was the deceased doing in your attic, Mr. Curry?"

"He and my daughter shared an interest in computers. It was the computer, I expect."

"But you say your daughter is visiting her grandmother."

"That's right."

"Your wife is researching an article."

"That's right."

"You are off on this island on business."

Curry took a breath, exhaled slowly.

"Then you came in," the detective said to Kim, "saw the light in the attic, found the rear door jimmied, went up to investigate and discovered Herman. Happened to be passing by?"

"Coming to see Mrs. Curry."

"Why?"

"We're friends."

Throughout, Curry watched him intensely. Kim kept his expression noncommittal.

"Who called the police?" the detective inquired.

"My assistant, Gwen Ackers."

"Why would she do that?"

"When there was no answer on the telephone, I became worried."

"You knew Mrs. Curry well enough to become alarmed? Let's see now, you say that you and Mr. Curry had never met before tonight?"

"That's right."

"What do you think about that, Mr. Curry?"

"What should I think?"

The detective looked down at his notebook and chuckled. He closed the pad and stood up on legs too thin for such a stocky torso. "Guess that takes care of it," he said. "Thank you, gentlemen."

"What next?" Richard asked.

The detective walked to a painting, speaking as he examined it, "The lab will do their thing. Fingerprints, blood analysis, hair samples—"

"Hair?"

"The boy had it stuck to his fingers."

"Then what?" Richard demanded.

"Homicide is mostly routine work," the detective moved to another picture. "Almost always it's somebody with a motive born out of passion—husband-wife-lover—"

"That is clearly not the case here," Richard declared. "What happens next?"

"Scientific investigation, Mr. Curry."

"Scientific," Kim advised. "They have a backlog at the FBI, so it will take weeks to get a report on fingerprints. The hair samples will go to Montgomery and languish for more weeks."

An officer shot an angry glance at them.

"Most homicides are solved when somebody confesses," Kim noted. "A drunk brags in a bar, a convict confides in his cell mate."

The detective side-stepped to another painting. "Seems that way sometimes," he said amiably.

"Are we through?" Richard asked.

"For now."

"Is there any reason I can't leave town?"

The detective spoke with his back to them, "Business?"

"Possibly."

"I think that would be all right. Your office would know how to reach you?"

"Yes."

As they moved toward the door, Richard said, "I want to talk to you, Jensen."

"My office is on Old Shell Road."

Car doors slammed, blue lights extinguished and vehicles pulled away from the curb. Gwen was in her automobile, waiting.

"Poor Herman," she said.

"Yeah."

"Such a funny boy, such a strange boy."

Kim looked back at Richard Curry standing in the door of the brilliantly lighted house.

"Do they know who did it?"

"No. Let's go home, Gwen."

They needed to think, Mother Meredith had declared. They needed time to distill their thoughts and reevaluate all they'd learned. She had suggested the family retreat near Front Royal, Virginia where the Blue Ridge Parkway began. It was where Ellen and Arnold had spent their honeymoon, his favorite place in the world. So much his, in fact, not even Mother Meredith had been able to go there after Arnold died.

The hazy blue mountains humped across the horizon, fields of sneezeweed cast yellow blankets along the highway. Driving with the windows opened, they caught the scent of honeysuckle and blackberries fermenting on the stem.

Ellen would have thought trauma upon trauma would bring a numbness, but her emotional pain continued, nearly unbearable. Blaise had poured forth her nightmares, tearfully apologizing after they left Wynette Weyman in Chicago. She spoke of horrible fantasies, "daddy," trousers wet from the knees down, his shirt soaked from elbows to wrists. Her recurring dream was of him, running from the scene, dust caking his cuffs, shoes muddy.

"But it was a dream," Ellen stated.

"I think so. I can't remember, mama. It must've been."

God it was awful.

Blaise repeated snatches of conversations with Betty Sue, lending a childish hue to black tales of poverty, babies with runny noses, bare feet, the cupboards with scanty provisions of macaroni, soups, saltine crackers and tins of sardines. "Can't we help them, mama?"

"I'm sure Richard will agree, Blaise."

And Richard. Ellen did not share Blaise's guilt for having joined this sordid search. As Mother Meredith had said, he had invited it with prevarication and secrecy. They were all awash with relief

226

that Richard was not guilty of murder, yes, but Ellen resented the deceptions that had induced this doubt and turmoil.

Blaise caromed from bitter accusation to aching doubts, even now. "I wanted to love him, mama. I did love him, because of you. Even when I thought he had done bad things, I saw how much he meant to you."

Yellow blossoms turned to tickseed sunflowers and golden ragwort, the valleys more open, the mountain drawing nearer. Blaise and Mother Meredith rode in the back seat, each absorbed in their own thoughts as Ellen drove.

Over and over, Ellen sifted through all she'd learned, from Betty Sue to Wynette and including herself. It was the history of a man burning with ambition, dedicated to success, not only financially, but socially. But then, having $32 million, he spent it sparingly. They did not participate in the very things wealth afforded.

Ellen remembered something her father once said, when she was still in high school. "Veneers are to cover cheap wood. Or cheap people."

With Richard, it was the veneer that was of lesser quality. He did not tout his money or his life. He aspired to no pretensions.

Everything she'd learned about him had only confirmed the essence of the man she'd married. He was honorable and generous. Two former wives spoke of him in glowing terms. Childhood acquaintances extolled his virtues.

Agonizing, Ellen stared ahead at the winding road, her hair blown by breezes through the windows. She glanced in the rearview mirror and Blaise was looking. They smiled at one another, sadly, painfully.

"Arnold and I came here on our honeymoon, Blaise."

"Mother Meredith told me."

"It was Arnold's place," Mother Meredith spoke, out of Ellen's field of vision. "He hunted and camped every inch of the twenty-five hundred acres. He named the gulleys and ravines, he knew the oldest trees, the best picnic sites."

Blaise peered out her window now, and Ellen thought she'd seen a wince.

"He loved it," Mother Meredith said, softly. "Loved it."

"I suppose Mr. Manx is dead by now," Ellen commented.

"Oh, no. He's the caretaker still. Over the years, as age crept up on him, we sold the livestock, the horses. His duties are restricted these days to just being there."

Ellen turned onto a narrow paved lane between two precipitous mountains.

"He doesn't know about Arnold," Mother Meredith said hesitantly.

"Doesn't know?"

"It's so remote up here," Mother Meredith said. "We came so seldom anyway. He was old. I didn't want to burden him."

Blaise looked at Ellen in the mirror.

"He wouldn't have remembered," Mother Meredith attempted to explain. "He goes back and forth in his mind. He thinks today is—well, you can see, can't you?"

"Yes."

Blaise turned away, looking down at a rocky creek of clear water. "How much further is it?" she asked.

"This is it!" Mother Meredith exclaimed. "Your great-grandfather cut this road nearly a hundred years ago. He wanted a visitor to see the most beautiful places before reaching the lodge."

Ellen slowed as they came to a roaring waterfall, the air noticeably cooler, moss forming a gray and green frame around the cascade. Rainbows evanesced, and spray rose in a fine mist to dew the leaves of ivy surrounding the pool.

As long as the water falls, I will love you, Arnold had vowed. They had swam naked, made love over there under the . . .

She shifted gears and drove on.

"I haven't been here in a long time," Mother Meredith said to Blaise. "Your grandfather and I went swimming there with no clothes on."

Blaise laughed with a blend of surprise and pleasure.

"Look, look!" Mother Meredith leaned forward and touched Ellen's shoulder. "That's where Arnold shot his first deer, Ellen. Did he ever show you where he marked the oak tree?"

Below which, their initials, A.M. + E.M.

. . . as long as the water falls . . .

It had taken Grandfather Meredith three years to construct this passage. Ellen remembered Arnold's tone of disdain as he described the number of laborers, the tons of dynamite, the teams of mules and wagons used to cart debris. "One helluva waste," Arnold had concluded. "But oh, what a masterpiece, isn't it?"

"It's beautiful," Blaise murmured. "How much of it is yours, Mother Meredith?"

"Ours, darling. One day, yours. All that you see is one day yours."

. . . Four square miles . . .

"We could be a hundred miles from civilization," Mother Meredith mouthed the words Ellen had heard Arnold speak. "In the wintertime you can hear the crack of a bough under snow, as sharp as a pistol shot. During the spring, when thunder rolls, it echoes up and down the valleys . . ."

. . . like tympanies and bongos, like kettledrums in some heavenly orchestra . . .

"Herds of deer come each winter to feed in the valley, which you will see when we reach the crest," Mother Meredith sounded choked, recalling Arnold's descriptions. "When they're startled, they turn en masse and flee in bounding leaps, their tails flashing white flags, their antlers like leafless trees . . ."

. . . We'll raise our daughters here, Ellen . . .

"The rains, when they come," Mother Meredith intoned, "are as pure as crystal and they strike the leaves and logs like fingers on a keyboard, the creeks rising, water swelling . . ."

. . . Music more lovely than any symphony . . .

"And when lightning strikes, the valley fills with ozone . . ."

. . . celestial flint, the air purified . . .

Ellen groaned and Blaise jolted, staring at the rearview mirror. Ellen leaned aside to hide her expression.

"The berries are sweet as sugar and make wine on the vine. Raccoons and birds get drunk, eating them. The smell of scuppernong and . . ."

"Should I stop at the gate, Mother Meredith?" Ellen interrupted.

"Oh, yes. We'll have to tell Mr. Manx that we're here."

They reached the crest, a fieldstone arch, an iron gate was open, permanently. The caretaker's cottage was of the same stone, covered by a cedar shingle roof.

The old man, hair askew and white as clouds, supported himself on a homemade cane, hobbling out to intercept them.

"Mr. Manx," Mother Meredith opened the car door, her voice raised, "It's Mrs. Meredith!"

"Ho so it is!"

"I've brought Arnold's daughter, Blaise."

"Ho so you did!"

"Blaise, this is Mr. Manx."

"Looks like Arnold!" Mr. Manx crooned, reaching in the window to touch Blaise's face. "And ho, who else have we here?"

"You remember Ellen—"

Ellen got out and took his quivering hand, flesh was loose on bone, cold to the touch. His eyes brimmed with tears. "Like old times, Mrs. Meredith! You and Mr. Meredith and Arnold and—"

"We'll be here a few days, Mr. Manx," Mother Meredith interceded. "Is the house in good order?"

"Ho yes! Ho yes! Like Mr. Arnold left it."

"Are you feeling well?" Mother Meredith motioned Ellen inside the vehicle.

"Ho yes. For an old man. Ninety, you know."

"Does your daughter come often?"

"Now and again. To clean and bring supplies."

"We tried to call," Mother Meredith was still shouting to be heard, opening her car door. "Why don't you have a telephone anymore?"

"I do."

"How is it listed?"

"Mr. Arnold be along soon?"

"I don't think so. How is the telephone listed, Mr. Manx?"

"Don't have no idea." He pronounced the word, *idee*. "It's my daughter's phone, she pays the bills."

"You should have a telephone up here."

"I do."

"But how—"

"How long before the rest of the family comes?"

"They won't be coming, Mr. Manx." Mother Meredith turned to Ellen, sotto voce, "Let's drive on, Ellen."

"Want I should call a maid, Mrs. Meredith?"

"No, we'll make do, Mr. Manx."

"My daughter will come today, if I ask her."

"No need, Mr. Manx." Aside, to Ellen, "Let's drive on."

Ellen started the car and the old man stepped back a pace as the vehicle trembled. "Like it used to be!" he cried.

"Does he have a telephone or not?" Ellen queried.

"Who knows, dear. I presume his relatives check on him now and then."

"Ninety years old?" Blaise marveled.

"He's been saying that since I was here, Blaise," Ellen laughed. "He doesn't know how old he is."

"He looks ninety," Blaise concluded.

As they wound down the descending side, Ellen fought a wave of melancholy. Her best hours with Arnold had been here. When they were young and blind to the world, when they were playing grownup and married, without children and with few cares.

"I can see why he loved it," Mother Meredith said.

"Yes," Blaise replied. "So can I."

Kim took his coffee on the back patio, a small enclosed rock garden accessible from the kitchen only. He wanted to be away from telephones ringing, the clack of typewriter keys, the tension of the office inside. Gwen had hired two girls from a secretarial service. They were preparing a sales presentation, contracts and payment schedules for a business that wanted protection.

He sipped coffee, sneakered feet on a low glass table. The sun felt good on bare legs. He unbuttoned his shirt to get more of the rays.

"Mind if I join you?" Gwen appeared at the exit.

"As long as you don't talk."

"That's okay," she replied, "as long as you do talk."

He sighed heavily. He hadn't slept well last night. Every time he closed his eyes he had vivid recurrences of Herman lying in a scarlet pool.

"What are we going to do now, Kim?"

"About what?"

"Hey," she urged, "come on! Let's not play games. I want to know whether to be frightened or not."

"I don't know."

"Did Richard Curry kill him?"

"I don't know, Gwen."

"Well," she whispered, "goddamn it, you look like you think he did it. Did he, or didn't he? A guess will do."

"I said, I don't know."

She clamped her lips, eyes darted. Now she smiled. "Here we go," she spoke as to a child, "all together now, Kimbrough. Put the positive things on one side, the negative things on the other side and let's see which weighs most."

"He might have arrived, found Herman, killed him, then jimmied the back door so entry would appear to be forced."

"That's what I think," Gwen concurred.

"But the expression on his face—"

"When?"

"When he thought, or pretended to think, he might find his wife and Blaise dead somewhere else in the house. It was—convincing."

"Desperation makes fine thespians."

"Yeah."

"We think he killed three children," Gwen remarked.

"Looks that way."

"Why would he hesitate to kill Herman, then?"

"His flight had just come in, he barely had time to get there. I felt Herman's body, looking for a pulse. He'd been dead a few hours, I think."

"But you don't know that to be a fact."

"In Nam I got to where I could tell by feeling the neck. Rigor mortis progresses from the face, the jaw, down the body to the toes. Blood gets sticky. The cops checked out the flight and time of arrival, and now, so have I. I don't think Richard Curry killed

Herman. But if he did, he's the coolest bastard that ever lived. He answered their questions, but he never whimpered, never whined. He kept his dignity, didn't get ruffled even when that stupid detective insinuated there was something between Ellen and me."

"This is a mess," Gwen shook her head ruefully. "Not only have we wasted an awful lot of time and money on a criminal enterprise, we find ourselves dealing with a psycho."

"Maybe."

"There isn't a glimmer of a chance we're going to get a contract out of this man!"

One of the hired girls came to the patio door, "Somebody is here."

"Did he give his name?"

"No."

"You should always ask who is calling," Gwen went inside, instructing patiently. "You should say, 'May I tell Mr. Jensen the nature of your business—'"

Kim gazed at his sockless ankles and sipped coffee.

Not much chance they'd get a security contract from Curry, that was true. But no man ever needed it more.

"Kim," Gwen came outside before speaking, "It's him. Richard Curry. What should I do?"

"Let him in, Gwen."

She hesitated.

"Show him in, babe."

T Chapter
WENTY-TWO

Without apology for his appearance, Kim received Richard on the patio where it was quiet.

"Would you care for coffee, Mr. Curry?" Gwen inquired.

"No, thank you." He assessed Kim, bare legs, tattered shorts, no socks, shirt unbuttoned. He sat, then intertwined strong manicured fingers.

After a long silence, Kim asked, "What may I do for you?"

"You tell me, Jensen."

Kim removed his feet from the glass table. "You need computer security, Richard. May I call you Richard?"

"I need this security because you had entry into my attic?"

"I was invited there. As was Herman Krause."

"Who extended the invitation?"

"Ellen hired me to uncover Blaise's access codes."

"Why would she do that?"

"Blaise had been examining your business records from Atlanta and—"

"In your opinion I must protect myself from my wife and daughter?"

"If they can violate your computer, anyone can."

"I'll have to restrict traffic in my attic."

"Anyone with a terminal and a telephone can reach your computers," Kim warned. "That makes you vulnerable to your competitors, the IRS, any investigative body."

"And my wife."

"Within the computers are your business records, but because of the way you've structured the program, it's also possible to determine everything from your net worth to the cost of operating your household. It may not be a state secret, but how many people do you want to know that?"

"Part of the purpose of computer accounting," Curry said, "is the ready availability of such data in a form the tax people can audit easily. Contrary to what you may think, there is little I have to hide."

"Look, Curry, I sell a service, the value of which is obvious to people who need it. If you don't need it, so be it."

Gwen spoke at the door, "Telephone, Kim."

"Take the number."

She brought an extension onto the patio and plugged it in. "Armand Joaquin with *Mobala News*," she said.

A flicker of distress in Curry's eyes. Kim took the call only for that reason. "Hello, Joaquin."

"Listen closely, Jensen," the voice was vibrant with anger, "the cops were here asking about Ellen. Richard Curry had told them she was doing an article for me that required travel. Something about minerals. Curry was here earlier, looking for his wife. That dead boy—what the hell is going on?"

Gwen had brought coffee to Curry anyway, trying to distract him with murmured conversation. But Curry was listening, his expression—alarm, fear?

"You know as much as I do, Joaquin."

"Where is she, Jensen?"

"How would I know?"

"Because your nose is in everybody's business. Now goddamn it, where is she?"

"I don't know."

"Is she working on the computer article?"

"I don't know."

"According to the cops, you were on the scene last night when Richard Curry came home and discovered the body."

"That's right."

"You went over there to find Ellen, you said."

"She wasn't there."

"Okay," Joaquin exhaled with finality. "Your ass is mine, sport. Whatever you're up to, I'm going to find out."

He hung up and Gwen took the extension inside. *So Curry didn't know where she was.* Kim sipped cold coffee, squinting against the glare of the sun.

"Police mentality is a pragmatic one," Kim said softly. "They gather and sift, check and recheck. Let's look at this from their perspective."

"What has that to do with computer security?"

"They're called to your attic to remove a boy brought there by your wife. Ellen will verify that."

Curry glanced toward the kitchen where Gwen was listening.

"You and I meet over Herman Krause, and I say I've gone there looking for Ellen."

"Is that true or not?" Curry questioned.

"As far as it goes, it's true," Kim replied. "You can prove your whereabouts, so you have an alibi. I had an alibi. Besides, they have a murder weapon with fingerprints, hair from Herman's fingers, so they're going to nail somebody. That doesn't worry you or me, we didn't do it."

"Have you a point to make?"

"You told them your wife was chasing an article for the newspaper. They checked it out. It isn't true. You went to the newspaper looking for Ellen, so you apparently don't know where she is."

Uncertainty was only a quick flash in Curry's eyes. "Jensen, have you anything more to add to your sales pitch?"

"The facts stand for themselves."

"And, if I say forget it, you'll forget it?"

"That's right."

"Then forget it," Curry stood up, straightened his suit jacket.

"Do you know where Ellen is, Richard? Think like the police. Given these circumstances, what would you believe?"

"I wouldn't know, Jensen. But don't worry on our behalf."

"They are probably going to interrogate Ellen. Where has she been? Who can attest to that?"

Curry hesitated.

"They may subpoena your computer records," Kim noted. "I could store sensitive material for you in my machines and you could erase it from yours."

"That won't be necessary."

"I could find Ellen."

"She isn't lost, Jensen."

"You could too, of course," Kim persisted. "You could go to your office manager and explain the predicament—"

"I haven't yet seen the predicament."

"Your computer man could put a flag on telephone calls made by Ellen or Blaise, charged to your home or office. If they're making credit card purchases, those will show up on your machine. Maybe Ellen and Blaise are together. Wherever they are, they are probably unaware of what's happening here."

"Ellen won't be accused of murdering that boy."

"Probably not. But she'll have to tell them what she has been doing, which means she has to tell them what Blaise has been doing, and that means explaining why Herman was in your attic and why Ellen hired me. The police mentality is, as I say, pragmatic. Gather, sift, check and recheck. Ellen will have to prove her whereabouts. It can be embarrassing, if nothing else."

Curry moved toward the door.

"As I say," Kim insisted, "your office manager can locate Ellen just as I would. But I can do it today. Perhaps within the hour."

Curry turned, eyes narrowed, "You locate Ellen and then we'll discuss a possible contract."

"Fair enough. Come back this evening."

"You said within an hour."

"One hour to locate Ellen. Three hours to check out things you may wish to know. With us on contract, you will find we can provide certain valuable services which go beyond security."

"Such as?"

"What the police are thinking, who they are suspecting. Answers to some critical questions."

"Such as?"

"Such as who may have killed Herman. And why?"

"Find Ellen Curry," Kim dictated, going upstairs.

"You made a lot of wild claims to Curry, Kim. Claims you can't back up."

"If she makes a telephone call charged to home or office, I want to know it immediately—where the call originated, and then run down the location."

"We've wasted a great deal of money already—"

"Call the credit card home offices and tell them we have an emergency, tell them we are the accounting office, give them the card numbers. If Ellen spends anything, I want to know where, how much, and time of day if possible."

He kicked off his shoes, shed his clothing. "See if you can get a line on this Meredith woman."

"That will take days," Gwen reasoned. "She's wealthy. She has accountants, attorneys, investment counselors, secretaries, and billing could go to any of those."

"You're right. Forget Mrs. Meredith. Concentrate on Ellen."

"Kim, will you listen to me?"

He started water running for a shower.

"We aren't going to get a contract from this man, Kim."

"We'll get it."

"He's stringing us along. And that crap you gave him about learning who killed Herman and why, that was not a smart thing to say."

"Somebody killed him because he was there, Gwen." He pointed at a bar of soap on the lavatory and she gave it to him. "Herman was the kind of twerp who would scrawl a clue with his own blood and his dying breath. When I got to the attic the CRT said 'I am Tony.' It all ties in, somehow."

"You're guessing, Kimbrough."

"Put those girls downstairs onto this," he stepped into the tub. "Have them monitor long distance calls."

"Kim, may I talk to you?" she asked pleasantly.

"Oil company credit cards," Kim mandated, "airline credit card vouchers, watch for electronic fund transfers on Ellen's bank account—"

"Richard Curry is not afraid of the police," Gwen said. "He isn't afraid of you. He is a dangerous man."

"He's afraid of something. His wife, maybe. Afraid he'll lose her. Afraid of what she can do to him. He's afraid of something. I've got to find out more about the guy. Jesus, he's cool. He could face a firing squad and never blink an eye."

"Remember, one time when we were having a picnic with your folks?" Gwen spoke on the other side of the shower curtain. "Remember what your father said about the two most dangerous people being the very poor and the very rich?"

"Gwen, get on it, will you?"

"The very poor have nothing to lose," Gwen recounted, "the very rich can do anything, and lose nothing—remember?"

She swept back the shower curtain and turned off the water. Kim wiped lather from his forehead.

"You see my face, Kim?"

"I see it."

"See my eyes, how green the fire?"

"I see, Gwen."

"You aren't a stupid man. We will not get a contract from Richard Curry. He may be a murderer, he positively is a criminal. No contract!"

"We're going to get a contract," he vowed.

"Do we want it? A man who killed children? A man who will surely be indicted for murder?"

"Even if Curry were eliminated from the picture, a business as large as his continues to operate with or without the owner. We'd be negotiating with Ellen, most likely."

Gwen averted emerald eyes. She took a breath, evoked a smile. "We didn't take Regalia boats when we discovered they were hustling drugs. We've always avoided the underworld. I vote to forget Richard Curry and drop the matter."

"Gwendolyn—"

"That's my vote," she said evenly. "What's yours?"

"Look, babe, I'll make a deal with you. I'll find out whether Curry killed his kids. If he did, we drop it. If he didn't, we go full steam ahead. Agreed?"

"You have no way of knowing such a thing."

"But if I do, will you stay with me on this?"

"Not guilty, we go on," she affirmed. "Guilty, we drop it instantly."

"That's the deal." He bent forward to kiss her and she put fingertips on his wet lips. "I'm not one of your wide-eyed students, or some yokel businessman who doesn't comprehend the limitations of computers, Kimbrough. There's no way you can know whether Curry is guilty or not."

"I'll crash the Medical Information Bureau."

She contemplated this a moment. "How?"

"I know someone in Birmingham, home office of a large insurance company. It'll cost us a few dollars, but we'll get the whole story. In the meantime, please start hunting for Ellen Curry. Check the rental car agencies, stay on the credit card accounts."

He completed his shower, considering the portent of what he was about to do. From the first application for insurance to the most recent, all information would have been fed into the giant data bank of the Medical Information Bureau, which was shared by the life insurance companies of America. If an applicant lied, the computer caught it. If he misrepresented health status, the computers revealed medical examination results from years past. The beneficiary would be listed.

If Richard Curry were suspect, the computers would know. If he had never been identified as a suspect, because of three marriages, different states, this telephone call would tip investigators and wheels would begin to turn. If Curry killed three children for insurance money, he was about to be exposed.

It had been easy to tell Gwen they'd drop Curry, if the man were guilty. Because, if guilty, his time was running out. And if he was not guilty of murder—well—then they weren't so different, he and Richard Curry. Both of them stretched the law, but neither broke the law in the areas where they operated. Who was he to pass judgment on a matter of ethics?

Wearing a fresh suit, Kim went into his office and dialed Birmingham.

"Angelo?" he began, "This is Kim Jensen in Mobile."

"What do you need, Kim?"

"Three children dead, three different marriages, one man involved."

"Murder?"

"That's what I'm trying to find out, Angelo."

"Cost you $500, Kim."

"You've got it. Okay, here is what I know . . ."

Mother Meredith went from room to room, throwing open leaded glass windows, turning on fans. The lodge had sixteen bedrooms, four suites if used that way, giving every guest a view of the blue hazy mountains circling the valley.

Everywhere was evidence of Arnold, his gun racks, mounted trophies, fly rods and tackle boxes. On the walls, photos of famous and near-famous visitors who had come here when the Meredith family was active in politics and business. Here and there, Arnold's grinning face as he held aloft that which he'd bagged or hooked.

Blaise lifted a framed photograph from the fireplace mantel. "Who is this?"

Ellen's breath caught. It had been a photo of herself, holding infant Tony, but now it was torn with only Blaise remaining. "That's you, Blaise. You were about four years old."

"I had skinny legs."

Mother Meredith was walking through the house, covering anguish with prattle, "Dust everywhere," she said. "They should've protected the furniture with slipcovers."

The building had an aching scent of familiarity. The liquor

cabinets were stocked, Arnold's favorites. On one shelf, several bottles only partially filled, lost to evaporation, perhaps.

"It's as if he were here only yesterday," Mother Meredith murmured, her eyes brimming with tears. Instantly, she snapped erect, "I'd better examine the sleeping quarters. We may wish we'd gone to a hotel, instead."

Mother Meredith went to the master suite, first. Dust covers were in place, the canopied bed draped, the French style furniture oddly out of place in such a rustic setting. She removed the cloths carefully, to avoid stirring silt. Ellen heard Blaise flush a toilet.

"Let's see Arnold's room now," Mother Meredith said, bravely. She attempted a smile when their eyes met, but neither of them could hide distress.

When the door was pushed open, a faint lingering masculine—

"Remember that rum cologne Arnold always—" Mother Meredith stared at a rumpled bed, head quavering. "That's the way it was when last I came here, Ellen. I couldn't bring myself to touch a thing. Forgive me, I'd forgotten."

"It's all right, Mother Meredith."

Exuberantly, Blaise bounded through the room into the bathroom, "First considerations first," she cried. "Is there any hot water?"

There was. The place kept, as always, ready for occupancy. She and Arnold had made love in that bed, with icicles along the eaves beyond the bay window, with the rustle of breezes to lull them during summer visits.

She saw Blaise in the bathroom, kneeling to examine the sunken Grecian tub. "Wow! Whirlpool baths! It needs to be scrubbed, though."

Mother Meredith stood a pace inside the door, chin quivering, struggling for composure.

"Whose are these?" Blaise queried, "brush, comb, electric razor, toothpaste—"

"Let's begin by cleaning the living room, shall we?" Ellen suggested.

"Are these daddy's?" Blaise extended toilet articles.

"Yes." Breathlessly.

Blaise turned the hairbrush, holding it toward better light.

On a bedside table, a novel lay face down as if the reader might return any moment to continue the tale. Blaise opened cedar closets and there hung clothing for all seasons, boots, galoshes, hunting clothes, flannel shirts. In the hewn oak drawers of the dresser were underwear, socks, a few pennies in change.

"Mama?" Blaise turned, blinking, "This glass is sticky. Somebody has been drinking out of it."

"Mr. Manx and his daughter come here to check on things," Mother Meredith explained. "They may have used it. Mr. Manx once had a liking for the grape. He and Arnold used to be drinking buddies, as Arnold put it."

"He's been using daddy's brush, too," Blaise said, "the hair is gray."

"Shall we start by cleaning the living room?" Ellen tried again.

"As if only yesterday," Mother Meredith whispered.

"Let's go back to the living room, Blaise. We also need to check the larder, Mother Meredith. We may have to drive to town for more groceries."

They walked the long hallway, Blaise stopping at every painting, scrutinizing each mounted photograph. "Here's another one with everybody torn off except me," Blaise said. "Who did that?"

Ellen did not recall the pictured instant. But only Blaise was there, the rest of the image thrown away.

"Weevils in the flour bin," Mother Meredith called from the kitchen. "But most of the canned goods seem all right."

"The cans aren't rusting?" Ellen joined her in the massive pantry.

"Looks good to me," Mother Meredith turned a tin of anchovies, looked at the cap of a jar of martini olives.

Along the lower shelves, airtight containers, crockery pots with anchored lids, provisions designed to last and be available when the owners arrived.

"Smells good in here," Blaise said. "It looks like a grocery store."

"Oh what parties we once held," Mother Meredith lifted her spirits. "Sometimes fifteen or twenty people would drive over from Washington. That was when your grandfather was going through his public service phase. A dollar a year man, they called him. That was his salary for slaving seven days a week, month after month."

"A dollar a year?"

"I once computed his wages to be less than two pennies a week," Mother Meredith laughed. She peeked into a large crock and bent to sniff. "Tea smells good," she said.

On a kitchen counter lay a few brown petals of some distant flower arrangement. Ellen swept them into one hand, turned to seek a trash receptacle.

By the refrigerator. She depressed a foot lever with a toe and the lid lifted.

Plastic liner. She dumped the dead plant inside and stood there a moment. She pressed the lever again, the lid lifted. Two plastic cartons. She retrieved one and examined it. Orange juice containers.

When she glanced up, Blaise was staring.

"Mr. Manx's daughter has been making herself at home, obviously," Ellen stated.

"Which I do not mind," Mother Meredith defended. "I haven't been here in years. Nobody comes here. A house needs human habitation to stay young. A home without the warmth of people soon begins to age and warp."

So intense was Blaise's stare, Ellen snapped her fingers, "Are you there, Blaise?"

The girl nodded, tight-lipped. She went to the refrigerator and opened it. "There're more cartons of orange juice," she said. "Probably soured, right?"

"I expect so, Blaise."

Ellen watched her open one, taste. "It's okay," she reported.

"Very well now," Mother Meredith wrapped her coiffure in a dishcloth. "Who sweeps, who carries out refuse, and who changes the bed linens?"

Ellen took the broom. As she moved through the living room, ghosts from youthful years seemed to smile down from photographs on the mantel. She could almost smell that rum cologne.

They had made it a point to get here for Christmas, when possible, secretly hoping they would become snowbound.

Blaise had a rocking horse. Ellen glanced around. It was still there! In a corner, Blaise as a toddler had called "a stable."

Through the rear windows, she could see the octagonal fence where they rode horseback to warm the steeds before going out for a day. The barns stood as mute testimony to a considerable equestrian investment from years ago. The tack loft was the repository for a special English saddle Arnold had given her, a larger hand-tooled western saddle abandoned because it didn't feel right.

She had become immobile, staring toward the paddocks. Now, aware of Blaise, watching, Ellen renewed her sweeping.

"Were you happy here, mama?"

"Yes."

"Was daddy?"

"Here above all other places," Ellen said.

"Who cleaned the place back then?"

"Mr. Manx was younger. His wife was alive. His children—he has several daughters and a couple of sons. They worked here full-time. It takes a large staff to keep a place of this size."

Blaise listened with troubled eyes.

"Did you get the beds changed, Blaise?"

"I did it." She strolled to the window, looking where Ellen had been looking a moment ago. "Did you ride horseback in those days?"

"All the time."

"Were you very athletic, mama?"

"You had to be, to keep up with Arnold."

"Were you happy?"

"I told you—"

"Happy!" Blaise said sharply. "Not what you think I want to hear, but really happy! Were you as happy as you are now with Richard?"

"Blaise, you've always called Richard 'daddy.' It would be such a shame if—"

Blaise wheeled, fists clenched at her sides, "mama, please, damn it—"

"Blaise!"

"I need to know!" Blaise shrilled. "How much does this daddy mean to you, compared to my real daddy?"

Mother Meredith appeared for a moment, saw the situation, and returned to a back room.

"When I was young, before you and Tony were born, when Arnold was young—we were very happy."

"When did that change?

"It came about gradually. It wasn't easy to pinpoint a day or a month—"

"When Tony was born."

"It came about while Arnold was overseas, I think."

"When Tony was born."

"Let me see, what year was that?"

"He tore Tony off the photographs, didn't he?"

"The photos may have gotten damaged and somebody was trying to salvage that part which was good."

"He tore off Tony and it *was* daddy, wasn't it?"

"Blaise—"

Blaise grabbed her arms and Ellen dropped the broom handle. "Mother, something was wrong with daddy, wasn't there? Something you never told anybody. He went to Vietnam to get away from us, didn't he?"

"Blaise, honey, he adored you."

"What about Tony?"

"Every father favors his daughter."

Blaise looked from one of Ellen's eyes to the other, probing, delving.

"He didn't love Tony as much," Ellen confessed.

"He hated Tony."

"When you study psychology, you will learn about silly rivalries between a father and a son. It's a normal thing."

"He hated Tony."

"Now, Blaise, that is unfair."

"His hatred was sick and his love was sick," Blaise gazed toward the fields, tears in her eyes.

Ellen pulled her under one arm, struck by Blaise's growth in recent weeks.

"I wasn't crazy, mom."

"Of course you weren't."

"But, daddy was."

Chapter
TWENTY-THREE

"She flew from Mobile to Chicago," Gwen jiggled a foot as she spoke. "She didn't rent a car, but she's traveling by automobile. They spent the night in Toledo—"

"They?" Kim questioned.

"Meals for three, a hotel suite," Gwen said. She checked her notes. "American Express card. I called the hotel in Toledo. It was two women and a girl."

"Mrs. Meredith and Blaise," Kim assumed.

"Mrs. Meredith is apparently paying for some things," Gwen surmised. "No meals charged to Ellen Curry in Toledo."

"Go on."

"The next night they were in Pittsburgh. Ellen's card paid for gasoline in Harrisburg, Pennsylvania and breakfast in Winchester, Virginia."

"Any long distance calls?"

"Not on the Curry telephones."

"Keep at it babe."

Alone, Kim ran his fingers through thick hair, leaning back, staring at the ceiling. Cobwebs in the corner. He made a note to call a janitorial service.

Somebody killed Herman and why?—he wrote that, too. The fingerprints would tell the tale. If it was a stranger, a burglar, bad luck—so much for that. But if it was anybody related to the Curry family, be it ever so remotely—

I AM TONY

He went through the kitchen, entered the computer room from the back way. Gwen was dialing access codes, tapping bank and telephone company computers, Curry's office machines.

"I suggest you ask Richard Curry who Ralph is," she said.

"I will."

"Look here," she typed RALPH CURRY on the keyboard. Data swept the screen. Gwen ran a slender finger down the video display. "Now look here," she typed RICHARD CURRY and a credit card number.

"Concentrate on Ellen, Gwen."

She put a finger on the CRT. "You see that, don't you? Richard and Ralph have been in the same places lately."

"Show me Ralph Curry's account again."

Gwen did so.

"Get me a printout on both those schedules, Gwen."

He went to the room where students worked during school months. He took out Blaise's floppy discs and began to run them. *Had to think like Herman thought. As Herman thought Blaise thought.*

He began at the beginning, when the Atlanta business was only a paper facade, a series of maneuvers designed to make it appear successful when indeed it was not.

Five thousand dollar check payable to—cash.

Kim scanned the text of Blaise's code, now translated. She had made note of the transaction and added, "genuine."

Yes. It was. The $5,000 was withdrawn.

A few weeks later, another $5,000 check, this one payable to Ralph Curry, also "genuine." Once a month thereafter, a like sum, identified by Blaise as "paid out, genuine."

Gwen placed a printout at his elbow. "I'd ask him who Ralph Curry is," she stated.

"I will, Gwendolyn."

She stood behind him, watching as Kim called up data from the nonexistent business. Amid the bogus transactions, the only ones Blaise marked "genuine" were those related to Ralph Curry.

"Wait a minute," Kim mumbled. He consulted Blaise's cryptic analysis again.

"Where is Bhat?" Gwen asked.

"It isn't a place, it's money."

"This says one million from Bhat," Gwen indicated the data showing.

Kim returned to Blaise's summation, "The only deposit that wasn't borrowed money came from Bhat," her notes stated.

"So where is Bhat?" Gwen queried.

"It is *money*, Gwen."

"I'm going to look that up in the dictionary," Gwen said.

One of the office girls appeared at the door, "Mr. Jensen, an insurance company in Birmingham is calling. Mr. Angelo."

"Have him wait a minute," Kim said.

"Bhat," Gwen read aloud, "is a member of an Indian caste of bards or entertainers."

"What!"

"That's what it says." She closed the dictionary.

"Blaise must have misspelled it. When I was in Vietnam, we ran into it every time we went near Thailand."

Gwen rifled pages, muttering the alphabet aloud as she sought the word. "Here it is! B-A-H-T—a basic monetary unit of currency in Thailand. Equal to one hundred satangs. Worth about half a penny in U.S. money. One million baht would be fifty thousand U.S. dollars."

Kim lifted the telephone receiver, "Angelo, what have you?"

"Ralph Richard Curry III, died of typhoid after an illness of two weeks. Positively verified. Cause attributed to polluted water and lack of adequate health care."

Obviously not murder. "What else, Angelo?"

"Son number two, by the second wife, also named Ralph Richard Curry but no numeral suffix, playing on a tricycle in a driveway and the mother ran over him with her car. Multiple trauma, crushed chest, death accidental."

"Okay, Angelo. What about Tony Meredith?"

"Drowned. Jurisdiction of the Cummings, Georgia police who investigated. Autopsy confirmed drowning. The boy fell in a lake. Due to the amount of insurance, an adjustor did a routine financial inquiry. Richard Curry had a business in Atlanta that was doing well. He paid $50,000 in taxes according to bank records. He was married to a prosperous widow, Ellen Meredith Curry, and she was the beneficiary, not him. The investigator determined that the sum received would not be considered great to people of such financial standing."

"Who bought the insurance, Angelo?"

"Curry never did."

"Who, then?"

"The first son was insured as part of company benefits by Curry's employer, Dawes Silica Mining, in south Georgia. Son number two: insurance purchased the year of birth by grandparents, making parents cobeneficiaries. As for the Meredith child, that claim was actually three policies. One, an endowment for future education automatically transferred to a sister, Blaise Meredith, and became a part of her estate when her brother died. It was put in trust. The second policy was paid from the family estate of a paternal grandmother, named Meredith of course, and the lady is pure gold, worth millions of dollars, old money."

"The third policy on Tony Meredith?"

"Part of a military policy bought by the boy's father, Arnold Anthony Meredith, lieutenant colonel, U.S. army career officer, killed in action in Vietnam."

"How much are we talking about?"

"The child, also named Arnold Anthony Meredith, was insured for a total of $500,000 with double indemnity payment included. I call it 'devil's indemnity' because it tempts people to do evil things."

"Thanks, Angelo."

"You know where to send my check?"

"I do. Thanks."

When he hung up, Kim found Gwen waiting for the verdict. "Typhoid killed the first son. The second son was run over by his mother while backing from her garage. If there's any murder involved, it isn't those two."

"And Tony?"

"If it weren't for the $50,000 taxes Curry paid, to make himself look affluent, I'd say that was accidental, too. But Richard wasn't faring as well as the insurance companies thought. To them, between Richard and Ellen, the sum of $500,000 didn't seem exorbitant enough to commit murder. They have it listed as drowning and an autopsy affirmed it."

"Mr. Jensen?" one of the girls again. "Mr. Joaquin is here from *Mobala News.*"

"Damn it," Kim sighed. "Okay. Send him into my office. I'll be there momentarily."

He turned back to the CRT. Blaise's translated text was there. The Devil hath power to assume a pleasing shape.

I AM TONY.

"Well, Gwendolyn," he flicked off the CRT. "Let's go see how deeply Mr. Joaquin intends to fry us."

Mother Meredith plopped into a chair, face flushed, arms hanging over the sides of the furniture. "Sweat is reputedly good for the complexion," she said. "Personally, I believe it tends to enlarge the pores. Where is Blaise?"

"Wandering around the grounds, I think."

"Coming here may be an adventure for her," Mother Meredith confessed, "but I regret it."

Ellen nodded, grimly.

"Everywhere I turn the past engulfs me," Mother Meredith said brusquely. "The whole Meredith male lineage, from daguerreotype images of great-grandfather Meredith to snapshots of Arnold, you and Tony."

"I know."

"I must speak to Mr. Manx, however," Mother Meredith assumed her managerial tone. "We've obviously had vandals. Did Blaise show you the torn photographs?"

Ellen wiped the kitchen bar, staying busy.

"One photograph was complete except the faces," Mother Meredith said. As if somebody had poked out the faces with a stick.

Bullet holes. Ellen had seen it, too.

"It was nice of the vandals to put them back into the frames again," Ellen suggested.

The ensuing lull was so heavy, she glanced at Mother Meredith. "What do you mean by that, Ellen?"

"The photos are behind glass, framed. Why would anybody mutilate a picture and return it to the frame?"

"I shouldn't dare to guess."

"We need certain items, Mother Meredith. Would you mind if I borrowed the car and drove to town for groceries?"

"I think we have plenty."

"We need bread."

"We'll bake some then."

"Mayonnaise, peanut butter, pickles. Those are Blaise's requests."

"That child consumes entirely too much junk, Ellen. Given a choice of a superb filet mignon in a first-rate New York restaurant, she insisted on french fried potatoes and a hamburger."

Ellen filled a sink with hot water, looking over the bar into the den at Mother Meredith. The woman was lost in thought, her head still swathed in a kitchen towel.

"It isn't likely a vandal would put the photographs back," Mother Meredith admitted. "And, so far as I have ascertained, that is the only damage in the building."

Ellen rinsed dishes, drying them, putting them back into the cupboard. *A box of oatmeal.* She took it down to inspect for weevils. None.

"I remember when we came here years ago," Mother Meredith reminisced. "The first day was always toil. The commodes would be rusty, stained by iron ore in the water. The men would flush out the pipes by leaving spigots open—"

Ellen looked into the sink. The water was clear.

"Ellen, dear, I've been trying to decide how to apologize for the inglorious faux pas of our situation."

"It's all right."

The woman stood and came to the bar. "It is obvious Blaise was caught up in fantasies about Tony's death."

"Things tend to the best, Mother Meredith."

"She presents quite a case, you know."

"Blaise does that."

"She asked me if I ever saw ghosts. *Real* ghosts, she said." Mother Meredith laughed mirthlessly. "I said, well, yes, I suppose I had seen a few specters in my time. Once when my husband and I had a touch too much ouzo in Athens, again when we overimbibed tequila in Acapulco. Those were younger days when we foolishly felt we had to present a democratic front by emulating the common man. Let me assure you, the reason peasants die young relates directly to the things they ingest. Ouzo. Tequila. There's nothing medicinal about plebeian alcohol."

Mother Meredith sighed, face pained. "I should've known Blaise was fantasizing, weaving her tales of sub rosa business undertakings, fraudulent taxes paid to create an impression of wealth, insurance—"

"I do understand, Mother Meredith."

"We left Mobile on what I presumed to be a lengthy vacation, a time to become closer, better friends. When we reached Atlanta, Blaise dragged out a spool of ruler—"

"A spool of ruler?"

"A reel with demarcations by the inch and foot," Mother Meredith explained. "She had us tramping through bramble measuring the distance from the cottage to the site where Tony drowned."

Ellen subdued a quiver.

"Blaise had me stand at that place while she went back to the cottage. Incidentally, it was occupied. Give Blaise high marks for bravado, I'll say that. She announced she needed to go inside and inside she went."

"What for?"

"So she could gauge how well she could hear me call."

Ellen closed her eyes a moment, quelling the tremble of stomach muscles.

"We had to go to Tennessee, Blaise said. To see some elderly man at a nursing home. I had steeled myself for the worst possible scene of deprivation, 'shuffling poverty' Arnold's father used to call it. There was none of it, thank goodness."

"I went there, too," Ellen precluded descriptions.

"The child had been preparing me psychologically from the instant we left Mobile, I see that now."

"Yes."

"Tiny remarks. Pieces of remarks, actually, a hint here, a clue there. Ellen, I thought I had come to the same terrible conclusions quite independently and I began to ask some pointed questions. That was precisely what Blaise desired."

"I'm sure."

"I lay awake all night long, Blaise tossing and turning in the next bed. By then I was positive Richard had fabricated his business in Atlanta merely to look good to you. I saw he had hidden much of his past. From the nursing home, we went to Ochlochnee chasing this Ralph person. We never did find him. Do you know who he is?"

"No."

"Exactly!" Mother Meredith said. "The conundrum spiraled and escalated and I came to the horrifying conclusion that Richard had—"

"Mother Meredith, please—"

"You see how I became enmeshed in it."

"I see."

"That pitiful woman, Betty Sue. Filthy children with phlegm on their faces, fingernails ragged, feet bare—"

"Please."

Mother Meredith shut her eyes tightly, opened them again, face contorted. "If you wish, I shall take the blame for all this when we sit down to explain to Richard."

"There's blame aplenty for everyone, including Richard. Let's not worry about that."

"And yet—" Mother Meredith walked away, speaking, "there are still things which don't—how does Blaise say it?—things that don't *compute.*"

"If I may borrow your car, Mother Meredith?"

"Oh, of course. But, Ellen, really, we can make do with what we have. You're too young to remember when women baked their own bread, concocted their own condiments. The pioneer spirit, Arnold's father used to call it. How the Meredith men treasured that quality."

"If we were here indefinitely," Ellen said, "I might yield. Or, if the Meredith men were here to boss us around, but I don't want to devote our hours to survival techniques."

"I can't argue with that." Mother Meredith produced keys to her Mercedes. "You know the way to town and back, don't you?

"Quite well. I'll be back in an hour and a half."

"Bring a dozen lemons, dear. I may try to make mayonnaise for the challenge of it."

Ellen went to the car, looking for Blaise. The child was probably exploring creeks and rills near the mountains. Out here, Ellen remembered, time became day and night, not hours and minutes. Solitary hiking would be good for her.

The valley was in the shadows of evening already. It would be dark within thirty minutes. Perhaps she should wait until tomorrow. No, she wanted to take the drive, be alone. She'd heard all of Mother Meredith's lamentations she could stand for the moment.

Ellen slammed the car door and turned the key.

Damn.

She tried the key again. *Nothing.*

A fine place to have a dead battery, or whatever. Ellen withdrew the keys, examined them. It was the proper one, but when she tried again, the motor did not turn.

All right, forget the shopping. Ellen got out, locked the vehicle and turned full circle. "Blaise!"

Her voice rippled away in echoes.

"Blaise!"

She heard the feral silence of creatures poised, unaccustomed to an alien sound. "Blaise!"

Her voice came back to mock her, *laise-aise-aise . . .*

Mother Meredith appeared at the door, "If you're going, Ellen, better hasten, it'll be dark soon."

"The car won't start."

"Dear, dear," Mother Meredith clucked. "Mechanical things always fail when needed most."

"Blaise!" Ellen shouted, *laise . . . aise . . . aise . . .*

Her voice bounced from land to sky, up the valley and home again.

"It looks like a storm brewing anyway," Mother Meredith put the best face on the moment. "Perhaps it's better to wait until tomorrow, Ellen."

"I have no choice, Mother Meredith."

"We will have Mr. Manx take care of it in the morning."

Irritated, Ellen went around the house to the back side. Sound here played odd games. A whisper could be heard a mile, but a shout up the same ravine was absorbed and unnoticed. "Blaise!"

"Here I am, mom."

Blaise stepped into view from the tack barn. Ellen saw a jagged twist of lightning, clouds pulsed within, but there was no roll of thunder. She walked toward the grinning girl. Blaise had donned a pair of dusty jodhpurs and she held a leather riding crop in one hand.

"How do I look?" she pivoted on one foot.

"Like a girl in need of a bath."

"There are drawers full of old-fashioned clothes in there, mom. Western blouses, boots, saddles and horse blankets. These fit me very well, don't you think?"

"They were mine."

"Really! How old were you?"

"Twenties, I guess. Come on, Blaise, it looks as if we're in for some stormy weather."

The first gentle rumble reached their ears, the next valley over catching the brunt of the front.

"I love it here, mom."

"We'll have to make do on supper," Ellen said. "The car won't start. No complaining, understand?"

"Mother Meredith said this place would be mine someday, mom. Is that true?"

"If she said so, I'm sure it's true. Hurry, Blaise."

"Let me get out of these clothes."

The sky flashed brilliantly and the landscape became a vivid reversal, like the negative of a photograph, whites became black, blacks became white.

"Whoo," Blaise shuddered. "That seemed awfully close."

"I said, hurry."

Blaise ran inside the tack barn and Ellen stood in the doorway, waiting. She heard a hiss of electricity and a fiery tongue licked a tree on a perimeter mountain. She smelled ozone.

Blaise came out, buttoning her blouse. She kicked shut the door and latched it.

Another hiss, like sticky adhesive being lifted from a surface. The sky went white and a crash of thunder shook the tack barn. The echo carried off the percussion and Blaise had taken several quick steps toward Ellen when it happened.

She stood transfixed.

"Blaise, lightning is nothing to dare. Hurry!"

"Did you see that, mom?" she asked softly.

Rain fell in massive drops, thunder rumbled.

Ellen grabbed her arm, prepared to run for the house. Another flash and Blaise said, "I thought I saw somebody."

T Chapter WENTY-FOUR

Armand Joaquin tossed an unsealed manila envelope on Kim's desk.

"What's this?"

"I always make it a practice to show a controversial article to the subject," the publisher said. "Anything you have to say will be printed as a rebuttal if you wish. Anything you want to contest, I'll discuss with you."

Kim shot a glance at Gwen and sat down. He pulled out typed pages. The headline: IS ANYONE SECURE?

"Catchy headline," Kim said.

"Catchy subject," Armand replied.

Kim read his own indictment. Kicked out of Cal Tech, freshman year, in trouble with the Marines, demoted from sergeant to corporal, again from corporal to private, time in the Saigon stockade. Joaquin had done his homework.

"Arrested on a charge of illegal trespass," he read aloud.

"That's what the bank said. They're quoted in there."

It covered Kim's parents, a biography of both, quoted mother, "Kim is a maverick, but we've never discouraged that."

"What did you think of my parents?" Kim smiled.

"Nice people. Your mother sold me an armoire."

Gwen took several pages, reading for herself as Kim continued. His grades from high school, including deportment. The financial status of his business.

"Your figures are off a few dollars."

"You may correct them, if you wish."

"Close enough." Kim shoved the remaining pages at Gwen, and troubled, she read slowly, eyes darting back and forth to re-examine certain passages.

"Any comment?" Joaquin invited.

"I think that about does it," Kim said.

"Is this an editorial or what?" Gwen demanded.

"I don't think it draws a conclusion, does it?" Armand observed.

"The damned headline is an editorial question," Gwen snapped. "It suggests the flavor, postulates a conclusion before the reader reaches the text."

"Then I will change it," Armand responded genially. "Anything else?"

"As I said," Kim lifted his hands, "that ought to do it."

"Do what?" Gwen railed.

"Ruin us. That's his purpose."

"Is there anything that you think is untrue?" Armand Joaquin lit a cigarette.

"All true," Kim said.

"Fine. Would you care to comment?"

"I don't think so."

"Then it will run in our Thursday edition, Jensen."

"Are you going to let him get away with this?" Gwen cried.

"The truth is difficult to counter, Gwen. The fact that it isn't the whole truth is a prerogative of the press. Right, Joaquin?"

"I have asked for a comment, that includes elaboration."

"I was arrested for illegal trespass because the bank in Pasadena was incensed by my youth. I was nineteen and I had penetrated their computers to prove it could be done. I did that at their invitation, but they tried to milk me for information without payment for services rendered. I took it to the newspaper. The bank had to do something to save grace so they swore out a warrant for illegal trespass. You could add a footnote if you wish. They settled out of court and paid *me* $10,000 to shut my mouth."

"I'll be happy to add that."

"Of the eight hundred people who had been apprehended for computer thefts at that point," Kim said, "most were caught by accident rather than design. Over $2 billion has been stolen by electronic data processing thieves during the past twenty years. That represents about fifteen percent of the total, because eighty-five percent of such crimes are never reported to police. Banks, like the one that charged me with illegal trespass, are very shy of publicity when they must admit they haven't protected their customers adequately."

"I'll make note of that," Armand trickled smoke toward the ceiling.

"Computer crime pays very well," Kim said. "While most American embezzlers take home $19,000, computer crimes net the average thief close to $500,000. It's safer than robbing people with a gun, less hazardous than mugging, and can be perpetrated with a minimal chance of prosecution. Most are never formally charged, to avoid unfavorable attention to the losing institution."

Gwen sat with the manuscript in her lap, reading it again.

"As for my high school deportment," Kim stated, "mother is right, I was a maverick. Restricted several times for skipping class or playing practical jokes on the faculty. I was expelled twice in my senior year. But I was also captain of the football team, a member of Phi Beta Kappa, and won first place in a statewide debating competition the same year. I was awarded a scholarship at Cal Tech—"

"Only to be thrown out in your freshman term," Armand interjected.

"That's true. I was one of twenty-six students who used the campus computer to print out 1.2 million McDonald contest entry blanks using a FORTRAN formula."

"What is that?"

"*FORTRAN is a type of computer program.* Anyway, since we held a third of the entries, we won a station wagon, a year of free groceries, about twenty pounds of $5 gift certificates and a great deal of publicity."

"They expelled you for that? What about the other twenty-five students?"

"They expelled *me*," Kim said, "because I penetrated the Strategic Air Command computers in Boulder, Colorado and the government had to revamp security to keep some student from shooting off atomic bombs as a class project."

"Where is Ellen?" Armand asked flatly.

"I told you, I don't know."

"What the hell is going on, Jensen?"

"I do not know, you sonofabitch," Kim said evenly. "But I'm not trying to harm Ellen Curry. I'm trying to help her."

"What were you doing in the attic of the Curry home?"

"Is this for your article, too?"

"It damned well may be, sport."

"I went looking for Ellen, saw the light in the attic and Herman's car parked in the driveway. The back door was broken. I went through the house turning on lights, calling out. I found Herman's body just as Richard Curry arrived. That's it, that's the truth, and that is everything I have to say."

"For what it's worth," Armand took back the article and stood up, "I don't believe that's all there is. I smell something rotten and I'm going to run this story as it reads."

"Would you consider waiting until you talk to Ellen?"

"If I could speak with her, yes. But her husband doesn't know where she is and you profess to know nothing."

"We're looking for her," Kim said. "Wait a week. What have you to lose in a week?"

The publisher met Gwen's distinctly antagonistic eyes. "I'll give you that," he said. "One week from Thursday. If I hear from Ellen by then, I'll reconsider."

Kim nodded, fingertips touching, elbows on his desk. "Show the gentleman the door, Gwen."

"Gladly."

Alone in his office, Kim gently massaged tired eyes. The newspaper article would impede, if not destroy what he'd managed to build here.

"Want some hard-boiled eggs?" Gwen called from the kitchen.

"No, thank you."

"Dratted shells stick to the eggs," he heard Gwen mutter. "Why do the hens make them this way?"

Curry hadn't returned. So that, probably, was the end of that. Unless he could think of a hook better than he'd been using.

"Want an egg salad sandwich?" Gwen offered, still in the kitchen.

"No, babe."

With the publicity about Herman plus that damning article written by Armand Joaquin, he'd better think of something, or plan to move all this expensive equipment to another city.

He dialed the Mobile office of the FBI. "John, this is Kim. I need a favor."

"Uh-huh."

"The Mobile police are investigating a homicide. Decedent was one Herman Krause."

"I read about it in the newspaper. What have you gotten yourself into?"

"The cops found a filet knife in a kitchen rack, bloody with prints of the assailant, they hope. I need to know whose prints. I need to know today."

"Why not order the White House delivered to your lot, Kim?"

"Tell them it's critical to something you are pursuing, John."

"Uh-huh, if I did this, it would have to be a trade."

"It will be. Call me in the morning."

"You jest, friend. There's no way I can get this by morning. The police may not have submitted the prints, yet."

"You can get it, John. It is *critical* to your needs."

John swore and hung up.

Gwen stood in the door, frowning. "What are you about to do, Kim?"

"Sell my soul to the FBI."

"For what?" she queried. "Curry didn't come back, Ellen Curry isn't going to put out and—"

"Hey!" he was on his feet, "let's say I'm doing it because of Blaise. Because I'm sick and goddamned tired of doing what's sensible. But I'm going to do it and that's that."

"I see."

"Gwen, I'm sorry."

"Don't apologize. Just answer a question for me. What are we, you and I?"

"What do you mean?"

"We're lovers, that's true," Gwen said conversationally. "We're friends as far as lovers can be. You're my boss, which is obvious, because you feel free to intimidate me."

"Babe, forgive me."

She held him off with a hand on his chest. "You allow me room and board, such as it is, I get to sleep in that atrocity you call a bed with all its leering statues staring down."

He laughed softly. She shoved him backward.

"When you need overtime labor I'm your partner," Gwen stated. "When you have the time and inclination, I'm your companion, your concubine."

"Ah, come on, Gwen."

"Don't touch me," she warned, "unless you want an egg salad facial. Let's see now, maybe this would be easier if we determine what I am not. I am not your wife. Except by common law statutes, but since Michelle Triola didn't fare well in court against Lee Marvin with her palimony suit, we live-ins have no court protection."

"Gwendolyn," he growled, "gimme kiss."

"I don't qualify for unemployment compensation, so I'm not salaried," she said. "Gee, I guess that settles it."

"Settles what?"

"What I am," she said. "A glorified educated whore."

"Gwen, damn it."

"Or, *stupid.*" She flung the sandwich at him and slammed the kitchen door.

"Gwen, baby, listen to me—"

"No, you listen to me! I want to know your intentions, Kimbrough, and I want them lucid."

"Okay, look, you want to be my partner? You certainly contribute your share around here."

"Bet your kilobyte I do."

"Consider it done," Kim said earnestly. "Fifty-fifty, you and me from now on."

"Is that it?"

"What else do you want? I'm giving you half interest in this building, $200,000 worth of equipment—"

"Not yet paid for."

"What is it with you!" he shouted. "You want me to drop the Curry thing? Right. To hell with it. I'll drop it."

They stood in the kitchen glaring at one another.

"Is that it?" Gwen asked, voice low.

"What else is there?"

She nodded, wheeled to walk out.

"Will you marry me, Gwen?"

She halted.

"Will you?"

"Yes."

Jesus. What had he done? She turned slowly, peering up at him with misty green orbs.

"On one condition," Kim hedged, "we see this thing through on Curry."

"Why?" Gwen shrieked.

"Because, if we don't, we aren't going to have anything, Gwendolyn. That newspaper article is going to finish us with most of our existing clients, and dry me up for potential in Mobile. I've gone too far to quit, now. If we don't get a contract from Curry, this business is over."

Gwen covered her eyes with the palm of a hand. "Kim, we won't get a contract, you know that."

The doorbell sounded. "That's got to be Curry," Kim said. "Answer the door."

"You have egg on your face," Gwen walked by briskly. "In more ways than one."

Water roared in downspouts, the shingled roof a drum for torrents falling from a coal-black sky. Lightning crackled, Ellen's hair seemed to rise at the nape of her neck as she prepared for bed.

. . . as long as the water falls . . .

There had been no discussion about who would sleep where. Mother Meredith assumed the master suite, Blaise was ushered into an adjoining bedroom to this one, and Ellen could hear the girl humming from a tub of hot water. She communicated by hollering through the open door which connected the two domiciles.

"I'll bet it's good sleeping here with all this rain on the roof!" Blaise called.

The remarks required no response. Ellen went into her own bathroom. Blaise had washed the tub, but a film of cleanser remained around the drain. Ellen got down on her knees to rinse it away.

"We ought to come up here more often, mom!"

. . . commodes rusty with iron ore . . .

She lifted the lid. The commode was clean. Toilet paper hung on the spindle. A monogrammed hand towel on the rack.

"If there *is* such a thing as ghosts," Blaise had said over supper, "this would be the place for them. The wind moaning, the rain falling, thunder crashing. Ouzo and tequila combined, right, Mother Meredith?"

"Electrical storms are not comforting," Mother Meredith said. "I had a great-aunt who was struck by lightning as she sat in a swing on her veranda."

"Did it kill her?"

"No, but it was a shocking experience."

Blaise let a finger fall toward Mother Meredith, and clicked her tongue. "That was good," Blaise said. "Not real good, but good enough."

"Levity in the face of a maelstrom," Mother Meredith had said. "You come by your liking of the elements from Arnold. If he'd had his way, he would be in the midst of all this, one fist lifted to challenge the fates."

Several times during the evening, Ellen had seen Blaise tense, staring down a dark hall, or looking out a window through sheets of water pouring from the eaves.

"You are going to spook yourself, Blaise," Ellen cautioned.

"I already have."

Up the mountain, they could see an occasional wink of light from the caretaker's cottage. Ellen had decided she would go up there first thing in the morning and use the telephone to call for a mechanic. She worried, stranded out here, what if one of them became ill, broke a leg?

"Is that you, mom?"

"I'm in my bathroom, Blaise."

"Mom? Is that you?"

"Blaise!" Ellen yelled, "I'm in the bathroom!"

"Mom!" Blaise shrieked.

An instant later, naked, the girl stood in the bathroom door, shivering.

"Blaise, I warned you about that ghost nonsense. Get a grip on yourself and calm down."

"I heard him whisper my name."

"Don't be ridiculous."

"He said, 'Bla-isssse,' in a low whispery moan."

"Blaise, will you stop it!"

"He said, 'I love you, Bla-isssse.' "

Ellen watched goose bumps erupt across the girl's shoulders, down her arms, across her thighs.

"May I sleep in here with you, mom?"

"If you stop the juvenile campfire talk."

"Let's lock the doors, all right?"

"Blaise, enough is enough."

But Ellen went to the adjoining door and latched it. Then to the hall door and turned the lock.

"I forgot my bathrobe," Blaise groaned.

"You may borrow one of mine. Good grief! You are beginning to affect me, too."

Blaise laughed nervously. "It was the wind, I guess."

"It was," Ellen declared gruffly. "Get in the bed. I'm going to take a bath."

"Leave the door open, will you?"

"Blaise, I've had enough of this."

"Please? Leave the door open at least part way."

Ellen submerged her body into warm water and heaved a sigh of relief. She ached in every joint, muscles protesting from days of sustained tension.

Call Richard, too. Tomorrow, when she went to the caretaker's cottage.

Rain was a muted tattoo, the high bathroom window flashing a brief announcement preceding each shuddering clap of thunder. Ellen watched blue light play upon the ceiling, warped by heavy leaded glass, distorted by rain twisting down the panes.

Dear God!

She sloshed water, scrambling for a towel to cover herself. She stared toward the window, waiting for another instant of illumination, waiting to see if she had seen—

"Mom?"

Ellen cried out as Blaise stuck her head through the door, "mom, are you all right?"

"I nearly slipped."

"Mom, were you reading this book?" Blaise held the volume that had been lying open on the bedside table.

"No."

"Who was reading it?"

"I don't know, Blaise. Would you please let me finish my bath?"

She bathed hurriedly, watching the window. Several short flashes came, but the storm was abating, rain easing.

A low moan rose in the ducts, ebbed away to silence, *Get hold of yourself!*

Ellen laved water over her body, shivering despite the warmth.

aaaaaaaaaaissssssseeeee . . .

"Blaise, are you in the bedroom?"

"Yes ma'am."

Ellen pulled the plug, letting water drain in throaty gurgles.

aaaaaaaaaaaisssssssseeeee . . .

"Blaise! What *are* you doing?"

"Looking at this book, mom."

Ellen stepped up on the commode to shut the vent. From the duct came a hollow exhalation, a pause as if taking a breath, another wheeze.

She closed it. Wrapping a towel around herself, she went into the bedroom and put on pajamas.

Blaise sat in the center of the bed, eyes wide, watching every movement.

"Blaise, I want you to stop acting so sophomoric. Is that understood?"

"Yes, mom."

"Have you ever sat around late at night with a group of children telling tales? It begins to work on your nerves despite what common sense tells you."

"I know."

"So wipe that expression off your face and turn out the light."

"May I ask one thing, first?"

"Ask in the dark and don't use the word 'ghost.' "

Blaise turned off the light and when Ellen got into bed, the child snuggled near, her breath rapid, warm on Ellen's neck.

"I love you, mom."

"Love you, Blaise."

"When are we going home?"

"I'll speak to Mother Meredith about it in the morning."

"Let's go home tomorrow."

"I'm willing. I'm sure Mother Meredith will agree."

"I want daddy to hold us for a long time, don't you?"

"Yes. Go to sleep."

The wind was dying. The rain subsided.

"If you're going to ask," Ellen ordered, "ask me now before I'm half asleep, Blaise."

"Ask what?"

"Whatever you wanted to ask a moment ago."

"About the book, who would have been reading it?"

Ellen thought to give the child a bit of the past here in the present. To give that sense of continuity which comes when the living touch that which the dead have touched. "Arnold may have been reading it the last time we were here," she suggested.

Blaise pulled covers over her head and pressed nearer.

"If not him, I don't know who," Ellen added.

She felt the child shiver.

"Blaise, I'm serious. You must cut this out!"

"I'm trying, mama."

But like paste to paper they lay there, Ellen plotting the degrees of Blaise's relaxation by wilting appendages, from feet to legs, hands to arms, Finally, Blaise turned aside, smacking her lips, and gave a sigh before slumber.

Ellen slipped out of bed, felt for her slippers in the dark and groped for the book Blaise had been examining. She went into the bathroom, shut the door, turned on the light.

She read the title, *Death Knell*. A marker held the reader's last page. She read a few lines.

Ellen closed it, grunting sardonically. The cover illustration suggested intrigue and suspense, typical of the novels Arnold used, to read himself sleepy at night.

Published by Putnam. She stared at the copyright. Two years after Arnold died . . .

T Chapter
WENTY-FIVE

Richard had changed clothes since this morning. Wearing an open neck shirt and sports jacket, he sat down and clasped his hands, waiting.

"Who is Ralph Curry?" Kim asked.

"None of your business, Jensen."

"You fly coach, stay in moderately priced hotels, eat and drink economically."

"Did you find Ellen or not?"

"You live unostentatiously," Kim pressed. "Your family home is modest."

"You didn't find her," Richard concluded.

"Ralph Curry costs you $60,000 a year," Kim tapped a print-out before him. "He spends more money on food and drink than you do on home and family."

Richard stood up, "Excuse me," he moved past Gwen toward the door.

"You've been where Ralph has been for the past several

weeks," Kim lifted his voice. "The police may raise some interesting questions."

Richard stood with his back to them.

"Ralph Curry flew from Mexico City to Miami," Kim deliberately lowered his tone, forcing close attention. "He rented an automobile in Miami and drove to Tallahassee. He ate his usual gourmet meal, drank a fine liqueur, and reposed in luxury accommodations. The next night, the night before Herman was killed, he was in Pensacola, an hour away."

Richard stood at the door, unmoving.

"See if anything else has come in on Ralph Curry, Gwen."

When she left the office, Kim said gently, "Sit down, Richard."

He watched the man sink into a chair.

"A computer is a tool," Kim observed. "A manufactured brain of sorts. It can do nothing but read num')ers. It can only identify a circuit that is open, or closed. A yes-and-no machine we call it. It adds and subtracts. It cannot multiply or divide. But because it can work at the speed of light it tabulates in fractions of a second. Instead of multiplying a six-digit number by a four-digit number, it adds until it reaches the same conclusion, instantly, it seems. Tiny impulses racing along thousands of miles of wiring. If it has been programmed properly, it can store millions of bits of yes and no, converting numbers into letters on a keyboard. Thereby it can 'talk' to us insofar as we've given it the answers. But never does it forget. It compares things. Your roast beef to Ralph's Peking duck. Your martini to his Dom Perignon champagne. Your second class accommodations compared to his sumptuous ones, always first class, crème de la crème."

He saw color drain from Richard's face, muscles drawn.

"Ralph showed up in your life in Atlanta, didn't he, Richard?"

Gwen placed a short printout on the desk and immediately left the room again.

"You gave him $5,000 cash for some reason," Kim elaborated. "Then you gave him your own name and identity. Your credit cards. Your past."

Richard was white, staring.

"You took his deposit of a million baht and put it in the business account, then wrote a check for American currency, to Ralph Curry. He had you by the jugular, didn't he?"

"Yes."

Gwen returned, sat against a far wall.

"Blackmail, Richard?"

"No."

"What then?"

Richard shook his head, silent.

"Blaise is a remarkable girl, you know. She put all this together using your old business files from Atlanta."

"Ohhh-h—"

Gwen was on her feet instantly, going to Curry. "Are you all right?"

"Get him a drink, babe."

Kim heard the tinkle of glass and bottle and Gwen brought the liquor, put a hand on Richard's shoulder as he drank.

"First I thought you'd murdered your sons for insurance, Richard."

Curry spilled liquor. "You sonofabitch," he seethed.

Kim's private telephone rang and he waited as Gwen answered. She murmured, "It's John Lawrence, Kim."

He took the receiver, "That was fast, John."

"The power of privilege, partner," John said.

"What did you learn?"

"You first, Kimbrough. If you were investigating Regalia boats, where would you look?"

Kim reeled off bank accounts, Nassau, Miami, Colombia. He dropped names of three principals he knew to be involved in laundering huge sums of illicit cash. When he finished, John said, "I didn't think you'd actually do it, Kim. I'm ashamed of myself. I hope this doesn't destroy our friendship."

"Tell me."

"There are no prints on the knife. The police are not publicizing that in hopes of keeping everybody shook up. Blood was the boy's. They do have hair from his hands, but they'll have to find a head to match it. I'm sorry."

"Okay."

"Is this matter anything we should know about, Kim?"

"No. And this trade was a onetime deal, John."

"If it's any comfort, the police don't suspect you or Curry of the murder."

"What about Mrs. Curry?"

"Does she have large hands?"

"No."

"They found a bloody palm print on the attic stairs, too big to be a woman. Sorry I duped you, pal. But we did need this stuff on Regalia."

"It doesn't matter, John."

After he disconnected, Kim rocked gently in his chair, looking at the stricken man. He decided to continue his bluff.

"Ralph could have been in Mobile the night Herman was murdered. Did you know that, Richard?"

"No."

"That was the FBI, checking out the prints." He paused for a reaction. Curry didn't bat an eye.

"They have no record of such prints. How would you explain that, Richard?"

An almost imperceptible tic in one cheek.

"Why would Ralph kill Herman, Richard?"

"You don't know that he did."

"When you and I reached the attic, the computer video had one sentence on it, 'I am Tony.' "

Richard's hand trembled as he accepted another drink from Gwen.

"I think Herman was trying to tell us something," Kim said.

Richard thrust the liquor glass at Gwen and made a move to rise. "Stay put, Curry," Kim growled. "I've told you I am not your foe. I've said we will help you, and we will."

"I've endured your insults, intrusions, insinuations—"

"This just came in on Ralph," Kim looked over the material Gwen had put before him. "Ralph had breakfast at the Governor's House hotel, turned in his rented car to Hertz, settled his account with his American Express card—"

"Where?"

"Montgomery."

Richard reached the door in two strides.

"He isn't there anymore," Gwen said. "He hired a private plane and pilot. I called a few minutes ago."

"Going where?" Richard rasped.

"Winchester, Virginia."

"Winchester?" Kim questioned. "Weren't they just in Winchester?"

"Yesterday."

"Who?" Richard demanded.

"Ellen, Blaise—Mrs. Meredith."

"My God almighty!"

"What business would they all have in that area?" Kim asked.

"It must have something to do with Mother Meredith," Richard quavered. "Let me use your telephone." He felt his pockets, withdrew a folded piece of paper. "I found this number on my desk—Mother Meredith's attorney. Hello, operator, this is an emergency—"

"Gwen, call the airport and see if you can charter a plane."

"It's late, Kim. There won't be anyone there."

"Call somebody at home, babe. Get a jet."

"I'm going with you."

"I need you here, on the phone, and monitoring computers."

"No answer," Richard hung up, stood there a moment, then lifted the receiver again. "Operator, I want to call the Meredith residence in Westchester, New York."

In the outer office, Gwen was on another telephone.

"Hello? This is Richard Curry, my wife Ellen is—yes, that's right—Mobile. I'm looking for my wife and daughter. It's an emergency."

Gwen whispered, "No jets."

"Any plane that flies, Gwen, the faster the better."

"I have reason to believe they are with Mrs. Meredith," Richard stated. "They are in or around Winchester, Virginia. Do you have any idea why they would be there?"

A moment later, Richard asked Kim, "Where is Front Royal?"

"Near Winchester, I think."

He saw Richard's knees bend slightly as he leaned against the desk.

"Get the airplane, damn it!" he railed at Gwen.

Kim pushed a chair toward Richard, touched his elbow, easing him down. Richard held the telephone as if in shock.

"Mother Meredith—family lodge—hunting preserve—twenty-five hundred acres—near Front Royal—God—oh, God, don't take them away from me—oh, God, please not again—"

"The fastest plane they have goes two hundred and twenty miles per hour, Kim," Gwen called from the telephone.

"Do you want a plane, Richard?"

"Yes."

"It costs $2,700," Gwen reported. "They can get you there in four and a half hours."

"Yes," Richard said.

"It'll be ready in thirty minutes, Kim," Gwen started upstairs.

"Where're you going, Gwen?"

"To pack your bag."

"No time!"

"You have to have clothes, Kimbrough. You can't go without brushing your teeth."

He yelled up the stairs. "Three minutes and we're gone, Gwen—three minutes!"

He returned to his office. Richard sat with shoulders rounded, head hung.

"Richard, who is Ralph?"

"I was trying to protect them."

"Who is he, Richard?"

"He got worse and worse—but this—Herman—"

"It's Arnold Meredith, isn't it?"

"Yes," Richard sobbed. "Arnold Meredith."

In the dark except for a sliver of light from the bathroom Ellen dressed hurriedly. She could hear Blaise slumbering, and once asleep, the girl was not easily aroused.

Ellen unlocked the door, felt along the hallway for a light switch and flipped it. The door to Mother Meredith's room was shut, the rain a lulling patter on the roof as Ellen walked the long corridor.

Something rattled in the kitchen and she paused, listening.

Mice? She illuminated the area, went to the bar and turned on those lights too. Imagination, perhaps.

She took a cue from Mother Meredith earlier in the day, using a dish towel to wrap her head. Then, out into the rain. She heard thunder echo from the front now departing, but behind her more pulses of electricity suggested another storm to follow.

For months after they buried Arnold, Ellen had dreams about opening a door to find him standing there. A ghastly mistake. A bureaucratic fumble. Later, visiting a psychologist, she learned that many war widows harbored secret wishes, or dreads, that their deceased husbands were alive somewhere.

Nobody had been to the lodge in the years since Arnold was killed. But the book on the bedside table was published two years later. So all right then, she was going to put this to rest immediately. Ellen pulled her jacket closer, the rain soaking through the makeshift bandana. To her rear the flash of lightning quickened, gained volume.

. . . saw daddy run away with trousers wet from knees down . . .

. . . why would anyone puncture the faces of a photo?

. . . thought I was crazy, mama . . .

Ellen stumbled in the dark, the lane muddy and slippery. She remembered the distance to the cottage as a fifteen minute walk. It seemed longer now. Mr. Manx would be sleeping.

She would telephone Richard in Aruba. Call Mobile, if he was there by now. *Come get us, please. Forgive us, please.*

She twisted her ankle on a stone and murmured a gentle oath, hurrying onward, the road ascending at last.

Breathless, at the crest, she turned to review her progress. The valley flashed under heavenly flickers, thunder rolled toward her from the lighted house below. Ellen rapped the door, the wind sweeping past, making slats of shutters hum and bang.

She knocked again, calling, "Mr. Manx! It's Ellen Curr—Ellen Meredith, Mr. Manx!"

She pressed near the heavy door, trying to hear. She felt around her feet for a rock and used it, the door reverberating with each blow.

"Ho there," the muted cry from within.

"It's Ellen Meredith, Mr. Manx!"

"Ho yes—"

She heard the clank of a bolt and the door opened to throw yellow light across her feet.

"Come in, come in!" The wind blew his nightgown between thin legs and his knees were like grapefruit in Christmas stockings.

"I'm sorry to disturb you, Mr. Manx. I'm Ellen Meredith."

"Ho yes."

"I couldn't get my car started."

"Shut the door, shut the door."

She bolted it, shivering, her raiment clinging to cold flesh. "Mr. Manx, may I use your telephone?"

He pointed his cane and she went to the instrument, dripping water across the floor.

"It's dead," she said.

"Storm does that," he pursed flaccid lips. She only now realized he was without dentures.

"No phone," Ellen said.

"Be up again tomorrow, maybe," Mr. Manx spoke too loudly, as if it were she who were elderly. "Come a wind like this one and down she goes."

"Mr. Manx—Arnold—have you seen Arnold?"

"Ho yes," he chuckled, the cane held a scant inch from the floor, tapping as muscles endured the spasms of age. "Good boy, Arnold," he said. "Changed, but that's what war does to you."

"You *have* seen him," Ellen whispered.

"Ho say what?"

Ellen raised her voice. "You saw him?"

"Ho yes indeed."

"When?"

"When when when," Mr. Manx squinted, cane pinned now, arm shaking. "Six, eight, ten hours ago, I guess. Is he all right?"

"Did he look all right?"

"Ugly mustache."

"He has a mustache?"

"White as snow. Like my hair. See my hair? Used to be a red-head but the heat drained out." He laughed at this, gums exposed. "All my children, red hair, too."

"Are you absolutely positive it was Arnold Meredith?"

"Ho hell yes! Knowed the boy since he was no taller than a buttercup. My drinking buddy, that's Arnold."

"He was here *today?*"

"Got here shortly before you did. Came in a cab."

"Mr. Manx—listen to me—Arnold may be ill."

"Ho no, healthy as a horse that one."

"In his mind," Ellen insisted. "He may be suffering from the war. Do you understand?"

"No, no," he shook his head, pale eyes mystified. "Comes here twice a year and we tie one on. He's all right."

"He seems all right," Ellen said emphatically. "But he isn't. He can't be. He's sick in his head, Mr. Manx."

She watched lips purse, relax, purse, relax. "If you say so, Mrs. Meredith."

"I want you to telephone the police."

"No phone. You tried it, didn't you?"

"I did. But will you try again and again until you get the police?"

"Arnold is my drinking buddy—"

"It's critical! Please—try over and over."

She moved for the door and he snatched a raincoat from a wall hook. "Better take this, little lady. Storm's a-brewing."

She threw it around her shoulders, stepped into a cutting breeze and halted.

In the valley below, the lights of the house went out, one wing at a time.

He was there. Ellen began to run.

The twin-engine plane threw back warm currents as Kim and Richard climbed inside. Navigational lights flashing, the pilot

279

closed the door, latched it. "We're headed for one hell of a front, guys."

"Bad weather?"

"May not get there," the pilot said. "A band of turbulence forty miles wide, running along the mountains going from south to north."

"Nevertheless," Richard said, "let's try."

"Makes no never mind to me," the pilot donned his earphones. "I flew through ack-ack in double-U-double-U-two so I don't get scared by any measly thing God has to throw at me."

The pilot pulled a curtain closed between himself and the passengers. Richard stared out a window as they taxied into takeoff position.

"Mind telling me what happened, Richard? How this got started?"

The engines reverberated and the pilot hollered, "Buckle up, boys, here we go!"

"Arnold found a charred body, rubbed his dog tags in the ashes, left Vietnam AWOL," Richard said. "He'd drawn money from his family account, sent it to Thailand. Caught a flight out. It was insane. Having trouble with Ellen, they were talking of divorce. He went off his head, he said. When he got here, a year later, he'd spent all his money, had no identification. I was dating Ellen in Atlanta and he got some perverse satisfaction from seeing her fall in love with me, marry me. Insane."

The city of Mobile fell away below them and the engines eased to cruising speed.

"If I would help him get his money from Thailand, he'd go away, Arnold said. He needed $5,000 until it came. To protect Ellen, I did it. He didn't love her. He detested his own son, Ellen told me. Tony was a wonderful boy."

Kim leaned nearer to hear the almost whispered words.

"I knew what it was to go through loss, to suffer like Ellen had suffered, I—I loved her—"

The drone of engines drowned all sound for a moment. Then Richard took a deep breath, continued.

"He thinks of nothing but himself. Milking me. Five thousand a month, he wanted. But it was never enough. He said, do it, or he'd go to Ellen."

"Then it was extortion?"

"Extortion of a kind. But as long as I had money, I would agree. The bastard. The *bastard*!"

"Is he a threat to Blaise and her mother?"

"Ellen, maybe." The man cupped his face with both hands, crying.

"Why the business sham in Atlanta, Richard?"

"I had to build a front. To do what I do now, I had to look solid. The banks loaned money and I borrowed, I never stole a cent—"

"I know that."

"Arnold said I had to share with him because he'd forfeited everything, the family fortune, his name, his wife and children."

The pilot struck his head around the curtain. "Either one of you fellows want a shot of hooch, it's in the rear compartment. Help yourself."

"Richard?"

"Not for me."

Patches of lights passed ten thousand feet below, man-made galaxies in a universe of black.

"Gwen will have rented a car for us by the time we get to Winchester," Kim said.

"Right."

"Get some rest. We're going to need it."

"Arnold had no way of knowing they'd be there," Richard said. "The state of his mind—he might stumble in on them, before he realizes. I've been chasing him since he got kicked out of a place near Nashville—he's erratic. He's volatile."

"I don't own a weapon, Richard."

"Neither do I."

A moment later, "We don't need a gun. I can reason with him. But by then, if they see him, the damage will be done."

The plane lunged, dived, engines racing.

"Buckle up back there," the pilot hollered. "They're sending up the ack-ack!"

Kim heard the man cackle as the craft dropped suddenly, bringing their stomachs into their throats. Morosely, Richard peered out at fiery gashes slashing through roiling clouds.

Caught in an updraft, the plane ascended, ascended, ascended, then dropped, plummeting so fast, Kim's ears popped.

"Shoot yer best, yer sons-a-beeches!" the pilot shouted.

"That's what I needed," Richard intoned. "A madman for a navigator."

They landed on a lighted concrete strip swept by rain and wind. The plane came in nearly sideways to compensate for crosswinds, then tires scorched and somehow the pilot wrestled them to a stop. Before Kim and Richard reached the terminal, they were wet to the flesh. Shoes squeaking, they hurried to the car rental agency.

"Vehicle for Kimbrough Jensen?"

"Yes. You have a message, too, Mr. Jensen. It's urgent."

He stepped into a booth and dialed his office number. The telephone rang once.

"Gwen?"

"Trouble, Kim."

"What?"

"Curry isn't rich."

"How can you know that since midnight?"

"I've been calling banks. Tokyo, Hong Kong, Taiwan—those bank accounts with millions of dollars."

"No such accounts?"

"The accounts are there, the money isn't. He shifts it around, uses it to pay local merchants."

Kim saw Curry pacing, clothes rumpled, watching the clock, waiting.

"The warehouse in Aruba is leased," Gwen said. "He still has a mortgage on his home. He paid cash for automobiles and household goods, but little else."

"Damn."

"He's doing it again," Gwen warned. "The same thing he did in Atlanta."

"But, why?"

"Has it occurred to you that Richard Curry hired this Ralph person?"

"To do what?"

"To do," Gwen said, "whatever Ralph is about to do . . ."

T Chapter
TWENTY-SIX

Her path punctuated by jabs of lightning, Ellen ran, stumbled, fell, arose to run again. Her legs felt leaden, her feet sheathed in concrete, her sides aching. *What good will I be exhausted?* she asked herself, but still, she ran.

Would Arnold be dangerous? Vicious? She had always had the capacity to argue and tease him out of a bad mood. Would he hurt her? Blaise, never. She was sure of that.

Then anger was a white hot emotion and she cursed him for this and all other ordeals he'd perpetrated. For hiding, allowing her life to become impossibly complex. Was she married to Richard now, with Arnold alive?

Was he alive?

Wait a minute—wait a minute! The telephone could be out because of the storm, so too the electricity in the house. Blaise had infected her with phantoms and scaremongering. Ellen's lungs seared with each inhalation, her knees buckled, and she arrived at the lodge, railing, trembling, hot flashes making her skin prickle, sweating despite the chilling rain.

She felt her way along the hall, trying each light switch. Her breath was gasping evidence of her presence. When she reached her bedroom door, she clamped her jaws to silence the sounds she made. She groped ahead, arms outstretched, heart hammering. She bumped the foot of the bed with a knee and circled to the side where she'd left Blaise sleeping. *There.* Ellen felt a hip, the girl's shoulder. She stilled her hand, waiting for movement. Breathing. Asleep. She debated waking her, but for what reason? Add to the child's fears needlessly? What could Blaise do? If—she forced herself to think it—if Arnold were here, what scene would transpire? Mother Meredith would first be shocked, then furious, and finally hurt that Arnold had let her grieve while he hid away.

Ellen paced her steps to the door, found it, and entered the hall again. She held her breath, but a pulse drummed in her ears and she heard nothing. Mother Meredith hated locked doors—she would wake her, tell her all of this—accept the inevitable chiding, welcome the rebuttal.

Locked.

Ellen put her head to the door, straining to hear. Sounds. Like water. Rain, of course. Or was it? She turned the knob again and pushed, but it was locked, not stuck.

She thought of calling out. But behind the door, inaccessible, suppose someone lurked, also listening?

She slid her hand along the wall, hurrying as fast as the dark would allow, bumping a small table in passing. She stepped to the bar and followed it, then to the rear door and surprised, found it unlocked. She had locked it before retiring. Locked and checked it—it had been locked!

She went out into sheets of rain, stinging her face like driven sand. Shrubs gone wild lashed at her face as she shoved through to the leaded glass window of Mother Meredith's room. If necessary, she would break a pane.

She stood there, her shadow a stark silhouette against the building with each successive strike of lightning. She could hear the roar of high water afar, the machine-gun pelt of falling rain on the tack loft, the swirl from the eaves forming a curtain between her and the window.

A gun. She needed a gun.

Would she shoot? Actually shoot? Certainly not in the dark at an object unseen. Certainly not until she was absolutely positive she was threatened.

By then—

She remembered the racks of shotguns, the rifles over the mantel. "Always loaded," Arnold once told her. "Never assume they are not loaded—they are always loaded."

Which meant, if she faced a criminal, he could have one of those weapons, too.

Damn fool! This is all imagination. Gibberish and ghost stories!

She penetrated the cascade of falling water and stood under a broad eave, drenched. Ellen felt for a toehold, found it, and pulled herself up to the window. She yanked hard, expecting resistance. The window opened easily, nearly throwing her backward.

She blinked her eyes free of water, clambered inside and on her knees paused to assess the room with diminished vision.

A flash of lightning gave a stroboscopic glimpse—Mother Meredith, sleeping, as always wearing a black nightshade, her ears plugged to insure total silence.

Ellen crawled away from the window to avoid backlighting. Another flicker, then another. The bathroom door was shut.

She heard water. Not rain. Not the eaves. Ellen reached over and pulled the window closed.

Water. Behind the bathroom door. The rush from a spigot into the tub, the churning noise of a bath being drawn.

"Mother Meredith," Ellen spoke into her ear. "Mother Meredith," Ellen shook her gently.

The woman sat straight up with a squeak and Ellen felt her snatching at the earplugs.

"Be quiet," Ellen whispered. "There's someone in the house."

"Are you sure?" Mother Meredith asked aloud.

"Shhh—" Ellen pulled her from the bed and holding Mother Meredith's arm, led the way to the hall door. She turned the key, opened it, the rush of water in the bathroom louder as they stood here.

"Shhh," Ellen cautioned again, and she urged Mother Meredith into the corridor.

Ellen probed for the exterior keyhold to lock the door. She heard a grate of plumbing fixtures, a turning faucet, and water stopped flowing.

Now she knew. Without doubt.

Someone was in there.

Sitting in the telephone booth, Kim saw Richard Curry pull back a sleeve, examining his watch. Nervous. Pacing the floor like a caged animal.

Kim took a small address book from his shirt pocket and thumbed through it. He put the long distance call on his credit card.

"Angelo?"

"Yeah."

"Sorry to wake you, Angelo. This is Kim Jensen. Emergency."

"What time is it?"

"Angelo, you remember the data you got on the Meredith boy?"

"Yeah."

"The sister, Blaise Meredith, was she insured?"

"Same kind of policies, I think."

"Half a million with double indemnity."

"Think so, Kim. What time is it?"

"One more question, Angelo. Is death by murder covered by double indemnity?"

"If the beneficiary didn't bring it about, yeah. Kim, where are you?"

"Is Ellen Curry insured?" He saw Richard coming, angry.

"I don't know, Kim. Damn it, call me at the office, later."

He hung up as Richard rapped the phone both.

"What's holding you up?" Richard demanded.

"Making sure they haven't gone somewhere else, Richard. A few more minutes."

"I can't wait."

"Better we go prepared, right? Do you know where this place is?"

"No."

"Call the police in Front Royal and ask for directions."

Richard muttered a vulgarity, patted wrinkled trousers seeking change. Kim gave him a dime.

When Richard went into another booth, Kim called his office again. Gwen caught it instantly.

"Listen to me closely, babe. Ralph Curry is really Ellen Curry's former husband, Arnold Meredith. Got that?"

"Got it."

"Extortion at the least, interstate laws violated since it was via mail, telephone, and international travel."

"Okay."

"Call John Lawrence and tell him. Have him check Arnold Meredith's military files. Tell him we're going to the Meredith hunting preserve near Front Royal, Virginia and I don't know what I'm walking into."

"Get out of there, damn you!"

"I can't babe. Too late to quit."

"Get a pistol, then."

"Where?"

"Get something, Kim, or don't go. You hear me?"

"I'll try. You get John busy. Tell him we think Arnold Meredith may be at this hunting preserve. Have him send the cavalry and don't spare the bugles."

"I mean it," Gwen shrilled, "you stay out of there!"

"I love you, babe."

"If you get killed, Kimbrough, I'll pour vinegar on your grave. The grass will never grow."

"Do as I ask," Kim replied, steadily. "Oh, and call the state police, the Front Royal police—the Marines, if you can do it."

"I will."

"Good girl. Gimme sugar."

She hung up.

Kim tapped the glass partition, "I left something in the airplane. Be back in a second."

"These people aren't going to help," Richard snapped.

"Call the fire department," Kim suggested. "Call the ambulance service. Wake up the county agricultural extension officer."

He turned up his collar, running into rain. He saw the airplane being refueled.

"You have a gun?" Kim questioned the pilot.

The man's hair was plastered to his face. He turned and spit. "Got a sawed-off 10 gauge loaded with double-ought. It'll take down a small tree at ten feet. Got a .357-caliber Magnum that'll core a canteloupe like a fist. Got a police special chrome-plated snub-nose .38-caliber which shoots true. Got a pump action Daisy BB rifle. Got a—"

"You have all that with you?"

"Yep. I switch around. Depends on what's chasing me as to what I use. If it's a sparrow, I use the BB rifle. If it's a narc, I use something else."

"Will you sell me a pistol?"

"No. But I'll rent you one. If you don't kill anybody with it, bring it back and you owe me fifty dollars and a case of hooch. If you get it hot, just throw it away and the price will be considerable."

Kim took the .38, tucked it in his shirt under his belt.

"Watch the quick draw," the pilot advised. "It has a hair trigger and you could go to soprano."

"Thanks."

Richard was waiting, overtly infuriated. "Damn it, Jensen. Let's go!"

Kim drove, headlight beams truncated by a torrent of rain, wind buffeting the vehicle, wipers frantically sweeping aside precipitation only to leave him blind a second late.

"Richard, what is your net worth?"

"You may have a contract, Jensen," Richard said, flatly.

"Your net worth, Richard?"

"I have no idea and this is not the time to discuss business. Watch for the Limeton Road. The dispatcher at the cab company said it was four miles down the Limeton Road."

"I need an answer, Richard. Your net worth?"

"I don't know."

"Ball park guess then. One, two, thirty million?"

Richard looked at him out of the side of his eye, "A lot closer to one than thirty, I'll assure you."

"You aren't rich, are you?"

"Who suggested I was?"

"Your computer."

Richard shook his head. "Serves you right," he said softly.

"Why the scam again? Building a front for banks as you did in Atlanta?"

"In Atlanta I was building a front to gain credit. I needed access to large sums of cash. But as the business evolved and I saw how people buy certain items for the pleasure of having paid exorbitant prices for it, I needed a front all right, but not for the banks. In my business, Jensen, the clients are criminals. They are buying counterfeit goods to sell illegally. Criminals can't be trusted. It's cash only, no credit. The only way to assure payment is with power. To people like that, the only power is money. They have to think I have politicians paid for, police bribed, a phalanx of attorneys ready to defend me. They have to believe I have the power to retaliate if they cross me. That's why the net worth is shown so high."

"No $32 million, then?"

"If I had $32 million," Richard stated, "I wouldn't be having trouble with Arnold. This all started when I couldn't send him his monthly $5,000. He called from Tennessee raising hell, threatening to come to Mobile for his money."

"You're broke?"

"I can meet my payrolls, pay for incoming merchandise, carry the business until we receive payments, but I am not worth $32 million. I've learned there is no such thing as enough money. A man might as well enjoy what he has."

Water flew from the sides of the car, tires sucking at puddles, gusts of wind making Kim keep a firm hold on the steering wheel.

"Stock wouldn't be worth much," Richard said, as if to himself. "Until it's put together, it's only bits and pieces of little value."

A Virginia State Police car passed, going in the opposite direction, driving slowly, a spotlight slicing the night off to one side of the highway.

"I should've killed him," Richard said. "I thought about it. Wanted to. But I couldn't. I should've. But I couldn't do it."

Kim saw the police car turn around behind him. Richard saw it too, in a sideview mirror. "What do you suppose they're after?" Richard remarked.

They topped a hill and the lights behind them disappeared. *Same as us, I hope.*

"There it is," Richard said. "Limeton Road."

Her fingers shook and Ellen fumbled the key and dropped it. She pushed Mother Meredith across the hall into the bedroom where Blaise was sleeping, and bolted the door from within.

"Where are the lights?" Mother Meredith complained, flicking a switch.

"Electricity is off. Listen to me, Mother Meredith. I have some astounding news."

"Mom?" Blaise called in the dark.

"It's all right, Blaise."

"What happened to the lights?" Blaise pulled a chain on the lamp.

"The lights are off, Blaise. Mother Meredith—" Ellen fought to control her tone, seeking words to say this. "Mother Meredith, I think Arnold is alive."

"I knew it!" Blaise shrieked.

"There was a novel on the bedside stand, Mother Meredith," Ellen held the woman's shoulders. "It was being read. The kind of book Arnold kept to read himself to sleep. It was printed two years after Arnold was supposed to have been killed."

"I saw him, mama!" Blaise cried, "—white hair and a mustache—"

"That's how Mr. Manx described him, too," Ellen related. "Mr. Manx said Arnold arrived here shortly before we did."

"Oh, mama," Blaise wailed, "I saw him! At bus stops, outside school, sometimes in a crowd, watching me. Then months would go by and I wouldn't see him. I knew it was him."

"All Arnold's favorite liquors, some of the bottles nearly empty," Ellen persisted. "His brush with white hair in it."

"Sometimes he didn't have the mustache," Blaise spoke from the bed. "Sometimes he dyed his hair. I would find him standing there, looking at me and when our eyes met, he'd disappear."

She felt Mother Meredith shivering.

"But I think he's ill, Mother Meredith. He and I were having marital problems, we had discussed a divorce."

"Ellen—"

"He so disliked Tony, Mother Meredith. Jealousy. You know how Arnold is, he doesn't want to share attention."

"Ellen, please," Mother Meredith pleaded.

"I knew that," Blaise's tone was utterly flat.

"I think it may have been Arnold who punctured the photographs of Tony and me," Ellen rushed. "I think he tore the image of us away from Blaise."

"I knew that," Blaise said in a monotone. "Crazy, I said. Crazy."

"He isn't the man we remember, Mother Meredith. He may need help. Psychiatric help."

"Ellen, Ellen—"

"We dare not rush out to him now," Ellen cautioned. "We dare not be unaware of what he is today. Would he hide his life and let us suffer grief, if he were well?"

"Mom, he killed Tony."

"Shush, Blaise."

"Ellen, please, stop, listen—"

"Mom, he did! I saw him run away. His trousers were wet from the knees down, his sleeves were wet from the elbows—"

"Blaise! You have imagined that."

"No. I swear it, mama. I saw daddy run away. He ran out of the woods and his cuffs got dusty because the road wasn't paved and—"

Ellen thrashed the dark to find her, to silence her.

"Ellen, Blaise," Mother Meredith choked. "Stop it!"

Something fell somewhere in the house. Ellen halted, as did Mother Meredith and Blaise, stock-still, listening.

"He was in your bathroom," Ellen stated. "He was running water in the tub."

292

"Ellen, dear, why would he do that?"

"To drown you!" Blaise said in tremolo. "To make it look like an accident, just as he did with Tony."

"Rubbish!"

Ellen felt the woman move and she grappled for an arm, held her. "You must not go out there, Mother Meredith."

"There are guns all over the house," Mother Meredith snapped. "I was once a fair shot for squab and I'm a fair shot for intruders, too."

"No," Ellen insisted. "I'm trying to tell you, this is not the Arnold we know."

" 'Tisn't Arnold at all, Ellen!"

"Did you hear the water running in your tub?" Ellen reasoned. "Did you hear the faucet being cut off?"

"Things are creaky in this old place—"

"He was running the tub," Ellen said forcefully. "He was in the bathroom. He had locked your door—did you lock your bedroom door?"

"No, but—"

"He was in there, with you, door locked, running a tub of water."

"He would've killed you, Mother Meredith," Blaise gasped. "Hit you in the head and drowned you. I did see him run away the day Tony drowned, I saw him run—"

"Nonsense!" Mother Meredith rebuked.

"Then how do you explain it?" Ellen demanded.

"A squatter may be on the premises," Mother Meredith rationalized. "Nobody has been here for years. Mr. Manx is not as agile as once he was, he may not have seen the man."

"His daughter comes here to clean, you said."

"One can spy a vehicle far enough to be warned to flee," Mother Meredith stated.

"You cannot go out there with him."

"We cannot stay in here, Ellen. Do you think barricading the door will keep out an intruder? The windows—"

Lightning flashed and they saw the head and shoulder silhouette of—

Blaise screamed.

"Get away from here," Mother Meredith said in stentorian tones.

With the next flash, he was gone. Blaise wept with terror.

"This has gone entirely too far," Mother Meredith dictated. "Listen to me, both of you. Arnold is dead. We buried him in Arlington National Cemetery."

"He's alive, Mother Meredith!" Blaise sobbed. "I've seen him."

"You've seen his photograph and he would not be the same today as then," Mother Meredith insisted.

"He watched me! I saw him run away from Tony—"

"Child!" Mother Meredith barked, "Your father is *dead.*"

"We don't know that," Ellen said shakily. "We buried a closed coffin. We took the military statement and personal effects."

"Arnold is dead," Mother Meredith enunciated. "Do you think I would take anyone's word that I was burying my only son? Do you believe for an instant that I would accept a charred body as my flesh and blood?"

"What else could you do?" Ellen cried. "They send a box and say he's ours!"

"And he was," Mother Meredith said. "I did not wish to burden you, Ellen, but I knew things—"

"Oh, God—"

"Blaise, if there were any way to say this," Mother Meredith agonized. "If you could go into the bathroom a few moments while I talk to your mother."

"No!" Blaise shrilled. "Tell us both!"

"Ellen," Mother Meredith's cold hand clasped Ellen's forearm. "Arnold was not a strong man, you knew that."

"Mother Meredith, he's out there."

"He couldn't compete, Ellen, dear. He couldn't compete with his father and so Arnold joined the military. He couldn't compete with Tony—"

Ellen sobbed and Mother Meredith squeezed her arm.

"He shot himself, Ellen. He was not a casualty of war. Family friends helped create the story because of—because of practical considerations. Benefits to Blaise and you. Widow's benefits and other purely financial considerations."

"He was burned, Mother Meredith."

"They think he set the building afire before he did it, Ellen, but he shot himself. The wound was self-inflicted. The—the—the instrument was at the side of his body. The best forensic men in New York examined him. I didn't want to put you through that. I ordered it done."

"They were wrong. Somehow wrong."

"No, they were not wrong. Arnold's teeth were perfect because of many dental efforts. We had absolute proof with dental charts dating from childhood. He broke his ankle riding a stallion out behind this building when he was eleven. They made x-rays. The break was there. It was Arnold."

"Then who—who is out there?"

"Squatter, prowler, burglar," Mother Meredith recited. "It could be anybody, but it is *not* Arnold."

T Chapter
TWENTY-SEVEN

Linked by touch in the dark, they sat on the bed, listening, waiting.

"Daylight can't be far away," Mother Meredith observed. "When it comes, we're going out to confront this person."

"I could climb out a window and run to Mr. Manx," Blaise suggested.

"What could he possibly do?"

"Call the police!"

"The telephone is dead," Ellen reported. "I went up there before I woke Mother Meredith."

Mother Meredith fingered Ellen's clothing, "You'll have your death of consumption, Ellen. Change into something dry."

"Why hasn't he broken in yet?" Blaise quavered. "What's he waiting for?"

"We are three to his one," Mother Meredith said.

"He isn't afraid of us! We don't have a gun, we aren't as strong as he is—"

"He doesn't know that," Mother Meredith replied sharply. "Let's not advise him, either."

"He was in your room," Ellen said, voice low. "I think Blaise guessed right. He meant to do you harm."

"Ellen, I will not participate in wild extrapolations. It is not logical that he would have a grievance against me. He has us where he wants us, bottled up in this cubicle while he ransacks the house at his leisure."

"No," Ellen said. "I don't think so. He's been here before, drinking, eating, reading. He was probably here when we arrived."

"I say again, stop the nonsense about Arnold."

"If he had only been trying to herd us together," Ellen said, "why would he run a tub of water with your bathroom door closed? Blaise is right, he was about to hurt you."

"*Kill* you," Blaise insisted.

"Why?" the grandmother queried calmly.

"I left the house," Ellen said, "he must have seen me go. He had ample opportunity to attack Blaise, the door was open, I was gone. So Blaise is right, he wanted it to appear an accident. As if you'd fallen and drowned in the tub."

"Absurd, Ellen."

"Then why would he do that?" Ellen murmured.

"Why indeed?"

"Mom—" Blaise's voice quavered softly, "mom, he wanted to make me rich. So all Mother Meredith's money would come to me. So this place would be mine."

"Of all the nonsense I ever heard," Mother Meredith said.

"He knew my name," Blaise whispered. "He called my name through the ducts. You heard him, didn't you, mom?"

"I think so."

"For what bizarre purpose?" Mother Meredith scoffed.

"How did he know my name?" Blaise insisted. "If it isn't daddy, why has he been places where I've been? Watching, disappearing—coming back to watch again?"

"It is not Arnold!" Mother Meredith said angrily.

"All right," Ellen reasoned, "let's assume it isn't Arnold."

"It *isn't*."

"Assume it isn't," Ellen persisted. "Then who is it? More importantly, what is his purpose here?"

"How could he know we would be here?" Mother Meredith argued. "We came upon the scene unexpectedly and surprised an intruder. He's now attempting to frighten us away. Some sort of psychotic, perhaps. Harmless, but possessive of this place."

"He did know Blaise's name," Ellen said. "He watched me leave without trying to get to me. If it were Arnold, I think he would've made his move right then—against me, or against Blaise. But he didn't. He went for you, Mother Meredith."

"Rubbish garbage nonsense!"

"To make me rich," Blaise said.

"Who—" Ellen felt her abdomen wrench. "Who would do that?"

"The same person who killed Tony, mom."

"Who would benefit from such a horrible—"

"Mom, it was daddy. He killed Tony for insurance. That's what I thought, at first. That's what I thought until I found out about *this* man!"

The lights came on and they blinked at one another.

The lights went out.

"He's still here," Blaise stated.

"The power company is working on fallen lines," Ellen said hopefully.

"No," Mother Meredith advised. "He's at the fuse box. I can see the caretaker's cottage lights. We derive our power from the same source. If there's trouble with the lines it would be between here and the cottage. He's manipulating the fuses."

Ellen's mouth was acid, tongue foul. She could smell their fear, a musky scent like the burrow of an animal. She heard things afar, the clink of a displaced pot in the kitchen, the scrape of a chair on flooring. Blaise's breathing was amplified as if through a microphone. Ellen thought she heard the whine of an engine, the squeal of tires, despite the dripping eaves and roll of thunder as the storm passed away. She went to the window, watching the mountain.

But who would it be?

He had cut the telephone lines. She was positive of it now. Mr. Manx could have called no one, she was sure.

Who would come here?

Who would know to come, except someone who knew the intruder?

Richard.

Ellen clasped her arms across her stomach, nauseated. Who would benefit from Tony's death?

Richard.

Who would profit from the murder of Mother Meredith?

Ellen retched and Blaise came to hold her. "I'm sorry, mom," the child wept. "I'm so sorry."

"The bastard!" Mother Meredith cried. "The unholy bastard!"

"Why didn't you tell me, Blaise?" Ellen asked, weakly.

"Mom, I couldn't. I wasn't positive. I couldn't!"

Ellen went into the bathroom, knelt at the commode and swept back her hair to vomit. Blaise stood behind her, a hand on Ellen's forehead, "I'm sorry, mama."

"Give me a wet washcloth, Blaise."

"There's no water."

"He turned off the pump," Mother Meredith noted.

They returned to the bedroom and Ellen gasped, sickly.

"Mom, look!"

Twin beams cut an arc in the sky at the top of the mountain. From the depths of the building came a masculine invective and Mother Meredith erupted, "He sees it too!"

They had found the lane at last, marked by stone columns overgrown with vines. Kim drove up a winding route through a valley. Fallen limbs dislodged by wind had littered the narrow passage and several times they had to drag away debris. A river roared beside the roadway. They rounded a sharp curve and the headlights exposed a shimmering waterfall, deafening in volume, flooding the pavement with overflow.

Richard waded ahead, feeling for macadam, gesturing for Kim to follow. Then they drove up a steep snaking incline, the road twisting ever higher.

As they gained the crest, Kim said, "What the hell is that?"

In the glare of the car lights, an old man in a flowing nightgown was shoving iron gates closed. His snow white hair askew, he tottered out of view a moment and returned with a shotgun cradled in his arms.

"He must be a watchman," Richard said. "I'll speak to him."

The windshield wipers squeaked back and forth as huge drops blew down from overhanging trees. Kim cut off the motor as Richard got out. He rolled down his window to hear.

"The reason they built the cottage here," the old man shouted, "was so I can hear a car coming four miles away."

"My name is Richard Curry."

"Turn around and get gone, Mr. Curry."

"Is Mrs. Meredith here?"

"She is."

"Blaise and Ellen are with her?"

"They are."

"I'm Ellen's husband. Blaise is my daughter. I need to get in."

"Ho no you don't," the old man shifted his weapon ominously, his legs spraddled, spindles in a sheet, the wind forcing the wet garment against his frame. "Turn around and go away," he hollered.

"Could you call them and verify who I am?" Richard asked.

"Phone is dead as you damned well know. You cut the lines. When I found that, I knew you'd be making your move."

"No sir, we didn't do that," Richard said. "But they may have been cut—"

"Go away, mister, or you're going to take a load of shot with you."

"It may be critical that we see Mrs. Meredith."

Kim slipped out the door Richard had left open. Hidden by the blinding lights in the watchman's face, he pushed through wet underbrush, circling the barrier and the cottage. As he rounded a corner, the old man was leveling his gun. "I'll blow that contraption to smithereens," he warned. "Turn about and be gone."

"Ellen is my wife and—"

"That done it," the old man yelped. He cocked hammers of the double-barrel shotgun and lifted it.

Kim shoved the shotgun up, twisted it from his hands and pinned frail arms. "Easy old-timer. We didn't come to do harm. We're friends."

"Claiming kin? Lying thieves! Cut my phone, come to plunder. I'm not alone, ho no!"

"We didn't cut the lines," Kim said. "We came to help Ellen and Blaise. You say they're here?"

"They're here."

Kim released him, but kept the gun. "And Mrs. Meredith?"

Richard was swinging open the creaking gate. "Get out of the way," he yelled.

"Who else is here?" Kim pulled the man aside so Richard could pass with the car.

Disarmed but not defeated, the old man warned, "The lodge is a fortress, I can tell you. Ho yes. Guns wall-to-wall and all loaded. You'll never get in."

"Arnold Meredith is here," Kim provided.

"And a crack shot he is. So's his mother."

The tires scratched gravel, the vehicle slipping as Richard accelerated. Kim turned to get in, deciding to take the old man with them, but Richard kept going.

He watched the taillights zigzag, the vehicle sliding. Only now did he discern the unlighted lodge in the valley below.

If he shut the gate, help could not come. If he left it ajar, Arnold might escape.

"Is there any other way out of here?" he questioned.

"Ho! You got to come out the same way you went in and I'll be waiting for you."

"He'll probably hike out a back way," Kim pondered aloud.

"River up, creeks running. You'll never make it."

"Do they have a four-wheel drive vehicle?"

"The fen is soggy," the old man delcared confidently. "Best tie me up or shoot me. You won't get away."

Kim saw the car halt, midway there, then heard the spin of tires as Richard gunned the motor seeking traction.

"Stuck," the old man snickered, smugly.

"If the police come," Kim ordered, "send them down."

"Phone is out as well you know!"

"We called the police!" Kim began to run. "Send them down." He threw the shotgun aside.

Richard regained firm ground and drove on. Kim paced himself for endurance, thankful for the hours spent on handball courts with John Lawrence. He was a clear target out in the open like this. He glanced back to gauge the light, but there was still no sign of day beyond the thick black clouds.

He saw the car halt, headlights on the door and a huge bay window. Richard ran inside. The first pang of muscle fatigue shot through Kim's sides. He slowed his pace, positioning himself so the headlights gave him advantage, the glare shielding him from a sniper.

"It's all over," Kim heard Richard say.

"You dumb freak!" a masculine reply. "We could've had a fortune if you'd stayed away."

"They know, Arnold."

Kim approached the lodge at an oblique angle to the door. His back against the building, he drew the pistol.

"How did you know I was here?" the man asked, suspiciously.

"We'll go back to the Islands, Arnold. It was nice there, wasn't it?"

"You stupid sonofabitch!" the man screamed. "Don't you see what you've done? Now I have to—"

Kim peeked through the window. In sharply defined rays of light he saw Richard's back, the white-haired man holding him with a shotgun.

"You shouldn't have gone to Mobile, Arnold."

"Curry, you're so dumb it's exhausting."

"You killed that boy—why?"

"He knew," the man said, evenly. "When I got there he was blabbing, Blaise knows her daddy killed—"

"Her daddy killed? *Who*?"

"How was I to live if you didn't get the insurance?"

"Tony? Arnold, you killed Tony?"

"You said you couldn't afford to pay me, didn't you?"

"Arnold, you killed your own son?"

Kim circled the building to another window and peeped in. *Couldn't see from here.*

"Well, all good things must come to an end," the man said, ruefully, "and this is the end of a lucrative relationship, Richard."

"But, why?" Richard wailed. "Why are you doing this?"

"No one knows Ralph Curry but you."

A chimney blocked his vision and Kim scampered along the wall toward the rear.

"I have to tell you how close you came to being rich, you dumb jerk. I went to Mobile to take out the kid, to prime the pump with more insurance. That was shortsighted of me, Richard. But ah hah! The old biddy with the millions came here. I was going to take her out tonight, but your wife must've gotten suspicious."

"My wife . . . *my wife* . . . "

"I planned to slip her into a long hot tub. The kid gets the fortune, you have unlimited funds, and we live happily ever after. But now, what can I do, Richard? You've screwed it up coming here. I'll have to waste you all."

Kim pushed open the rear door and crawled toward an overstuffed chair. Now he faced the light, less than the best, the two men like shooting range cutouts in sharp relief against the rays from the automobile. He had only the chair to shield him, and a shotgun would cut through upholstery. He lifted his head, daring to look. If he missed, Richard was just beyond—if he missed, the shotgun would take off his head.

"So long, sucker," the baritone lamented. "It was good while it lasted."

"Arnold, no!"

"Freeze, Meredith!"

Instantly the man dove to one side, and Kim ducked as the shotgun exploded, the chair torn away above his head. Ears ringing, he heard a second shot and sounds of scrambling behind the bar.

"Richard, you all right?"

"Yeah."

"Meredith, there's no way out of here," Kim said. He heard a soft chuckle, and hugged the floor as the shotgun flashed red against the wall, the chair raining cotton over him.

Three shots. How many did he have? Kim cursed himself as he heard another weapon being snatched from the wall.

"I'm going to kill you, Arnold," Richard said, so calmly it carried finality. From the far side of the room came two quick shotgun blasts and glass shattered behind the bar, liquid trickling in the dark.

"When you go for the door, Arnold," Richard said, "I'm going to kill you."

Kim heard the *goop-goop* of shells being drawn from a barrel. He fired three shots toward the dark corner, dived for the bar. In the same instant, Richard must have run into the hall, firing once as he escaped.

"Sonofabitch," the man muttered, firing down the hall. Kim shot to the right of the muzzle flare.

"Son of a *bitch*!" the man seethed. "All right, you guys, let's talk."

No reply.

Kim assessed his chances for reaching the back door again. The headlights cut clean brilliant slices, broken by furniture into white rays which made the dark all the blacker.

"I'll take the car and go, Curry," the man bargained. "What do you say?"

Silence, except the patter of liquid. Kim smelled rum.

"Curry? The women aren't hurt. No harm done. I'll get my ass out of your life. What do you say?"

"Give it up, Arnold," Kim said.

The blasts that followed shredded the bar, shattered glassware.

"The police are coming," Kim said. "You might as well give it up."

He heard an obscenity, the sound of something dragging. If Arnold fired behind this bar, that would be it. Kim drew himself up at one end of the bar, now cursing the headlights.

"Turn on the lights, somebody!" he yelled. He could hear the man grunt, dragging nearer . . .

"Turn on the lights!" Kim screamed.

"Mom," Blaise cried, "that's Kim!"

They clung to one another, the reverberating gunshots escalating terror to the point of panic, the men screaming, cursing.

"We could jump out the window and run," Ellen said.

"Not in that marsh," Mother Meredith declared. "We'd be in the open and if they saw us sloshing across—"

Kim's anguished cry came again, "Richard! Turn on the lights!"

"Mom, what can we do?" Blaise shrilled.

"Out must be better than in," Ellen said. "Out the window we go. Run for the woods."

They helped Mother Meredith by holding her arms, lowering the woman as she whimpered with the strain. Mother Meredith was out of the underbrush only to come back, instantly. "Richard!" she alerted Ellen. "He's outside the front door."

They heard Kim swear and a blast flashed crimson. Ellen saw Richard inch foward, shotgun in hand.

Mother Meredith shoved through shrubbery, sputtering, Blaise and Ellen behind.

"Where're you going?" Ellen cried.

"To turn on the lights."

They reached a utility room and Mother Meredith flipped switches.

More blasts came from the living room and kitchen.

"Look," Blaise announced.

Revolving police lights fast approaching.

"Now they come," Mother Meredith sneered.

305

Siren piercing, the police car turned broadside and officers took shelter behind their own vehicle. Mr. Manx fell on his knees beside them.

"Drop it!" an officer yelled. Richard put his weapon on the ground and crawled backward.

Each officer alternately covered the other. They moved to the car at the front door.

"Police!" one yelled.

Another vehicle raced toward them, siren blasting.

The second car disgorged two more troopers and one put handcuffs on Richard.

"This is Mrs. Meredith!" Mr. Manx said, as they converged in the living room.

Blaise stared at the man. "He looks like daddy."

"No he doesn't," Mother Meredith scoffed. "He hasn't the breeding or character of Arnold."

"No," Ellen agreed. "He doesn't even favor Arnold."

Richard staggered. "That isn't Arnold?"

The man laughed. "You stupid sonofabitch. So close to a fortune and you blew it."

"He isn't *Arnold?*" Richard screamed.

"Most assuredly not," Mother Meredith declared.

Richard lunged, despite his shackles, and the police restrained him.

"Can anybody explain what in the name of Jehovah is going on here?" an officer demanded.

"I'll kill you!" Richard shrieked.

The man smirked. "Sucker," he said.

Ellen and Blaise rode in the rear of the Mercedes, Kim driving, with Mother Meredith at his side. They had found the distributor cap beneath Mother Meredith's car. Before them, one state police car in which the imposter was chained and caged. Behind them, a second police vehicle followed with Richard also in handcuffs and under arrest.

"Arnold always loved it here when it rained," Mother Meredith intoned.

Blaise wept softly, Ellen holding the girl's head in her lap, both of them stunned by news of Herman's murder.

"Why did he do that?" Blaise cried out.

"I don't know, Blaise," Ellen murmured.

Blaise sat up suddenly, glaring out a window, "I hate this place," she sobbed. "I hate everything about this place!"

Ellen saw the grandmother waver, eyes aqueous. "Look how bright the leaves," Mother Meredith said to Kim. "Rain cleanses. I suspect that is what Arnold liked most. He wanted everything neat and in place. Military life suited him fine."

When they reached the caretaker's cottage, the leading car stopped to let out Mr. Manx. He still wore his nightgown, colorless hair thatched and tangled. The old man hobbled to the closed rear door and shouted, "See you, Arnold! Come on back and we'll tie one on, ho!"

"I don't suppose he'll ever retire willingly," Mother Meredith noted, sadly. "His daughter asked me to let him die here and so he shall."

The vehicles moved again, downhill, trees dripping crystal droplets into sodden undergrowth. The falls fed a roiling river. Kim activated the windshield wipers as they passed through mist.

"Look Blaise," Mother Meredith spoke without joy, "there goes a doe and her fawn."

But Blaise was slumped again, weeping inconsolably. Ellen stroked her head.

"If that isn't Arnold," Kim asked Mother Meredith, "who is he?"

"Who cares?" Blaise screamed.

"Blaise," Mother Meredith reproved, "chin up and chest out, dear. Mr. Jensen doesn't deserve abuse."

"I'm sorry, Kim."

"Forget it, babe."

They reached the main highway and turned toward Winchester, picking up speed.

Ellen remembered Betty Sue, the banker in Ochlochnee. Wynette, horrified and defensive of her former husband.

"You would have liked Arnold," Mother Meredith spoke to Kim. "Men found him wonderful."

Ellen thought of all they had learned, how damning was the knowledge. Dead children . . . Richard's business in "simulated" products, he called it. *Counterfeit.*

He was not who she'd thought. But then, none of them were.

"Kim, I want to stop," Ellen said. "Stop now, please. Stop here."

The vehicle hesitated, eased, hesitated as Kim warned the following car by flashing brake lights. He pulled to the side of the road.

"Mom, what are you doing?"

"Suppose we're wrong," Ellen said. "Richard is confined back there like a criminal. Suppose we're wrong?"

"Mom!"

"Ellen, don't be foolish—"

"Even if we're right," Ellen said, "he'll never need me more. But suppose we *are* wrong? If I don't support him now he will never forgive me."

"Mom, please—no!"

"Until proven otherwise," Ellen said, "I must assume the best."

"Mama—he killed Tony!"

"He says he did not," Ellen opened the door. "Mother Meredith, will you come and sit with Blaise?"

"Mama, don't go."

"I must, Blaise."

Ellen walked to the police car. "I want to ride with my husband."

"We can't allow it, Mrs. Curry."

"Why not?"

"He's under arrest. You'll have to ride with the others."

"Then arrest me," Ellen insisted. "I want to ride with him."

The policemen exchanged glances and the driver stepped out. "I have to search you," he said hesitantly.

He patted her sides, face red. "I'll have to put you in cuffs too, Mrs. Curry."

This done, he opened the door and she sat beside Richard.

His eyes were rimmed, cheeks gaunt. He hadn't shaved, his clothes were filthy and he looked at her with such pain, she leaned to kiss him.

"I love you, Richard. You resurrected me. My life began when you came into it. You have given me more happiness than anyone deserves."

He hung his head, chest heaving.

The shortwave radio crackled in staccato bursts, the officers riding in silence.

"I believe you," she whispered. "I believe you thought he was Arnold."

He made a strange sound, inhaling, then sobbed again.

"Know what I want, Richard?"

He shook his head.

"I want a beach house." She slipped nearer. "And a garden of rich soil, and all your waking hours for the rest of our lives."

"I was trying to protect you, Ellen."

"I know."

"He knew everything about you, about Blaise. He had money in Thailand, and you'd told me Arnold withdrew money before he was killed. I thought—"

"I know, darling."

"I wanted to kill him."

"Hush, Richard."

"I love you, Ellen."

"Yes," she said. "I know you do."

T Chapter
TWENTY-EIGHT

As the doctor probed with a cold stethoscope, Ellen thought not of the examination, but of the past seven months. Their ordeal had not yet ended—

"Weight, heartbeat and blood pressure good. You look good. How do you feel, Mrs. Curry?"

Nervous. Frightened. Ellen said, "I feel all right."

He pressed her feet and ankles. "Do you have any problems with water retention?"

"I don't think so."

Blaise was out in the reception area waiting for an answer. "May I go to Switzerland?"

Mother Meredith had made the offer to Blaise. Then she'd appealed to Ellen. "Finishing school, that's what Blaise needs. A touch of polish. The panache that international experience will give." *Preparatory school.* "For college," Mother Meredith said. For wealth, she meant. For a life Blaise had only recently glimpsed.

"Would it not ease things emotionally, Ellen?" Mother Meredith reasoned, persistently. "To let wounds heal, time for Blaise to reflect and mature."

Blaise felt alienated from students at St. Paul's. The continuing publicity made her uncomfortable. Herman's murder—

"No emotional trauma?" the doctor smiled. "If you intend to become pregnant, handle it with care."

"Then, you think it'll be all right?" Ellen asked.

"You're hale and hearty and you want a baby," the physician said. "Why not?"

"Pregnant!" Blaise had reeled incredulously with the revelation. "You're going to have a baby on *purpose*?"

"We're considering it, Blaise."

"Is that what daddy wants, a baby?"

No, Richard hadn't wanted it. Not at first. Not without fear, even now.

"Blaise," Ellen had said, "marriage is based on sharing. The good and bad, the ups and downs. Love is the residue of shared experiences. A child is the ultimate act of sharing."

"Then it's your idea," Blaise had sulked. "You think a baby will make everything all right."

"Do you think it will be a complicating factor?" Ellen had countered.

"I know it will be. Babies always complicate things."

As Ellen entered the waiting room, Blaise put aside a worn copy of *Good Housekeeping*. "What did he say?" the girl questioned.

"Hale, hearty and ready to be a mother," Ellen reported.

Blaise helped Ellen don her coat and they stepped into a cold January wind. When they reached the car, Ellen let the motor idle to warm the heater.

"Have you made a decision, mom?" Blaise spoke with an accusatory tone.

"We're going to have a baby."

"I don't mean that, and you know it."

"I've decided it isn't my decision to make," Ellen said. "You are the one who will be an ocean away. You will be leaving your friends and loved ones—"

"You do that very well, mom," Blaise smiled falsely.

"Do what?"

"Make me feel guilty. Make me feel it's my fault I feel guilty! Leaving my friends, going an ocean away. Leaving my loved ones, which is to say, leaving those who reputedly love me."

Ellen snatched up the emergency brake and the car lurched. "Reputedly, Blaise? To whom are you referring?"

"I'm sorry, mom."

"We all harbor some guilt, Blaise," Ellen said hotly. "But a mark of maturity is one's capacity to come to grips with it. There's no doubt that you are loved. Mother Meredith loves you. I love you. Richard loves you. But I want you to know something, Blaise. The one thing love cannot long endure is punishment. Don't you think you've punished Richard enough?"

Blaise blinked hard, then put a finger to her eye. "My contact lens slipped," she said.

Ellen released the brake, backed from the parking place.

"There's the trial to think about," Blaise stated.

"Well, you can't run away from that, Blaise. If you are in Switzerland, you'll have to come back. That's one of the unpleasantries in life that you must see through."

"I dread it."

"We all dread it."

"I read in the newspaper he's still fighting extradition."

Ellen turned toward home, traffic creeping along Airport Boulevard.

"Mama, I can't help it," Blaise said softly. "I tell myself that daddy didn't mean to cause all of this. I tell myself he didn't hurt Tony, that he loved Tony. I tell myself he loves me and he loves you."

"Correct."

"But I can't force myself to touch him. I can't talk to him. I feel guilty and I feel guilty for feeling guilty! You did right, going back to ride to the police station with him. I wish I had been that wise."

"Why don't you say that to Richard?"

"I tried. I stammered and stuttered and ended up shaking his

312

hand. Shaking his hand! Like a truce or something. I was embarrassed to death. I just can't, that's all."

After a moment, Blaise said, "You could tell him for me."

"No, I can't. The genesis of all our problems has been a lack of communication. That's a burden you and Richard must bear."

"How does he feel—watch the traffic, mom!"

"Ask him, Blaise."

Blaise sighed dramatically and stared out her window. They passed a bank with a sign which stated coldly, *forty degrees.*

"Guilt is a canker, Blaise," Ellen suggested. "You must forgive."

"I forgive daddy."

"I wasn't speaking of Richard. I meant you must forgive yourself."

Blaise sighed again. "That's even harder. I hate myself for doubting daddy, but he asked for it. I hate it that I thought he'd killed Tony, but it wouldn't have happened if daddy had answered my questions!"

"Richard is a victim here, too, Blaise."

"We're all victims. Even Mother Meredith."

When they reached the house, Blaise said, "Kim is here. That's his car."

Ellen heard men's voices in the kitchen as she hung her coat in a hall closet.

"Ellen," Kim stood as she entered, "this is John Lawrence with the FBI. He was responsible for the Virginia State Police arriving at the lodge."

"Has anybody made coffee?" Ellen asked.

"I'll do it," Blaise offered, giving herself the excuse to stay.

"I was telling your husband," the agent said, "we've completed our end of the investigation."

Richard put his hand atop Ellen's and squeezed gently.

"Kim asked me to come over with him," Lawrence said. "I must tell you, most of what I have to say is supposition."

Ellen watched Blaise scoop coffee, losing count and putting in too many.

"The man who called himself Arnold Meredith is, as you know, not Arnold Meredith. Nor Ralph Curry, of course. We've managed to identify him as Randall Zakowski, but that was an assumed name, too."

"Then who is he?"

"We don't know. Probably never will know," the agent said. "He served in Vietnam as Major Randall Zakowski. From his fingerprints we know he and Arnold were in the same outfit. We've gotten a deposition from fellow officers who described Zakowski and Meredith as friends. One comment caught my eye, a fellow officer said they drank together and shared foxhole confessions."

"What is that?"

"Intimate personal details of their lives," John Lawrence replied. "Now for the supposition. We think Arnold must have related his personal problems. He was distraught over a pending divorce. He wanted to get leave, to come home and argue his case, but the military wouldn't allow it. We suspect Arnold and Zakowski dreamed up a way, by faking Arnold's death and shipping home an unidentifiable body. Zakowski had a reputation as a con man in Saigon and it's reasonable to assume he had connections to pull it off. We know Meredith withdrew considerable sums of money from American accounts and had it deposited in various banks. Thailand was one such place. Whenever possible, to cover his escape, Arnold Meredith established accounts with numbered codes, so anyone could withdraw the monies if they knew the code. But Zakowski may have had other plans. We'll never prove it, but we think he murdered Arnold and burned the corpse, letting it go home while he retrieved the money Arnold had transferred to the area. But then, he found himself in an awkward position. If anyone found out he had personally removed the money, wouldn't they suspect him of murder?"

Kim caught Blaise's eye and winked. The girl grinned, returned the gesture.

"A personality like Zakowski," John said, "is never going to confess anything. But he can't resist boasting. He does it with innuendo, admitting nothing, but letting us know how brilliant he thinks himself to be. He went to Atlanta and spied on Ellen. He saw her getting married. He discovered Richard had a business with international connections. Zakowski figured, what the hell, if he presented himself as Arnold Meredith, the worst would be if Richard threw him out or called the police. But to forestall that possibility, he came asking for nothing except Richard's help in retrieving 'his' money from Thailand. Richard fell for it. Zakowski knew details about Arnold which he passed along conversationally, things Ellen inadvertently confirmed, and now the scam was in motion. He cannot resist telling how Richard gave him an identity, all the while protecting Zakowski from those who could prove that he was not Arnold Meredith!"

"Damn him," Richard swore softly.

"How much of this will come out in court?" Ellen asked.

"It is in the hands of the Mobile police," John said. "The charge is the murder of Herman Krause. That means they must prove Zakowski had opportunity to commit the crime."

"We can prove he was in Pensacola the night before, and Montgomery the night after," Kim interjected.

"Then," John continued, "they must prove he had the means, which is to say, the weapon. The knife was found in this house, hair was found on Herman's fingers which will prove he engaged in a struggle. But then they must prove Zakowski had a motive."

"That means telling about Tony," Ellen said.

"Yes. Mr. Curry will have to testify to the extortion. Blaise will be asked to say she saw Zakowski leave the scene where Tony drowned, and that she saw him again in subsequent years. The fact is, if you three didn't stick together, they might not convict the man. The evidence is primarily circumstantial, except the hair found on Herman's hands. That alone would not be conclusive."

The percolator bubbled, uninterrupted.

"When will the trial begin?" Blaise broke a lull.

"He'll use every legal maneuver to delay and complicate," John said. "He hopes your resolve will weaken, your anger will diminish."

While they drank coffee, the discussion turned to business, computers, and Kim's forthcoming marriage. Blaise lingered at the kitchen bar. Several times, the girl and Richard glanced at one another. Like strangers, it seemed to Ellen, touched not by words or flesh, but signals that were implicit.

Ellen escorted Kim and the agent to the door.

"My personal advice would be," John said, "keep your memory of that murdered boy. As time elapses, it is easier to shrug away the past. Our judicial system encourages it, but I don't know of any other system I'd use to replace it."

"Thank you for coming to see us, Mr. Lawrence."

She stepped outside. In the lee of the house, the sun was warm, air stilled, the sky so blue it didn't bear scrutiny. She waved as their car drew away.

Inside again, she returned to the kitchen.

Blaise and Richard were gone.

Ellen gathered cups and saucers, took them to the sink. Through the window, she saw Richard down at his garden, turning soil with a spade. On the patio, Blaise stood as she'd stood a year ago, assessing, spying—

Breathless with déjà vu, dread mounted, Ellen's heartbeat ascending. Blaise moved to a concealing post as Richard turned. Seeing, but unseen, the girl observed Richard's winter ritual of aeration and fertilizing, preparing for his spring garden.

With aching helplessness, Ellen subdued anger, then frustration. How could a family exist with distrust and misgiving?

She loved them. Differently, but equally. She ached for them to love one another, to love a new baby, if it happened.

Her eyes stung and Ellen held the counter grieving for what could not be.

Blaise stepped into warm sunshine again. She had grown—taller, older than the months warranted, accruing maturity. Mother Meredith's influence was taking effect. Blaise had recently said she never discussed how much things cost anymore.

"Why not?" Ellen had asked.

"It makes me feel hypocritical," Blaise had rejoined. "When my friends talk about wanting something their family can't afford, it embarrasses me."

The stain of wealth. Alterations in perception.

316

"Blood does not make the son of a king worthy to be king," Mother Meredith once quoted Arnold's father from years ago. "Being raised as royalty is what makes a monarch."

Perhaps it was inevitable. Perhaps unrealistic to think Blaise could resist a pending fortune.

Ellen started to turn away, depressed—but Blaise moved, going down to the winter-parched yard, walking toward Richard.

Please God. Are you there?

Blaise halted, watching Richard work, but then she must have spoken. He wheeled, and it seemed to Ellen, neither said a word.

Blaise went to him hesitantly and put her arms around him. Thus they stood.

Finally, Richard dropped the spade and took her in his arms . . .